The
Hidden
Child

Louise Fein holds an MA in Creative Writing from St Mary's University. Her debut novel, *People Like Us* (entitled *Daughter of the Reich* in the US/Canada) has been published in thirteen territories, was shortlisted for the RSL Christopher Bland Prize 2021 and the RNA Goldsboro Books Historical Romantic Novel Award 2021. Her books are predominantly set during the twentieth century and all of her books seek to explore issues that continue to be of relevance today.

———

Also by Louise Fein

People Like Us

The Hidden Child

Louise Fein

For Millie, Josh and Lottie

This novel was inspired by the author's own experience of raising a child affected by epilepsy. In imagining she had been born one hundred years earlier, into an era which believed in a flawed science, itself shaped by xenophobia, prejudice and fear, she hopes to raise awareness of the attitudes and stigma which persist and continue to impact our society and language today.

'A learned man is an idler who kills time with study. Beware of his false knowledge; it is more dangerous than ignorance.'

George Bernard Shaw

PART I

July 1928

I

Eleanor

Mabel grips Eleanor's arm tight as they bowl fast along the country lane, Dilly's hooves kicking dust into sultry July air. Limbs of the trees which stand like sentries beside the lane reach out and curl above them, joining like the high arches of a cathedral to form a cool green canopy, shading the little pony and trap and its occupants from the fierce heat of the afternoon sun.

'Faster!' giggles Mabel, glancing up at her mother with sparkling eyes. 'Make Dilly go faster!' She turns back to look at the road, laughing with glee as the wind lifts her curls, almost translucent where the sunlight catches them, her little bottom bouncing with excitement on the seat beside her mother.

Eleanor steadies the reins in her hands. There is a creak of leather and the faint tang of equine sweat. The pony is trotting fast enough for this heat. Besides, they are plenty early enough to meet the 4.25 from London.

'Dilly can't go any faster, Mabel,' Eleanor answers. 'It's too hot. And besides, she's quite old now, so it wouldn't be fair.' Dilly's chestnut sides are darkening with sweat, but she maintains her fast pace, pulling eagerly against Eleanor's hands; ears pricked, head raised, as though she is as elated as Eleanor at the thought of Rose coming home. Happiness swells as she thinks of her sister's reaction when she shares her news. News even Edward doesn't know yet.

Mabel pouts and drops Eleanor's arm. 'How old is Dilly?'

'Around thirteen, I believe.'

'Is that old?'

'Middle-aged for a pony, I should think.'

'How old are you, Mama?'

Eleanor laughs. 'You should *never* ask a lady her age, Mabel.' She leans down and kisses the top of her daughter's head. 'But, as it's you, I'll tell – as long as you keep it a secret between us,' she says, tapping the side of her nose, keeping her expression stern.

Mabel nods, her face solemn.

'I'm twenty-seven. Actually, almost twenty-eight,' she adds in surprise. How did she get to be so old? She was twenty only last year, or so it feels. And why does twenty-eight sound so much older than twenty-seven? Thirty is just around the corner, she realises, with a sinking feeling. Is thirty old for a woman? A man of that age is considered to be just entering his prime of life, but a woman...

Beside her, Mabel lets out a little gasp. 'That's so old! Will you die soon, like Patch? You won't die, will you, Mama?'

'Goodness me, no! People live much longer than dogs, and ponies, darling. I'm really very, *very* young for a person.'

Mabel looks relieved. 'Is Aunt Rose twenty-seven too?'

'Aunt Rose is only eighteen, soon to be nineteen,' Eleanor says, 'and now that she is suitably educated, well-travelled and polished into a smart young lady, your papa is rather keen to find her a nice, rich husband.' She bites her lip. Too much. Such things tend to be regurgitated by her daughter, usually to the wrong person. She glances down at Mabel's countenance. She seems firmly focused on the road ahead. The little girl is completely still, presumably contemplating whatever age-related questions that go on in a four-year-old's mind. She looks pretty as a picture in her Sunday-best cream dress, decorated all over with tiny yellow and pink flowers. Eleanor had agreed with Mabel earlier that it was just the thing to greet Aunt Rose from the station in.

Mabel shifts and looks up at Eleanor. There's a darkness in the little girl's eyes. She has noticed this a few times before. So imperceptible, she wonders if it's her imagination. In a flash it's gone and Mabel's face lights up.

'Can we sing a song?' she asks, smiling.

'Good idea,' Eleanor nods.

'What shall we sing, Mama?'

'Let's see...'

Eleanor takes a deep breath, and along to the rhythm of Dilly's clip-clop on the lane, she begins to sing and sway, Mabel quickly joining in with the swaying and the chorus:

O dear what can the matter be?
Dear, dear, what can the matter be?
O dear what can the matter be?
Johnny's so long at the fair.

He promised he'd bring me a bunch of blue ribbons.
He promised he'd bring me a bunch of blue ribbons.
He promised he'd bring me a bunch of blue ribbons.
To tie up my bonny brown hair...

Eleanor can't remember all the words, or the order of them, so she makes some up. Mabel doesn't seem to mind and joins in happily, singing tunelessly at the top of her voice. Dilly twitches her ears back and forth.

He promised to buy me a crunchy green apple.
He promised to buy me a crunchy green apple.
He promised to buy me a crunchy green apple.
To eat while I sit on my chair...

The trees peter out and the lane runs beside a field. A group of slow-moving, shaggy Belted Galloway cows and calves graze close to the ditch at the side of the road, tails flapping at their round, hairy sides, the long grass sweeping their low-slung, white-striped bellies, heads lowered as though it is too hot to hold them high. Swarms of gnats hang in the air and Eleanor swipes at them as they pass through. Up ahead, the lane shimmers in the afternoon heat haze. Eleanor glimpses the distant church steeple through the treetops beyond the field.

'Almost there,' she tells Mabel, who is still singing to herself, O dear, what can the matter be?; the same words, over and over, with little pauses now and then before she starts again.

Rounding the corner at the end of the field, the station comes into view, with the White Hart public house opposite. Beyond, over the brow of the hill and out of sight, lies the village of Mayfield, quintessentially English, with its picturesque village green, complete with cricket pitch, duck pond and maypole. Its timber-framed historic houses, some dating back to Tudor times, are arranged in an undulating hug around the green, the whole village nestled close amongst the beauty of the Surrey hills.

Eleanor twitches the reins backwards and the ever-obedient Dilly slows to a walk. They're a good ten minutes early.

'Woah!' Eleanor calls and the pony and trap lurch to a halt. She steps down from the trap, keeping hold of the reins, and guides Dilly to the water trough outside the pub where she takes a long drink, sucking the water noisily through the metal bit in her mouth. The pony rubs her head against Eleanor's shoulder, almost knocking her off balance.

'Got an itch, girl?' In response, Dilly snorts and Mabel giggles. 'Come on, you silly old thing.' Eleanor gives her a fond pat and leads her into the shade beneath the branches of a huge beech tree near the pub building. Dilly lowers her head and rests one hind leg.

Eleanor lifts Mabel down from the trap so she can stretch her legs in the lane. While they wait for the train to arrive, she watches the little girl as she wanders, examining a beetle here, picking up a coloured stone there, all the time chattering to herself. Once or twice she stops mid-chatter and is completely still. It's as though she has just remembered something... Then, a second or so later, she continues on her way.

'Afternoon, Mrs Hamilton,' Ted, the postman, calls from across the lane. He gives her a wave as he pushes his bike towards the postbox outside the station. 'Hot one today,' he adds, pulling his keys from his pocket.

'Isn't it?' She wipes a gloved hand across her brow as if to demonstrate how close to melting she really is.

The postbox door creaks open and Ted's head disappears behind it as he empties the letters into his waiting mailbag.

She watches him idly, her mind drifting in delicious anticipation to her sister's homecoming. How she has missed her! Rose is all Eleanor has left of her childhood, and the impulse to keep her close and safe is almost unbearable. Perhaps because their two brothers failed to return from the war, and following the tragic deaths of *both* of their parents, Eleanor is naturally fearful to let her sister out of her sight. It took a supreme effort of selflessness to allow her to go off to Paris for so long. Until Edward, it was just the two of them against the world.

Edward really is so good to Rose. Darling Edward, what a burden they have been to him. When he married her, he took on far more than just a wife. It's right that Rose should find a husband now and relieve Edward of the responsibility of two women to take care of, especially with a growing family. Her hand finds its way to rest against her belly as her eyes drift back to Mabel, crouching beneath the tree collecting twigs. She tries to imagine her sister on the arm of a handsome young man and the pang of loss hits her hard in the chest.

She shakes her head. She cannot keep Rose all to herself. Besides, her sister has every right to a happy family. She thinks, for a moment, what her life would be without Edward and feels a little sick.

Eleanor's first encounter with Edward is seared so deep into her mind; the clarity of the memory takes her breath away, just as he did when she first set eyes on him eight years ago, in 1920. The broad shoulders beneath the sharp cut of his uniform; the medals lining his chest. A quick glance and she had recognised the Military Cross, awarded for exemplary gallantry. From behind her typewriter she had wondered, as he folded his tall frame into a chair outside the brigadier general's room in the War Office, just what acts of bravery he had undertaken. Those haunting eyes which fixed on hers, just a little longer than strictly appropriate for a captain waiting for his decommissioning appointment. She remembers the effect he had on her, the hot fluttering in her chest and how the words she was typing melted and swam on the page in front of her. She could still feel the soft spring breeze from the open window touch her skin; the grind of traffic rumbling along Horse Guards Avenue below, the press of his eyes on her flushed cheeks as she tried, fruitlessly, to concentrate on her work. From the corner of her eye, she'd watched him take a pen and notebook from his top pocket and, forehead wrinkled in thought, begin to write. She'd wondered if he was a poet or perhaps planning his words for the brigadier.

'*He promised to buy me a shiny green apple,*' Mabel sings suddenly, looking up at Eleanor. 'Is that how it goes, Mama? That song?'

'Yes, darling,' Eleanor murmurs absentmindedly.

When Edward had disappeared behind the brigadier general's closed door, Eleanor became aware of the strong thrum of her heart, the prickle of sweat on her skin, the rasp of her breath in her throat. The knowledge he would walk back out at some point had her patting her hair, smoothing her blouse, pinching her cheeks. It had felt like hours before he reappeared. It was ridiculous, she knew. She, just a young, ordinary girl – a secretary; he a military man, a *much* older man. He must be, what, thirty, thirty-five, even. She only nineteen! And pretty much destitute, now that she and Rose were alone together in the world. Someone so smart and self-assured, so brave and handsome, would never be interested in her.

He reappeared, turned, and the brigadier general shook him by the hand, saying, 'Best of luck with it all,' pumping Edward's hand so vigorously his moustache had wobbled. A Temporary Gentleman, Eleanor surmised. A man given a temporary commission to serve as an officer in the war, now released to return to his former profession. Back to what? she had wondered, unable to resist staring at him as he prepared to leave the room. Before replacing his cap, he turned and smiled. A warm, wonderful smile which lit up his face. Passing her desk, as he'd left, he slipped a folded note next to her typewriter, unnoticed by the brigadier general whose mind was undoubtedly on the hundreds more he had to decommission in the coming days.

I'll be at the Café Bru, corner of Whitehall Place, at six this evening if you would care to join me for a cup of tea? Be reassured that my invitation is purely professional. Yours, Edward Hamilton, the note had read, which set Eleanor's heart racing all over again.

There's a jangle of keys as Ted locks the postbox, the bulging sack resting in the basket between his handlebars. He turns towards Eleanor, touching his cap as though to say goodbye, but instead, his vision darts over her shoulder and he lets out a yell. His hands leave the handlebars, the bike crashing to the ground, mail pouring from the sack. Eyes stretched wide, mouth agape, he is pointing at something beneath the tree.

Eleanor turns in confusion.

Mabel! Sticks scattered, she's sitting on the dusty ground, face twisted, her eyes rolling back. Her chin drops to her chest, once, twice, hands twitching.

Eleanor's feet are rooted to the ground in horror. Her daughter looks as though she's been possessed, her normal sweet expression vanished behind the contorted features of her face. Ted moves first, walking slowly, hands extended.

'What's the matter with her?' he says. 'What's happening...?'

His words snap her into action and Eleanor runs to her. 'Mabel?' She takes her in her arms. The little girl doesn't respond. 'Mabel!' Eleanor cries. *What is wrong with her?* It's as though she's not there, a strange creature inhabiting her daughter's body in her absence. There's a roar in Eleanor's head, panic closes her throat and she slaps Mabel's face. Hard. Anything to rid her of the hellish grimace, the other-worldly look in her eyes.

'Shall I fetch the doctor?' Ted's voice, his hand on her shoulder.

And then suddenly Mabel's face returns to its usual self. Her eyes focus on Eleanor's and they fill with cloudy confusion. Eleanor's heart is beating hard, her breath shallow. The ground shudders beneath her feet. 'It's OK,' she whispers into Mabel's ear. 'It's OK.' She sweeps the dust from her hair, her dress.

'Mrs Hamilton?' Eleanor looks up into Ted's worried face. 'I said, shall I get the doctor?'

Eleanor looks back at her daughter who has now popped her thumb in her mouth and is sucking hard on it.

'No,' she says, without any real conscious thought as to why not. 'She's quite all right, now,' she says. 'I don't know what happened. She—'

'Cooee! Eleanor!'

Rose.

Eleanor staggers shakily to her feet, and turns to see her younger sister, a wide, wide smile beneath her floppy-brimmed straw hat, rosy-cheeked and beautiful, striding towards them up the slope from the station, a vision of perfection, carrying her case in one hand, waving with the other.

Mabel shifts in her arms and points at Rose.

Eleanor turns back to Ted. 'Really. Mabel is fine. She was late to bed last night and she's very tired. I'm sure that's what it was – just a funny turn. You know children! I'm so sorry about all the letters. We'll help you pick them up.'

'Not to worry,' says Ted. 'Long as the little 'un's OK...' He looks uncertain.

'Please,' Eleanor says. 'Don't worry. Mabel is completely fine. There is absolutely no need, *no need*,' she insists a second time, 'for you to mention this to anyone.'

Ted nods and bends to right the bicycle. He props it against the tree and gathers up the strewn mail. 'Forgotten about already,' he says, giving her a flash of a smile.

Rose is crossing the street. Sprinting the last few yards, she drops the case and launches herself straight into Eleanor's arms. In a swirl of fine cotton and her sister's flowery scent and laughter, she is swallowed into Rose's embrace, Mabel squeezed between them. They pull apart as a whistle sounds from behind the station building. A cloud of steam rises and the sound of the train, cranking and straining hard out of the station, fills her ears. Mabel is too heavy and Eleanor puts her gently down.

'Oh, Rose! How good it is to see you. I didn't hear the train arrive!'

'And you, dearest Eleanor. Now, how is my favourite niece?' Rose gently pinches Mabel's cheeks and the little girl buries her head shyly in Eleanor's skirt. 'Goodness, how you've grown!' She turns to Ted, who is picking up the scattered contents of his mailbag. 'What's happened, can I help?'

'It's quite all right,' he says, crouching to refill the sack. 'I was being clumsy. Nice to see you back, Miss Carmichael. How long has it been?'

'Nine whole months!' she laughs. 'Can you believe it?'

'Welcome home,' says Ted, picking up the last of the letters. 'Well, I'll be on my way.'

'Yes. Thank you, Ted, for earlier.'

'Hope she's OK,' he says again, giving Mabel a concerned look as he passes. 'Good day to you both.'

'Good day, Ted.'

He swings a long leg over the back of his bicycle and, knees bending outwards to avoid the bulging mailbag, he peddles away.

Eleanor holds her sister at arm's length. 'How well you look,' she smiles. Rose has filled out. She really does look the picture of health, her light-blue eyes shining, her cheeks flushed. Edward will have no trouble securing her a suitable spouse.

She reaches down for the case Rose dropped during their embrace.

'Come on, let's get home,' Eleanor says. 'I expect Mrs

Bellamy has made us all a nice Victoria sponge cake, with strawberry jam inside just for you and Rose, Mabel.'

The little girl licks her lips and rubs her belly. 'Yummy,' she says, her earlier shyness melting away as fast as it arrived. 'I *like* strawberry jam.' How normal she sounds. How ordinary. Is it possible that she just dreamt up that awful episode? Had Ted not also witnessed it, she might just be convinced of that.

'I love strawberry jam too.' Rose smiles at her niece. 'See? We're just the same, you and me,' and Mabel curls her little fingers into Rose's gloved hand.

'It's so good to be back,' Rose exclaims as, seated in the trap, Eleanor turns Dilly to head home to Brook End, Mabel in the middle.

'It will be an adjustment,' Eleanor says, 'to be back in quiet old England after your travels.'

'Of course, but I've missed it. And *you*, dear Ellie. We've never been apart for more than a few weeks before.' She smiles. 'But... Oh, Paris really *is* wonderful. It was so generous of Edward to let me go.'

'And did it do the trick?' Eleanor asks with mock seriousness. 'Have they turned you into a chic and fluent Parisian? Edward will want to see evidence of his investment.'

'I shall have to let *him* be the judge,' Rose laughs.

Dilly breaks into an eager trot and Eleanor glances at Rose's profile. She truly does look radiant. Her months in Paris and the weeks travelling around Italy have clearly suited her.

They fall into a companionable silence, lulled by the sound of Dilly's hooves, her smooth coat gleaming and dulling as she passes through patches of sunlight and lengthening shadows, the sun dipping lower in the sky.

With Rose beside her, her secret bubbles and rises like hot air. She can't contain it. Somehow it feels so right to share this with her sister first.

'Rose...' she whispers above Mabel's head, 'I have news.'

Rose's eyes widen. 'Oh! Really? How far gone... Are you OK?' Her forehead creases with worry. After three lost babies, the caution in her face at the news is no surprise.

Eleanor feels her eyes fill with tears as she returns the smile. 'Three months. The doctor is confident this time. B-but I can't help but be afraid. I haven't even told Edward. I don't want to tempt bad fate.'

Rose reaches over and squeezes Eleanor's shoulders. 'If he says it's going to be fine... Well, that's wonderful news! You didn't get past two or two and a half months those last times.'

'Yes, I know. But still... It's hard to relax.'

'Of course,' says Rose. 'That's understandable. But you must take care of yourself. No stress or strains.' She waggles her finger at her.

'I'll try.'

'What does that mean, Mama? What is stress-or-strains?' Mabel looks up at her, saucer-eyed and hopeful to be included in the adult conversation.

'Oh, it means Mama mustn't get too tired or upset.'

'Why not?'

'We'll talk later,' Eleanor mouths to Rose, then to Mabel, 'Oh, just so that Mama doesn't get too tired or a headache.'

'I get headaches,' says Mabel.

'What was it that happened just before I arrived?' asks

Rose, clearly trying to change the subject, 'when Ted asked you if the little one was all right?'

'Oh...' Eleanor feels the joy seep away, like a balloon slowly deflating. 'It was just that Mabel...' *What was it?* She can't think how to describe what happened. 'Oh, nothing,' Eleanor says at last, looking at her daughter. There is no sign of anything wrong at all. 'She's fine,' she says.

But as Eleanor guides Dilly through the stone gateposts and up the sweeping drive towards the sprawling Edwardian façade of Brook End, the shine of the day is gone, replaced by an unease which settles over her like a damp, unwelcome cloud.

2

Edward

The air has a stickiness to it when Edward steps off the delayed 18.40 onto the platform at Mayfield. Strolling towards the waiting car, swinging his briefcase, he wonders if a thunderstorm is brewing. Usually there's a marked coolness here in the deep green of the Surrey Hills, away from the heat and fumes, the grime and bustle of London. In the country, a man can *breathe*.

But this evening Edward's shirt sticks resolutely to his back and sweat trickles down his temples and beneath his armpits. He shrugs off his suit jacket and slings it over his arm.

Wilson raises a hand in greeting as Edward approaches. He's smoking, leaning on the bonnet of the Sunbeam and Edward's heart flutters at the sight of his new car. Its cream bodywork gleams; the black trim and interior is smart and modern. He'll take it for a spin this weekend, just him with Eleanor at his side. He finds he is smiling as he pictures the scene: the wind plucking at their cheeks, her hair smooth and neat beneath her hat, clasped with one hand so it doesn't blow away, passers-by gaping at them.

'Good evening, sir.' Wilson greets him, quickly stubbing

out his cigarette and tapping his chauffeur's cap with two fingers. Edward runs a hand over the Sunbeam's paintwork and clicks open the passenger door, stepping lightly onto the footplate and swinging himself into her plush interior. Wilson cranks the engine and she judders into life.

'Good week, sir?' Wilson asks cheerily as he expertly manoeuvres the car out of the station. Edward will need to work on his handling of her. She responds so smoothly to Wilson. In Edward's hands, she is decidedly jerky. There are some awful grindings and screechings when he operates the gears.

'Yes, indeed. Very good. Successful,' Edward replies, settling back in his seat as they set off down the lane towards home. There is a pregnant pause, as though Wilson expects him to elaborate the reason for a week's stay in the London flat. Normally Edward tries to be home at least once or twice mid-week. 'I gave another series of lunchtime lectures,' he offers, 'at the Queen's Hall.' There is no response from Wilson. 'Do you know it – on Langham Place?'

'Of course, sir. The concert hall.'

'Exactly. That's the one. A large, prestigious venue.'

'Glad to hear they went so well, then, sir. Interesting topic, was it?'

'Inheritance and the Stream of Life.'

'An... expansive subject, that sounds. And were the audiences large?'

'Most pleasingly, Wilson, yes. Each day, a sell-out!'

Wilson smiles, 'Quite the celebrity, then, sir.' Edward wonders if the man is overstepping into sarcasm.

He chooses to take the remark at face value. 'Men of science like myself, in the main, but many more besides.

This has been an international event. We've hosted experts from all across the globe who are interested in learning more about the science of eugenics. America. France. Scandinavia. Germany. Members of Parliament, ministers, too.' The day had been a success. Dare he even say, a triumph? *Five* Members of Parliament in the audience, no less, and several prominent gentlemen and ladies of society so enthused by his talk that they have pledged funds and signed up to join the Eugenics Society.

Edward shifts in his seat to turn his gaze out over the fields in the hope it will discourage more questions. Who wants to make polite chit-chat with his driver? He sighs. 'I'm certainly in need of a relaxing weekend. This evening marks the end of a busy and tiring week.'

'Of course, sir.'

Edward peels his shirt away from his chest. 'Will there be a storm tonight?' Best change the subject. Wilson was country-born. These salt-of-the-earth types know. Garson, the gardener, could sniff out rain twenty-four hours before it happened. Even Mrs Bellamy, the cook, could predict sunshine or rain, nodding sagely at pink-tipped clouds in the morning, or the evening, and at cows lying down – or is it standing up?

Wilson accelerates along a straight stretch of the lane, handling the gears with such ease the Sunbeam's engine throbs with pleasure. 'I would imagine so, sir.' Wilson raises his voice against the increased thrum of the engine. 'This interminable heat must end sometime. A good soaking will do the parched ground the world of good.'

'It's even worse in town, I can tell you.' The breeze slaps like a cool, wet cloth on Edward's hot skin.

The gates of Brook End are upon them too soon. The journey from the station is barely two miles and for one crazy moment, Edward considers instructing Wilson to drive on past so as not to end the liberating, childish glee that soars. Just to be here, riding high in his new car, the wind in his hair, fresh, country air filling his lungs.

Brook End is a big house, by most people's reckoning. It's not a stately home, as such, but a handsome, brick-built, sprawling villa, four storeys high, and a mere twenty years old. A suitable residence for a respected member of the upper-middle classes, with a growing family and an even faster-growing reputation for being *the* expert in his field of psychology and education. It's quite the ticket. Modern is far more suitable for a Man of Science. Edward could undoubtedly have picked up a mansion steeped in history, with a large estate, had he been minded so to do. As soon as he and Eleanor had become engaged, he'd searched in earnest for the right country house for his bride-to-be. He had wanted to give her the very best he could afford, especially after all that she had been through, coming as she did from a good, professional family. Her father had been a financier in the City of London and she had grown up with money until the devastating loss of all the male members of her family during the war had sent their fortunes spiralling downwards, forcing her mother and Eleanor herself to seek work.

Five years ago, there had been a fair few stately homes going on the cheap, but Edward's private bankers, Coleroy & Mack, had advised him against taking on such a venture, and their financial acumen, their hunch about the British economy and the increasing tax burden wealthy landowners would have to carry, had been proven right.

With the aristocracy selling up in their droves and investing their money elsewhere, he is happy not to have assumed their hefty tax burden, not to mention the social and economic responsibility they were all busy extricating themselves from. No, Edward congratulates himself for not falling into that trap. He might be considered by some to be nouveau riche or, as Barton Leyton once called him, a wealthy upstart, and stately home or no stately home, the people of polite society would continue to sniff down their haughty noses at him. But, unlike Barton, who moans regularly about the cost of keeping Mayfield Manor from crumbling around him, Brook End requires little maintenance and boasts both modern conveniences and ample space, as well as a beautiful location. Besides, Eleanor, who is of far better breeding stock than Edward, seems perfectly content with the house. At least, she never says she isn't.

'Evening, sir,' Alice greets him at the front door.

'Good evening to you too, Alice,' he replies, noticing her round and freckled face is flushed with excitement.

'Mrs Hamilton collected Miss Carmichael from the station earlier today,' she gushes. 'Lovely to have her home, isn't it? She's told me all about her tour around Italy. It sounded wonderful. And you must hear her speak French! Like a native, she is.'

'Indeed? And what did she say?'

'Oh, heavens, I've no idea. She could have been telling me I'm the queen of England for all I know, but it did sound lovely, like.'

Edward smiles indulgently. 'I see. And where are the ladies now?'

'Changing for dinner, I believe. It'll be served in fifteen minutes.'

'Excellent. I just have enough time to wash and change myself.'

Taking the stairs, he notices how empty the house is without a dog. A house really isn't a home without a dog in it. It's been over a month since Patch died. He must look into replacing him.

'My darling!' And there she is, standing arms outstretched at the top of the stairs. Eleanor. His beautiful wife.

He bounds up the last two, grabs her and pulls her into an embrace. 'Oh, how I've missed you!' he says, breathing in her lily-of-the-valley scent. He picks her up and swings her around, making her shriek and giggle.

'Edward!' she cries. 'Put me down!'

'Never!'

'Urgh, it's making me dizzy! Someone will see!'

'Who cares,' he laughs, and releases her.

'Go and wash and change,' she smiles up at him. 'You smell of London.'

'I do? And how does that smell?'

'Like old boots!' she laughs. 'Scrub it off and put on some of that cologne I gave you for your birthday. That will be a great improvement!' She blows him a kiss and skips downstairs. 'I must speak to Mrs Bellamy before she ruins the soup!'

During dinner, the first rumble of thunder growls over the clatter of cutlery and clink of glasses.

'Is that thunder?' Rose peers over her shoulder through the window and into the darkening garden beyond. She turns back to the table. 'We had such a *terrific* storm in Venice. Rain like stair rods. I was quite certain we would all be washed away, if we weren't struck by lightning first, because our funny little *pensione* was perched right up at the top of a rickety old building.' She tears the tiniest piece of bread from her roll and pops it into her mouth, chewing quickly, lips pursed, like a mouse. 'The old *signore* had to administer several glasses of Moscadello to Madame Martin, Clarissa and I, to calm our nerves. You should have heard our squeals!' She giggles at the memory.

'Well,' says Eleanor, 'you are quite safe here. There's no need for the fortification of anyone's nerves.' She takes a long drink from her water glass as if to prove the point.

Rose merely shrugs and nibbles on another morsel of bread.

Edward imagines that now Rose is home, he will retreat to his study more often, simply to avoid the overwhelmingness of too much female company. There is nothing wrong with female company, per se, but when there is an imbalance, a man must have a place of sanctuary. Marrying Eleanor had meant taking on so much more than just a wife, and Edward had done so gladly, willingly. Rose really has turned out rather well. There is no doubt she will make someone a decent proposition of a wife.

Rain begins to patter against the windows and the thunder rumbles closer.

Edward sniffs. 'If it clears up enough by Sunday, how about a picnic by the river? To celebrate Rose's safe return.' He smiles at her and raises his glass.

She beams and raises her own. Edward studies her as she replaces her glass and lifts the soup spoon to her lips. Bright and full of energy after she'd finished her schooling, she had begged Eleanor to let her go to Paris to immerse herself in the French language. The idea of taking up French was spun by a teacher at the Blofield School for Young Ladies, who had impressed upon Eleanor that Rose had quite a flair for foreign languages and that she shouldn't waste her talent. Rose is nothing if not determined.

Edward takes a swig of claret.

She *is* an attractive girl, if rather stubborn and overly confident. Nothing compared to Eleanor, of course. His wife still turns every head whenever she walks into a room. Whilst Eleanor tends to think too much – to take the weight of the world upon her shoulders – Rose has a certain *joie de vivre*, a vivaciousness which makes up for the irregularity of her features. She was too thin before her travels, but now she has a pleasant figure and her hair is cut into a sleek, modern style. She has become *à la mode* in Paris, it seems.

'You know her, don't you, Edward?' Rose is saying, tuning Edward back into the room. 'You must have met her too, Ellie?' Eleanor nods her head. 'Well, my advice,' Rose continues, 'don't! It's truly awful. Boring, old-fashioned – and damn it, the *women*! How can such an enlightened woman like her write a book about such pathetic creatures! And as for the men, well, don't start me on those!'

'Who? Which book?' asks Edward.

'*Love's Creation*, by Marie Carmichael. I mean, I had to read it, given the pseudonym. Coincidence, don't you think?'

'Pseudonym for whom?' Edward looks to Eleanor for help.

Eleanor sighs. 'For Marie *Stopes*. Her novel, *Love's Creation*, which, incidentally, Rose, took her *years* to write, is being slated by the critics.'

'Fairly,' says Rose. 'I think next time you see her, you should encourage her away from fiction.'

'We hardly have that sort of relationship, Rose. I'm not her editor – I've only met her through Edward's work.'

'Well, someone should,' Rose mumbles.

Eleanor frowns at her. 'Perhaps she *is* better at non-fiction work. With a second book out this year, she should be admired, not criticised. It's entitled *Enduring Passion* and follows on from her previous book, *Married Love*, dealing with matters pertaining to the bedroom and—'

'Yes, yes, I think we understand the subject matter, Eleanor. Not one for the dinner table.' Edward shifts uncomfortably in his seat, acutely aware of being the only male in the room. 'Besides, you should remember how much good she does in the world. All the work she has done on making birth control available for those least well equipped to have children is rather more important than her observations of what should or shouldn't take place between man and wife.'

'But that's the very point!' exclaims Rose, thumping the table with her free hand. 'She is a feminist and a progressive and yet her novel is about the most conventional of couples.'

'Feminist?' Edward wonders. 'Well, I suppose—'

'Now, if you really want to read something fresh and different,' Rose interrupts, 'I recommend Hall's *The Well of Loneliness*. Much more risqué! About a couple of lesb—'

'*Rose!*' hisses Eleanor, then there is a suppressed giggle from them both as Alice enters the room.

Edward's collar is too tight around his neck and the room is suddenly overly hot. What does Rose know of sexual inversion? It really *is* time to find the girl a husband. Alice silently removes his empty soup bowl and replaces it with a plate of sliced chicken.

'Potatoes?' she offers, returning with a bowl and serving spoons. He nods and she places tiny, perfectly round, buttered new potatoes on his plate. He adds a pile of green beans and carrots from the side plates on the table.

'Let's invite a party down from London next weekend. Now that Rose is back.'

Rose and Eleanor pause in unison and look at him.

'I thought you didn't like having people down, Edward,' Eleanor says, fixing him with a steady look. 'You usually say you come down here to escape people.'

'Well, yes... That's true, ordinarily. But shouldn't we be introducing Rose into some sort of decent society?'

Eleanor's eyes sparkle beneath the electric lights. They really are quite extraordinarily beguiling. Almost violet in this light. He wonders for the thousandth time how he ever managed to capture such an exquisite creature. How fortunate he was to encounter her that day he went to decommission at the War Office. He'd pulled out all the stops to entice her to come and work for him. He'd told her his invitation was purely professional, which was not exactly true, but as it turned out she had become a rather brilliant research assistant for three years, until he finally plucked up the courage to ask her to marry him. Truly, he doesn't deserve her, but with deft practice, he shoves that thought aside.

Rose drops her cutlery. Did she just roll her eyes? 'I've plenty of friends,' she protests. 'I don't need introducing to any stuffy—'

'You need a husband,' Edward cuts in, silencing her. If he is forced to take on the role of Rose's father next to Eleanor's mothering, well, so be it. He is, furthermore, at forty-three, old enough to *be* her father, although he finds the role uncomfortable. She must understand she can't cavort around Paris, Venice, Rome and London forever. She should marry well, which will be good for her and, in turn, quite possibly good for him too, if she finds a *somebody*.

'It's a bit late to invite anyone from town next weekend. Let's get some local people over for a tennis party, if you like,' Eleanor says smoothly. 'The Leytons, of course. And how about the Taylors and the Blythe-Etheringtons? Or the Millers? Rose, you'd like to catch up with Iris Miller and the Leyton girls, wouldn't you?'

'Yes! A tennis party would be fun. Could Clarissa come down from London too?'

'I don't see why not,' Eleanor agrees. 'I could invite Sophie and Henry too. Provided you don't talk constantly about Italy and bore everyone silly.'

'There is nothing boring about Italy.'

'Unless you weren't there.'

The rain intensifies against the windowpanes; thunder grumbles ever closer. Just as Alice is clearing the dessert plates, a flash, brilliant and white, momentarily illuminates the garden, the lights flicker, then go out altogether. A crack of thunder, shockingly loud and unexpected, sends the women shrieking to the window as another flash lights up the garden and the fields beyond.

Alice leaves to fetch the gas lamps, returning with two just as little Mabel arrives, shivering with fright, huddled in the arms of her nanny, Miss O'Connell.

'Apologies for the intrusion, sir,' Miss O'Connell says, her tongue curling around her words. 'The child refuses to settle, what with the storm and the lights out an' all. Screaming for her mother, so she is.' There is something mesmerising about Miss O'Connell's gentle Irish lilt, her whispery voice being so at odds with her looks. She's a heavy-featured woman. Strong bones, too, he can hear his late mother say, sizing up her thick waist and solid bust with a wrinkle of her nose and the arch of her eyebrow.

'That's perfectly OK, Miss O'Connell,' Eleanor says, pushing back her chair and opening her arms to take Mabel. Grace O'Connell is her full name. It, he muses, being at odds too. Graceful was something Miss O'Connell was most certainly not. 'I'll comfort her and get her off to sleep. You may get your supper, now.' The nanny, relief slackening her cheeks, her mouth folding up into a smile, turns and leaves the room.

Mabel clings to her mother and stares around with huge, blue-black eyes.

'Hello, little one,' Edward says, leaning across the table and stroking a hand over her hair, fine and delicate as spun silk. 'The thunder won't hurt you. It's just noise.'

'Nanny says it's God getting angry up in heaven at the bad people. He roars and thunders after them with a big, big hammer if He finds out you are evil on the inside, like

28

I can be sometimes,' she says, trembling. 'And He made the lights go out.'

'Ach, that's nonsense, Mabel. Whatever is she thinking, filling your little head with such rubbish?' Edward says; Eleanor shakes her head, pursing her lips.

'Am I bad, Mama?' Mabel asks. 'Is it my fault the lights went out?'

'No! Of course not, Mabel.' Eleanor throws Edward a look and takes their daughter's fat little hand in her own. 'Papa is right. Thunder is just the sound of the lightning in the sky. It can't hurt you. I shall have stern words with Nanny in the morning about all this.'

'Why would she frighten poor Mabel like that?' Rose tuts.

Mabel covers her ears with her hands and yelps at another, sudden, loud crack of thunder. The room flickers and flashes bright as daylight.

'Let's get you back to bed,' Eleanor says softly, placing the child on the floor.

'I'll take her up,' says Rose, picking up a lamp and leading Mabel with the other hand to the door. 'We'll have the lights back tomorrow, I promise. I'll tuck you in, safe and warm, and stay until you fall asleep. Would you like a story? Or I can sing you a lullaby. What would you like best?'

'Sing,' Mabel says, delight in her voice as the door to the dining room swings shut behind them.

Later, the storm spent, Edward smokes a cigarette on the terrace. The air is rich and earthy. Perfume from the jasmine growing beneath the terrace rises, pure, strong and sweet. The storm has washed away the hot, sticky air and it's pleasantly cool. Rose and Eleanor have already gone up to bed and Edward revels in the peace and solitude.

Cigarette finished, he climbs the stairs and knocks quietly on Eleanor's door. A week's absence, the pent-up electricity released by the storm and the need for oblivion, have intensified Edward's desire for his wife.

She is wearing her cream negligee, bare-armed, and tantalisingly see-through.

'My darling,' he says, taking her in his arms, the skin of her naked shoulders satin beneath his palms. 'I've missed you.' He cups her chin with his hand, raising her face upwards, kissing her warm, pliant lips. She responds briefly, then pushes him away, but smiles up at him, her cheeks flushed.

'Edward!' She grasps his hand. 'I've been desperate to speak with you all week, alone.'

He reaches for her again, pulling her close, this time kissing her throat, a feather touch, just as she likes it. But she brushes him aside and he laughs now at this strange game she is playing.

'No,' she says firmly, squirming from his embrace. 'You need to listen. Come, sit.'

She leads him to the bed, where he sits, pressed close to her. She strokes his hand.

'I have the most marvellous news.' She looks up at him coquettishly from beneath her lashes, biting her lip.

'Well, don't keep me in suspense,' he laughs, pushing a strand of her hair from her cheek.

'Can't you guess?'

His breath catches.

'Do I dare to?'

'Yes, I really think it's safe to dare this time!'

'Have you seen the doctor?'

'I have, and he is confident, now that I'm past three months. I've been feeling ghastly too, which he says is a very good sign. Can you believe it! The worse the nausea, the better, apparently.'

'You've kept it quiet all this time.'

'I didn't want to get your hopes up, didn't want to tempt fate. Besides, I've only really known myself for sure this last week.'

Edward kisses her, tenderly. Gratefully. This time, she doesn't push him away.

'I know we have been... But the doctor said, just to be safe, I should avoid... Well, you know. Because of the last three times... Do you mind awfully, Edward? I'm sorry. I just wouldn't want to risk...'

Did he mind? Of course he minded.

'I wouldn't dream of it,' he says. He places a light hand on her belly. 'This baby is the most important thing. It really is the best news, Eleanor.' He looks deep into her eyes. 'I'm happier than any man could be. Truly.' That part *was* true, wasn't it? 'You must get your rest.' He sighs and pats her knee. In the lamplight, she is more beautiful now than ever. His heart lurches.

'Stay, Edward.'

'No. You'll sleep better by yourself. I don't mind sleeping in my own room,' he lies. The dreams are never as bad when Eleanor is close. But it's only right that he should let her rest properly. Since Mabel, there have been three miscarriages, at around two months. The loss Eleanor had felt each time was a shocking blow. His guts contract at the thought of it happening all over again, especially if it were to be his fault. *Please let this one stick. Please let this one be a boy. A healthy boy.*

Maybe a healthy boy would be enough to dispel the bad dreams and haunting shadows for good.

I

*A*llow me to introduce myself. Or perhaps we've already met? It's quite possible. Diseases like me are hard to avoid. I hide away in the shadows until one day, it begins. A feather touch. Light as the brush of a moth's wing or the faintest breath of a newborn. Then, gaining strength, like the unfurling of a leaf, I take shape. An unwanted guest, crawling through the dark recesses of a loved one's mind.

At first, I'm dismissed as something other. For me, the subterfuge is all part of the game.

Can you see me?

Here I am: behind that blank stare; beneath the slack cheek. The relaxed button lips allowing a trail of saliva to ease its way out.

Finally, the realisation hits, and you know it's me – Epilepsy!

Then comes your frown. The purse of lips, tilt of head. The horror of it all.

A hand of sympathy from a loved one on your arm; a pat which says a thousand sorry words. The shrinking and shrivelling, the must stay away in case it's catching.

The shame and then the hiding.

After that, whatever harm I do, you do far worse. Oh yes,

you humans think yourselves above the animals, with your clever brains and fancy morals; but really, it's your inhumanity that sets you apart.

I understand what drives you. No single creature knows you better than I, for we go together, we two, however hard you try to order the world and rid it of me. Hand in reluctant hand. From Dostoevsky to Gershwin; Caesar to Joan of Arc to Vincent van Gogh; unknowns to kings and the sons of kings. There's no rhyme or reason. No pattern to comfort you. Rich or poor, young or old, genius or simpleton, I care not. They are all mine for the taking.

So, what am I, this creature of the mind you so dread?

I am anti-order. I am chaos. I disrupt and disturb. I'm the power of deception. A noise not there. A strange flavour on the tongue. A vivid pulse of light. The smell of hellfires; a kaleidoscope of colour. I'm an apparition; a clarity and a dissolution. You'll see me in the twitch of a hand, the fall of a chin. A darkness behind the pupils. The twist of a mouth, the jerk of a limb. The crack of a head; the falling, falling. I'm right there, behind those blank, dead eyes; that slack expression. I am the stuff of nightmares; the destroyer of memory. I'm inspiration and hallucination. Creation and destruction. For when my power is unleashed, your ordered world unravels.

But one thing, my friend, is certain. Whatever mischief I may make, it's nothing to the folly of your meddling.

Come. Let me show you where your arrogance and foolishness can lead.

3

Eleanor

'Have you seen Rose?' Eleanor asks each member of the household as she trails from room to room. The sun is high in the sky and Rose is nowhere to be found.

Eleanor's legs are shaky and her stomach queasy after the drive with Edward this morning. He can do many things well, but driving isn't one of them. Sitting beside Wilson at the wheel is one thing, beside Edward is quite another.

In the kitchen Mrs Bellamy is almost done plucking a chicken, its naked skin fresh and pink, like a goose-bumped baby's. Eleanor gags. She turns away quickly and helps herself to a glass of lemon water.

'She appeared briefly after breakfast, looking for something to eat,' Mrs Bellamy says, wiping her hands down the front of her apron. 'I've not seen her since, mind.'

The cook sighs and stretches her arms out wide and back as though easing her aching shoulders. Chicken plucking must be a strenuous task. Red and gold feathers lie in a heap on the table and a few of the finest down float on the light breeze from the open back door.

'This one's a skinny runt,' she says. 'I'll 'ave to send Bertie out for another. I'll never get enough meat off this one to feed all those mouths tonight. What was 'e thinkin', bringin' me this pathetic thing? And on top o' the electricity goin' off n'all.' She stares gloomily up at the dulled lights hanging above her head. 'Any ideas when they'll get it goin' again?'

'They're working on the generator now, I believe. Won't be long,' Eleanor says. She eyes the chicken. 'I'm sure that will be quite enough meat, Mrs Bellamy.'

'It'll be me who gets it in the neck if it isn't,' Mrs Bellamy sniffs and Eleanor wonders if the irony is intended. Mrs Bellamy herself could do with feeding up. Cooks are meant to be wholesome and round – Mrs Bellamy is all sharp edges and sinew. She certainly bears more than a passing resemblance to the skinny runt lying on the table before her.

'Whatever you think best,' Eleanor says, her voice light as the breeze stirring the hairs on the back of her neck. She tries not to think about another chicken having its neck wrung. 'I must find Rose...'

She leaves the kitchen, her glass of lemon water still in her hand. Best not to see what goes on behind the scenes of food production. If she thinks about it too hard, she is tempted into the notion of vegetarianism. And that wouldn't do, not right now, in her condition. Perhaps after the baby is born.

She stands in the hallway, sipping the water, the sharp tang of lemon calming the rolling sickness in her belly. Sunlight filters through the stained-glass windows either side of the front door, painting coloured reflections on the walls and splashing them onto the polished oak floorboards. The grandfather clock ticks loud and reassuringly beside her.

Edward scolded her this morning during their drive, gently and kindly, but all the same, his message was clear:

she must rest more and take care to look after herself and the baby. What does she think he pays Miss O'Connell for? The nanny must get fed up, Eleanor stealing her charge away from her whenever she fancies it.

She wonders at herself and what she has become. Refusing invitations to parties in town, on account of Mabel. She used to be a different sort of person altogether. She had taken the job at the War Office because she had had to earn a living, but she had come to enjoy it, had loved the buzz of office work, the feeling of being useful and playing her part in something bigger than the home. Working for Edward had been even better. She shared his passion for advancement in science and her feeling of usefulness increased. But once she married him, that had to stop. She thinks back to those early days and suddenly yearns for them. She'd loved working for Edward, collating all the complex data from his research, being in the thick of it, being near to him all day, every day.

She wonders how different her life might have been if she hadn't been brave when he'd handed her the note in the War Office. At the end of that day she had walked into Café Bru feeling outrageously brazen, although seeing him smile and wave at her from the table by the window, she had almost turned around and run straight back out. But his easy conversation and confidence had soon made her forget herself. He was a fascinating, clever man. She'd never met a psychologist before. A man of science; knowledge flowed out of him and into her eager ears. She was overwhelmed by his certainty, by the power and drive in him to change the world. He was looking for a research assistant, someone young, bright. Male or female, it didn't matter. Women, he told her, from the research he had conducted, and quite contrary to what some men thought, could be equally as clever as men. He was struggling to find the right person and the brigadier general had told him that once he'd finished his decommissioning, he would be packing up that office. Edward surmised, correctly, that he might not have any more need for her once that time came and the brigadier general had given her the highest of praise, he had said. Might she possibly be interested? The first thing she told him about was Rose. How she had to earn a decent wage to support them both. Six months later she was installed at a desk in his office at the university. And the rest was history. Edward had paid her double his other research assistants; nobody could have been more compassionate or caring.

She's happy with her life now, of course she is. What could be better than watching Mabel play on the lawn with her nanny while she sat on the terrace with the latest Agatha Christie in her hand? But still, there's a part of her that misses the feeling of doing something important, of using her mind and having a job, of lunching at the Savoy Grill or sipping champagne at the Ritz with Sophie and the cream of London society.

'Rose?' she calls hopefully, turning her face to the upper floors of the house. Surely she can't still be in bed? As Eleanor begins to climb the stairs, she thinks of herself at nineteen. Back to a time when she too might have spent an entire Saturday morning in bed. Utterly exhausted, having stayed up until the small hours with Sophie, dancing with young men at the Hammersmith Palais.

Until that day in 1920 changed her life forever.

'Rose!' She shouts this time, irritation rising.

At the top of the staircase, she vows to write to Sophie this afternoon. She will know some eligible young men.

Eleanor bursts into Rose's bedroom and there she sits, her back to the door, leaning over her writing desk, still in her night things, not even dressed!

'Here you are, Rose, darling! Almost lunchtime and you've not left your room,' she can't help but tut.

Rose swings around to stare at her, a flash of guilt in her light blue eyes. 'I'm sorry! Have you been waiting for me? I wanted to write a letter...'

'But it's your first morning back! Are you missing the girls at Madame Picard's already?' Images of Rose sharing a room with Clarissa and an assortment of other girls fills her head. The camaraderie, the larks – the freedom of being young and unmarried with everything still to come. She imagines the excursions around Paris, the shops and chic cafés...

Rose turns back to her desk, gathering neatly written pages together and turning them face-down on the blotting paper.

'That's a long letter, Rose dear,' Eleanor says, crossing the room and placing a hand on her sister's shoulder. 'Who are you writing to?'

'Oh, just a friend,' Rose says lightly.

'Come on,' Eleanor gives her shoulder a squeeze and laughs. 'Spill the beans. Perhaps we can invite your new friend down here for the weekend, with Clarissa, if you like.'

'Well...' Rose places a hand on the pages, as though worried Eleanor will snatch them up and read them. What is she hiding?

'Rose?'

'Oh, Eleanor! I suppose you shall find out soon enough anyway. And I know Edward has plans for me. It really is very awkward...'

'What is? What's awkward?'

'Edward wanting to marry me off, like some burdensome daughter in a Jane Austen novel. But it's the 1920s for heaven's sake, and while I know he's been awfully generous and everything, I simply don't want to marry. Not right now, anyway,' she adds in a rush. 'I want to live a bit first. I'm only nineteen and I want to work in town, like you did. You had to give up work when you got married and I don't want to do that. I want to have fun. I want a career. I should use my French. I'm pretty much fluent now, you know. And I speak passable Italian. I was thinking of journalism...'

'Journalism,' Eleanor repeats, gripping the bedstead beside her.

'And... Well,' Rose continues, 'I've met somebody. Formed an attachment.'

'What on earth do you mean?' Eleanor laughs. 'How can you have met someone? You've been at school all these months. With girls! You've been travelling with Clarissa and that Madame Martin, who was supposed to be keeping an eye on you. You can't possibly have met someone.'

'Well, I have. So there it is.'

'Who?'

'Sorry, Ellie, but you are behaving like my mother. And you aren't. You're my sister – you should be on my side.'

'There are no sides, Rose. I am on it!'

'It's simply that I have met the most dreamy man and – and I'm in love.'

'Oh!' Rose's gaze is steady and obstinate, her cheeks

carry that flush again. It's not a flush of good health. Of course it isn't. It's a flush of love. Of happiness. How did she not spot it before? 'But that's wonderful! Only, you just said you didn't want to marry?'

'I don't. That doesn't mean I don't want to form an attachment.'

Eleanor's smile dies on her lips.

'Just exactly how attached?' she asks, her voice hoarse.

'Seriously. As in: we are lovers attached.'

'Good lord.'

'His name is Marcel Deveaux. He's French. Oh, Ellie, he's the most devilishly handsome man. The most intelligent, lovable man you will ever meet!'

'Lovers.' Eleanor sinks down onto the end of the bed. 'Oh, Rose, how could you? Surely you are engaged? And what exactly does Monsieur Deveaux do for a living?'

'He's a painter and thinker. Writing and suchlike. He's part of the Paris set,' Rose says, her face lighting up with pride. 'And he is completely, utterly penniless. Which is why I need a job, Ellie. So I can support him while he gets established. I know I've a lot to thank Edward for and I'd not dream of expecting anything more from him because he's already done so much for me. But this is what I want, Ellie. You *must* tell Edward I'm not getting married to one of his rich friends!'

Eleanor lies down, her head propped up against the two cushions Edward fetched from the car after they finished the picnic lunch. It's nice of him, but he is fussing and clucking around her as though she's as fragile as a painted eggshell.

It was altogether more pleasant when this baby was her secret; when she could hug the notion of it to herself. Now she is other people's business: Edward with his fussing, Mrs Bellamy telling her what she should and shouldn't eat, Rose instructing her not to lift even the lightest of baskets. They should all just leave her be. She and the Grub, as she's named the baby, were doing just fine without *anyone's* interference, thank you very much.

The sun is warm on her face. The day has turned out fine, and thankfully a little fresher after last night's storm cleared the sultry air away. Before her the meadow, thick with wildflowers and yellowing grass heads, slopes steeply away, down towards the woods and the winding river, where it flows far below, out of sight between the trees. She closes her eyes, her body relaxing onto the picnic blanket. Edward has ambled off for a smoke with Wilson by the car and Rose has wandered away with Mabel. When Edward returns, she'll break the news. Always best to save unpalatable things until he has a full stomach and is relaxed after a smoke. Above the whisper of the breeze comes the rising shrill of a blackbird, the sweet trill of a song thrush, the rattling caw of a crow. She would be truly content, were it not for the bombshell Rose dropped this morning.

How on earth is she to tell Edward? Anger at her sister's stupidity rises inside her and her eyes ping open. What was she thinking, getting mixed up with a penniless Frenchman? How naïve to think she can support the two of them. What a dreadful money-grabbing, good-for-nothing sort he must be. Taking advantage of a young, well-to-do English woman. Perhaps he has heard of Edward and thinks he can get his hands on his money? How could he, this Marcel character, bear the indignity of being supported by a working woman? Clearly, he must be some sort of revolutionary socialist, seducing Rose as part of his grand scheme to live off her while he lazes around all day playing with his paints. Revolution is in the Frenchman's blood, if she isn't much mistaken. She shudders at the idea of Rose bearing his children, of lowering the quality of her excellent genes.

Eleanor begins to sweat at the thought of Marcel, his dirty hands wandering all over Rose. And what of Madame Martin, her supposed chaperone? She clearly hadn't been doing her job. She will write a letter of complaint, as well as to Madame Picard's school. Poor Edward, all those fees! Perhaps they could demand a refund. What good was it, grooming Rose for a good marriage if she went off and ruined her reputation like this? No one who is anyone will want her now. She'll be Spoiled Goods. Unless it is all hidden under the table. She'll ask Sophie's advice. Lady Grant-Parker, as she is these days. Things are different for girls now, Sophie often tells Eleanor, with a knowing wink. One must simply be *discreet*. Men have been at it forever, of course. Bloody hypocrites, the lot of them. Perhaps it isn't a *complete* disaster.

Eleanor props herself up on her elbows. There are Mabel and Rose, walking slowly towards her through the long grass, hand in hand, Mabel holding her butterfly net aloft, her face knotted in concentration. Eleanor smiles. It's a picture of summer beauty. Rose crouches and points, whispering urgently to Mabel. A flutter of creamy white as a butterfly rises a few feet in front of the pair and Mabel lunges with her net, thrashing it wildly from side to side, missing the butterfly by several feet. She falls head first into the grass, giggling.

'Come back!' she shouts. 'Butterfly!'

Rose helps her to her feet. 'Ah! Better luck next time, little lady. One must be quiet and stealthy to be a good hunter. Loud noises frighten the prey away,' she laughs as Mabel stamps her feet.

'I'll never catch one!'

'Of course you will. Patience. That's all you need.' She pinches Mabel's cheeks. 'Come on, my little hunter, I think we've earned ourselves a nice glass of lemonade.'

They flop down beside Eleanor and she pours two glasses of the cloudy, sweetened lemon water from the flask, handing them to Mabel and Rose.

'So refreshing, thank you,' says Rose.

'Did you two have a lovely adventure?' Eleanor asks Mabel.

'We didn't catch any butterflies,' Mabel says pouting, throwing down the net.

'Never mind,' Eleanor says, patting her knee. 'Butterflies like to be free in any case. They look so pretty fluttering about – look! Isn't that a Red Admiral over there?' She points to a large brown butterfly with flashes of red passing close by. Butterfly Meadow, they call this place, on account of there being so many of them when the grass, punctuated with wildflowers, gets long and before it's cut at the end of August.

'Yes, I think it is.' Rose watches it rise and fall, darting this way and that. 'Are you still mad at me?'

'I'm not prepared to discuss it now,' Eleanor replies quickly, looking at Mabel. 'I'm not going to spoil a wonderful afternoon. Once Edward knows...'

Rose sighs, throws her hat to one side and flops dramatically onto her back. 'I really think you're being terrifically old-fashioned and beastly, Ellie.'

'*Rose*,' Eleanor barks.

Mabel jerks and drops her glass of lemonade. The liquid soaks her dress and the glass rolls away. Mabel's head flops forward, snaps up. Her eyes roll and her breath is sharp, jagged, mouth pinched. Her head snaps again.

'Mabel!' Rose shouts, rolling away, pulling the hem of her skirt away from the puddle forming at Mabel's side. Mabel doesn't react.

Eleanor stands and plucks Mabel from the puddle, dabbing the wet fabric with her napkin. 'That was your fault!' Eleanor throws at Rose.

'No it wasn't! It was you shouting at me – you frightened her, the poor mite.' She sits up and grabs the cloth covering the picnic basket and uses it to mop up the spreading pool of sticky liquid.

Mabel glances around, looking dazed. 'Has she gone?'

'Who, darling?' Eleanor holds Mabel firmly. She's heavy in Eleanor's hands, floppy, as though she hasn't the strength to hold herself upright. The dark patch of wet on her dress stretches from her belly to her knees. They will have to go back now to get her a change of clothes. She was silly to have given Miss O'Connell the afternoon off. If she'd let her accompany them, as the nanny had wanted to do, Eleanor could have sent *her* back to the house to get Mabel changed, without spoiling the whole afternoon.

'The lady,' Mabel says, looking around with strange, blank eyes, 'the one with the fire hair. She smells funny.'

Eleanor meets Rose's eyes and she shrugs.

'I'm not sure who you mean, poppet,' Eleanor replies. 'It's just us, Rose and me. Come on, let's get you back to the house and changed out of those wet things.'

Mabel looks down at herself as if surprised to see she is covered in lemonade.

The little girl yawns. 'I feel sleepy.'

Rose stops wiping up the spillage and peers at Mabel. 'Ellie, do you think there's something wrong with her?'

'What do you mean?' Eleanor asks, looking down at her daughter who is leaning her head into Eleanor's chest, her eyes flickering. 'There was an accident. She's just tired, that's all.'

'Are you sure?' Rose looks up at her, brows knitted in concern. 'Her eyes looked so strange – her pupils all big and black. It was only for a few seconds, but... She was there, then she wasn't there. Did you see that?'

'No,' says Eleanor stiffly. 'I have no idea what you are talking about. Listen, if Mabel is tired, she'll fall asleep anywhere. It was just an accident. You're fine, aren't you, darling?' She gives her a little shake to wake her and puts her down. Mabel's legs buckle to start with, but then she straightens and stands, leaning against her mother's legs.

'Rose...' Eleanor turns to her. 'You stay here otherwise Edward won't know where we've gone. Tell him I've taken Mabel back to the house to clean her up as she's soaked in lemonade, and Wilson should bring the picnic things back in the car. I'll see you later at the house. Come on, Mabel, best foot forward.'

'Why don't I go and fetch the car?' Rose persists. 'Perhaps Mabel has a fever coming on. She did say some odd things, Ellie, about fire hair.'

'Do stop fussing!' Eleanor hisses. A tight knot has formed inside and won't release. She'd been looking forward to Rose's return for weeks. This picnic should have been perfect, the two of them together again. She looks down at Mabel then pulls her by the hand to start her walking.

They climb the steep hill and reach the path which leads through the woods around the back of Brook End. It's not a long walk but Mabel is dragging her feet.

'Carry?' Mabel reaches up her arms.

Eleanor sighs.

'You're too big and heavy for me now. Would you like a piggyback?'

She crouches down and Mabel clambers onto Eleanor's back, slumping against her, a dead weight as Eleanor tramps along the wide path between the trees. Sunlight dances through the branches and the leaves shift in the light breeze. A shape flashes at the corner of her vision. She stands still, heart thumping, peering between the silver trunks. She holds her breath. Wings flap, a branch bends. Something scampers in the undergrowth. No, there is nothing there. She exhales and walks on again, faster now, her senses on high alert. Forever jumping at shadows.

Eleanor puffs up the slope of the lawn towards the house, the sticky wet of Mabel's dress seeping through onto Eleanor's own clothes. She sees once again the sickening flop and snap of Mabel's head, remembers Ted's words of concern, Rose's poke and prod at her. She pushes them firmly out of her mind.

A warm bath and a sleep will see her little girl as right as rain in no time.

4

Edward

'Well, she will have to *disentangle* herself, won't she?'
Edward says dismissively. 'It must be done swiftly,
decisively, before any real harm is done.' He stands in front
of the mirror, legs spread, fixing his collar onto his dinner
shirt, pushing the studs firmly into place. 'Certainly better
this "attachment" was formed in Paris, not London. Less
likely to get out that way.'

Eleanor, dressed for dinner in her simple midnight-blue
gown, all long-lines and elegance – no visible signs of
pregnancy yet – sits in one of the armchairs in his room,
cross-legged, swinging one foot back and forth. Her face
is pale and she fingers the long string of freshwater pearls,
the ones he brought back from a conference in Bielefeld,
Germany.

'What form is this *attachment*, exactly?' Edward asks.
She meets his gaze in the mirror. 'Are they engaged?'

'I don't believe so. But she plans to move in with him. To
keep him.'

'What do you mean, keep him?' He maintains a calm
tone. Level. In spite of the irritation rising inside him like
an itch. Eleanor doesn't need this. Not now. She looks so

worried and so he can't let her see he's riled too. It would cause her even more stress and anxiety.

'I know, it's utter madness. She thinks she can get a job, as a journalist of all things. She plans to support him, and he plans to while away his days painting or some other nonsense. She tells me he is from a good family – there may even be some wealth – but Rose says he's turned his back on all of that, is some sort of bloody socialist. Apparently considers it vital that we should move to a planned economy – like Russia. Capitalism is dead, that sort of thing. Worldly goods apparently mean nothing. Love is enough. She says they will be happy with very little.'

He snorts. 'That's easy to say now, when she has all the greatest comforts provided for her. I suspect she thinks that if we meet her beau, we will be as entranced as she is, and that I will provide them with a comfy little *pied-à-terre*. Well, she can think again.'

'Oh, Edward! Don't be too hard on her. I'm afraid we will drive her away.'

Edward clips the last collar stud in place and snorts again. 'Nothing will come between the two of you. Look, she is in the first flush of romance. It's her first love! She knows nothing. It won't last, trust me.' He reaches for his black bow tie, doesn't say what they both know: that he is Eleanor's first and only love too. *His* past love affairs, sparse but a little messy, are kept strictly to himself.

He loops the tie around his neck. Perhaps he should find himself a valet. Would that be too much? He rather fancies the idea, but Eleanor would say he is perfectly capable of dressing himself. Besides, it would be an unnecessary expense. And devilishly difficult to find a good one. These days, without status and title, it's hard enough to attract any good domestics.

'What should we do?'

'We should,' he says, shrugging on his jacket, 'write immediately to this Monsieur Deveaux, and tell him to break off this nonsense. Has Alice taken today's post or is it waiting until Monday?'

'It's on the hall table. She'll take it to the post office first thing Monday morning.'

'Good. I'll find his address. Leave it to me. It's the last thing you need to be worrying about, especially now that...' He glances at her flat belly, hardly daring to believe the pregnancy is real. How wrong of Rose to put this stress in Eleanor's life at this very moment when she should be at her happiest and most content. 'I plan to make it very clear the pair won't be getting a penny from me. I doubt very much whether his family are any more pleased about all this than we are. Knowing there will be no money in it for him will cool his passion, I'm sure of it.'

'What if it doesn't?' Eleanor asks, her voice soft, frail.

'I suspect we will have to make some sort of compensation.'

'But what if what Rose says is true, if he really *doesn't* give a damn about money?'

Edward sighs. *What if.*

'He will.' He goes to her and lays a reassuring hand on her shoulder. 'Trust me, Eleanor, money can buy anything, if the price is right.' He pulls her up, looks into her eyes, sweeps a stray lock of hair from her forehead. He has the overwhelming urge to hide her away from all the bad things in life. She's been through so much. But she is strong, intelligent. She's had to be.

'Almost anything,' she says.

'Indeed.'

'I do hope it doesn't cost you too much, Edward. I'm so sorry about all this.' Eleanor looks utterly wretched, tears in her eyes as she looks into his.

He cups her face in his hands. 'Sweetheart. It's not your fault. You've done your very best to be sister, mother *and* father to Rose these past eight years. Don't let this worry you. I will deal with Rose and this Marcel. I promise.' He strokes his fingers across her cheek. 'The only thing *you* need to do is focus on this baby. Now, our guests will be waiting.' He kisses her forehead. 'If we don't go down soon, Mrs Bellamy will be huffing about her ruined supper. And we can't risk the wrath of Mrs Bellamy, now can we?'

Rose is already entertaining the guests in the drawing room by the time Edward and Eleanor come down. Their neighbours, Barton and Lizzie Leyton, have brought their two eldest daughters, Charlotte and Lilly, the younger two having been thankfully left at home with their governess. Also in the room are the great American, Harry Laughlin, and his wife Pansy, and two of Edward's most promising psychology students from the university, Leslie Hearnshaw and Peter Reinhart. Hearnshaw and Reinhart have already made the acquaintance of the girls, and the five of them are grouped in one corner of the room. Finally, Marie Stopes and her husband, Humphrey, who are house-hunting in the area, make up the party.

'Good evening, everyone,' Edward says, 'I do apologise for my tardiness.'

'No need, my man!' Harry smiles his broad smile and offers a warm, firm handshake. He is almost bald, but with a neat crop of white hair just about clinging on, making him look older than his forty-eight years. 'We're being well taken care of.' He raises his glass.

Pansy nods and smiles. 'We've been getting to know your delightful neighbours.'

That's perhaps not the description Edward would use. Barton, as usual, is holding forth. 'We've installed electrics in the downstairs rooms too,' he says in his deep-toned boom, 'at the cost of a wretched small fortune, I might add.' He scowls, his bald head shiny beneath the light of the once-again-working electric lights of the drawing room. 'Shan't bother with the upstairs. One only sleeps there, after all,' he sniffs. Barton, ten years Edward's senior at fifty-three, balances the loss of the hair on his head with an increasingly splendid hirsute face. Complaining about the cost of things is the favoured topic of conversation amongst the Leytons, with their large clutch of daughters and ever-dwindling income.

'Don't be absurd, Barton,' Elizabeth Leyton – Lizzie, as she insists – says. She turns towards first Pansy, then Edward and Eleanor, laughing merrily and loudly, as though her husband has cracked a most hilarious joke. He cannot imagine how it must be to live with these two, who blare when they could just as well talk. He feels a sudden pang of sympathy for the daughters. 'Of course, we must electrify the upper floors of the house,' she snaps. 'Simply everyone is electrified these days.' Her ample bosom jiggles along with her enthusiasm beneath her satin blouse. 'Don't you agree, *everyone* is electrified?' She glances around the assembled party, eyes imploring their support. 'I mean, whatever would people think if we only had the ground floor done?'

'Oh, absolutely,' Pansy chips in, regarding Lizzie with ever-widening eyes. 'How could *anyone* survive without electricity?'

'You English with these great, ageing piles of stone!' Harry cackles. He turns to Marie and Humphrey. 'And you? Do you have an ancient property around here too?'

'Not yet,' Marie says without humour. 'But we did see a most promising house in Dorking today. Didn't we, Humphrey?' He nods obediently. Where Marie is all voice and forceful energy, Humphrey is silent and discerning.

'Drink, sir?' Faulks, the butler, glides between them.

'Ah, a little tot of that nice Glenfiddich, if you please, Faulks.' Barton is all smiles now. 'The one I had last time I was here. So mellow and woody. Make it a large one, would you? Don't water it down with ice or whatnot, there's a good chap.' He settles himself back into Edward's favourite armchair. Short and stocky, he might once have been useful on the rugger field, but Barton has a clear weakness for the better things in life. He reminds Edward of a horse put out to spring pasture, his paunch a little rounder, his beard a little longer, every time he sees him.

'Yes, sir,' says Faulks. 'Madam?'

'Gin and tonic for me,' says Lizzie. She is taller than her husband by half a foot. She is well meaning, but a little silly and given over to expansive emotions. 'Slice of lemon and double tonic,' she says.

Edward watches her waving her arms about as she talks

Pansy through the problems of having friends with the very modern of modern conveniences and a spendthrift husband who prefers to live in the past.

Lizzie looks around the gathered group with a wide smile. 'So, tell me, Edward, how is it you know such delightful Americans? Barton only ever mixes with stuffy old Englishmen. What a refreshing change to meet some foreigners!'

There is a polite tinkle of laughter.

'Harry and I have a common interest in science,' Edward explains. 'In particular, in the field of eugenics. Harry is one of America's leading experts in this new and exciting field of study.'

Lizzie's eyebrows are travelling up her forehead. 'How impressive,' she says, bobbing with enthusiasm. 'Isn't it, Barton?'

'What the devil is *eugenics?*' Barton asks, looking perplexed.

'Put simply,' Edward says, giving his well-rehearsed answer to the uninitiated, 'it is a science inspired by Darwin's theory of "survival of the fittest". The aim of the Eugenics Movement is to improve the human population by increasing reproduction of the most desirable characteristics in human beings and suppressing reproduction of the *least* desirable – for example, inheritable diseases, mental retardation and so forth.'

'Sounds like it makes some sense.' Barton tilts his head, ruminating on the idea.

'But why would you want to get involved in all that?' Lizzie asks, her nose wrinkled as though they are discussing something rather distasteful. 'I thought you were something big in psychology or education, Edward?'

He laughs. 'I am, but these things are all connected. Besides,' he glances at Eleanor, who gives him the tiniest nod of approval, 'we have rather personal reasons for our deep interest in this work. Both Eleanor and I wish to see dangerous undesirables off the streets to avoid tragedies like the one which befell dear Eleanor's mother.'

There is a moment's awkward silence.

'Of course,' Lizzie says swiftly. 'I do understand. But it sounds like quite a task. How will it be achieved?'

Marie Stopes sidles closer to Edward. 'Birth control is one way,' she says.

'Ah, Mrs Stopes, I almost forgot,' says Harry, smiling at her. 'Miss Sanger specifically asked me to remember her to you.'

'Hmm,' Marie says, puckering her lips. It is no secret that Marie and Miss Sanger were not entirely at ease with each other. 'Thank you,' she says finally.

Getting on for fifty now, Marie is showing no signs of slowing down. Edward gives her a placatory smile. 'There could be no greater supporter of any negative eugenics model than Mrs Stopes here,' he tells the others. 'So great is her passion for curbing over-breeding by the lower orders and the inferior races that, in the absence of forced sterilisation being an option, she has funded the expansion of her clinic to offer free birth control for any woman who would qualify as a defective.' As far as Edward can see, that includes any woman who isn't rich.

'Ah, Edward! You are too kind,' Marie laughs. 'I hope

Miss Sanger is well?' she says to Harry. 'She has a fight on her hands over in New York. I feel for her.

'Now,' she turns to Edward, 'I hear your wife's sister has an interest in *journalism*. I have a proposition – how about she comes to work for me at *Birth Control News*? I really could do with some help. I'm rushed off my feet.'

'I've no doubt about that,' Edward answers, glancing towards the girls who are giggling, heads together on the other side of the drawing room. Why does he get the feeling they may be laughing about Marie's book. Rose was awfully cruel about it. He cannot for a single moment see Rose working with Marie, who is a woman of firm and, some say, extreme views about population control. Something tells him this would not be a match made in heaven. 'But Eleanor and I are rather hoping to dissuade Rose from the occupation. I'm sorry to disappoint you. I'm not sure Eleanor is ready to let her loose on the streets of London yet. She's had – well, in many respects at least – a sheltered upbringing. Whilst in Europe, she was, of course, accompanied by a chaperone. She'll be living here with us for the foreseeable future, which is too far to travel to London every day in any event. I wouldn't want her living alone in London in some ghastly boarding house.'

Marie shrugs and knocks back her gin and tonic. 'Ah well, it was just an idea. The offer is there if you change your mind.'

'We're being taxed out of existence,' Barton is grumbling to anyone who will listen. 'Nothing is sacred any more. Our very way of life is under threat. Wealth. It's a dirty word, these days. I should've thrown in the towel. Sold up and got out while I could. Moved to America. Or India. Or the Continent.'

'Pff. They're in a worse state than us,' Edward puffs. 'Especially France,' he adds through gritted teeth. 'And Germany worse still.'

'Are things better in America?' Lizzie asks.

Harry rocks back on his heels. 'Well, the economy isn't really my territory,' he says slowly, 'but I think it's fair to say my country has boomed since the war, where England and Europe have, well, stagnated. We're a nation who aspires. Wealth is *not* a dirty word where I come from. But of course, what happens in Europe, and to our closest allies, is of utmost importance to us Americans. It is in *all* of our interests to protect our democratic, capitalist system from the very real threat of communist revolution. We see that.'

'See?' Barton looks at Lizzie. 'Haven't I been saying this? You only have to read the papers!'

'I think we *all* here have the same interest at heart,' Edward agrees. 'The problems are complex and we certainly need to pull collectively together. In this country,' he addresses Harry, 'we have a stagnating economy because, with rising unemployment and reducing wages, people don't have enough money to spend on goods, hence the falling demand. Plus, our exports have been hammered thanks to Mr Churchill and his colossal mistake in 1925 to try to turn the clock back to before the war!'

'How so?' asks Harry.

'By returning us to the gold standard at a ludicrously high exchange rate. I even agree with Keynes on this point – as he says, fixing our currency value to gold is a barbarous relic. Still, like Harry here, I'm no economist either. *My* speciality relates to something much more far-reaching and valuable to us all.'

'Which is?' Lizzie asks, leaning towards him. 'Your work is always so mysterious, Edward. Do tell!'

'There's no mystery in what Edward does.' Eleanor laughs, winking at Edward. 'He's in the paper every other day, or so it seems.'

Edward smiles at her, then turns to Lizzie. 'The human mind,' he says with a flourish, tapping his own forehead for effect. 'It is the key to all of our fortunes, and of course it is much related to what we were speaking of earlier – eugenics and the *improvement* of the human mind; it's a fascinating topic.'

Marie steps forward, waving her empty glass for emphasis. 'But, as Harry here has alluded, we, our *race*,' she speaks expansively, like a preacher to his flock, 'is at a critical, pivotal point. It seems we have possibly reached the pinnacle of human intelligence. Our very civilisation itself is under threat as a result. We can do nothing and allow it to deteriorate. Or we can take action, now, and halt the inevitable decay. Save civilisation from an almost certain self-destruction.'

'Goodness!' exclaims Lizzie, hopping from foot to foot, sloshing gin and tonic out of her glass. 'That sounds awfully extreme. How can we be at the pinnacle of intelligence? Edward, you are the mind person, do you agree with...' she looks at Marie, so stiff and plain next to her voluptuous, frivolous self, 'her,' she finishes, with a curl of her lip and a wrinkle of her nose.

'I'm afraid,' says Edward, assuming the grave tone he

uses at his lectures, 'I do. It is an unfortunate fact that over-breeding by the *lowest* stratus of the population, in particular, the unfit, the feeble-minded, the criminals, alcoholics, epileptics and so on, combined with under-breeding by the *most* able – those of higher intelligence – creates an imbalance. Left unchecked, this leads us, as will be blatantly obvious, towards a disastrous future.'

Marie nods. 'If you think your taxes are bad now,' she waves her glass at Barton, 'they will become ruinous in the future. Imagine the cost of the hordes of defectives we will have to support? I can tell you, there are already young, married men today of the professional classes forced by this very fact to remain childless, because they simply cannot afford them due to the burden the underclasses are putting on society.'

'God, how depressing,' says Barton, staring gloomily into his glass. 'The end of civilisation. Not much we can do about that, I suppose.'

'All civilisations come to an end,' Harry says. 'The Greeks, Romans, you name it. This is not an over-exaggeration, I'm afraid. Western liberal democracy is on a slow, steady decline. Communism and the planned economy, autocracies, all on the rise around the world – and it's this population imbalance which is the root cause of the problem. Some say it's too late to save our dying democracies. But I remain optimistic. We mustn't go down without a fight, eh?'

Barton grunts. 'Another drink, Faulks, please.'

'And you, Harry,' asks Lizzie. 'What is your role in all of this?'

'I'm Director of the Eugenics Record Office at the Carnegie

Institute,' Harry explains. 'Edward and I – Mrs Stopes too – have much in common,' he adds. 'We've worked in parallel for a long time. We are both psychologists, educators, and above all interested in improving the health and wealth of our nations.'

'And what brings you to England?' Lizzie asks, all big eyes and ears.

'Well, as Edward says, our work overlaps. By sharing our knowledge and working together in the new and growing scientific field of eugenics, we can give the movement momentum in Europe. Our interests here are aligned and, let's face it, we need urgent progress on this now, more than ever.'

Harry sips his glass of water, eyeing Barton's refilled whisky with a frown. 'Indeed, I'm keen to push for a world government, so that these international issues of interest can be dealt with at a macro level involving all wealthy nations.'

'How would that work?' asks Eleanor.

'Along the lines of the League of Nations and the US constitution. This would, of course, be dominated by Europe and North America,' Harry explains, 'but it would be key in the battle to protect racial purity, in particular of the Nordic race – the most ideal race, so to speak. We are funding research in Germany with this in mind. Indeed, Pansy and I will visit the Kaiser Wilhelm Institute in Munich once our business in London is complete. The wealthy of America see philanthropy as a responsibility. To give back, you understand.' He turns to Barton. 'And what is it you do, sir?'

'Me?' guffaws Barton. 'I don't have a profession! I'm what we used to call in this country a *gentleman*. A dying breed… I *should* be able to live off the fruits of my land, but that is becoming increasingly difficult these days, thanks to wealthy upstarts, like Edward here.'

'I am a man of *science*, Barton,' Edward sighs, smoothing out the wrinkle of irritation at Barton's attitude. His upper-class snobbery for the fact that Edward is the son of a self-made man is unlikely to ever change. The brilliantly able John Hamilton, himself the son of a Durham-born miner, a fact Barton is unaware of and Edward has no intention of highlighting, put himself through night school to become a civil engineer. A man of prodigious intelligence, his work on laying regional railways and building bridges made him a fortune, which Edward, as his only son, luckily inherited. It is this which has allowed him to pursue his academic and research interests for the good of all mankind. But still… Edward carries the whiff of *new* money about him, something the Americans rejoice in, but the English aristocracy regard with varying degrees of disdain and suspicion.

'The one promising prospect,' Barton continues, brightening a little, 'is that we've bred rather a lot of pheasants this year. Thousands of birds, in fact. It's a decent way to generate a little extra income, you see, all that woodland lying idle otherwise. Adaptability, my man. That'll see us through. One can make a nice bob or two from shooting these days. London-types, pardon the expression, who like to host weekend shooting parties.'

'Talking of parties,' Eleanor says, 'Edward and I were planning to have a tennis tournament next Sunday. Rose's great friend, Clarissa, is coming down for the weekend. We could make a party of it – to celebrate Rose's homecoming.'

'What a wonderful idea!' exclaims Lizzie.

'Even Mabel can come out and join in the fun,' Edward says, cocking an eyebrow at Eleanor. She nods her agreement.

'She loves to dress up for a party. Already has quite the fashion sense at only four,' Eleanor laughs.

'Oh, and I nearly forgot,' Lizzie exclaims. 'Would Mabel like a puppy? I rather thought she might be missing dear old Patch. Our gamekeeper's retriever, Goldie, has five pups. He's keeping one and I promised the girls one. Would you like another? They're pure bred – I'm sure we'll find takers easily enough.'

'Edward?' Eleanor's face is eager and his heart softens at the thought of the joy a puppy would bring to the household. Mrs Bellamy probably won't be pleased, but then there isn't much which does please Mrs Bellamy, when one comes to think about it.

'Agreed. A home, after all, is not a home without a dog,' Edward acknowledges, just as Mrs Faulks bustles in to tell them dinner is ready.

Perhaps a new puppy might take Rose's mind off a certain Frenchman too.

II

You call it war.
     I prefer game.

For it is I, like the cat who toys with the helpless rodent, who holds the power. Despite your years of study and solemn institutions; despite your scientific advances and understanding of nature, you've not conquered me yet. If I choose to tease and taunt you, I will, and I do. Your pathetic, misguided attempts to get rid of me simply boil down to arrogance and false confidence. Oh, what diversion!

We've been at it for thousands of years, you and I, and I never bore of it. You see, you are so full of fear and superstition and religious fervour that I am easy to dismiss as something other.

It's an unfair game, or war, or whatever you want to call this thing between us. But, just like the cat with the innocent little mouse, that's half the fun! I love to lead you a merry little dance, concealing or revealing myself whenever I choose.

Can it really be me, responsible for that person not there? For the flash of light, the peculiar cloud on a sunny day? That broken sentence, the blank stare? Am I behind the misplaced object? The how did I get to be here? *Is it me who's responsible for the burnt arm, the cut lip, smashed head, broken rib? Your loved one's confusion, hysteria or aggression? Or could it be down to something else entirely?*

You cannot know, because I am a genius of subterfuge, deception and confusion.

Let's face it, you'd rather explain away your loved one's odd behaviour through any means but me. It's the hand of God, the Devil himself, witchcraft or sorcery.

And yet, in spite of all the incantations and the burnings; the drownings and the torture; the locking up and ostracising; the sterilising and euthanising – I'm still here!

Oh, how it suits me to have you fumbling in the dark for the light.

Well, my friends, so now you know: I have a new plaything. Fresh prey. This one malleable and young and open to visions and sensations.

You don't detect me here, behind the girl's strange ways.

You simply laugh and deny. In this twisted game you do not seek, while I hide.

For I am the master of disguise – and that is the beauty of it all.

5

Eleanor

Eleanor is putting the finishing touches to her display of home-grown roses on the hall table when the unexpected and loud *toot toot* of a motor car horn outside the front door makes her jolt and almost knock the whole lot on the floor.

Her face breaks into a huge smile as she swings the door wide. 'Who else...?'

Sophie's face is a white-toothed grin from where she sits, almost hidden behind the wheel of an exceedingly large motor car, her husband stiff and looking slightly green beside her.

'What do you think of my new motor, darling?' she yells above the purr of the engine. 'It's a Mercedes-Benz, no less. Birthday present from Henry,' she adds, patting him on the head as one might a pet Labrador.

'Eleanor!' Henry grins broadly and raises a hand in greeting. 'Bloody relief to be here. It turns out my wife drives insanely fast. Women drivers! They aren't safe on the roads. Should be bloody banned.'

'You haven't experienced Edward's driving,' Eleanor murmurs beneath her breath, smiling and waving back.

Lord Henry Grant-Parker jumps down from the car and walks languidly around to open the driver's door for his wife. He has an easy grace, a birthright, like all of those of his class, suave sophistication and certainty of their own superiority being served up alongside their morning milk.

Sophie peels off her driving gloves and unties the ribbon securing the hat to her head. She mimes a kiss against each of Eleanor's cheeks.

'Did you drive that thing all the way down from London?' Eleanor asks, staring at the car, its bonnet impossibly long, sleek and silver. It looks fraught with danger. 'You *are* brave.'

'Oh, I don't mind. Gives one a rush, this driving lark. Have to sit on a cushion, mind you, or I can't see over the top. Damn pedals rather a stretch too, but I love it when everyone jumps out of the way, seeing me roaring towards them. What japes! Henry likes to be driven really, though, don't you, darling? Anyhow, are we the first? Who else is coming?'

'Wonderful day for it,' Henry comments, stretching his arms out wide. 'Edward out on the court already, is he, getting in some early practice?' He laughs and mimics a tennis swing.

'No, he's—'

'Look at you!' Sophie loops her arm through Eleanor's as they make their way inside. 'Hiding away down here in the bloody depths of bloody nowhere. Why haven't you come to a Friday night soirée for ages? Are you avoiding me, dearest chum?'

'No! It's—'

'And where's that sister of yours? Back from her travels?'

'Ah, Rose, yes, I need to speak to you about her—'

'Dying to hear about her time in Paris. And Italy – where

was it she went? Rome? Florence? She *must* have done Florence – and Siena, my *absolute* favourite. Come along, Henry…'

Rose and the elfishly beautiful friend, Clarissa, are in the kitchen imploring something of Mrs Bellamy, who has her hands on her hips and is shaking her head violently.

'I am *not* cooking any foreign muck. If you want to eat such things you'll 'ave to go to them fancy restaurants in London. I'm a good cook, and I'm sticking to proper food, *English* food,' she says firmly.

'But Clarissa has the re—'

'Look who's here,' Eleanor breezes in, giving Rose a sharp *stop it* look. Upsetting Mrs Bellamy must be avoided at all costs, or the entire household will suffer from her bad temper. They had a week of overcooked, dry, salty meat and watery vegetables only last month after Edward made some ill-judged remark. 'Rose, Clarissa, please go and entertain Lord and Lady Grant-Parker on the terrace.' Clarissa flickers her large eyes over Henry and bites her lip. 'Mrs Bellamy, please ask Alice to bring out a jug of lemonade and some glasses, thank you. And the champagne on ice. Oh, and the lunch smells truly spectacular!' She flashes her most warm and grateful smile at the cook.

The guests gather on the back terrace beneath a pale blue sky and whipped-cream clouds. Below them is the croquet lawn and Eleanor's rose garden. Beyond that, the main lawn slopes away towards the tennis courts and the sweep of rhododendrons. Beneath the wisteria-clad pergola, Faulks and Bertie are putting the finishing touches to the table decorations where lunch will be served after the tennis.

'What was it you wanted to say about Rose?' Sophie asks, a champagne flute dangling from her fingers.

Eleanor checks no one is listening and sidles closer to Sophie's ear, filling her in on the French lover, Marcel, Edward's disappointment and Rose's ridiculous notion of becoming a reporter and supporting him whilst he satisfies his inner artist.

'How very decadent,' Sophie comments, squeezing her eyes half shut and giving Eleanor a sideways look. She takes a drag on her cigarette. 'I rather like the sound of him. Suave, sexy Frenchman, eh? Bit of a cliché, but whatever. I'm sure she'll bore of him soon enough. I expect we can find some equally charming Englishman to lure her away. Leave it to me, darling. So, how about you both come to London next weekend and I can make some introductions?'

'Oh, not me. I can't leave Mabel.'

'Why ever not? I leave my two horrors at every opportunity.'

Eleanor does not expect Sophie will be any closer to her children, Sebastian and Freddie, than she is to her own mother. Eleanor had met and become friends with Sophie at boarding school before the war. She'd glimpsed Sophie's mother only once or twice, a frightening and distant matriarch, during the school holidays. The maid, nanny and chaperone were the constant familiars in Sophie's young life.

'Once they are older and a bit nicer,' Sophie is saying, 'I expect I shall want to spend more time with them. Boarding school will sort them out – it'll turn them from monstrous beasts into tame and elegant young men. The least exposure to them now, the better, in my view. Three and two really are most tedious ages.' She lets out a tinkle of laughter.

Eleanor takes a deep breath.

'I'm expecting again, Soph. I can't risk losing this one,' Eleanor says, skirting the topic of Mabel.

'Oh, bad luck!'

'Congratulations would be a more usual response.'

'Well, that too, of course. Goes without saying. But bad luck all the same. Hateful for the figure and made me feel rotten for the whole damned nine months.' Sophie raises her champagne glass as a toast. 'Well, best of luck, old chum. And to the good old times,' she smiles. Then, 'How's Edward?' Sophie asks, squinting into the sun as she watches the first raft of tennis players make their way across the lawn towards the courts.

'Working all the hours,' Eleanor sighs. 'He's so busy. Taking on too much, if you ask me. He's been staying up at the flat all week these days.'

'Oh?' Sophie pauses and studies Eleanor's face, a slight frown appearing on her forehead. 'You know, perhaps you should drop in on him in Bloomsbury now and then. Surprise him. Keep him on his toes. A man left up in town all week must be subject to all sorts of temptations.'

Eleanor laughs. 'Edward wouldn't... He isn't the type...'

'All men are the type, Eleanor. Trust me.' Sophie throws a look towards Henry, whose mouth is so close to the impish, giggling Clarissa's ear, he appears to be lapping it. Eleanor blinks and looks again. No, she didn't imagine it. The two are unquestionably flirting. Why would he, when *Sophie* is his wife? Sophie's pale nostrils flare when she sees what Eleanor is looking at. She lets out a breath. 'Just another of Henry's little diversions,' she says, and sucks hard on her cigarette.

Dressed in white silk, trimmed with lace, Sophie is a vision of sophistication. Not beauty, exactly, but style and grace. She looks distinctly out of place at Brook End. Too smooth, too grand for its rustic, middle-class attitude, if a house can have an attitude. It's definitely no morgue like Henry's grand country house in Gloucestershire, filled with priceless antiques, laid out to wow its visitors. Brook End is a *home*, not for show. It's all honeyed wood and comfy sofas, books piled high on coffee tables, begging to be read. There's an easel set up in the morning room with a half-finished picture of the garden which Eleanor can't quite get right, and the detritus left by Mabel that Eleanor doesn't bother about, knowing Miss O'Connell will clear it up at the end of the day.

Henry has slid his arm around Clarissa's waist. Eleanor curls her toes. How awful to be humiliated like this in public. Poor Sophie, the woman who appears to have it all. Married to Lord Henry Grant-Parker, once the most eligible of bachelors, until she snapped him up. The newspapers love her. Lady Grant-Parker, leader of fashion and style, is often photographed for the gossip pages during the Season, wearing Chanel at Royal Ascot, Schiaparelli at Goodwood, Lanvin at Henley. Whatever Sophie has, others want too. Including her husband, it seems. Eleanor turns away in disgust.

'Shall we go down and watch the tennis?' Sophie asks, stiff-backed, head held high.

'Good idea.' Eleanor touches Sophie's arm, hoping she

can feel Eleanor's solidarity through her fingers. She searches the guests for Rose and spots her talking to the Leyton girls. She waves her over. 'Would you go down to the courts with Sophie? I promised Mabel she could come and join in the fun. I'll be back soon, I promise,' Eleanor tells Sophie.

She darts back into the house and climbs the stairs to the nursery, the unpleasant images of Henry draped over Clarissa, a girl half his age, playing through her mind. What a disgrace. And the girl? Her parents should be keeping a closer eye. She'll be spoiled goods now. Like Rose. Dear God, Rose! How could she? Sexual deviance wherever one looks. She shudders, glad that Rose's misdemeanours at least are not on public show. She will do everything she can to make sure it stays that way.

'There you are!' She smiles at Mabel who is playing on the floor in a patch of sunlight. Her ragdoll, Prudence, is being held upside down by the ankles, her yellow-wool hair dangling.

'Mama!' Mabel scrambles up to greet her. 'Prudence was being very naughty so I said, "You are a bad, bad dolly. You have the devil inside you, you are so bad."'

'Oh! I'm sure Prudence doesn't have the devil inside her.' She wonders where on earth the child gets this stuff.

'Oh, she does,' Mabel says gravely. 'That's why I have to hold her upside down, so the devil falls out, see?'

'I do.'

Mabel throws herself into Eleanor's arms. She smells faintly of warm milk and sweet lavender.

'Would you like to come and watch the ladies and gentlemen play tennis?' Eleanor releases her to the floor and crouches to be at Mabel's eye level.

'Can I play?'

'Not this time, my darling. You're too little.'

'Oh.' Mabel's lower lip juts out and her face folds into a frown. 'That's not fair.'

'Mabel! Do not speak to your mother like that!' Miss O'Connell, her face fierce, is folding Mabel's clean clothes and putting them away in her wardrobe. 'Apologise, or you shan't be watching the tennis at all!'

'Sorry, Mama.' Mabel's cheeks redden.

Eleanor glances up at the nanny. She seems very cross today. 'Hush,' she says, squeezing Mabel's chubby arms and smiling at her so she knows Mama isn't cross, even if strict Miss O'Connell is. 'I'll play tennis with you another day. Now, would you like to come with me and watch the tournament? You must promise to be a good girl, though, and stay quiet and not disturb anybody.'

Mabel nods her head vigorously, just as Miss O'Connell says firmly, 'Tennis tournaments can go on for an interminably long time when you are only four. I'll bring Mabel down soon enough and it will give you a chance to mingle with your guests, as every good hostess should.'

Something snaps in Eleanor's chest. Damn the woman for telling her how to behave at her own party.

'I'll take her now, Nanny,' she says firmly. 'She can have something to eat with us, and if she gets bored, well, I can send her back to you.' She smiles sweetly at Miss O'Connell. 'Come along, Mabel.'

As they leave the room, they find Edward, changed into his tennis gear, at the top of the stairs.

'Papa!'

Mabel takes his hand and they walk down side by side counting stairs, two by two.

On the top lawn, Mabel darts off to play hide-and-seek as they head down the garden, disappearing behind shrubs and hollyhocks in the borders, shrieking with laughter each time Edward discovers her. Eleanor smiles, the sun warming her shoulders, the muted sounds of ball on racket, laughter and a yell rising from the direction of the courts.

But now Edward is crouching in front of Mabel. She is standing unnaturally still, one arm outstretched, her finger pointing at something unseen. Eleanor's heart plunges.

'I don't know what you mean,' Edward is saying to Mabel. He looks in the direction she is pointing. 'Lady with the fire hair? I can't see anyone. But I think you mean *red* hair. That's what we call it.'

'Don't like her,' Mabel says, and Eleanor feels sick. They don't know anyone with red hair.

'There's nobody there, Mabel.' Edward stands and puts his hand out again for her to hold. She takes it, still pointing with her other hand. 'Now,' says Edward, 'if you play your cards right, your mother *might* let you have a slice of Mrs Bellamy's honey cake.'

Mabel smacks her lips. Then, as sudden as if she'd been shot, she is down, sprawled and jerking on the grass.

Edward lets out a yelp. 'Eleanor!'

Her mind moves slowly and is strangely detached, as though watching the scene through a mist, or from behind a curtain. She told herself the incidences at the station and the picnic were nothing. Three times now. It's hard to ignore. She watches Edward give Mabel a short, sharp slap across her cheek as though to rouse her. At first she doesn't respond, then she opens her eyes and looks dazed.

'There's something wrong with this child!' Edward stares at Eleanor, wild-eyed. 'Do you think she's coming down with something?'

Eleanor shakes her head and crouches down next to Edward.

'Edward,' she says softly as they both stare at Mabel, 'it's not the first time this has happened. I've seen it before.'

'What? Why didn't you say? *When* did it happen before, Eleanor? How many times, for goodness' sake?'

'I thought maybe – maybe it was nothing.'

The little girl turns and looks at her, her eyes swimming into focus. 'Mama,' she says, trembling slightly, reaching her arms out.

Eleanor sits on the grass and pulls their daughter onto her lap. She meets Edward's eyes. They are both thinking the same thing.

'I'll take her back to the house,' she says, her voice breaking. 'Get Miss O'Connell to put her to bed for a couple of hours.'

'That would be for the best.' He looks at Eleanor, his face tight, and her heart crashes. 'We cannot tell anyone about this,' he says. She nods dumbly. 'Not until we... Get some advice.'

'I-I'll tell Miss O'Connell and the guests that she tripped and banged her head when she fell.' She brushes the child's hair from her eyes. 'That she needs a rest.'

'I still don't understand why you didn't tell me,' Edward says, his voice low.

'I was afraid. And besides, she has a vivid imagination.

74

I thought that maybe she was just overtired and it would pass. I didn't want to call the doctor in case...'

Edward nods. 'Has Miss O'Connell not mentioned anything?'

Eleanor shakes her head. 'No, absolutely not.'

'Well,' Edward smiles thinly, 'perhaps it is nothing.'

'Edward!' Barton is yelling from the tennis court. 'We need you to make up a four!'

'Coming!' he yells back.

'You'd better go and enjoy the tennis,' Eleanor says, controlling the wobble in her voice. 'I'll fetch Mabel some honey cake on the way back to the house. Oh, perhaps that's it. She hadn't had any lunch! It's my fault. I should have let Miss O'Connell feed her before...'

Edward puts a hand on her knee. 'Don't go blaming yourself, Eleanor. But perhaps you are right. Cake. Yes. A little something sweet might do the trick.'

She watches Edward walk towards the tennis party. He glances back, just once, and gives a little wave. She knows she must get Mabel back to the house before anyone asks questions, knows Sophie will be waiting to talk to her, but she is just so weary.

She pulls her daughter in close, hugging her tight, rocking her until her head comes to rest against Eleanor's chest. Within seconds, she is fast asleep, rosebud lips parted, eyes flickering gently beneath the closed lids. Her skin, peachy-cream, is smooth and soft, a hint of flush now appearing again on her cheeks after the earlier pallor. She will never tire of looking at this face. Every line, every curve of her features, as familiar to Eleanor as her own.

6

Edward

The offices of Coleroy & Mack at Number 24 Cheapside are housed in a building with discreet, blanched stone from the outside, solid, dark teak on the inside. As a bank, they are small, in comparison with the joint-stock giants, but here every client is special. A niche bank for the wealthy, for those who need to know their money is in good, safe hands, where few questions are asked, but every care is taken to look after the client's best interests. Coleroy & Mack were banker to Edward's father before him, ensuring his hard-earned fortune multiplied satisfactorily, mostly with investments in the burgeoning electronics and steel industries in America. Now they are looking after Edward's funds with equal shrewdness in the financial marketplace.

'I don't like risk,' Edward impressed on Mr Coleroy many times when the man had mooted the idea of speculating on the stock exchange.

'Everyone is a speculator these days,' Mr Coleroy told him. 'A very good way of making fast money.' But Edward has never been tempted.

'I have plenty of money,' he also impressed on Mr

Coleroy, 'and I want to keep it that way.' Anything fast sounded risky and made him nervous.

With mutterings of 'As you wish,' Mr Coleroy agreed to stick to real investments in real companies and solid government bonds and left the speculation on flimsy things like paper and futures and options to braver souls than him. What Mr Coleroy could not know and would never understand, since he had undoubtedly come from a well-to-do family which never worried about having enough money, was that Edward had every reason to think differently. As James Joyce so succinctly expressed in *Ulysses*, his father was one of those who had forced his way to the top from the lowest rung by the aid of his bootstraps alone.

Edward's father had been sent down the coal mines at the age of twelve and had looked after every penny of his hard-earned cash with a care and dedication Scrooge would have deeply admired. It was ingrained in Edward to take great care of his money, to never risk it slipping through his fingers, the hovering possibility of poverty being all too well understood.

Through sheer brainpower and working all hours of the day and night, his father had accumulated a good deal of money and they had lived modestly, in an ordinary small house with simple clothes, simple food, simple furniture. As a young child, Edward had been happy – he'd known nothing else. The only extravagance his father indulged in was to spend money on his son's education with the one intention of elevating him from the working classes.

But the reaction of his new school chums to Edward's inelegant background had been brutal. Edward quickly became ashamed of his rough parents and small house.

Ever since, he had done everything he could to hide his origins, compensating for his family history by speaking out against the underclass to leave no one in any doubt of his allegiances. Even Eleanor had no idea just how humble his beginnings were – she would never have married him if she'd known, he is certain of it. Even if her family had hit on hard times because of the deaths of her brothers and her parents, they had at least been of decent, good breeding.

He, on the other hand, was an anomaly. A bright spark amongst the ash and grime of the lower classes.

'Good morning, Mr Hamilton.' He is greeted by a middle-aged receptionist, sporting a neat grey bun, who looks tiny behind her oversized desk. It gives him a warm rush to be recognised on sight. 'Do you have an appointment?' she asks, running her finger down a list of neat writing in her large leather-bound desk diary.

'Good morning. No meeting today – I'm here to make a withdrawal.'

'Ah, yes.' She looks up at him and smiles. 'Certainly. Come through.'

He wishes he didn't have the dull throb of a headache as she leads him through a large door to a room where a number of clerks are seated, working through ledgers. The headache is hardly a surprise. He suffers from many of them, clusters of pain, pounding against his skull, which go hand in hand with the worst of his nights. Last night, as is often the case before a day like today, he barely slept at all. And now, after the tennis party weekend, he has the added worry about Mabel to add to the normal turmoil in his brain. He even found himself praying to the God he can no longer believe in, that what they witnessed was really nothing at all.

The receptionist leads him over to a cashier.

'I'll leave you here, in the safe hands of Mr Jones,' she says with a smile and heads back to her oversized desk.

Jones stands in a rush, shoving the papers he is working on to one side, his pen dropping to the floor as he leans across to shake Edward's hand.

'Good day, Mr Hamilton. Is the family well? Will you be withdrawing the usual sum?' he asks, retrieving his pen from where it rolled behind his chair. Jones is of a nervous disposition. A thin and sallow-looking young fellow, wearing a crumpled shirt and thin tie. Devil only knows why he should be so nervy around Edward – they go through the same transaction every month so he should be used to it by now. Edward watches as the lad's hand trembles a little as he writes the withdrawal sum in sloping letters on the cheque for Edward to sign. It suddenly hits him that perhaps the lad thinks these regular, large cash withdrawals have some sort of criminal connotation. But that's ridiculous. Edward is a well-known man. He is often quoted by the British Broadcasting Corporation on the wireless, no less; his reputation is impeccable.

'Excuse me for a few moments,' Jones says, taking the cheque and disappearing behind another door to fetch the cash. The room is quiet, bar the scratch of a pen, the shuffle of a clerk in his chair and the clearing of a throat.

Edward leans back in his chair and checks his watch. His temples throb. He reaches up and kneads the tight knot of muscles in his neck and shoulders. Ten thirty. He has time to walk. He'd rather do that than face the grimy, airless tunnels of the tube. A pleasant stroll along the river will be just the ticket; perhaps the fresh air will rid him of the darned headache.

He imagines Eleanor calling Dr Hargreaves, as they agreed in the end she should. Dear God, he needs a cigarette. He reaches for his cigarette box in his jacket pocket, snaps it open, pulls one out. He promised he would be home for the consultation, even though his week is chock-a-block with meetings and lectures and letter-writing. He strikes a match and lights up, his palms clammy. Drawing the smoke into his lungs, the hit of the nicotine calms him.

The door bangs, making Edward jump. Jones is back.

'Here we are, Mr Hamilton, sir. Apologies for the wait.' He seats himself back at his desk, pushing an ashtray in Edward's direction, and, breathing heavily, counts out the one-pound notes. 'It's all there,' he says, when the last note has been placed onto the pile. 'Twenty-six pounds.'

'Perfect. Thank you, Jones.' He stubs out the cigarette and picks up the pile, feeding it into the large envelope he has brought for the purpose, then slides the envelope into his slim briefcase. He stands and holds out his hand for Jones to flap with his cold, limp fingers. Edward places his hat on his head. 'See you next month, Jones. Have a good day – goodbye.' With a brisk smile, he heads back towards the reception area.

The doorman nods as Edward approaches and pulls the door wide for him to pass through. He steps out onto the pavement and takes a long, deep breath, his heart beating a steady thud, thud in his ears. The headache tightens its grip.

The street is crammed with motor cars, trucks, bicycles, the odd horse and cart. Horns are blowing, people yelling.

The traffic is almost at a standstill. As he makes his way toward the Thames, he sees the river, too, is busy with barges carrying coal, logs and consumer goods; with sailing vessels, steamboats, pleasure cruises, fishing boats. London has become a sprawling mass of humanity, a boiling pot of wealth and poverty, class and the absence of it, brains and brawn. The whole city, in its frenetic effort to put the horrors of the war behind it is careering, full-steam ahead towards – what? Something better? Or something worse? Whatever it is, Edward, like everyone else, flows with it, helpless against the rip tide of its frantic energy.

But the past, he thinks grimly as he quickens his speed, one can never be truly free from the past. The heavy weight of its grip, however hard he and this beloved city try, will slowly but surely suffocate them all until, one by one, silently screaming, this broken generation is dead.

Only then can there truly be peace...

Violet is waiting, as arranged, on the bench behind Black-friars Station. They meet here in the summer months; in winter, their preferred place is the saloon bar at the Queens Head pub where they can warm themselves by the fire, Edward with a coffee, Violet with a gin and lime. Edward prefers the summer arrangement. This way they can sit, side by side, watching passers-by and Edward doesn't have to meet her eyes.

'Morning, Captain... I mean, Mr Hamilton,' Violet says, making to stand when she sees him approach.

'Please. Don't get up.' Edward raises his hands to emphasise the point. He stands awkwardly before her. She is a small-boned, slim woman, of seemingly indeterminant age. He knows she is around thirty, but she could be older, judging by the looseness of the skin around her mouth and eyes. Her mousy-brown hair is long and wound into a tight bun at the back of her head, her clothes functional rather than fashionable. But her face is pleasing – regular-featured, pretty. He never knows what is quite appropriate. Should he shake her hand? Kiss her cheek? 'How are things?' he asks instead, avoiding all contact and taking his place beside her.

'Not so bad, sir,' she says. 'And yourself? How is your family?'

Edward can feel Violet's gaze take in his expensive clothes, his well-polished shoes, the sharp features of his face. He cannot bring himself to look properly at her. Not yet. Instead, he stares straight ahead, ignores the continuous thud, thud in his temples. He takes in the scenery; the London plane trees in full, splendid leaf. On the other side of the street, a man is selling roses from a bucket, holding out a stem to people passing on the pavement. *Half a dozen for six pence!* A newspaper stand is set out next to the kerb and he can see the headlines pasted to the board above the stand from where he sits:

LONDON AIR RAIDS. Final Attack Last Night – Fighter Machine In Flames. Ministry Admits London Inadequately Protected After Defences Put to Test In Mock Air Attack.

MORE UNEMPLOYED! 1,354,000 registered on July 30.

STABILISATION OF COAL INDUSTRY – Negotiations for extending five-counties scheme to halt reduction of prices and end market surplus.

It's the top headline which holds his interest. *Air Raids.* London has been subjected to mock air raids the last few nights, preparations for another war when the country is still reeling, unrecovered, just ten years after the last one. That war had promised to be the war to end all wars, but promises, it seems, like men and ancient books, are fragile and liable to crumble into meaningless dust. He tears his eyes away, aware of his quickened pulse, shoves the wretched thoughts to the back of his mind.

He glances at his companion. 'Things are fine with me, thank you, Violet.' He hesitates. How much is appropriate to share? 'I'm to be a father again,' he finds himself confessing. He needs to keep the conversation going, avoid any awkward pauses.

'My congratulations, then, sir. Pleased for you. I see you're a busy man, these days. Seen your name in the papers, once or twice. Not that I understands any of it!' She shuffles her feet. 'Anyroad, as it happens, I'm expecting too. Fifth time for me.' She huffs. He shifts to look and realises he had failed to notice her rounded shape when he'd approached the bench. 'Too many mouths to feed already, what with my Bob laid off again,' she tuts. 'I bloomin' hope this is the last one...' Her voice fades away, embarrassment taut between them.

'There are ways, you know.' Edward feels his face flush, but pushes on. This is important and men like him can't afford to be squeamish. 'There is a book entitled *Married Love*—'

'Not so good with readin'. No time, you understand.'

'Of course. Well, the author is a friend of mine, as it happens. She has a clinic, a Mother's clinic, here, in Central London. Stopes is her name. Marie Stopes. She helps women like you. I can write a letter of introduction—'

'I wouldn't be able to afford the fees.' Violet shrinks beside Edward on the bench, her head lowered, fingers twitching in her lap.

'No, no,' Edward says. 'The clinic is free for all married women. She can help you with methods of...' He can't think in the moment of a polite way of saying it. When he is lecturing, or in a clinic situation, he has no problems with the words 'contraception' or 'birth control', or even, if there are Americans in the room, 'planned parenting', but here, sitting in the sunshine on a bench with Violet, the discussion is acutely uncomfortable. 'Well, I would be most happy to write you a note of introduction,' he repeats. 'I'd have thought five children is more than enough for a family of limited means.' He bites his lip. 'What I mean is—'

'That really is most kind, Captain... Mister... sir,' Violet interjects, her cheeks scarlet. 'I – um. Perhaps I will take down the name and address after all.'

'Of course.'

There is a pause in the conversation.

'But still,' Edward says at last, 'many congratulations on this child. Each one should be seen as precious.' He speaks slowly, noticing his jaw is tight. He stops to work it loose. Somehow, face to face with a person like Violet, it seems the right thing to say. When speaking of her sort in the abstract, it is rather easier to speak of the catastrophe of too many children born to families who can ill afford them. And too few children in those families who can, and should, afford them. A longer pause. They both know what must come next. 'So,' Edward begins, 'how is he?'

Violet shakes her head and sniffs. 'Not so good.'

'Oh. I'm sorry to hear it.'

'It's up and down, as you know. But he's very low at the moment. Depressed, I'd say. That's the heart of it. Needs something to cheer him. A visit from you would do it...'

'I don't have the time!' Edward's voice is harsher than he intended. He clears his throat. 'What I meant was, I don't have time at the moment. Work is terribly busy and I'm conducting a host of lectures to promote my latest book. I also have busy clinics and, on top of that, I have my research work, both at the university and for the London County Council. Plus, of course, I am also a family man. At weekends... Well, I'm needed at home, with a young child and another on the way. Eleanor, my wife... She would wonder...'

'Of course,' Violet speaks quickly, apology lacing her voice. 'I understand. You are an important man. I should never have had the presumption—'

'It's fine, really. I would very much like to visit. Just not now.' In all the years he has been married – five, to be precise – he has not found the time.

'I feel so sorry for 'im, that's all,' Violet says, her voice shaky. 'And soon I won't be able to go so often, not with this one due in a coupla months. I go every Sunday, after church, even though we can scarce afford the train fares.'

'That's... That's really very good of you, Violet,' Edward says, his voice soft.

At last, Edward turns to face her. She still has the same pretty eyes which struck him when he first met her, but she looks years older. It's as though all the worry has pulled her features down a fraction, just enough to take the shine off her youth. Her eyes crinkle at the edges and a frown sits between her brows. Her lips have lost their full, ripe curve. He looks away.

He searches his mind for something more to say. Something neutral to keep the conversation going. To delay the humiliating finale of their rendezvous. But his brain is dulled from pain and lack of sleep and it remains stubbornly blank. He manages a few banalities about the weather, the London traffic.

Finally, Edward gathers himself, pulls his briefcase onto his lap and pulls the manila envelope from it. The moment they have both come for.

'Well, my dear...' He places the envelope in her warm hand, closing her fingers around it with his clammy one. It is easier this way. A cash transaction. Nobody can trace it, nobody can question it. 'Here is the allowance for this month.'

'Much obliged, sir.' Violet quickly shoves it into her handbag, snapping the clasp shut and clutching the handles tight enough to whiten her knuckles.

He hesitates for a moment. 'Perhaps I can give you something extra this time? To help with the little ones?'

'No, Capt – Mr Hamilton. You're generous enough as it is,' Violet says. She sits up taller. 'We don't need charity. We can manage, thank you all the same.'

He stands, stretching his hand out to Violet. She stares at it for a moment, then takes it, allowing him to help her off the bench. The familiar twisting and churning he gets in his belly whenever they meet is back. He has an overwhelming urge to turn and run, to never come back and have to look at the gratitude in her eyes. But he will, because he must. It's the chain which will tie him forever to his shameful past.

'I'm afraid I have another meeting to go to,' he says in the pause, 'but I wish you and your family well. Until next time,' he adds, donning his hat.

'Yes, sir. Until next time. And I thank you from the bottom of my heart,' she says, patting her handbag.

Edward walks swiftly away.

'I'm telling you,' Edward says, glancing around the bank of pallid faces staring at him in the airless committee room on the fourth floor of the Palace of Westminster. 'The data is all here. Science cannot lie.' He taps the thick block of reports from his latest educational study which sit in front of him. He is presenting the results to a committee set up by the Board of Education to deal with the problems of trying to educate the growing numbers of mentally defective children in the classroom. 'I have additional material from studies conducted in America, by the eminent researcher Carl Brigham, who sees a similar decline in American intelligence. In the case of America, however, I'm told the decline in intelligence across the population is due, largely, to the increase of immigration and the integration of less intelligent races. Brigham's work has led to legislation in America to restrict immigration and a successful policy of sterilisation and incarceration to ensure defective genes are removed from the population of future generations. It is vital, if our great nation is to halt our own decline – and I don't think I would be over-exaggerating if I were to say *demise* – to put in place far-reaching policies of our own.'

The room is stuffy and hot. Any breeze coming off the Thames is too weak to reach them through the open window. Edward would dearly love to remove his jacket, as a few of the other men have done, but he resists the informality. He tries to ignore the sweat forming on his back, beneath his armpits and in the creases of his elbows.

'Sorry,' says Arthur Wood, chair of the committee, 'but I'm not sure what all this has to do with the matters at hand.' He drums his fingers on the table. 'Professor Hamilton, I thought we were here to discuss education policy?'

Why can't these people see that everything is connected? That we wouldn't *have* all these problems if... He sighs and explains in a slow, steady voice, 'I'm afraid, Mr Wood, it has everything to do with it. If we merely deal with the *symptoms* of the disease in our population – and I shall come to those in a moment – that won't present a cure, gentlemen, will it? No, we must stem the rot. Unfortunately, the rate of breeding of the, for want of a better word, *underclasses*, far outstrips that of the able, intelligent members of society.' He pauses to allow that fact to settle. 'Science has proven, beyond doubt, that a propensity to alcoholism, criminality, sexual inversion, weak-mindedness, violence, epilepsy, depression, sexual deviance – you name it – are inherited tendencies passed, generation to generation, through bad germ plasm in our genes. But, most importantly, and for the purposes of *this* discussion, you will see from these reports that intelligence itself is 100 per cent inherited from one's parents. The potential of each and every child is set at birth – and no amount of education is going to change that.'

He stares around the room at the blank faces before him. He clears his throat. 'I'm sure you will agree, gentlemen, once you have studied this report,' he taps the papers again with his fingertips, 'that given what we now know about the inheritability of ability, we must make a complete overhaul of our educational system.'

'How so?' asks Wood, ceasing his drumming and leaning back in his chair.

Edward smiles his most indulgent smile. 'May I firstly refer you to my work published a few years ago, *Mental Testing for Schools*, which I'm sure you will be familiar with. What, in essence, I am advocating, is systemic change in our schools. We must identify the most intelligent children at age eleven by nationwide testing, along the lines I have advocated in my book. The brightest children can be placed in the most academic schools amongst peers of similar ability where they can thrive. The rest, for whom academic attainment and leadership will never be an achievable goal by virtue of their birth, will receive a basic education and must be directed to more practical learning. For these children, the goal will not be the professions, but they will fill the ranks of workers the country will need if it is to build a healthy future.'

'And the mentally defective children?' Wood asks.

'Those with only mild deficiency will be accommodated in the mainstream schools so they can achieve some sort of low-level qualification. Separate provision should be made for retarded children. Those classified as idiots, imbeciles or feeble-minded – those uneducable – must be placed immediately into public care and control. These children of the lowest abilities should be retained in residential institutions or colonies provided by the local authorities, to take them off the streets and, importantly, to prevent any risk of them breeding and passing on their defective genes. That is, unless a programme of sterilisation can be introduced to deal with this problem.'

'What sort of numbers of defectives are we talking of, Professor Hamilton? The expense surely could be prohibitive,' asks a worried-looking, snowy-haired gentleman whose name Edward cannot remember.

'Until we implement nationwide testing, I won't have those figures to hand.'

'But,' presses the man, 'I was always of the understanding that the point of testing the intelligence quotient of children was to give *additional* educational support and input to those who were identified as lacking in attainment, within our existing school system, rather than to weed out the weakest and place them in institutions. By taking out the brightest too – I'm not sure how this will be beneficial overall?' He raises one of his bushy brows halfway up his forehead. The overall effect is rather comical and Edward suppresses the desire to laugh.

'In a nutshell,' Edward patiently explains, 'I'm afraid this is a rather outdated hope. We prove here,' he points to his papers, 'and many other recent studies have shown, that nurture can make very little difference to intellectual ability. No amount of decent schooling, improved nutrition or any other benefit poured into the lower orders will make a jot of difference. It is, therefore, an ill-use of resources to direct them to attempting to improve these children. My proposal will be to test *all* children at age eleven, by which time their intellectual abilities will be more than measurable, and the results will guide us as to which type of educational establishment they should be directed to. We, as a nation, can ill afford to waste resources in times of such high unemployment and downward pressure on wages, which, of course, reduces tax receipts. Indeed,' he adds, 'over a generation, the cost will naturally reduce if we can prevent the feeble-minded from having children at all.'

There is a collective shuffling and murmuring around the table. Edward drinks from his water glass.

'I'm sorry, Professor Hamilton,' says the man with bushy eyebrows, 'but I and several of my colleagues here,' a few of them nod encouragement, 'fail to be convinced that there is enough evidence to support your findings. To change our entire education system, to forcibly lock up children and to begin a sterilisation programme, seems to us to be an enormous gamble without irrefutable evidence to back up your assertions. For instance,' he continues when Edward doesn't respond, 'exactly how reliable *are* these tests at age eleven? How can you be certain it is the underlying intellect and not tutoring driving the results?'

Edward looks around the twelve sets of eyes trained on his face. There is a collective holding of breath as they await his response. Irritation rises at their inability to see reason.

'May I suggest you *read* the evidence here, before you write off my recommendations? This is just one small part of much larger steps we must take as a society to improve *all* of our lives and to ensure future prosperity. We don't have the luxury of time to commission more and more lengthy studies when the action we need to take is crystal clear and *now*.'

'But,' persists Bushy-Brows, 'if you and your eugenicist friends are *not* right, then the negative implications for many, many children and families will be immeasurable! Such concepts are unpalatable to many people, Professor Hamilton,' he adds, adopting a grave expression.

Edward opens his mouth to respond but Wood holds up his hands and interjects. 'Gentlemen, I think this discussion is in danger of straying further than the matter immediately at hand. Let us remember that the remit of this committee is to discuss education policy alone. Let us read the evidence the good professor here has put in front of us and reconvene once we have done so.'

There are nods of approval, although he catches Bushy-Brows mumbling something further about how the evidence must be *irrefutable* to his neighbour. Edward chooses to ignore him and gathers himself to leave.

'Well, gentlemen...' He beams around at them all. Really, he cannot abide this stuffy little room any longer. 'If there are no more questions for now, I have a luncheon engagement. Once you have read my report, please do get in touch. I would, if I'm permitted,' he looks to Wood, 'like to be consulted on the recommendations which are to be made by this committee *before* they are put forward to the Board of Education. I believe this, and other proposals I am working on for the Ministry of Health, should work in conjunction. And if anyone is interested in learning more, my latest book, entitled *The Delinquent Youth and the Criminal Mind*, is out and on sale in all decent book shops.

I think you will find it most enlightening.' He addresses the last point towards a stony-faced Bushy-Brows.

A few other members chuckle and nod their approval.

'On behalf of the committee, thank you very much for coming and presenting us with your findings, Professor Hamilton,' says Wood. 'As always, cutting edge and enlightening stuff. We are most grateful for your time and dedication.'

And Edward is heartened by the round of applause, the warmth of the admiring looks, the nods of approval from many around the table.

7

Eleanor

'Eat up your porridge now, darling,' Eleanor tells Mabel. The little girl stirs it round and round her bowl, talking quietly to Prudence, who is balanced on the arm of her chair.

'Prudence says *she* only eats her porridge with extra sugar.'

'But that porridge is for you, not Prudence,' says Eleanor. 'Come along, eat up quick or Nanny will be here to take you out to play and you'll be hungry.'

'I only like what Prudence likes,' says Mabel, kicking at her chair and sticking out her lower lip.

'For heaven's sake, Ellie, just give the child a little more sugar,' Rose says with a sigh. She winks at Mabel. 'Aunt Rose agrees with Prudence: the more sugar the better.'

Eleanor gives Rose a hard stare. But her will is gone and she sprinkles an extra layer onto Mabel's rapidly cooling breakfast. 'It seems I'm outnumbered by three,' she says. 'But it's Aunt Rose's and Prudence's fault if all your teeth fall out.'

'Thank you, Mama.' Mabel's smile is wide as she offers her first spoonful to the doll, then swiftly pops it into her own mouth.

Eleanor spreads marmalade, thick with peel, on her toast. Edward's empty chair nudges at the corner of her vision. *Are his now regular week-long absences solely work related? Does Sophie know something she doesn't? Or perhaps there are other reasons he is avoiding Brook End.* She watches Mabel, now concentrating hard on scraping off the sugary top of the porridge.

There is a light knock on the door.

'Good morning, Mrs Hamilton. Is Mabel finished with her breakfast?' a sullen-faced Miss O'Connell asks.

'Good morning. Yes, I think she's all done.' Eleanor turns to Mabel. 'Wipe your mouth on your napkin, Mabel,' she instructs. 'Are you quite all right, Miss O'Connell? You look a little tired.'

'I'll be grand,' the nanny replies, tight-lipped. She doesn't look grand. She has dark shadows beneath her eyes.

Mabel slides off her chair.

'Wish your mother a good day.'

'Have a nice day, Mama,' Mabel says quietly, and follows Miss O'Connell out of the room, dragging her feet along the carpet.

What's up with those two?

'So, what do you think?' Rose is asking.

'Hmm?'

'Ellie, did you hear anything I just said?' Rose drops her knife onto her plate with a clatter.

'Er, I'm sorry, my mind was elsewhere.'

'I *said*, there's an advanced shorthand course in London I'd like to take – I need to brush up my skills. I mentioned it to Sophie and as the Pitman's School is in Southampton Row, she said I could stay with her during the week for the three months the course is running. Of course, I shall come home to Brook End every weekend, just like Edward.' She stares at Eleanor, as though waiting for a reaction. But Eleanor is far from here. Far from the dining room, Brook End and Rose and her plans. Instead, she is buried inside herself, trying to understand the vague, murky feeling in the pit of her belly as it amplifies. She waits for it to solidify into something real, but it remains stubbornly nebulous and she cannot grasp what it means. She forces herself back to the present.

'Rose,' she says carefully, 'I have no issue with you taking the course – and staying with Sophie would be a far better prospect than lodging in a boarding house. I understand your desire to work. Truly. I enjoyed working before I was married. But...'

'But?'

'But couldn't you consider a secretarial job, or – or something more fitting for a girl of your class? Journalism is a *man's* domain. And certainly not suitable for someone like you. I would worry so much for your safety and your reputation.'

Rose rolls her eyes. 'I'm sure Mother would have wanted me to do it,' Rose says.

Eleanor looks at Rose's eager face and wonders what indeed their mother would say. Their mother *before*. Before The Tragedies, as she has come to think of it all. She can barely remember her mother before the war, that carefree, happy and vivacious woman, so reduced by each loss she suffered. And Rose? Well, she would remember even less. She'd been only four years old when war broke out. Seven, when both older brothers were lost in action within only

96

a few weeks of each other. She'd watched her father die a slow and agonising death as his lungs, damaged by poison gas, gasped and fought for breath for months. And then, as if that weren't enough in any single young life, when Rose was ten years old, their mother left for work one morning but was never to return. The Tragedies. Unable to process such intense grief and devastation, she and Eleanor had spun memories of their parents and brothers which were far more fantasy than reality. Eleanor alone has brief flashes of the true versions, which she keeps entirely to herself.

'She would want me to be happy,' Rose says stubbornly.

'But not at any cost,' Eleanor says. 'She would want you to keep from harm,' she adds. 'Besides, despite engaging a very expensive chaperone to watch over you in Europe, that didn't exactly save you from trouble, did it?'

'Oh, so is that what this is really about? You're still mad at me for falling in love with Marcel!'

'I...' Eleanor bites her lip. 'Edward and I feel that you could do better with a—'

'*Edward* and I? Don't you think for yourself any more Ellie?' Rose's voice climbs and her cheeks redden. 'Who I fall in love with is not *his* business.'

'Rose! After all he has done for us! For *you.*' Eleanor feels anger ball in her own chest. 'You know perfectly well why Edward did what he did. How could we possibly allow you to go off and marry a penniless – by your own admission – Frenchman, whom you barely know!' Eleanor stops, breathless, and glares at her sister.

Rose stares at her defiantly but has the sense to keep quiet.

'Besides,' Eleanor continues, catching her breath, 'you also know perfectly well that it is *precisely* because of the terrible thing which happened to our dear mother,' her voice cracks, 'that I don't want you to work in London. You can't stay with Sophie indefinitely and you'd end up in some awful boarding house. Men prey on single women, walking home alone on dark nights. Truly, Rose, as I say, it isn't that I don't want you to work. I enjoyed it, even though I *had* to, and you do not. It's that you, living alone, working in the *newspapers*... It just seems so risky and *wrong*.' A knot forms in her throat and she slumps back in her chair.

The dark shadow of their mother's death silences them both like a frigid winter frost.

'Look, for now it's just a course. I'm not proposing anything more dangerous than sitting at a typewriter, you know,' Rose says finally. 'And I shan't walk about the backstreets of London on my own, I promise you.' Rose looks pleadingly into Eleanor's eyes.

Rose cannot possibly remember. She must have blocked out that terrible day in February 1920. But for Eleanor, who was nineteen at the time, it is seared into her memory, branded, so she can never forget the horror of it.

It was old Mary, the knocker-up, who had found their mother at first light. Tube held to her lips, Mary had shot dried peas at the upper windows of workers who slept in the back streets of Soho to rouse them for work. From the corner of her vision she had spotted their mother's skirts, draped over the dirt like a dead butterfly's wings, in a narrow alleyway. A brief glance at her glassy eyes and marbled skin, at the scratches and deep purple marks on her neck, told Mary all she needed to know. That a life had been stolen before her owner was ready to willingly give it up.

Later that same day, two bearded policemen had come. Eleanor and Rose had been mad with worry since because Mother had not returned home from work the previous day. Gently, the elder of the two men had broken the news. A dangerous vagrant had escaped the workhouse and their mother had had the misfortune to be in the wrong place at the wrong time, encountering the murderous delinquent as she took a shortcut home.

Eleanor had stared at the front door she had just closed behind the policemen and wondered what on earth to say to her ten-year-old sister. As she fought back tears and refused to allow panic to erupt inside her, she'd turned to face Rose's pale, silent shock. *We'll be fine,* she had told her as she held out her hands to clasp her sister's fragile fingers, and mentally composed a letter to their cold, remote aunt and uncle, their only relatives, who lived in Edinburgh. *I have a decent job and I'll find a way to manage,* she had told Rose, adding to her mental composition the impossibility that the pair should move up north to live with them. She had doubted whether the aunt and uncle would want that any more than Rose or Eleanor would.

And in that moment Eleanor threw off the last vestiges of childhood innocence, and in her chest was ignited a flame of hatred towards the cursed underclasses, the criminally-minded in particular. Something must be done about them roaming the streets, terrorising innocent women. And that was how she found the Eugenics Society, filled as it was with people who shared her vision for a safe and vagrant-free future.

'Ellie,' Rose says patiently now. 'I know you worry about me. I know how much you care, and I love that. But,' she takes Eleanor's hand, 'you have to let me live my life. I'm serious about becoming a journalist. I know it will be hard, and most newspapers won't want me. But we women have the vote, so surely we women can do so many more things than before? I really do want to do this. So very much. The course starts on the second of September. And Sophie says I can stay as long as I like and she would be delighted to have my company. What harm can come to me there? She has offered to introduce me to Roger Fry and Clive Bell – you know, the art critics. If I could work for them, initially at least, it could be terribly useful for—' she bites her lip before the name *Marcel* escapes. Eleanor decides not to mention it either. '*And* Sophie knows Leonard Woolf!' Rose continues, excitement seeping into her voice. 'I mean, she said he might be able to get me a job at Hogarth Press. I know it wouldn't be for a newspaper, yet, but it would be a start and Sophie says I should keep an open mind. Anyway, the point is, she knows *all* the right people.'

'Marie Stopes has offered you a position at *Birth Control News*,' Eleanor says, remembering the conversation from the dinner party. 'You wouldn't even have to do a course to begin there.' She doesn't add that there would be the benefit of working amongst women, not men.

Rose wrinkles her nose. 'No chance,' she says. 'Don't get me wrong, I think birth control is a wonderful thing, but I can't stand the woman. And even *you* have to admit, Eleanor, her views are pretty extreme. She hates everyone, from Jews, to Italians, the French, even. And God forbid that you should be *poor*. Really, Ellie, I don't know how you and Edward tolerate her.'

'Well, I—'

'Sophie thinks it's a good idea I do the course, and she'll help me,' Rose presses. 'I'll be quite safe with her. *Please, Ellie!*'

Eleanor smiles. Dear Sophie. Perhaps she will try to funnel Rose into something altogether more befitting of a girl of her class and social standing. Publishing would be more suitable and such a job would expose her sister to all manner of eligible men. Yes, her friend won't let her down and she can see Rose is not going to change her mind. 'OK, fine. But only if you stay with Sophie, and she knows exactly where you are at all times and—'

There is a sharp knock on the door.

'I need a word, please, Mrs Hamilton,' Miss O'Connell interrupts, marching into the dining room, holding Mabel tightly by the hand. She's only been gone a quarter of an hour or so!

'Can't it wait until after lunch?'

Miss O'Connell shakes her head. 'Not really, Mrs Hamilton. I've bad news to impart,' she adds, stiff and straight with it. They all glance at Mabel, who is pale-faced and sucking hard on her thumb as she leans against Miss O'Connell's skirts. 'Wouldya take that thing out of your mouth,' the nanny hisses. She leans over and tugs Mabel's thumb forcefully.

Rose pushes out her chair. 'Come along, Mabel.' She holds out a hand to the child who is looking bemused. 'Let's go outside and get some fresh air. Come now.'

Mabel takes Rose's hand obediently, tucking Prudence

under her arm. She moves as if to put her thumb back in her mouth, then thinks better of it and her hand drops to her side. 'I'm sleepy, Aunt Rose,' she mumbles.

'Well then, let's go and sit on the patio and you can have a little rest there?' Eleanor hears Rose say before the dining room door clicks shut behind them.

She turns to the nanny. 'Now, what is it? What's happened?'

Miss O'Connell stands stiff as a fire poker, chin jutting, fingers twitching.

'Do sit down.' Eleanor indicates the chair opposite. 'You are making me nervous.'

Miss O'Connell licks her lips. She's breathing heavily, her chest rising and falling, breath catching in her throat.

'I'm very sorry to do this with no warning, Mrs Hamilton,' Miss O'Connell begins in a rush, 'but I'll be handing in my resignation. I'll work my notice…'

Eleanor stares at her. Dread of what is coming next mounts in her belly. Looking after Mabel should be a doddle and Miss O'Connell spoke with excitement only two weeks ago about the prospect of the baby coming next year.

Eleanor clears her throat. 'B-but, I had no idea you were unhappy,' she begins. 'If only you'd spoken to me about it! On our side, we are very content with your work. If it's a matter of money, I'm sure there is something we can do. It's a good time with the new baby coming. I'll speak with Edward. We'd all be devastated if—'

'Mrs Hamilton,' Miss O'Connell looks as though she's been stung by a wasp, 'it isn't about my wages. You've been good to me and Brook End has been a happy place…'

'Then please don't leave!' Eleanor hates the pleading desperation in her voice.

'It's the child. Mabel. I can't look after her.' The woman rocks in her seat, her face drained of colour.

'What has she done?'

'She's not *done* anything, Mrs Hamilton. I think you know to what I'm referring. It's what she *is*.'

'You're not making any sense, Miss O'Connell,' Eleanor persists. Perhaps if they all continue the pretence, none of this will be real. 'What she is?'

'For the good grace of God!' She crosses herself. 'I know you're her mother and it's hard for you to take. I'd have thought you would've noticed yourself, you being an attentive mother.' She sits up straighter. Braces herself. Her eyes protrude from her head, ugly. 'The girl,' she says, her teeth barred like a fox, voice a hoarse whisper, 'is *possessed*. The devil has taken her into his clutches.'

Eleanor's mouth drops open at her words.

'It's true.' The nanny nods her head vigorously. 'It's in her eyes – the darkness. Ignore it all you like, but he's there all right. It's *chillin'*.'

Eleanor's insides curdle.

'She's starting to fit, proper-like now, big 'uns. Every day. You *can't* have missed it. She's done it just now – right after breakfast. I can't look after her, Mrs Hamilton, really I can't. Not long till she'll be foamin' at the mouth, too, I reckon—'

'How dare you!' Eleanor snaps. She glares at the woman. Miss O'Connell is a Roman Catholic. Eleanor's not a believer herself, though she doesn't mind Miss O'Connell's faith one bit. Edward is a man of science and, as such, he has an oddly confused relationship to God. He doesn't speak of it, but she knows he has an internal battle with Him, one where his logic struggles with the concept of a higher being at all, one where he blames God, should He exist, for what happened in the war. One of alternate blame and contrition.

Miss O'Connell, on the other hand, is deeply religious. Eleanor knows she reads the bible each night and Eleanor would never put anything in the way of her beliefs. And now this bloody nonsense. She suddenly remembers Mabel holding Prudence upside down to let the devil drain out of her.

'It was you!' she exclaims. 'You who has been telling Mabel she's got the devil inside her. That she's *bad*!'

''Tis the truth, Mrs Hamilton. However hard it might be to accept.' Miss O'Connell is flapping her hands, purple blotches spreading across her cheeks. 'The girl has visions. She sees a flame-haired woman. She *talks* to her, this invisible, flame-haired woman, see? The devil! Same thing! Real conversations when all I can see is empty air. It terrifies me, Mrs Hamilton. I can't sleep for the fear she puts in me.'

The room lurches and Eleanor grips the arm of the chair to steady herself. *Flame-haired Woman.* Images of Mabel flicker through her mind. She can hardly bear to think of it, but she knows exactly what Miss O'Connell means by the darkness in her daughter's eyes. She's seen that many times but brushed it off as her own imagination. Then, the trips and falls. She is supposed to be calling Dr Hargreaves but she can't bring herself to do it. *The Flame-Haired Woman.* Who the hell is she? Eleanor's body feels cold.

It's been easier to ignore and hope and pray Mabel's condition will go away all by itself. But now Miss O'Connell's hateful, spiteful words are making her face whatever it is Mabel has, with full, horrifying force. Her pulse soars, blood crashes in her ears. But worse still, what if the nanny were to let the hateful secret out? What if she *tells*.

This cannot get out!

She turns on puff-faced Miss O'Connell. 'There is *nothing* wrong with Mabel.' Her voice cuts like a knife. It would be her word against theirs. Eleanor and Edward could ensure she never gets a job in polite society again. 'How *dare* you accuse her of having fits? You are supposed to be taking care of our daughter, not inventing this preposterous devil-nonsense. Filling her head with it. Frightening her. It's probably *your* fault. She is terrified!'

'No, Mrs Hamilton, I've not—'

'Get out!' Eleanor says, her voice low with rage. 'Get out of my house. Mabel is a sweet, innocent, healthy, four-year-old girl. Do you understand? The devil? That is *you*, Miss O'Connell. *You* are sick. *You* need help.' The rage rushes up like boiling water, shoving aside the icy grip of fear. A mother, whose child is threatened, can react in only one way. 'You will not work out your notice. I can no longer trust you with my daughter. You must leave immediately!'

Eleanor is trembling from head to foot as she tries to stand. This shock, this disgusting assertion; it cannot be good for her unborn child. She must protect her Grub. Get a grip. Calm down. But the terror, the anger and confusion refuse to subside. *Question her*, cries a tiny voice. *You know she is right! Get every detail. Store it up, work out what to do with it*. But the questions won't come. She stays silent, her chest heaving, watching Miss O'Connell shrink in the face of her anger.

Every pore of her wants to run to Mabel, scoop her up. Wrap her arms about her and keep her safe. *I will never let any harm come to you, you precious, precious darling.* She remembers whispering that in Mabel's ear the day she was born. She'd cradled her tiny body in her arms and crooned the words to her. She should never have left her with this woman. She should never have let Edward convince her she needed a nurse from day one. She *could* have taken care of her all by herself. They would have been fine, just the two of them.

'As you wish,' Miss O'Connell is saying, turning stiffly. 'But there's no use hiding from it, ignoring the facts. There's none so blind as those who will not see,' she adds, her voice sour as acid as she makes for the door.

'Who have you been speaking to?' Eleanor shouts after her, terror of discovery crowding into her mind. If this can be contained, perhaps all is not lost. She is crying now, hot tears running down her cheeks, her throat tightening, strangling her words.

Miss O'Connell stops and turns to face her. 'No, Mrs Hamilton, I've not told a soul. I keep my thoughts and suspicions to myself, so I do. But it's plain for all the household to see and I can't speak for other folks who lives here.'

'Oh.' The wind rushes out of Eleanor and suddenly she feels old and tired. Could this, whatever *this* is, be kept a secret? Is it she who has lost command of her senses? She sinks back to her chair. She shouldn't have fired her nanny on the spot, seeing as she was resigning anyway. She should never have shouted at her in that way. Now she will be bitter and angry and tell the newspapers. Then what would happen to Edward? Oh God, Edward!

She looks up at Miss O'Connell, who stands, one hand on the door handle, looking uncertainly at her. She can see the woman's hand is unsteady and her heart softens. Miss O'Connell has been with them since Mabel was tiny and everything had been fine until today. There is static in the air as she waits for Eleanor to speak.

'I'm sorry,' she says at last. 'I spoke harshly. I shouldn't have done, but what you said – it has come as a shock. You understand?'

The woman lets her hand slide off the door handle. 'I do,' she says, her features dropping as though with resignation that *this thing* has defeated them both. 'I shan't speak out of turn, Mrs Hamilton. I'm a professional, so I am. Anything I learn about any of the families I work for is strictly confidential, so it is. Never broken my own rule on that, I can tell you.'

Embarrassment stiffens between them.

'I want to be fair, Miss O'Connell,' Eleanor says wearily. 'I would appreciate your... confidence about Mabel. I will pay you until the end of the month, and of course provide you with full references.' She pauses. 'I will also give you the week's bonus you'd have had at Christmas.'

'Thank you, Mrs Hamilton,' Miss O'Connell says, head bowed. 'Much appreciated. I'll pack and go and stay with my sister in Shepherd's Bush and look for a new position from there. Or perhaps I'll go back to Ireland for a while. My mammy is old and sick.'

'I'm sorry, Miss O'Connell, that it must end like this.'

'I'm sorry too,' she says, finally turning the handle and opening the door. 'I was fond of little Mabel, so I was. But Mrs Hamilton,' her tone is pleading, 'she needs help, that one. There's something rotten in her, there's no doubt. And the sooner you accept that truth, the better for you all.'

Miss O'Connell leaves the room just as Rose returns, Mabel at her side looking a little better than she did before. At least, she has some colour in her cheeks. Rose takes one look at Eleanor and runs to her.

'Whatever has happened?'

Eleanor sinks into her sister's embrace, wondering what on earth she is going to do.

8

Edward

It's past seven o'clock in the evening by the time the doctor stands, leather bag at his side, apologising on the doorstep.

'Emergency over at Standon Farm, I'm afraid. I had to wait for the ambulance. Cowhand crushed in the milking parlour.' He shakes his head and holds out a hand to Edward. 'Doesn't look good.'

'Well, thank you for coming. And apologies for causing further disruption to your evening.' He steps back to let the doctor pass into the hall, where he hands his hat and scarf to Alice.

'Now, who amongst you is the patient?'

'It's Mabel,' Edward explains and leads the doctor into the sitting room, closing the door behind them. 'I must speak with you first in confidence,' he explains, indicating a chair for the doctor to sit on, but they both remain on their feet. Edward pulls at his cuffs. 'I've had to return from London to a hysterical wife and I'd appreciate it if you could look her over too.'

The doctor says nothing and Edward takes this as a cue to continue.

'According to the nanny, who has since left, the child has

been having some strange… turns,' he explains. 'Visions of some sort; conversations with people who aren't there.' He pauses. 'Eleanor tells me *she's* also seen odd movements – with her mouth, eyes and chin. Eleanor is most upset about the manner in which the nanny left, making ridiculous claims that the child is possessed.' He rolls his eyes and laughs a hollow laugh. 'She's a rather strident Catholic, given over to melodrama and odd superstitions,' he adds.

'Well,' the furrows on Dr Hargreaves' brow deepen, 'I'd better have a look at Mabel.' He makes a move towards the door.

Edward places a hand on the doorknob, blocking his way. 'I can rely on your absolute discretion and confidence in this matter?'

Dr Hargreaves meets Edward's eyes with a steady gaze. 'Without question,' he replies.

'Thank you.' Edward opens the door and the doctor follows him in silence as they climb the stairs to the nursery.

Dr Hargreaves, a calm middle-aged man with a smattering of grey around the temples, delivered Mabel early one chilly morning in March, four years ago. Edward recalls the moment he first saw his daughter, tiny, red-faced and bawling, fists pumping, tongue quivering in her open mouth. The doctor had been smiling. He seemed to think her anger at the world was a good sign.

'Plenty of spirit in this one,' he'd said, as he had deposited her carefully into Edward's awkward arms. He'd rocked her gently and miraculously the squawks subsided. Her dark, dark blue eyes had looked around and finally met with his. From that moment, he was smitten.

A ball of pressure grows in Edward's chest as they reach the door of the nursery.

Eleanor sits with Mabel, her thumb in her mouth, on her lap. Miss O'Connell had tried in vain to rid Mabel of her thumb-sucking habit. 'Tchah, thumbs are *dirty*. And they're for *babies*,' she'd scolded, pulling the offending digit out with a pop.

Edward's heart pumps harder at the sight of his wife and daughter together like this. The little girl is in her nightdress, her eyes fixed on the book Eleanor is reading from. It's the perfect scene, and hard to imagine the fracas which must have occurred between Miss O'Connell and Eleanor, which she had tearfully reported to him the moment he had arrived back earlier this evening. It's not like Eleanor to lose her self-restraint like that.

Dr Hargreaves walks across to the pair and smiles broadly. 'Well, hello there, young lady. Do you remember me?'

Mabel fixes him with her big blue eyes and shakes her head.

'My name is Dr Hargreaves and I'm not surprised you don't remember me. It must be over a year since I last paid you a visit. I'm here to give you a little check-up. Is that going to be OK with you?'

Mabel glances at Edward and he nods encouragement. 'Yes, all right,' she says, the thumb removed, held aloft, shiny and wet.

'Good, good. Now, come and sit on the edge of the bed here for me.' He taps the eiderdown, slings his bag on the bed and opens it, pulling out his stethoscope.

Mabel sits quietly and attentively while the doctor listens

to her heart, tests her reflexes, and looks into her ears and eyes. She opens her mouth and says 'aaahhh' obediently while he looks at her throat.

Dr Hargreaves sits back on his heels, arms crossed and asks her some questions. How old is she? Does she have any friends? Can she count to ten forwards and backwards? What noises do pigs, ducks, cows, dogs, cats make? Where do frogs live? The questions go on. Mabel answers each one, perfectly.

At last the doctor stands up and says, 'Well done, Mabel. You've done wonderfully well. Now, you must be tired. It's past your bedtime, I expect.' Mabel gives him a shy smile.

'Can I speak with you a moment?' Dr Hargreaves motions Eleanor to join him at the window to speak out of Mabel's earshot.

Edward sits down next to Mabel on the bed.

'Hello, princess,' he says, stroking her soft curls.

'Hello, Papa.' She looks up into his face with earnest eyes. 'Why is the doctor come to see me?'

'To check you are fit as a fiddle.'

'Oh. Where is Nanny?'

'Didn't Mama tell you?'

Mabel shakes her head.

'She had to go away for a while, to visit her own mother, as she isn't very well.'

'When will she come back?'

'I don't know. Perhaps you shall have a new nanny.'

'I don't want a new nanny, I want Mama.'

Edward laughs. 'You'll still have Mama, princess. You'll have Mama *and* a new nanny. Mama is far too busy to look after you all the time.'

'But I like Mama best, then you, then Alice. No. Dilly then Alice. I liked Patch better than nearly everyone but he's dead so I can't like him any more. Can we get a new doggie, Papa?' Mabel asks, pulling at Edward's sleeve with her chubby fingers.

Dr Hargreaves and Eleanor make their way back across the room.

'I'll tuck you in,' Eleanor says to Mabel, and to Edward, 'I'll join you downstairs in a moment.' She pulls back the bedclothes for Mabel to climb in. Edward watches as his wife tucks the blankets up beneath Mabel's chin, then sits on the bed and tenderly begins to stroke her blonde mop of hair. His heart squeezes.

Downstairs in the sitting room, drapes drawn, fire and lamps lit, Edward pours Dr Hargreaves a glass of claret. When Eleanor joins them, he pours one for his wife too.

The doctor clears his throat. 'Mabel appears fit and well,' Dr Hargreaves says in a grave tone. His face is serious, the easy smile gone. 'But I must come straight to the point. Given the symptoms you've described, I strongly suspect Mabel has some form of epilepsy. It is not uncommon in children.'

Edward catches Eleanor's eyes. He can see the fear and shock in them, mirroring his own.

'But it can't be serious!' she says. 'Will she grow out of it?'

Dr Hargreaves runs a hand through his hair. 'That I don't know. It's possible. She isn't displaying any sign of mental impairment, yet. I'm not an exp—'

'What do you mean, *yet?*' Edward asks sharply.

'Look,' Dr Hargreaves' voice is gentle, placatory, 'the chances are, this is nothing serious. Mabel is as bright as a little button, but I have to be honest with you, the description of the symptoms you have described to me are... Not typical. These hallucinations – the woman with the fire hair. I've heard of such things, but I've never seen them before in such a young child. What it means, what effect it has on her growing brain, or what the ultimate outcome will be, I cannot tell you.'

A sickness rises inside Edward. He takes a large swig of wine in a vain attempt to bury it.

'But,' Eleanor says, turning her wedding ring round and round on her finger, her eyes darting between Edward and the doctor, 'neither Edward nor I have...' She can hardly bring herself to say the disgusting word, '... Epilepsy. I mean, it's an inherited condition, isn't it? How could she possibly have it?'

'Is there a history of it in either of your families – aunts, uncles, brothers, sisters, grandparents?'

They both shake their heads emphatically.

'It is most definitely not in *my* family,' Edward says.

'Nor mine!' Eleanor says. 'Children have imaginary friends, don't they? Rose, when she was small, had an invisible friend called Lavender.' She laughs at the memory. 'Lavender accompanied Rose everywhere for a year or two. She must have been Mabel's age. Perhaps even older – five or six—'

'Yes, but such imaginary friends are brought to life by the *conscious* mind. From what you have told me, this fire lady of Mabel's seems to be conjured from her *un*conscious mind. It seems clear to me that this, taken together with the other symptoms, would all point towards an unusual type of epilepsy. How often is she having these... episodes?'

'I'm not entirely sure, but I think they have increased in frequency. Possibly every day. A couple of times a day, maybe more.' Eleanor's face is pinched, her eyelids rimmed red.

Dr Hargreaves nods, his usual smile absent. Edward stares hard into the ruby contents of his glass. The usual mellow comfort is missing; it's as tasteless as water on his tongue.

'OK,' he says, thumping the useless glass onto the table and jumping to his feet. 'What can we do? In this day and age there must be something. I mean, it cannot be untreatable. And it *cannot* be epilepsy. There is no way Mabel has epilepsy. It isn't in either of our families! Whatever it is, we will solve this. I'll pay for whatever treatment is necessary, and damn the expense.' He lights a cigarette, offering one to the doctor, who declines.

'It is true that there are a variety of conditions which mime epilepsy. But this is an area of medical practice which is beyond my skills, I'm afraid,' Dr Hargreaves replies in gentle tones. 'I will write first thing in the morning to an acquaintance of mine, a doctor in Harley Street, who knows more than I do about the complicated matters of the child's mind. He is very well regarded. I strongly suggest you take Mabel to see him, sooner rather than later. Best to nip these things in the bud before they take real hold. I will, of course, mention that the matter must be treated with the utmost discretion, given your position in society, Professor Hamilton. Between now and your appointment, I suggest you note down all the symptoms she displays on a daily basis. Build up a record, so to speak.'

There is a moment of stillness. What more is there to be said? Edward's mind is numb. He knows there are a million questions yet to be formed in his mind, but for now there is simply the stultifying effect of shock weighing him down like a boulder.

'Should we stop Mabel from playing outside?' asks Eleanor in a small voice. 'Should we be doing anything differently?'

Dr Hargreaves shakes his head. 'No. You are clearly devoted parents. Seeking the best medical advice is the only action I can advise, for now at least.' He looks at Eleanor. 'It is vital that you take good care of yourself, Mrs Hamilton. You must not allow yourself to become too upset or anxious as we wouldn't want to cause harm to your unborn child, now would we? I advise you to replace that nanny as soon as you can find a suitable candidate. You look worn out and peaky. Your husband is keen that I take a look at you to make sure all is well.'

'Oh please, not now, Dr Hargreaves. I'm simply tired, that's all.'

'All right, you get some rest and I'll come back in the morning and check you over.' He drains his glass and, smiling at last, shakes Edward's hand. 'I'll write to Mr Silverton, a neurologist, first thing.'

'That's very good of you. Thank you,' Eleanor says.

'Please, I'll see myself out,' he says, as she makes to stand.

Once he is gone, the silence in the room is unbearable. The clock on the mantelpiece ticks louder and louder as Eleanor stares sightlessly into the middle distance.

Epilepsy. The word fills Edward with utter dread. But it cannot be. It simply cannot.

'Cooee!' The booming voice of Lizzie Leyton sounds from the hall, making both of them jump. 'Anyone here?' she calls.

'I'll go,' Edward says, taking in Eleanor's red eyes and pale cheeks. He squeezes her shoulder as he passes by.

Lizzie stands in the deserted hallway, dressed for dinner, beaming up at him. She is hopping from foot to foot with an energy Edward cannot imagine possessing. He forces his face into a welcoming smile. The woman has a bundle of blankets tucked beneath her arm.

'Ah, Edward!' Her voice is too loud and echoes around the hall. 'I came through the back door,' she explains, 'thought I'd find Mrs Bellamy there but the kitchen was empty.'

'Oh, she must be...' He stops and scratches his head. He has no concept of the time and his head whirls with weariness. 'I've no idea.'

'Well, never mind. I expect Eleanor is resting, yes? And Mabel – I suppose she's in bed, hmm? Of course she is. Is it rude to call so late? Barton and I are just off to the Churches for supper.' Edward is silent as she poses, then answers her own questions. 'Anyway, I didn't want to wait a day longer!'

The bundle in Lizzie's arms gives a violent jolt and a yap and a whine emanate from beneath the blankets.

'Oh, shoosh,' Lizzie pats the blankets, 'You've given away the surprise!' She sighs and unwraps a fat, pale yellow retriever puppy, black-nosed and pink-tongued. It scrabbles out of her arms to the floor and treks, splay-legged, as though drunk, across the hall floor, sniffing and wagging its stub of a tail.

'Isn't he a darling?' she says, watching the puppy slip-sliding across the floor. 'Mabel will adore him. I wish I could see her face when she first claps eyes on him.' She laughs, 'We have reached a point where we just want rid of them. Fell over one of the little mites this afternoon. Could have done some damage, I tell you, if the chaise longue hadn't broken my fall. Well now, I'm already late and Barton will have my guts if I chat any longer.'

She sweeps out of the front door and into the waiting car. Edward waves to a shadowy shape in the car he takes to be Barton, hidden in the darkness behind the headlamps. The car pulls away and he turns to watch the exploring puppy who has left a puddle behind it.

He forgot to ask Lizzie if the puppy had a name. Well, Mabel can name him in the morning, he decides.

Perhaps this will be just the thing to cheer everyone up.

III

I am found out, it seems. Well, so be it. You do not frighten
me. And so, on we move to the next well-worn phase in our
convoluted game. In this part, you still think you can get the
better of me. But I know you can't.

Strange how this should still amuse me so. But it does. Every
time.

And oh, the girl! Just like the cat, who teases the mouse again
and again by setting it free, so with the girl.

But she is good and rare. I grant her my very best of treats.

Like Joan of Arc, I give her visions.

I'm an energy, you see. Electricity. That's all I am, if you
break it down. And what is there to fear in that? If only you
would try to widen your mind. A distinguished few see me as
inspiration. Revelation. Epiphany, even. Painters, authors,
soothsayers, leaders. They won't admit it, of course. They are
ashamed of me. You make them that way – yes you, with your
judging and your ignorance.

But the girl. There is no resistance from her. I am free to toy
with her, to open her mind to the ferocity of my imagination.

And so I allow the electricity to burst forth, for the normal
patterns of the girl's mind to shatter. Arhythmical sparks fly

outwards as I send them down the highway of her nervous system, shooting with the speed of light through her spine and out into the muscle fibres bunched beneath her soft, pale skin. Her nose and mouth twitch as the muscles contract. A small hand extends as if to clutch at empty air. She grips the windowsill tight and folds inside herself, trying to make sense of my interference.

And what of you? Oh, you do what you usually do. You stand and stare, faces white masks of horror, while you watch the girl's arms fall limp and the side of her mouth drop.

Like a crack of gunfire exploding into the silence of a summer's day, I let my power loose with full force. My disguise is gone, and I no longer try to conceal myself. The girl takes a sharp intake of breath and I snap her mouth shut, roll her eyes back. Her head falls forward, chin to chest, as though bowing to her master. Again and again the pulse of my energy snaps her head forward, arms and legs stiffening with a force which sends her ricocheting through the air, banging her head on the wall as she falls to the floor, twitching.

As fast as it came, my power is spent.

The girl curls up, warm and safe, to sleep in her weeping mother's arms.

The girl is empty, and I am gone.

PART II

January 1929

9

Eleanor

Eleanor woke early this morning, sleep difficult now the baby is getting big. The Grub is always so active at night, kicking and moving around inside her. With Edward away at a conference in New York she has been feeling gut-achingly alone. She thinks back to the discussion they had had just before he left.

'Are you quite sure you don't mind me going?' he had asked as they lay in bed together that Sunday morning. He'd crawled in beside her in the early hours, cold and trembling, and she'd known he'd had one of his nightmares. He had finally calmed and drifted back to sleep in her arms. They'd both woken late.

'Of course I don't mind,' she'd said blithely. 'This eugenics conference is an important one, isn't it?'

'Most important one since 1923,' he'd confirmed. 'Representatives from all over the world will be there.'

'Then you must go. The conference was booked before you knew about the Grub. And you will be back before it's born, with a couple of weeks to spare, in all likelihood,' she'd said firmly.

Besides, she thinks grimly, even when he is in England, he seems to spend less and less time at home. His full weeks in London are now the norm, not the exception. She gets the feeling he returns to Brook End for the weekends merely because he feels obliged to. And when he is at home, he's always out with Byron, the damn puppy. The puppy who was supposed to be Mabel's, but who has become Edward's, even down to choosing its name, having dismissed all of his daughter's suggestions as ridiculous. *He needs training, Eleanor. Can't you see?* The harder she tries to engage with him, the more, she is certain of it, he withdraws. *No man is immune to having an affair.* Sophie's all-knowing drawl is in her ears, and she tries not to imagine Edward in his hotel in New York being comforted by some shadowy, scarlet woman.

Meanwhile she, Eleanor, is increasingly becoming a recluse, shut up within the walls of Brook End, terrified of Mabel's fits being discovered if she invites anyone to the house, yet unable to leave her in the sole care of the new nurse Edward has employed to look after her, the rather strict and haughty Miss Cartwright-Jones. Two months ago, Mr Silverton, the neurologist recommended by Dr Hargreaves, had confirmed a diagnosis of epilepsy, cause unknown, and started Mabel on a course of bromide salts, which, so far, have resulted in no improvement whatsoever. Despite going back to see him twice in the interim, the fits are more frequent by the day and Eleanor can only watch, helpless and desperate, as Mabel slides inexorably backwards and inwards. During their last visit Mr Silverton told them he doubted increasing the dose would work, but they have to reach maximum dose before declaring a medicine a failure, no matter the hateful stuff gives her stomach pains and makes her vomit.

At least she has Rose back at home while Edward is away, now that she's finished her shorthand course. Last night, she poured her heart out to Rose over dinner about their latest visit to Mr Silverton and Rose's eyes had filled with tears at the bad news.

'The doctor doesn't seem to hold out much hope,' Eleanor confided. 'Says it's one of the worst cases he's seen.'

'Dear God, no! Surely there is something they can do,' Rose had said, as she always did when they discussed Mabel. Eleanor shook her head, that familiar physical stab of pain in her belly. She really wasn't sure just how much more she could bear and wondered, for the thousandth time, what negative effect it might be having on the Grub. They had sat in silence for a while, appetites lost.

'Ellie, I'm worried about you,' Rose had said, studying Eleanor closely. 'You look so tired and... sad...'

Eleanor had let out a wry laugh. 'Oh, I'll be all right.'

'You need to talk to someone about all this.'

'I'm talking to you now.'

'I know. But someone else too. What about Sophie? I wish you would let me tell her. She would do anything she could to help you.'

Eleanor shook her head vigorously. 'No! You know what Edward would say if we told anyone!'

'But the staff know.'

'We *had* to tell the staff, they can see it for themselves,' Eleanor had said. 'They're all terribly upset and know that it must stay within our four walls. Apart from them and you, only the Leytons are aware. Lizzie knew something was up

– that woman has a sixth sense, I tell you. She came over on a particularly bad day and I had no choice but to tell her – they are our closest neighbours and they were bound to find out. But they are totally trustworthy.' Eleanor had implored Rose to change the subject. 'I'm sick with worry and I need distracting. Tell me, what have you been doing in London?'

Rose had brightened a little and began to tell Eleanor about an art gallery she had discovered in London, but let it slip that it was Marcel who had introduced her to it in a letter he had written.

'But Edward told him not to contact you any more!' Eleanor had exclaimed in shock at this revelation.

Rose's lips had twitched. 'Do you seriously think Marcel is going to drop me, simply because Edward tells him to?'

'Do you mean to tell me you are still in some sort of relationship with him?'

'Yes, Ellie, I'm sorry, but we are still writing to each other.'

'And what now?' Eleanor choked. What would Edward make of all this when he returned from New York? Edward had questioned the sanity of letting her do this course in London, and it seems he had been right. It had given her the opportunity to strike up a correspondence again. This is the last thing she needed to worry about, what with the baby and the ever-present shadow of Mabel's illness. 'Where does that leave your plans for a job?'

'Ellie, for goodness' sake, I'm not exactly engaged, not even close! I still plan to become a journalist, if that's what you are worried about. I can't just sit around and do nothing with my life.'

They had stared at each other then, the sting clear. 'What, like me you mean?' Eleanor had thrown at her.

'No!' Rose slapped her napkin on the table. 'Actually, Eleanor, this isn't about you at all.' And with that, she had stormed out of the room.

This morning, the row still playing on her mind, she had been desperate to leave the confines of the house, so had come out for an early morning walk. Now, wrapping her coat tighter around her, she begins to wonder if this was a sensible decision after all. High up on the chalky ridge she is far from home and a biting wind whips her thin skirt around her calves. Turning towards home, needles of sleet sting the bare skin on her face as she trudges heavily into the wind.

She has a horrible feeling that, as soon as Edward returns, Rose will be hot-footing it back to London to get a job in goodness only knows whatever irreputable outfit she can find in Fleet Street. The idea of being a reporter is so grubby and distasteful it sticks in Eleanor's throat. It has the same unpleasant connotations as a policeman, or prison worker or train driver. She imagines Rose hanging around street corners befriending prostitutes, alcoholics and petty criminals, with her notebook and pen at the ready, while Marcel the Frenchman charms and worms himself into her bed and Edward's bank account.

She shudders, wishing their mother were still there to advise her. She finds herself thinking more and more of her mother these days, aching for her presence, feeling, as always, the familiar stab of anger at the lowlife who so cruelly and violently tore her away, especially now, when her need for her is acute. She hopes fervently her killer is suffering every day of his miserable life in whatever hateful prison he is languishing in.

She layers her arms beneath the swell of her belly which grows heavier with every step. She should never have gone so far. Tomorrow, she will limit the extent of her walking to inside the house. A wave of weariness threatens to overwhelm her. Edward is due home in ten days and there are only four more weeks until this baby will finally be born. She cannot wait for that day to come.

The path winds down through the woods until it becomes slushy mud, levelling off by the river. Eleanor follows it, her shoes slipping and sinking, her feet becoming damper with every step. The river, sluggish and rusty red-brown from the high iron content in the local soil, flows silently beside her. She crosses it via a narrow, rickety bridge, hanging onto the wooden rail with freezing, numb fingers. Her pace becomes painfully slow and for a moment she considers collapsing onto the soft earth at the base of a large tree to rest, but it's too cold and wet and she doubts she would be able to get to her feet again.

The pain in her belly is getting worse and she is so tired. She's wet through and so cold her teeth are beginning to chatter. Why do her legs feel like rubber? She's starting to lose feeling in them and wonders if they will be able to hold her upright, all the way back to Brook End. Keep going. Keep going.

Her breath is becoming rasping and ragged and she fights back useless tears.

By the time she is back at the garden gate, the pains are coming regular and hard, so when each one strikes she is forced to stop, bend double and wait for it to pass before she can continue her slow, laboured walk up the garden. Labour! Because, even though the baby is not due for another four weeks, she is certain that this is what this is. Numb with cold when she reaches the house, she is suddenly surrounded by the combined shrieking fuss of Rose, Mrs Faulks, Mrs Bellamy and Alice.

'Wherever have you been, Mrs Hamilton?'

'We were sick with worry!'

'You're soaked to the skin – lordy, look at ya! Shivering from head to foot...'

'What got into you, Ellie? You might've said you were going off walking the hills in a blizzard before breakfast. Like normal people in control of their senses might do.'

'Whatever will Professor Hamilton say?'

'Alice – run a hot bath, would you? Mrs Faulks, be a dear and call the doctor. Are you in pain, Ellie?'

Even Mrs Bellamy looks almost pleased to see her back, thrusting a cup of hot sweet tea into her hands, muttering about people taking leave of their senses.

By the time her teeth have stopped chattering she is able to say that under no circumstances are they to tell Edward. She doesn't want to worry him, but yes, please, please ask the doctor to come quickly!

The grandfather clock chimes three in the morning and, with a final searing flare of pain, Eleanor pushes a baby boy out into the world. Dr Hargreaves proclaims him a little on the small side but otherwise healthy, while the midwife washes him down, swaddles him tight in blankets and places him, light as a bundle of rags, into Eleanor's arms. Blotched and red, his face puckers and wrinkles like that of a tiny, ancient man. He opens his eyes wide and tries to focus on Eleanor's face.

'Hello, Grub,' she smiles down at him. 'How nice to meet you.'

His eyes fix on her mouth and he purses his lips as though trying to mimic hers. Tufts of brown hair stand up on his head, still damp from his wash.

Eleanor looks to Dr Hargreaves who has instructed the midwife to wrap up the afterbirth for burning, declaring that too, to be healthy. 'Is he really OK?' she asks hoarsely, her throat inexplicably sore. 'There's no sign of any...' She finds she cannot say the word. 'Anything wrong?'

'Nothing at all.' The doctor gives her an indulgent smile over the top of the baby's downy head.

'Are you sure he is quite well?' she implores, again without wishing to mention Mabel.

'He really is in tip-top shape,' he reassures her with a squeeze on her arm. 'From the looks of him, I'd suggest he is only a couple of weeks early, rather than a month. Due dates are not an exact science, you understand. But, of course, it is early days.'

She nods, swallowing the lump in her throat. Mabel had been born perfect too, so who is to say what the future holds for this child?

'There really is no reason to be fearful,' Dr Hargreaves adds, his firm hand still on her arm. 'We have no idea what caused Mabel's affliction. It could have been something you don't even remember. A bang to the head, a shock, a childhood illness. There is every chance your son will be entirely normal.' He releases her arm. 'Would you like me to ask Faulks to arrange for a telegram to be sent to the professor?'

'Yes, please,' Eleanor nods her agreement, resting her head against the pillow.

'You should get some sleep now,' he says.

'But could you send up Rose first? I'm sure she would like to see the baby.'

'Of course.' He pats her hand and leaves the room.

For the first time, she's alone with Grub resting in her arms. They will have to find a proper name, of course. Grub won't suit him for ever, she supposes, even though it seems quite appropriate for this little wrinkled scrap of a thing. She stares at him, waiting for the overwhelming love she had felt for Mabel to flood through her. She shifts her position, continues staring at the baby, who has now drifted off to sleep. But there is... Nothing. Blank, emotionless, nothing. Through the open bedroom door she hears music floating up from the sitting room. Rose is playing Fats Waller's 'Squeeze Me' on the gramophone. She hears Dr Hargreaves announcing, 'Miss Carmichael, I'm delighted to tell you, you have a healthy nephew,' and then laughter and excited chatter.

It'll come, she tells herself, pushing down a sudden spike of panic in her belly. The love thing – it can't be forced. And she's exhausted. It's been quite a day. She'll feel differently after a good sleep.

Fats Waller croons about little Cupid from the living room. The song, with its teasing and squeezing and cheering notes fails to lift Eleanor's spirits.

'Oh, darling Ellie, well done!' Rose skips in and sits on the bed next to Eleanor. She kisses her sister on the forehead then looks down into the crib, her face lighting up at the sight of The Grub who is sleeping now, swaddled tightly against the January cold. For an exquisite moment she feels sure everything will be OK, but then Mabel floods back in, together with Edward's yawning absence, and gloom settles back over Eleanor like a blanket of freshly fallen snow.

'He is beautiful,' Rose whispers. 'So tiny, so perfect.' She smiles and traces the baby's cheek with the gentlest of strokes. She comes back to the bed and puts her arms around Eleanor, kissing her sister's hot cheek with smooth, cool lips.

'Ellie, darling,' Rose says, settling herself on the bed next to Eleanor, 'I'm sorry for our row last night. Truly. You know I love and admire you more than anything or anyone else on earth.'

Eleanor pats her hand, resting her head back against the pillows and closing her eyes with exhaustion.

'I know you do, and I you,' Eleanor says. 'I'm sorry too. But I do worry about you. It's only because I care so much…'

'I know, Ellie, and that's why I wanted to say, please don't worry. This thing with Marcel. It's just letters. We aren't planning to get married – and whatever I said last night, it isn't serious. I was just angry. I have no intention of seeing him. Look, since being in Paris, since studying in London, I really do want to become a journalist. Our mother couldn't have ever dreamt of a job like that. But now, we women, we can. We *should*. Marrying Marcel would get in the way of that, wouldn't it?' She laughs. 'So see? You needn't worry. It's much more important you focus on Mabel and your new baby. They are the most important of all.'

'Yes,' Eleanor agrees, although wondering which is the worst evil, Marcel or being a journalist. Probably Marcel. 'That's true.'

There is a short pause.

'Ellie, I don't want any more rows with Edward. Would you not mention the letters? They are just letters. *Please.*'

'All right. If you promise that is the truth.'

'I do,' Rose says. She kisses Eleanor again on the forehead. 'Now, I think you need to get some sleep.'

The morning sun is already streaming between the curtains when Eleanor wakes to the baby's snuffling cries from his cradle. He stops when she lifts him out and he falls back to sleep as she gently rocks him. She opens the curtains and stands for a moment in the cold by the window, looking out over the back lawn, now covered in a thin layer of snow.

'Well,' she says, peering down at her new son's tiny features, 'we really weren't expecting to see you quite so soon.'

She wraps a shawl around her shoulders and climbs back into the warmth of her bed, ringing the bell for tea.

Instead of Alice, Rose appears, sleepy-eyed and tousle-haired, with a tea tray laden with toast, a boiled egg and a large pot of tea.

'Morning,' she smiles. 'I wrestled this off Alice in the hall. I'm not sure which of us is more desperate to see the little fellow, but, as you can see, I won! How are you both?' she whispers.

Eleanor returns the smile. 'We are doing well, although a little tired and bruised, I think!'

'Of course,' Rose says, placing the tray on Eleanor's bedside table and leaning over to pick the baby out of Eleanor's arms. She hugs him close, peering at him with adoring eyes. 'Dr Hargreaves and the midwife will be here soon to check on you both,' she says after a few moments, 'but before they do, I know there is a little girl who would love to meet her baby brother!'

'Oh, do bring her in,' Eleanor says, sitting up a little taller, manoeuvring the tray onto her lap.

Rose places the sleeping baby carefully in his cradle and returns a few minutes later, Mabel clutching her hand, her eyes all big and dark beneath the mop of fair curls. Prudence, as ever, dangles from the other fist.

'Is baby in there?' she asks, pointing at the crib. 'Why isn't it in the nursery with me?'

'When he's a little bigger,' Rose says.

'Come here, my darling,' Eleanor calls out, and taps the bed beside her.

Rose helps her scramble up and she climbs under the covers next to Eleanor, helping herself to a finger of toast from Eleanor's tray.

'After Dr Hargreaves and the midwife have checked you over, shall I get in touch with the nurse who was due to start once the baby was born? I'll tell her he's arrived early and see if she can start immediately. That way you can get some sleep at least.'

'Thank you, Rose.'

Mabel strokes Prudence's woollen hair with her fingers, chewing thoughtfully on her toast. 'Where's baby?' she asks finally, looking up at Eleanor.

'In here, like we said earlier.' Eleanor points to the cradle.

'Would you like to see? I can carry you,' Rose offers.

Mabel nods vigorously and together they lean over the wooden side of the crib and stare at baby's sleeping form in solemn silence. Rose plonks her back on Eleanor's bed.

'What's his name?' she asks.

'He doesn't have one yet,' Eleanor says. 'We will have to think of a name for him, but I suppose we should wait for Papa to come home first. What do you think?'

'Papa,' she repeats. 'Papa, Papa,' testing the word on her tongue. As though she doesn't quite remember him. 'How did baby get here?' She turns to her mother and she and Rose exchange a look over the top of Mabel's head.

'Well,' explains Eleanor, 'a kindly stork – that's a big type of bird – delivered him to us, all wrapped up in a blanket and popped him beneath the gooseberry bush in the garden. What do you think of that?' Mabel's eyes widen. Eleanor smiles. 'And here he is, like magic! Do you like him?'

Mabel thinks about this for a moment. 'I don't know yet,' she says. 'But how did he get here?' she repeats.

'Erm... Well,' says Eleanor. 'You'll learn all about that when you are much older. For now, I simply need you to be a good, big sister to the baby. Can you do that?'

Mabel nods. 'Yes.' She is silent for a moment then says, 'He can play with Prudence.' She holds the doll out and Eleanor feels tears well and a lump grow in her throat. Mabel pops her thumb back into her mouth.

It takes Eleanor a few moments before she is able to reply. 'That's very kind of you, Mabel. So very sweet and kind.'

And she wishes Rose would take her daughter away so she can let the tears flow freely for a few self-indulgent minutes before she lets the doctor and the midwife in to see her.

IO

Edward

The huge atrium of the American Museum of Natural History is abuzz with activity as Edward and Leonard Darwin step out of the wind and rain on West Seventy-Seventh Street. Edward wipes the damp from his forehead with his handkerchief and smooths his hair.

'Now, where have I put my speech...?' Leonard pats all of his pockets. For a moment he looks all of his seventy-eight years. 'Damnation, I must have left it in the hotel!'

'I'm sure you, of all people, Leonard, will be able to say what needs to be said without a written speech. Relax, come on – you're the guest of honour. They'll be hanging off your every word.'

'I hope you're right, Hamilton, old chap.'

'Ah! There you are gentlemen. Major Darwin, Professor Hamilton – welcome!' Charles Davenport, a tall, thin man, immaculately dressed, takes long strides towards them. He sports a luxuriously thick moustache and curious triangular snowy beard. His eyes, bright and sharp, belong to a much younger man. He firmly shakes each of their hands. 'Delighted, *delighted* to have you both here. Now, Darwin and I go way back, but I've heard so much about your work from Harry Laughlin, Mr Hamilton, that I feel I know you already.'

'Edward, please,' Edward says.

'Come, let's go somewhere quieter and have coffee. There are some people I want you both to meet,' Davenport says, leading the way through the hum and buzz of workers putting their finishing touches to stands and displays before the doors open within the hour. The sign at the far end is suddenly illuminated as the electrics are switched on. *The International Federation of Eugenics Organisations – Eugenics Congress 1929* it proudly announces.

Edward follows the two father figures of the movement – in Darwin's case, Honorary President of the British Eugenics Society, and in Davenport's case, the President of the International Federation of Eugenics Organisations – into a conference room off the main atrium. Four or five men and two women stand drinking coffee and chatting as they enter the room.

They are gathered around a stand on which is propped the schedule of the three-day conference, a floor plan of the exhibits and a typed list of the three hundred or so representatives attending from countries as far afield as Europe, Latin America and even Japan.

Harry Laughlin smiles and waves at Edward. 'Coffee?'

'Please.'

'Do you know Junior, Edward?'

'I'm sorry?' Edward is facing a vaguely familiar, tall, neat-haired, broad-shouldered man, definitely middle-aged rather than young as the name would imply.

'It's a term of endearment,' the man explains. 'And to distinguish me from my father. John Rockefeller at your service.' He extends a hand for Edward to shake. Edward grasps it, warm and firm in his own.

'Oh!' Edward recovers himself and closes his mouth. 'Of course. I do recognise you. I, er, had no idea you'd be attending the congress in person. I am, of course, aware of your great support and all that your foundation is doing to further the eugenics cause.'

'I can't stay too long, I'm afraid. It seemed the right time, however, to announce the expansion of our research funding. Will you be visiting the facility at Cold Spring Harbor Laboratory on Sunday? We're collaborating with the Carnegie Institution on various projects. As we see it, it's our duty to have philanthropy at the heart of all that we do. It would be great to have as many of our foreign delegates come and see what we are doing and hopefully we can increase our international collaboration further. We're in talks with the Kaiser Wilhelm Institute in Germany to fund some extensive racial science research there. I find it fascinating, this theory of racial improvement. Vital, in fact. I mean, think of the benefits – the possibility to wipe out certain diseases, to improve intelligence, to prevent birth defects and deformities. Its potential is extraordinary, don't you agree?' Junior's face is alive with what Edward can only deduce is genuine excitement for the future. 'We're particularly interested in twin studies at the moment; so much to be learnt from them in terms of the nature versus nurture influence.' Edward nods his agreement. 'What's your area of expertise, Edward?' the great man asks.

'Psychology,' explains Edward, 'as well as education policy and intelligence testing. But my wife and I have been members of the Eugenics Society for years. I agree – the work of the movement is very exciting. I'm keen to do whatever I can to support the move in England to adopt a eugenics-based approach to government policy in several areas, as you are so successfully doing here in America. Indeed, that's really why I'm here. Unfortunately in England... Well, let's just say there are those who don't agree, or *understand* the possible benefits we could reap as a society. Some people see compulsory sterilisation or incarceration of the unfit as cruel or wrong. And on the individual level... well, that of course is a valid argument, but for the greater good...?' He laughs. 'I don't need to explain that to you.'

'No, indeed,' laughs Junior too. 'But we do have voices of dissent here too. The church, the liberals...'

'Ah, yes. That old chestnut. The state having ultimate power over individual rights.'

'Look, there will always be opposition. But it's too important, the *science* of the benefit too well-proven, in my view, not to go ahead with these policies. We must be bold. Difficult choices for the greater good, eh Edward?'

'Yes – absolutely!'

'Well,' Junior gives a slight bow, 'it's been a delight to meet you, but you must excuse me, I have several people I must speak to before I go. Harry here will keep you company. International collaboration is the way to move things forward, isn't that right, Harry?'

'Absolutely, sir!'

Rockefeller claps Harry on the back. 'You heard about

the success of the Buck vs Bell case last summer? We owe that to Harry. It's allowed many states to steamroller forward in their own programmes of sterilisation – vital work to improve the health of the gene pool. He's a real force of nature,' he adds, smiling in Harry's direction. 'We must all work together to stem the flow of bad germ plasm from inferior races.'

'The world is in crisis,' grunts Darwin, who, like everyone else in the room, has melted closer to the great Junior Rockefeller to hear his words of wisdom. 'What you are doing over here is to be greatly admired.' Junior takes a small bow as though he is personally responsible for all of it. 'But in my opinion, we, especially in Europe, are not acting quickly enough if we are to avoid a planetary disaster.'

'That's an extreme view, sir,' interjects a voice. Everyone turns and looks. A young man with a tag sticking out of his breast pocket stating PRESS in large letters, smiles. 'Ed Winslow, the *Daily News*.' He is carrying a camera on a tripod over his left shoulder.

Darwin gives him a withering look.

'Who let you in?' barks a man in a dark suit, moving himself between the journalist and Rockefeller.

Winslow indicates behind him at some invisible authority as the doors to the room are now closed. 'I was scheduled an interview and a photo. My boss...' Beads of sweat break out on his forehead.

'Ah! The *Daily News*, of course,' Davenport says, snapping his fingers. 'That's right. You were supposed to be here at nine thirty.'

'There was a big hold-up outside, some sort of demonstration. Sorry I'm a little late, sir.'

'Actually, it's perhaps better this way,' says Davenport. 'You have everyone worth photographing here in one room.'

'Except me,' Rockefeller says, 'I really must go.' He raises a hand in farewell and leaves, the dark-suited man a few paces behind him.

'Great.' The young man puts down his tripod and begins fiddling with the camera to set it up for a shot. 'So, um, you were saying, Mr …? About a world crisis?'

'Darwin. Leonard Darwin,' Darwin says. 'You can put this in your newspaper for the doubters to dwell on: we are heading towards a planetary disaster because the population of mankind is exploding and we can't allow it to go on increasing unchecked! Resources will run out, economies will dwindle, democracy will be defeated and autocracy will reign. It will end in some horrific war if we go on as we currently are.'

'I think, though,' the reporter says, pulling a pencil and notebook from his pocket, 'you are talking about population increase only of a certain kind.'

'That's quite right, young man. It's the population of the *lower* orders, the races carrying inferior germ plasm, which need controlling. If we don't do this, future generations of man will be of lower intelligence, more predisposed to disease, feeble-mindedness, criminality etc., etc.'

'That's a real doomsday, end-of-the-world prediction, sir! I mean, this great country has been built on the entrepreneurial nature and ingenuity of our immigrants, no?' He is scribbling furiously into his notebook.

'Well, yes, but there are immigrants and *immigrants*,' interjects Laughlin. 'We are simply sorting the less desirable from the desirable and, at the same time, encouraging those from the better gene pool, who rightfully *should* be having more children, for the future security of the race, to have more of them. It's unfortunate that those are the very people most likely to practise birth control methods.' Laughlin turns to glare at a tall, middle-aged woman who shakes her head at him.

'If it were my decision alone,' Darwin is saying, 'and you can write this down too, I would have strict segregation of the classes. There should be no intermixing, or the risk of lowering the biological stock is simply perpetuated.'

'The same goes for racial intermingling,' adds Davenport. 'Those of the lower racial orders should be prevented in large numbers, whilst those of the higher orders must be encouraged to breed more – four to six children at least!'

The journalist flicks over a page and continues his scribbling, his forehead wrinkled with concentration.

'Progress would be too slow,' pipes up another man. 'Euthanasia is the way to go. The cost of institutionalising the enormous and increasing numbers is untenable.'

Ed Winslow stops scribbling and looks up from his notebook, his eyebrows disappearing into his fringe of hair. '*Euthanasia?*' he exclaims, pencil held aloft. 'You cannot be serious about that?'

'A step too far for most people,' Davenport says, hastily. 'And not something we are proposing, for now.'

The journalist mumbles something, shakes his head and goes back to his scribbling.

'Which is precisely an argument for planned families,' interjects a female voice. 'Margaret Sanger,' the woman Laughlin had glared at earlier, steps forward and introduces herself. The name and face are familiar and Edward suddenly remembers that he met her in London some years ago with Marie Stopes, their work being along similar lines. If he remembers rightly, she had had to flee New York on account of her being hounded out for the work she was doing on birth control. 'Most of the poorer families with limited funds would dearly like to have fewer children, if only they had the means and the knowledge to do so. That would assist greatly in the drive to a better population.'

Davenport pipes up now, eyeing Margaret Sanger with suspicion in his eyes. She appears to have few friends in the room. 'But,' he says, 'what *you* preach is dangerous. The planned parenting practice is unbalanced, with those we would like to reproduce *more* being those who practise it the most. Look what birth control has done to the French! The upper classes are decimated.'

'That is simply not the case, sir,' Sanger says, raising her voice over the chatter breaking out in the room. 'It should be a *woman's* choice whether she has children or not. I'm as keen as you are to ensure the unfit have as few children as possible and, as you well know, support sterilisation in those who shouldn't have children at all. But this does not have to be to the detriment of women who must be permitted to make decisions about their own bodies.' Sanger is becoming animated, slopping coffee into her saucer. Winslow scribbles faster.

'Women,' says Darwin, 'are *more* essential to the survival of our race than men. What will become of human beings,' he laughs, 'if every bright and able, well-educated woman decides she does not wish to give up her freedoms for the constraints of motherhood? What then?'

Margaret opens her mouth to reply, but Davenport claps

his hands. 'I must draw this lively discussion to a close, I'm afraid. I've an opening speech to make.' He smiles.

'Oh, one moment!' Winslow cries, shoving his notebook and pencil back in his pocket. 'I need the photograph.'

The group stand together as instructed, Winslow fiddles with his camera and, with a brilliant flash of the bulb, the picture is taken.

Davenport disappears to give his opening address, Winslow following behind with his camera slung over his shoulder.

Edward wanders the main exhibition hall alone, noting down the articles and exhibits of interest he plans to come back to later. *Alcoholism and Heredity. Mental Disorders in Twins. The Era of Superman. Crime and Race Descent. Eugenics For Schools. The Perils of Birth Control. Institutions, Colonies and Sterilisations – The Way Forward.*

Looking at the exhibits, he realises with some dismay that America is so much further ahead in this race to a superior population. England must do better if the country does not wish to be left behind. *He* must do better.

Suddenly unaccountably tired, he makes for the café and buys himself a black coffee and fried doughnut to bolster his energy. Tucking himself in a quiet corner, home feels so impossibly far away. How he wishes Eleanor were sitting opposite him now. She would be stirring a little sugar and cream into her coffee saying, *Oh, I know I really shouldn't, but what's bad for the waist is good for the soul. Don't you think, Edward?* He smiles to himself. He really couldn't care less about the size of her waist, and especially now, when she is carrying his child.

And he says a little prayer that this child won't carry the defective genes affecting Mabel, poor Mabel. And there it is, the twist of the knife in the open wound. Mabel, whom they must hide away from the world in her nursery. Mabel, who won't be able to attend the girls' school she was supposed to start later this year. Mabel, who cannot be allowed to see the village children and must make do solely with the company of her rather sullen and strict nurse, Miss Cartwright-Jones, who can, at least in return for an extortionate salary, be trusted for her discretion. How ironic it all is, given the subject matter of the conference he is attending now. But that is different. Of course it is. Mabel is not at all the same as the people being discussed here. No, they are something else entirely. They are freaks and monsters. Criminals and good-for-nothings. They are the type who murder innocent mothers, like Eleanor's, who leave years of grief and despair in their wake.

'Edward!' He looks up with a jolt, surprised to find himself here, far, far away from the troubles of Brook End. It's Harry. 'So this is where you're hiding! You OK?'

'Oh, yes. I, er, just stopped to refuel. Would you like to join me?'

'Sure is busy out there.' Harry jerks his head towards the exhibition hall. 'But that's good, huh? I think it's going to be a big success, Edward. People are really beginning to get it. I think we're on the brink of a bright new era. Yes, I really do. Waiter! Yes, another coffee over here, please!'

Later, back in his sumptuous room at the Waldorf-Astoria, Edward exhales the exhaustion of the day. He decides that, given he is here all alone, it will be acceptable to bathe in the morning, and slips on his silk pyjamas. He pours himself a small nightcap from the decanter of bourbon on the bedside table, takes a sip and feels the tension seeping out of him.

He sinks onto the bed and stretches out his long limbs, easing away the knots in his shoulders with his fingers. Since he arrived in New York a few days ago, it's been a relentless round of meetings, breakfasts, lunches, dinners, speakeasies and jazz clubs; of schmoozing, smoking, smiling and too many bee's knees to bolster his flagging spirits. But it does seem that on this side of the pond there is less morbidity of thought than he senses in Blighty. The upbeat energy, the optimism of the people he has encountered in New York, is in stark contrast to that of the downtrodden streets of London. With the extraordinarily bright illuminations of Times Square, the soaring heights of the Chrysler Building and the other skyscrapers climbing higher and higher above the crowded streets below, New York is a world away from the slow, crumbling rot of London's low, grey cityscape.

The London view is that the civilised world is in free fall. Capitalism is doomed and nobody, on the left or the right, can agree on a cure for the disease. The socialists, of course, believe a planned economy will stem the decay.

Edward sighs and drains his glass. The answer, as the Americans seem to have worked out so much better than the British, is in the radical. Where the English muddle about and debate, the Americans are all action. It is time to be decisive. Time to lead. A vision flashes before him. Himself, a Captain, caked in mud and horror. His men, boys, shivering with cold and terror staring up at him. Reliant.

Trusting. He shudders involuntarily, pushes the thought aside, pulls up the covers and snaps off the lamp, suddenly thinking of Barton and wondering what he would make of all the electric lamps which are everywhere in Manhattan. Dear, parochial Barton. He would be most uncomfortable with the modernity of America.

Edward is quivering from head to toe. If only he can stop the violent waves of shaking and trembling, preventing him from climbing to his feet, cancelling all sensible thought.

It's dark. Flares of light pass overhead again and again. There's a rumble – not thunder. It's gunfire. Rapid. Close by. Machine-gun fire. He needs to move! To stand and take control, get out of the liquifying mud before he is sucked into its depths where he will die of agonising suffocation.

He pushes his upper body away from the mud until he is half-sitting, half-lying, propped up against the trench wall. He has no more strength in him. The waves of shaking become violent and he's powerless to stop them. *Don't want to die! Not here. Not like this!* In the distance, the repeated, *boom, boom* of falling bombs, deafening even here. A bright orange flare lights the sky and the renewed crack of machine-gun fire rattles his skull, crashes in his teeth. There's a metallic tang of blood in his mouth. It's close. Too close.

The noise is too much. He is mad with it. It's inside his ears, his brain. Louder and louder and louder until he can bear it no longer. He clamps his hands against his skull. Curls up amongst the tangle of legs belonging to the boys around him. Barely old enough to shave, the lot of them.

They stand, fire, crouch, reload, fire, reload. There are shouts and yells along the trench. Mud, stones, bullets rain down. There is no protection in here. They are sitting ducks, waiting for slaughter.

A thought slices through. A memory. *He* is in command. These are *his* men. *His* boys. *He* should be leading *them*. He summons every ounce of strength to grip his rifle with frozen fingers and tries to hall himself to his feet, but there's a rip of fire and the legs next to him buckle. The slight figure is down, falling against Edward, who pushes against the body and it rolls away. A bolt shocks through him when he sees the boy's face – *dear God, it's Private Avery! Burt bloody Avery. New arrival. Sixteen years old! Bloody sixteen.* The boy is violently twitching, eyes wide with terror, mouth agape. Edward is frozen in shock as the boy's blood and guts spill from a gaping wound, wet and white and red onto the mud; onto Edward's coat. Avery clutches at air, gasps, and then Private – his name hovers just out of reach – grabs Avery and holds him tight until the boy lies still.

'*Sorry*,' Edward says, or does he think it? *Sorry*.

What a fucking useless word.

The private – the boy, because that is what he is, not much older than Avery – squeezes Edward's shoulder. '*It's OK, Captain. I'll get the effin' bastard Huns what done this.*' And then he's gone.

Screams, shouting, more gunfire, more bodies falling back. More twitching, shitting, bleeding and crying. Will it ever be over?

Edward's guts squirm. He must take control. He's the officer in charge, he has to save his men. But the mud is too thick; he hasn't the strength to fight it. He cannot get up. Cannot save them. It's pulling him down, further and further. But it isn't mud sucking at him, dragging him under. It's the mangled body parts of his boys. He is lying in their thick, glutinous blood, gallons and gallons of it, pooled together and strewn with severed limbs and twisted guts. Their faces flash in front of him, alive with light and life, greeting him with smiles and winks and *oy, oy, sir, time for a chat? C'mon, give us a snifter, sir! Just the evening for a smoke on the terrace. C'mon sir, what's 'er name then? Betcha she's a looker'n all.* There is Butler and Crouch; Spencer and young Dean. There's the Miller twins and...

Edward wakes, sodden with sweat, disorientated. Where's the mud, the cold, the blood and shit? The stench of the dead?

No, he's here, lying in his vast bed, the covers rumpled and twisted around him. The curtains are open to the New York night and beams from the headlamps of passing vehicles crawl across the ceiling. His brain, still half immersed in his dream, tries to make sense of distant rumbles and crashes. Thunder? *Not guns. It's not guns.* He fumbles for the cord to light the lamp beside his bed, switching it on with shaking fingers. He checks his pocket watch. Six a.m. Not night after all. The noise outside begins to make sense. It's the sound of early-morning street cleaners and gas lighters, of the city waking to a winter's morning.

Edward eases himself onto the edge of his bed, waiting for the horror of the nightmare to subside. The galloping of his heart slows and he pulls his dressing gown around his shoulders and lets his head sink into his hands. He has not experienced such a vivid reliving like this for years, had kidded himself they were behind him – but of course they weren't. How could they be? His past lives inside him, squirming and rotting like the sludge at the bottom of a stagnant pond.

Self-loathing rises inside, like vomit.

He stands shakily. He needs to get clean, to bathe away the sweat and the memories.

He's trained his conscious mind to forget and it's his unconscious one he is most afraid of. Only Eleanor has the power to soothe him. Gentle, steadfast Eleanor. How he aches for her.

A knock at the door rouses him. Who the devil is that, at this time of the morning?

The bellboy hands Edward a telegram and his heart hammers. Telegrams mean only one thing – bad news. He tips the boy and shuts the door, ripping open the envelope.

BABY HAS ARRIVED EARLY STOP A HEALTHY BOY STOP MOTHER AND BABY WELL AND RESTING STOP CONGRATULATIONS STOP DR HARGREAVES.

The baby came early! A month early. Edward sinks onto the bed, his heart dancing in his chest, tears unexpectedly in his eyes. But it's OK. The doctor says they are both OK.

A boy!

I I

Eleanor

```
MY  DEAREST  DARLING  ELEANOR  STOP  SUCH
WONDERFUL  NEWS  STOP  I  AM  ONLY  SORRY  TO
BE  THIS  FAR  AWAY  STOP  I  DO  HOPE  ALL  IS
WELL  THE  BABY  BEING  SO  EARLY  STOP  I  MISS
YOU  VERY  MUCH  STOP  WILL  WRITE  IMMEDIATELY
STOP  YOUR  LOVING  HUSBAND  EDWARD.
```

The telegram sits on Eleanor's mantelpiece, propped against one of many vases of flowers. The flowers are being added to, almost by the hour, from well-wishers near and far, ever since the notice of the baby's unexpected arrival went in *The Times*.

'We're running out of vases, Mrs Hamilton!' gasps Alice breathlessly. 'Never seen so many bunches of flowers in all my days!' She blusters off in search of jugs and other vessels in which to place the bouquets.

Rose has been kept busy writing letters of thanks to friends, acquaintances, associates, students and colleagues of Edward's. Neither of them have mentioned the prospect of her returning to London anytime soon, but Eleanor rather suspects that, in amongst the letter writing she is doing on Eleanor's behalf, she is also sending clandestine letters of enquiry to newspaper editors. Eleanor imagines them, the grubby creatures wearing horribly creased suits, opening the letters gleefully in dingy offices, imagining all the disgusting things they would like to do to her nineteen-year-old sister.

Today Rose has gone off shopping in the county town of Guildford with the eldest of the Leyton girls, Charlotte. No doubt they will have lunch and a gossip while they are there, which leaves Eleanor to receive a long-overdue visit from Sophie alone. Perhaps Rose organised this on purpose, to give the old friends a chance to catch up without her muscling in.

After a soak in the bath and trying – and failing – to get into most of the clothes in her wardrobe, Eleanor resigns herself to having to don one of her shapeless pregnancy dresses, and finally makes it downstairs, carefully carrying the cradle, just in time to see the large silver Mercedes-Benz turning into the gates of Brook End at a rather alarming speed.

'He's the *absolute* spit of Edward,' Sophie announces, peering at the baby, as he frowns and screws up his face in his sleep. 'I'm sure he'll be thrilled when he finally gets to meet him. What's his name?'

'The Grub.'

'Ha!' Sophie turns to Eleanor. 'I meant his real name.'

'It's all he has at the moment. I'm waiting for Edward to come home and then we shall decide together. Or at least, Edward will say what he likes and I'll agree.'

'Oh dear!' Sophie wrinkles her nose a little in distaste. 'Is that really how it is?' She turns back to the baby, this time giving him a little glare, as though he represents the failings of all those of his sex.

'I can't see it,' Eleanor replies. 'The likeness to Edward, I mean. And anyway, why does everyone say a baby has to look like the damned father, when *his* contribution to its existence is pretty much over in a flash?'

'Genetically programmed that way, my dear, so the father has no doubts about its parentage. That said, *I* have doubts about Sebastian's parentage, but fortunately he has Henry's colouring so nobody mentions a thing.'

'Good lord. You don't mean...?'

'Darling,' Sophie says, with a tinkle of laughter, 'you didn't think I was going to let Henry have all the fun, did you?'

Eleanor feels her jaw drop. 'But you were so upset about Clarissa!'

'Only because he did it right under my nose. Doesn't give a hoot about who knows any more. And there are rules to this game. Discretion being the first. Not falling in love, the second. Little misdemeanours are easy to ignore – nobody gets hurt if nobody knows.' Then Sophie says, 'Any chance of a drink?'

'Heavens,' Eleanor says, beginning to wonder if she is the only person left in England to have had sex with only one other person: her spouse. She suddenly feels terribly old, prudish and Victorian. She rings the bell for Alice.

'So... Do you have some sort of *misdemeanour* going on at the moment,' Eleanor enquires, wondering if this is the reason for Sophie's high spirits.

'Perhaps,' she says with a wink. 'Speaking of misdemeanours, where's the lovely Rose?'

'She's gone out for the day with a friend. I think she needed a break from domestic monotony for a while.'

'*Quite* understandable.'

'Ah, Alice,' Eleanor says, at the sight of the maid. 'What would you like to drink, Sophie?'

'Oh, anything with alcohol in it. You choose me something, darling.' Sophie flops dramatically onto one of the sofas and stares out across the garden.

'How about a sherry?' Eleanor suggests.

Alice goes to the drinks cabinet and pours a small one for each of them. 'Shall I tell Mrs Bellamy you'll be ready for lunch?'

'Yes, please. Thank you, Alice,' Eleanor smiles. How good it feels to be back downstairs, vaguely normal again; she cannot imagine where Sophie finds the energy and inclination for her *misdemeanours*, the birth still so wincingly vivid in her memory and in her body. Still, she remembers thinking it an utterly preposterous proposition that she would ever go to bed with her husband again after giving birth to Mabel. She glances down at her son, pink cheeks just visible between the crocheted hat on his little head and the bundle of blankets tightly binding him up to his chin, and acknowledges that she evidently did just that.

Miss Harding, the nurse who arrived two days ago at Brook End, appears in the doorway after a perfunctory knock. Fresh out of Norland's, she is a green-eyed, baby-faced, slight girl, with a smattering of freckles which spread from ear to ear across her button nose. Eleanor wondered, when she first met her, if she was even old enough to be out of the nursery herself.

Miss Harding's looks, however, are deceiving. The girl

is flawlessly efficient and has immediately begun whipping The Grub into a strict routine of feeds and sleep and walks and lying on his back with his arms and legs free to kick, before being swaddled up again for the next round in the routine. Eleanor had been run ragged by the long nights before Miss Harding swooped in and rescued her. Now, Miss Harding does everything for the baby during the night, bar nurse him, which Eleanor can do without even leaving her bed. Before her arrival, The Grub, angelic during the day, was not so much a baby at night but a tyrant who thrashed and screamed unless he was attached for hours to Eleanor's breasts until her nipples cracked and bled. Mabel had never been like The Grub. In retrospect, she'd been the perfect baby.

'Time for the young man to get some fresh air,' Miss Harding proclaims, checking her watch. She picks the bundle out of the cradle and smiles at Eleanor. 'We'll be back in an hour for his next feed,' she says, closing the door behind her, and Eleanor feels her spirits inexplicably soar at the prospect of an hour free of The Grub to enjoy lunch and adult company.

'*Cheers.*' They clink glasses.

'Miss Harding believes in fresh air for babies and a strict routine,' Eleanor tells Sophie. '"The healthy outdoors is essential for a happy, settled child",' she recites. 'So out he goes, however cold it is. Unless it's raining, of course. I don't believe she puts him out in the rain.'

Sophie jerks her head towards the door Miss Harding walked out of a few moments ago. 'That's a bit of temptation under Edward's nose, isn't it? Pretty little thing like that...'

'Don't be ridiculous. Look at her, she looks like a child,

even if she isn't one. Why would Edward be interested in her? She certainly wouldn't… Anyway, why do you think everyone is so obsessed with sex? We're not all like *you*.' She sniffs and takes a sip of sherry.

'Oh really, Eleanor, sometimes you are awfully naïve.'

'And *really*, Sophie, right now I couldn't care less what Edward does as long as the nanny stays here and takes care of the tyrant in that bloody pram.'

Sophie giggles. 'I take it he'll be the last, then?'

'Edward's already muttering about having another. To make up for Mabel's—'

'Mabel's what?'

Eleanor sighs. It's so hard to keep quiet about it all. It's bound to slip out one day.

'Oh, nothing. Come on, let's go in and have lunch. I'm ravenous.'

'What's wrong, Eleanor? Is something the matter with Mabel? Where is she anyway? She's usually drifting about somewhere close by. She *is* a darling.'

'She's just a little under the weather, that's all,' Eleanor says vaguely, leading the way to the dining room. She rings the bell for the food to be served.

Over lunch, Eleanor tunes in and out of tales of Sophie's London life. Her mind is fogged with tiredness and thoughts of Mabel, alone with Miss Cartwright-Jones at this very minute, hidden away in the nursery, in case Sophie should catch sight of her fitting. Faulks, Mrs Faulks, Alice and Mrs Bellamy know, of course. Even Bertie. Nobody says anything but Edward has taken them all aside to ensure nothing is said outside the home. They give Eleanor sad glances and sidle around her respectfully, quietly, as though noise might for some reason upset her. Only Mrs Bellamy has surprised her. Mrs Bellamy who really didn't seem pleased with anything or anyone, had broken down in tears when she heard the sad news about Mabel.

Sophie is dropping in names like Vita, Virginia and Ottoline, who seem to be increasingly influencing her views on life, but are only known to Eleanor through the society pages in the newspapers, or on the covers of unread novels on her bookshelf.

'Oh, she's not having any of it,' Sophie laughs, a delicate portion of ham and salad, no potatoes, thank you, sitting untouched on her plate. She takes a long slug from a glass of chilled Blanc du Châteaux Margaux. 'Honestly, I can't work out if it's because she is *so* committed to the idea of doing good in the world, you know, exposés and all that, or whether it's because she's just utterly besotted with Marcel. What do you think?' At the mention of Marcel, Sophie's words sharpen into focus.

'Hmm? What do I think about what?'

'About the job Rose has landed. I feel partly responsible, seeing as I orchestrated the introductions to the Webbs and all that, but I do hope you and Edward don't mind *too* awfully? I just hadn't realised her politics were so left wing. Which is why I wondered about Marcel?'

'Please, Sophie, you are speaking in riddles. What job?'

'Oh lordy! She hasn't told you has she, the little vixen?' Sophie laughs and puts a hand over her mouth. 'She's got a job at the *New Statesman*! She's going to be assisting Charles Lloyd, the editor. Nice man, although a little misguided on certain things. Now you mustn't worry. She absolutely *must* continue to stay with me.'

'That's – that's very generous, Sophie. But I'm confused. Has she *seen* Marcel?'

'Only two weeks ago, darling.' Sophie's fingers touch her lips, eyes searching Eleanor's face.

Anger wells, hot and sudden. All these little secrets her best friend is suddenly letting slip about her own sister! And to think Rose is keeping all of this from her! She takes a deep breath to try to maintain calm. 'Why do I only find out about this now?'

'Honestly, I'd have mentioned it before, only then you went and gave birth, dearest, and I clean forgot. But Marcel was in London on some business or other and he asked if he could visit Rose at Berkeley Square. I didn't see any harm in it, so—'

'*You* didn't see any harm in it?' Eleanor is unable to hold her temper any longer. 'You didn't *think* to mention it to me, hmm? For God's sake, Sophie, I don't care about *your* lax morals but Rose is only nineteen!'

'Nothing terrible happened!' Sophie is on the defensive, waving her hands in protest. 'He simply came to a Friday night soirée as my guest… Well actually, in truth, he ended up remaining as a weekend guest—'

'Sophie! How could you, when you *knew* our feelings about Rose and this man! You are supposed to be my friend, you were supposed to protect Rose from someone who is no good, and *this* is how you behave?'

'But how do you know he is no good? You've never even met him.'

'He's a penniless French artist, Sophie, with a questionable background. *You* of all people should understand one cannot live on *love* alone.'

Alice's head appears again around the dining-room door. 'Shall I clear the plates, Mrs Hamilton?'

'Not now, Alice. Give us a few minutes.'

'So sorry, of course.' Alice closes the door behind her.

'I-I was protecting Rose. *Am* protecting her. I felt it was important to see for myself, to check this man out, before writing him off without ever having met him. Just because he is penniless now, doesn't mean in the future... And anyway, he really isn't entirely penniless. Besides, it was in the safe environment of my home where no harm could possibly come to her.'

'It wasn't your job to make such a judgement. I'll bet you won't take such a liberal and Bohemian attitude when your own children are looking for spouses. Urgh, sometimes you can be so infuriating!' The pressure is rising in Eleanor's chest. How easy it is to be liberal and free when you are staring down at the world from the lofty heights of the treetops. Sophie is frozen, a tomato pronged on her fork, held aloft and forgotten in her hand. 'You've let her see him before,' Eleanor breathes with sudden realisation, 'haven't you?'

Sophie leans forward and looks Eleanor squarely in the eye. 'Eleanor,' she says, her voice firm, 'I had no intention of upsetting you, or going behind your back. Indeed, I really wanted to discuss this whole Rose and Marcel situation with you, as did Rose herself, but you, dearest Eleanor, have been so distracted with – heaven knows what, but *something* – and the pregnancy, and we certainly couldn't tell Edward because he would have none of it... It was *impossible*. I thought I would do the best thing a friend *could* do in the circumstances, and do what *you* should have done. That is, to meet the damned fellow and come to your own conclusion. To keep an open mind and not judge a chap you have never met, conversed with, or even set eyes on.'

Now Sophie's becoming heated, her cheeks flushing the same pink of her nails. But she is being so utterly, completely unfair. How can she, *Lady* Grant-Parker, of all people, condone Rose's fixation with a nobody French artist? Tears begin to well in Eleanor's eyes. She rubs them away before Sophie can see them.

'Well, whatever am I to tell Edward now?' she demands.

'You needn't tell him anything. There is nothing to tell.'

'But... Are they secretly engaged? Are they planning to wait until Rose is twenty-one? Or are they not even planning on getting married at all!'

'In all honesty, Eleanor, dear, I have no idea. Surely that is for you to discuss with your sister? I am merely a concerned friend who has tried to do her best. I have made sure to be in the background when they have been together, acting as a responsible chaperone, if you will. Marcel has slept in the furthest bedroom away from your sister and I have enjoyed tea, wine and liqueurs with him and have come to think... Well, it is not for me to say.' Her tone is crisp, her back straight as a broom handle. She replaces her napkin on the table. 'All I can say is, marrying for money, or title – or *both* – is not necessarily all it's cracked up to be. Rose's happiness should also count for something.'

Eleanor is at a loss to know what to say. Sophie's words are harsh. Bruising. In the silence, the ticking of the clock over the mantelpiece grows louder.

'If you would prefer me to leave, I will,' Sophie says quietly.

'Perhaps it would be for the best,' Eleanor says, not meeting Sophie's eye.

'Fine.'

Eleanor watches as her friend twists the corner of her napkin between her fingers. She opens her mouth as if to speak but closes it again.

Eleanor rings the bell for Alice to come and take the plates. 'Would you care for a coffee before you drive back to London?'

'No, thank you.'

'It was good of you to spare the time to visit.'

'Eleanor, I know you are angry with me,' Sophie says, meeting Eleanor's eyes. 'And whatever it is you have going on, you can tell me, you know.'

'There is nothing. I'm simply tired. And upset about Rose.'

'Of course, but I'm sure once you have had a chance to reflect you'll see that you needn't be angry. I really think you should meet Marcel, Eleanor. Give the man a chance. For Rose's sake.'

By the time Rose arrives home in the late afternoon, overflowing with bags and good humour, dusk is falling and Eleanor has been crying for three hours straight. *It's the baby blues combined with an absent husband,* everyone agrees, and Mrs Faulks has Alice running about fetching cake and hot, sweet tea to cheer her up.

Eleanor can't tell them the truth, of course, which is that her tears have nothing to do with Edward or the baby.

Rose flounces into the sitting room, her cheeks flushed

with the cold, looking impossibly glamorous in a slim-fitting, salmon-pink suit. 'I've bought you a present which may lift your spirits,' Rose announces, removing her scarf and hat with a flourish and flinging them on a sofa. Eleanor sits in Edward's armchair beside a crackling fire, her tea growing cold in her hand, refusing to smile. Rose produces a wrapped box and holds it out to Eleanor.

'I'm not in the mood for presents,' Eleanor says miserably, thinking of her swollen, blotchy face and excess baby weight.

'Fine,' Rose says, clearly not going to be put off, 'I'll open it for you then!' Opening the box, she pulls out a beautiful bottle of Guerlain's Shalimar, and sprays the lemony bergamot scent around the room. 'Perfect to wear when Edward arrives home,' she adds. 'Not long to wait now!'

'Thank you,' Eleanor says curtly.

'Don't you like it?' Rose asks, shoulders finally slumping, smile fading from her face.

'It is *not* baby blues,' Eleanor announces with a sniff, twisting her sodden handkerchief in her hand.

'Darling, I—'

'It's *you*.'

'Pardon?' Rose sits on the sofa now, facing Eleanor, confusion clouding her eyes.

'Sophie told me everything. The job. The visits from Marcel. Why did you keep it all from me?' She chokes on her words. Eleanor hates the bitter neediness rising up inside her. The hurt of being excluded from all the big things happening in Rose's life when they have always shared *everything*, mixes with a flare of anger at Rose breaking her promise about Marcel.

'Ah...' Rose says, looking at Eleanor warily. 'I-I'm sorry,' she mumbles. 'I didn't want to upset or anger you with all of it. The job happened so suddenly – I was going to tell you, of course I was, but I didn't want you to think I was going to run off back to London as soon as Edward got back and—'

'And will you?'

'Well, soon, yes. They have been very good to me. I should have started already but they have kept the job open for me, given what happened and how I was needed here. They didn't have to, Eleanor, and I am terribly grateful.'

'I suppose it is good of them. But I do wish you had told me. I try to be supportive of all that you do, Rose.'

'I know, Ellie. But not with Marcel.' Her tone is bitter now.

'No, not with Marcel. I'm angry with Sophie for keeping it from me. We fell out.'

'Oh Ellie! That was silly. Is that why you are so upset?'

'Partly.'

'Well, you mustn't fall out over me. You must make it up with her. But you see, *this* is precisely why I kept it all secret!'

'But that *hurts*, Rose, can't you see?' Eleanor cries. 'You made me promise I wouldn't tell Edward because it was nothing. Now what am I to do? He will be *furious*!'

'Exactly! Ellie, I think it's unfair – Edward is so against Marcel, and neither of you has even met him.'

Eleanor is quiet; there is a lump in her throat and she is exhausted from the crying. A log drops in the grate sending a spray of sparks up the chimney. The fire leaps and brightens.

'I wish you would just *meet* Marcel, give him a chance,' Rose says.

'That's what Sophie said.' Eleanor lets her head sink into her hands and begins to sob again. 'Oh Rose, I've made such an almighty mess of everything, haven't I? Sophie hates me and now you do too...'

Rose runs to her, slides her arms around her and pulls her in close. 'Oh Ellie, you silly old fool. Of *course* I don't hate you, and nor does Sophie. You are my everything, you know that. And Sophie loves you to bits, I promise. You've got so much on your plate right now and I *do* think you might have a little bit of those baby blues everyone is talking about, even if you don't realise it. Listen, how about I put on some cheery music and get you some fresh tea? I'll get Alice to run you a nice, hot bath and afterwards you put on some of this perfume and you will feel a whole lot better.'

Eleanor nods, sinking further against her sister's warm and comforting body.

'That does sound rather lovely,' she says.

'Ellie?'

'Yes?'

'Not yet, but maybe in a few weeks when you're fully recovered and not feeding the baby. When Marcel is next in London... I'd like you to meet him. Before you mention anything to Edward. Please. I really do think you would like him.'

Eleanor pulls away and looks into her sister's eyes. She sighs. 'Maybe.' She sinks her head back onto Rose's shoulder. 'Ask me again when I'm not so tired.'

'OK,' Rose says, a smile in her voice. She rubs Eleanor's back. 'That's good enough for me,' she murmurs. 'For now.'

12

Edward

Edward opens the morning edition of the *Daily News* as he waits for his fried eggs and bacon. Still buzzing from the news from home, he wonders how Eleanor and the baby are doing. The conference is over and people will soon be heading back to wherever they have come from. For him, there is just one more place he must visit before travelling home. His bags are packed and late this afternoon he will be boarding the SS *New York* bound for Southampton.

Around him are the muted sounds of his fellow hotel guests at breakfast. Silver cutlery against bone china. The hum of conversation. The clink of coffee cup against saucer. He leans against the cushioned back of his chair, indicating to the hovering waiter to refill his coffee. He flicks over the pages of the newspaper and gives them a shake. He recognises the name of the journalist from the conference.

Closing of the 1929 International Congress of Eugenics
– By Ed Winslow

'During the last two decades, the new eugenics has risen from a mire of ridicule to the solid foundation of a recognized and important social factor,' Dr Charles B. Davenport, president of the International Congress of Eugenics, said last night at the final gathering of 200 geneticists from different parts of the world assembled in the American Museum of Natural History. He predicted that within two decades it would rise still further in public esteem and be regarded as the most important influence in human advancement. The same point of view was expressed by Dr Henry Fairfield Osborn and Major Leonard Darwin.

It seems Mr Winslow might have been won over from the initial scepticism Edward recalls from his attitude that first day. He reads on.

Analyzing an unfolding world crisis, from observations on a recent tour around the world, Dr Henry Fairfield Osborn said the situation resolved itself into six 'overs' – overdestruction of natural resources; overmechanization of industry; overconstruction of means of transport; overproduction of food and other commodities, overconfidence in future demand and supply; and overpopulation, with consequent permanent unemployment for the least fit. 'Prisons, reformatories, asylums, great public financial offerings, great national and local appropriations, great tides of human kindness and generosity are merely palliatives and temporary expedients,' Dr Osborn said. 'They may for a time gloss over the cataclysm; they cannot permanently cure it or avoid its recurrence. The only permanent remedy is the improvement and uplift of the character of the human race through prolonged and intelligent and humane birth selection aided by humane birth control. This is the keynote of this International Congress.'

Very true, thinks Edward. The young man has faithfully reported the very central theme of the conference. Good for him!

'In application there has been a slow but steady spread,' said Dr Davenport, reviewing the advance of the years in eugenics. 'Sterilization as a useful aid in negative eugenics has been adopted in Denmark. England and the Netherlands are considering legislation on the subject. The seriousness of the act of mate selection is, I think, becoming increasingly recognized partly as a result of more instruction in eugenics given in the schools. Marriage advice stations have sprung up in Germany, and we have an active center in Los Angeles.' Dr Davenport said he was optimistic enough to believe that young people more and more would be guided consciously as well as instinctively in making marriages that would ensure physically, mentally and temperamentally well-endowed offspring. 'Can we by eugenic studies point the way to produce the superman and the superstate?' Dr Davenport went on. 'Progress will come slowly. Man is a poor subject for experimental study; still worse to get to apply to himself established principles. But I think we are justified in having faith that the future will bring precise knowledge in human biology, and education will establish the desired mores.'

Couldn't have said it better myself, Edward thinks, nodding at the article. He folds the paper and checks his watch. Good heavens, is that the time? He doesn't wish to miss the transport which is to take him, and other foreign delegates, for a tour of the facility belonging to the Eugenics Record Office at Cold Spring Harbor on Long Island. The centre, financially secure and well-funded by wealthy benefactors, Carnegie and Mary Harriman, has become the home of American eugenics, and arguably, the whole of the Western world, spearheading research, data collection, education. Of course, its work spreads far wider than human genetics, with much advancement also in the field of animal breeding.

Edward folds the paper and hurries to join the others in the hotel foyer, his mind abuzz with the possibilities of setting up a similar research facility in London. What was it Darwin had mentioned over drinks the other day – the strong possibility of a knighthood? If he was instrumental in something like this, well, that would settle the matter. His spirits lift at the prospect of Sir and Lady Hamilton. Lady Hamilton? He has a little laugh at that and imagines Eleanor being equally amused by the connotations of the name. His own work to conquer the downfall of mankind, perhaps an analogy to that of Nelson's against the French and the Spanish.

Cold Spring Harbor turns out to be rather beautiful. A few buildings clustered around a grand clapperboard house, which, their driver points out, is the home of the ERO and its assistant director, Harry Laughlin and his wife, Pansy, all of it surrounded by trees on a hillside overlooking the bay.

It is cold, very cold, but the smattering of snow on the trees and the high ground gives it a fresh, clean glaze. The wind whips off the sea and hits him full in the face, making him gasp and his eyes water.

'It sure is beautiful up here in the summer,' someone comments. 'But cold and bleak in January!'

Edward tries to imagine the place in the summer. Warm wind replacing cold, the trees in full leaf. Boats bobbing in the blue of the bay. He has a fleeting vision of Eleanor and many future children living here, in all this space. Not Mabel; he tries not to think about her. They could build a beautiful, American-style house here. In the summer they could sail a boat in the harbour, he could make a name for himself. He could work much more closely with Laughlin and Davenport, attract funding from Carnegie or Rockefeller. Of course there are detractors here too, but their voices are quieter, more disparate; their influence less. He takes in a long, deep breath. Here he could leave his past behind, once and for all. Oh, the thought of no more secret meetings with Violet, no more guilt. But what about Mabel? The only inkblot on the otherwise fresh new sheet.

'Edward! Welcome!' Harry is striding towards him with his wife and another man, then shaking his hand warmly. 'Delighted to have you here. Now, have you met Heinz Kratz, representative from the University of Heidelberg?' A squat, balding man gives Edward a stiff and perfunctory bow. 'There is much interest in our work from our German friends, Edward. Come, let me show you both around. You remember Pansy?'

'Of course.' He gives the woman a peck on the cheek.

Harry talks them through some of his triumphs displayed

proudly on the walls of the offices. 'This is my pedigree model – you will appreciate this, Edward. Look at this...' The model shows the superior family characteristics of the Galton-Darwin-Wedgwood family pedigree. 'And then compare it with this,' he sweeps his hand across the display immediately next to the superior Darwin lineage which shows the hideous images of unfortunate families with various mental and physical disabilities, as well as those of different, inferior racial origins. 'We use these images widely in our education programme. Educating the population to ensure they seek out the best possible mate to breed with is of key importance. We find that the visual persuasiveness of pictures like these are important in winning hearts and minds.'

Edward studies the photographs.

'It's not enough simply to legislate. We also try to encourage and engage the public. We run competitions such as "The Better Baby" contest, or "The Fitter Family" contest, where we seek to identify the most eugenically perfect family.'

'As I understand things,' Heinz says, his hands behind his back, 'you have legislation to severely restrict the immigration of unwanted races, yes?'

Harry nods. 'Yes. Unfortunately, we had far too open a policy until the 1924 Immigration Restriction Act, which thankfully put a plug in the gush of Italians and Jews pouring into our nation. It's now reduced to a dribble. It's plain to see that the quality of the American race is under severe threat from inferior quality genes, and something radical had to be done. Just as we breed quality into racehorses, or higher yields into pigs and cattle, so we must breed higher quality into humans, the Nordic race being the pinnacle, the unfit and the lower quality races being undesirable.' He clears his throat. 'We cannot leave self-selection to the population alone – I needn't tell *you* that,' he laughs. 'Humans, as we both know, are rather bad at seeing just what is best for them. So, we, the intelligent and knowledgeable, must step in to prevent the explosive growth of the unfit.' He waves a hand again towards the photographs of the grotesque figures pinned to his board. 'Euthanasia being, in probability, a step too far to be publicly palatable, compulsory sterilisation *has* to be the answer if we are to prevent a rapid downward spiral of the human race.'

'Hmm,' Edward frowns. 'Unfortunately, we have a good deal of suspicion and opposition from all quarters in my country. For differing reasons, certainly, but it all adds up to an impasse on our ability to move forward. Other countries – yourselves, Germany,' he nods at Heinz, 'Denmark, Sweden, Australia, Canada – even those in the Far East are moving ahead of us.'

'Like I said to you before, Edward, give them *anything* they need to hear to convince them of the merits of your case,' Harry says. He waves a hand at a picture on the wall. In the picture, Harry is standing outside a courtroom, smiling and shaking hands with another man. 'Our victory at Buck vs Bell last year,' Harry says, and Edward remembers Junior Rockefeller referring to the case on the first day of the conference, 'has paved the way to roll out sterilisation programmes across the country.'

Edward recalls the case last summer when Harry had been asked to be an expert witness by the State of Virginia. It had concerned a girl, Carrie, herself the daughter of a poverty-stricken woman, who, after being abandoned by Carrie's father and left in abject poverty, became a woman of questionable morality. Carrie was removed as a toddler from her mother's care and placed into that of a wealthy couple. She progressed well at school until she was removed by her foster family to clean their homes and those of their neighbours. At seventeen she was found to be pregnant – she claimed to have been raped by the nephew of the foster couple. They then declared her mentally deficient and she was sent to the Virginia Colony for Epileptics and Feeble-Minded. Clearly the girl had heightened sexuality, common in the mentally deficient, the defective genes obviously being passed from mother to daughter, and would be passed on further to a third generation – Carrie's child. That infant did not need to be tested to ascertain if it was unfit – it obviously would be, and therefore should be placed in an asylum. Carrie herself must either be kept in an institution for the rest of her life to avoid her polluting any purer bloodline with the dangers posed by her defective genes, or be sterilised.

Harry had told Edward that he didn't *need* to meet the girl – the facts spoke for themselves. Her protestations of rape were just an excuse. During her short-lived freedom out of the asylum, she had led a life of immorality, prostitution and untruthfulness. She belonged, Harry had informed the court, to the shiftless, ignorant and worthless class of anti-social whites of the South. Sterilising her would prevent any further socially inadequate or defective offspring. Edward recalls the words of the judge in the case. *Three generations of imbeciles are enough*, and so, despite her objections, she had been forcibly sterilised. Mabel pops unbidden into his mind and he wonders where on earth the defective gene causing her terrible epilepsy could possibly have come from. It is most definitely not from his side, and he wonders whether there are any secrets in Eleanor's family she has chosen to keep hidden from him.

Five days later, Edward is standing at Eleanor's side in the darkness of her bedroom, the drapes still pulled tight shut against the winter cold and damp. It's not yet seven, but he couldn't wait a moment longer to see her and the baby. He clicks on the bedside lamp, but she doesn't stir.

She is sleeping, curled beneath the pile of blankets, hair tousled, her face half obscured by the covers. He smiles and sits beside her, stroking her hair to wake her as gently as possible. She opens her eyes slowly, as though pulling herself with extreme reluctance from the delicious world of her dreams. He watches her eyes swim into focus and then the realisation of his presence as consciousness, and the real world, returns. A warm smile lights up her face, her skin creased with marks from the pillow.

'Edward!' she exclaims. 'You're back!' She pushes herself upright and leans towards him, pressing her bed-hot body against his. He feels the stirring of desire and wraps his arms tight around her, kissing her again and again.

'Welcome back.' She pushes herself away and smiles into his eyes. 'Would you like to see your son?'

'May I?' Edward remembers how it had been with Mabel. Eleanor was so reluctant to let him hold her precious baby. She'd given him sharp instructions about supporting her head and clucked at his fumbled first attempts to carry their child. 'Don't drop her!' she'd screeched, more than once, as if he would! He'd borne her paranoia that he would somehow, inadvertently, hurt his own child with extreme forbearance, never uttering anything in response, assuming that this was a natural motherly response – protective, like a dog with her new puppies, or a cow with her calf.

She points to the cradle. 'I only finished feeding him half an hour or so ago. Go ahead and pick him up.' He glances back at her uncertainly but she nods at him.

He peers down at their son. His first thought is how unbelievably tiny he is, his fuzz-covered skull not much bigger than a cricket ball. Edward's second thought is how utterly perfect he is. The puckered lips, the swell of his cheeks, the fluttering pale eyelids. His skin has the lightest covering of down. He grimaces in his sleep.

Edward reaches down and slowly, carefully, pushes his hands beneath the blankets wound tightly around him, then lifts and cuddles him in close to his body. *His son!* How bloody marvellous to think those words – he will never tire of them. He doesn't stir from sleep. Lighter than a brace of pheasants, Edward notes as he stares down at him in wonder.

He strolls around the room, gazing at the baby's face, trying to imagine how he will look when he's older. Will he have Eleanor's fair hair, or his – albeit greying now – dark? The boy will be tall and athletic; clever, no doubt about that. But will he become an intellectual, like Edward, or an entrepreneur like his grandfather? He'll excel at cricket and rugby at prep school. Perhaps they will be able to secure him a place at Eton. Charterhouse, if Eton's a stretch too far. Unless of course Edward is awarded that knighthood, in which case, Eton *might* be suitable after all. Then it will be off to Oxford, whichever school he ends up at. Edward pictures himself taking the boy to Lord's cricket ground; or rowing on the Thames, teaching him to shoot pheasants. Together they will debate the state of the nation over a decent glass of red, Cuban cigars in hand.

How even more important than ever before, his work seems. He must do all that he can to ensure the world his son will inherit will be a better one. Not the one they seem destined to descend into.

'Look what we made,' Edward says to Eleanor, coming to sit beside her again, the baby still fast asleep in his arms. 'How unbelievably perfect is he?'

'Let's hope,' Eleanor murmurs, and Edward reaches for her hand, giving it a reassuring squeeze. But he wonders again about Mabel and if there is anything Eleanor could be hiding from him. There are no other relatives. No cousins or grandparents or aunts and uncles other than the cold and distant ones, as Eleanor refers to them, living up in Scotland, and whom Edward, in all his years of marriage to his wife, has never once set eyes on.

'And how are you, my darling?' He kisses her cheek. 'You look wonderful!'

'I hardly think so!' She lets out a laugh and tugs at her hair. 'You should have warned me you'd be here – I could at least have made myself look a little presentable.'

'But this is how I love you best. All tousled and sleepy and *you*.'

'Oh Edward, don't be kind. I look ghastly.'

'No, you look beautiful. Truly.' He holds her gaze so she knows he is being sincere, but she looks down at her hands.

'And everyone else? How is Rose, the staff?'

'Everyone is fine.' She smiles and looks at him again, now the focus is no longer on her. 'Rose has a job at the *New Statesman*. They held the position for her so she could stay with me until you were back. I think she will start on Monday.'

'Good lord,' Edward says, 'are we quite all right with her working for a socialist paper?'

Eleanor sighs. 'Sophie tells me it will be fine. I think... Edward, I think we have to let her find her own way a little. If we don't, she will simply rebel and I'm afraid I will lose her.'

'Don't be daft. You'll never lose your sister!'

'Well I nearly—' Eleanor stops, and Edward is sure she wants to say something more, but she turns her gaze to the baby and changes the subject. 'He needs a name,' she says as they both stare at him. 'Or I shall end up calling him *The Grub* forever, and that won't do.'

'No,' says Edward, 'it won't.' He's always hated that nickname. 'How about James?' he asks in a nonchalant manner, as though it just popped into his head, rather than him having decided on it days ago as he leaned over the railings of the ship, retching his empty guts into a heaving sea. Eleanor looks back at him, blank-eyed. 'My father's name,' he adds, imagining she might be awaiting explanation. 'Jimmy to his friends. Would that be all right with you?'

Edward strokes the soft fuzz of hair on the baby's head, his fingers huge and long against the boy's miniature skull. He marvels how it could be possible that this fragile and delicate mite will one day grow up to become a man. Eleanor is silent and he wonders if she will contest his choice. Maybe she would prefer it if they named him after her own father, Robert. He tenses, waiting for her to suggest it. If she does, he will reply that Robert will be a great name for their *second* son. He would very much like to have more than one. A clutch of sons, and daughters too. A horde of perfect children to fill Brook End with laughter and energy and fun. To load it to the brim so that beneath the chatter and the fun, the sad absence of their eldest child will dissipate and disappear...

Because, of course, that is what must happen. Mabel cannot stay here. That he decided too, as he contemplated his future over the side of the ship. The danger of her discovery and the consequent question mark over the quality of his genes and Eleanor's is simply too great. Surely Eleanor must see that too?

He can only hope that Mabel's affliction is a one-off, and any defect in Eleanor's line, because it certainly isn't in his, won't be passed to their other offspring.

He also imagines that with each child will come new pleasure and love and happiness to fill the void in his heart. The void which opened in the freezing mud of a Belgian battlefield in 1917. The void which has widened into a bottomless chasm since the onset of Mabel's illness, and with it, this unremitting, unreachable pain which sits at the core of him. No matter how hard he tries, what pleasure, amusement or distraction he seeks, still the pain stubbornly sits, ripening, growing in his heart until some day it will surely be impossible to bear.

The baby's face has become weirdly distorted, as though Edward is seeing him through bevelled glass, and it takes a moment to register that he has tears in his eyes. He turns from Eleanor and wipes them quickly away with his handkerchief.

'James it is,' he hears Eleanor say in a weak voice. He turns to her, smiling.

'Really? You don't mind?'

She shakes her head. 'No. I don't mind. Jimmy to his friends.'

'Would you like him back?' Edward says, offering the baby back to her.

She shakes her head again. 'I'm really awfully tired,' she says. 'Would you mind if I slept a little now? Perhaps we can have breakfast together when I've rested and you've bathed. I should like that.' And she lies down, turning away from Edward and Jimmy.

'Of course.' Edward lowers Jimmy carefully back into his cradle. As he tiptoes quietly to the door, he says, although he isn't sure she hears as her shape beneath the covers doesn't stir, 'Thank you, darling. Thank you for giving me Jimmy.'

IV

Imagine, if you can, you are like me. With the freedom to travel through space and time, from human mind to human mind with the ease of moving from room to room.

Can you feel it? The soaring, reckless joy of it?

Oh, the grace and the wisdom. The past, the present, the glimpses of the future, all within your sight and in your grasp.

There, now you have a taste for how it is for me.

But listen. I am here to give you a kindly warning, my friends, although I know you will pay little heed to me. Let's just say, I've seen the worst of you in the past, your inhumanity to your own kind when you suspect my presence, the women you have burnt at the stake; the small children, marked by their imperfections and taken to the woods in the still, dark hours of the night; abandoned for the wild animals to gnaw. I've witnessed your fumbling, misguided searches for a cure — the holes drilled into children's skulls; the electric shocks; the pulling of teeth and the infections with malaria. Laughable, really, were it not so very sad.

But I can see the worst yet is still to come. This obsession of yours with breeding a race of perfect humans. Imagine that! Humans free of disease, physical imperfections, feeble-mindedness and mental illness. Humans, but better ones, revitalised and cleansed of decay; each one full to the brim with physical perfection, intelligence and wisdom. How that idea – and your inability to see the impossibility of your vision – amuses me beyond measure. You humans and your quest to conquer nature! Don't you understand you are doomed to fail? Nature will always find a way to get the better of you.

Be that as it may, in the spirit of generosity, I must tell you this quest of yours will not lift the human race as you think it will, but instead it will lead you to horror and depravity of a scale you cannot, with your limited imaginations, foresee.

If only you would stop and think further and wider than the vision you have for a better world. Everything has a consequence, you should know that. With light, comes dark. With joy, comes pain. And of course, with every so-called advancement of man, comes a downside.

Think about it. How many times do you humans believe you have it all worked out, only to find you understood but a tiny fragment of the whole? But you are too certain of your power to look beyond the realm of your own knowledge.

And so it is with every man, who thinks he has the measure of me. It is such temptation to prove you wrong. It happens time after time, and so it will here, in this time and this place, just like it has in all the years which came before and it will in all the years which are to follow.

You cannot get the better of me.

Remember this in the future, my friends, remember this.

13

Eleanor

'Would you like to have a little time with young Jimmy on your own?' asks Miss Harding.

With her perfect skin, wide eyes and ready smile, it's hard not to notice her attractiveness. Since Sophie's flippant remarks the day she visited, Eleanor has watched Edward carefully, to see if his eyes linger upon the nanny just a little longer than they should. Not that he has been home terribly much. Jimmy's arrival doesn't seem to have altered his time spent at home which has shrunk now to one night a week. Eleanor wonders if Sophie is right and he has installed a mistress full-time in his London flat.

'It's such a mild day and it's only the first of March,' Miss Harding is chattering as she wraps Jimmy, sleepy and satiated from his feed. They are in a former guest room, now turned into Jimmy's nursery. Everyone agreed it was better for Jimmy to be kept away from Mabel and her disturbing turns. So the large nursery has now become Mabel's room, the place permanently smelling vaguely of borax and Lysol, filled with all the paraphernalia of a sick child, medicine bottles lined up along the top of the dresser where the toys should be. 'It is perfect weather to take young Jimmy here out for a walk. Look, even the sun is coming out!' Miss Harding nods encouragingly at the window.

Eleanor looks out across the orchard, with its bare-limbed cherry, apple, pear and plum trees, stretching away in ordered rows to the boundary with Mayfield Manor and its dense woodland beyond the fence. She pictures herself pushing the large silver and blue pram along the path, listening to the birds singing in the trees, talking conversationally to her baby. They could drop by at the stables and visit Dilly. She might even be kind to Byron, the half-grown dog, and let him come too, his tongue lolling, tail waving happily.

But inside she is cold and unmoved. The picture comes with no desire. Better that Miss Harding takes him. That's what they employ her for, isn't it? Besides, it's costing Edward a small fortune to pay for a nanny *and* a nurse for Mabel.

'Oh no,' Eleanor says, waving a dismissive hand, 'I'm actually feeling a little tired. You take him, please, Miss Harding.'

'Righto, Mrs Hamilton,' Miss Harding says, giving her a quizzical look. 'If that's what you'd rather.'

'It is.'

'Come along then, Jimmy lad. You can come down to the village with me. I need to post a parcel to my sister. It's her birthday. Rest well,' she says as she leaves the room, Jimmy cuddled in her arms.

In the drawing room, Eleanor rings for tea and tries to read *Mrs Dalloway* but really, it's too bleak and depressing. She looks at the half-finished watercolour of her roses propped up on the stand in the bay window but it doesn't call to her and she realises she can't concentrate on anything at the moment. A restless energy sits in her chest, along with a sick churning in her belly. She *has* to leave the house, get some fresh air in her lungs, but not with Jimmy. It's Mabel she is craving.

She climbs the stairs to Mabel's room. She saw the little girl for only ten minutes at breakfast, but the child was tearful and off-colour. The latest medicine prescribed by Mr Silverton, the neurologist, does not agree with her, and makes her vomit. Miss Cartwright-Jones had had to take her out of the dining room and back to the nursery for fear she might bring up the small amount of toast and boiled egg she had reluctantly consumed.

The fun they had together last summer feels so long ago it might have been another lifetime. All those picnics and lazy afternoons stripping off their stockings and paddling in the icy cold river water. Mabel hunting for butterflies, worms and creepy-crawlies while Eleanor tended to her flower beds. Hours spent curled on a blanket beneath the big beech tree near the tennis courts, Eleanor reading to Mabel or telling stories of magical other worlds while Mabel rested her head on her stomach for a pillow, listening as she stared up at dappled sunlight through the thick green canopy overhead. Her heart aches to have those times back. How she misses her darling Mabel. Jimmy, with his hungry wailing and lack of conversation is no substitute. A vision comes to her of Mabel sitting in the pony trap, singing along with Eleanor to the rhythm of Dilly's hooves. At the time she had not recognised the sensation of pure, unsullied happiness. Now it is no longer here, she feels the physical agony of its absence.

She reaches the second storey of the house and knows *exactly* how she will spend this afternoon. Miss Harding is right to extol the virtues of fresh air for young Jimmy, so why shouldn't Mabel benefit too?

'Oh, I'm not sure that's such a good idea, Mrs Hamilton,' Miss Cartwright-Jones says, when Eleanor announces her plan, glancing between her employer and her charge, who sits motionless against the wall, staring into the middle distance and sucking hard on her thumb. Prudence is clutched to her chest in a tight grip, her head lolling to one side, legs dangling beneath Mabel's arm. The child looks so pale she might have been made from alabaster.

'I think Mabel will benefit from some fresh air,' Eleanor opines. 'It is essential for all children,' she parrots Miss Harding.

'We could take a turn around the garden,' Miss Cartwright-Jones says without conviction. She glances out of the window, up at the grey clouds gathering and threatening to block the earlier promise of sun. She screws up her nose and announces, 'Although, I do declare that it is very likely to rain this afternoon.'

'I'll take my chances,' Eleanor says firmly. She won't leave without Mabel. She won't. 'We can wrap ourselves up in warm coats and hats, can't we, Mabel?' She addresses her daughter with false cheer, who, she realises with a stab, appears not to have noticed her arrival at all. Normally either one of her parents' presence in the nursery is enough to send the little girl into paroxysms of pleasure.

'But Mr Hamilton specifically said not to take Mabel out of the house or gardens...' Her voice fades and she doesn't look Eleanor in the eye.

Eleanor knows she is right, but she's fed up with complying with Edward's wishes. He is up in town all week, after all, leading a good life, heaven only knows with whom, while she is stuck here, like a prisoner, at Brook End. She breathes deeply. She has never once in her life before thought of Brook End as a prison.

She bristles against the nurse. 'Really,' she tells Miss Cartwright-Jones, 'it's what she needs. What we *both* need right now. Please get her dressed in warm things and meet me at the stables in fifteen minutes.' She turns and leaves, feeling a soaring sensation at her assertion of authority. She's been too meek with the offish Miss Cartwright-Jones, who needs to remember just who is boss.

At the stables, Bertie has Dilly harnessed in only a few minutes, the pony snorting and pawing the ground with her front hoof as he manoeuvres the collar into place and buckles the leather straps around her.

'Excited to be going on an outing, eh girl?' Bertie chuckles, clapping her smooth bay neck with a large, paw-like hand. 'Barely get out these days, do ya, lass?'

He backs her expertly between the wooden shafts then peers at the sky. 'Looks like rain later,' he says. 'But you'll be good for an hour or two.'

'Oh, thank you, Bertie,' Eleanor watches him, relieved. She trusts his weather forecasting to be more accurate than that of Miss Cartwright-Jones, who appears at that moment with Mabel who, despite the mildness of the day, is bundled into her winter coat, hat, scarf and gloves.

Bertie hoists her into the trap next to Eleanor and she tucks the thick rug around their legs.

'There,' says Eleanor. 'Warm as toast! Do enjoy a break

for a couple of hours, Miss Cartwright-Jones,' she calls down to her. 'I'm sure you would like to put your feet up for a while. The rest will do you good.'

'I will,' she replies. 'Do take care and keep an eye on her all the time.' The woman turns sharply on her heel and walks stiff-backed towards the house.

Eleanor huffs. As if she needs telling how to look after her own daughter.

Mabel looks up at her and grants her a weak smile. 'Dilly,' she says, pointing down at the pony, who moves eagerly off and down the driveway at a fast walk.

'That's it, Mabel! You remembered her name. Well done.' The way Mabel hardly speaks any more fills her with sick dread. Where will it end? With every seizure, she seems to lose the ability to say yet another word.

'Dilly,' she repeats and leans into her mother's body. Mabel was always such a chatty little thing, and now she barely expresses two words together. She used to bounce and sing and ask question after question until Eleanor could no longer bear it and begged her to stop. *Why are Papas taller than Mamas? Why do the birds sing? Do God and Santa Claus live together? Why can't you see the wind?* Always why, why, why? How tedious the questions had become!

Now Eleanor would give anything to have them back.

It's the medication dulling Mabel. That awful powder they mix with water and make her drink until she gags and sobs for them to stop. Eleanor cannot bear to witness it, so she lets Miss Cartwright-Jones administer the stuff with the door to the nursery firmly shut to muffle the cries and desperate protestations. And this is the result, this shadow, who was once her bright little girl.

Eleanor slides her free arm around her daughter. How lovely it is to be here, just the two of them. She has missed this intimacy. It's as though Jimmy or Miss Cartwright-Jones or both have come between them. No wonder her nerves are on edge.

Once out on the lane, she allows Dilly to break into her easy trot. The pony holds her head high, her ears pricked forward, clearly as pleased as Eleanor to be away from Brook End for a while.

'Let's sing,' she says to Mabel as Dilly pulls the trap between skeletal trees and naked fields, the drab view as devoid of colour as if it had been washed and rinsed away. Mabel looks up at her, her face as pale as the moon, her eyes dark pools. 'Perhaps something quiet and gentle today,' Eleanor says, remembering Mr Silverton telling them firmly they must avoid excitement as it might bring on a fit.

The Owl and the Pussy-Cat went to sea
In a beautiful pea-green boat:
They took some honey, and plenty of money
Wrapped up in a five-pound note.

Eleanor half says, half sings the poem in a soft voice as Mabel relaxes beside her. She goes to put her thumb in her mouth, realises the glove is on and pulls it off, flinging it onto the floor of the trap. Eleanor doesn't tell her off.

The Owl looked up to the stars above
And sang to a small guitar,
'O lovely Pussy, O Pussy, my love,
What a beautiful Pussy you are,

You are,
You are!
What a beautiful Pussy you are!'

Eleanor takes a breath to begin the next verse when she feels Mabel stiffen. She is concentrating on something and smacking her lips, her little fingers gripping hard on Eleanor's arm.

'Oh God, no! Please, not now. Woah!' she calls to Dilly, tugging hard on the reins. 'Woah!' The pony slows to a walk. Thankfully, they have not yet reached the village so there is no one to witness this devastating moment of shame.

Beside her, Mabel suddenly looks up at her mother. The slow mistiness in her eyes has cleared and been replaced by something else. In the inky darkness of Mabel's eyes is a terror which makes Eleanor's heart bang.

'Mabel?' she says, reaching towards her daughter to grab her arms. 'Darling, are you OK?'

But Mabel's mouth twists into an ugly grimace. Her eyes roll back in her head. Mabel is gone and a monster has taken her place. She jerks, her arms and legs shoot out, smashing hard into Eleanor. With a sickening crash, her head thrashes into the wooden back of the seat. Eleanor had no idea such a small body could contain so much strength. The force of the next seizure lifts Mabel inches off the bench. She crashes back to the wood with an almighty force and Eleanor tries to pin her to the seat to stop her from hurting herself, but Mabel continues to thrash uncontrollably beneath her hands until her face turns red, then blue. Eleanor releases her in horror.

'For Christ's sake!' Eleanor cries out in desperation. *She isn't breathing.* Mabel is suffocating right in front of her and she is useless. She has no idea what to do. 'Mabel!' she screams, 'Mabel, breathe!'

And as if she heard her mother's plea, the child, with an animal-like noise in her throat, gasps in some air before the next seizure hits. Her jaw clamps shut. Her limbs jerk, straight and rigid, as if made of the toughest steel. This time, the side of her face bangs into the wooden seat. Eleanor is powerless to stop her daughter from hurting herself.

In the next lull, Eleanor pulls Mabel onto her lap in an attempt to cushion her with her own body. The thrashing and jerking continues, Eleanor doing her best to absorb into her flesh the shocking power of each seizure. It takes her a few moments to realise that the sudden wet warmth on her legs is the result of Mabel releasing the contents of her bladder.

'Oh no,' she sobs, as the liquid swiftly cools and the tears stream freely down her cheeks, 'oh no, no, no!'

And then, as suddenly as it started, it stops. Mabel's body relaxes, her gasps slow and her breathing returns to normal. They sit in silence for a few moments, Eleanor stroking her hair and whispering in a shaky voice, 'It's OK, Mabel. It's OK.' And despite the cold, wet urine soaking them both, Mabel, exhausted, sinks into a deep sleep on her mother's lap, while Dilly stands and waits for instruction, clinking the bit between her teeth, flicking her ears back and forth, swishing her tail.

Eleanor sits, frozen, her arms wrapped around Mabel in the dark shadow of the seizure; trembling. Broken.

14

Edward

The large salon at Queen's Hall is heaving with people. Every chair is taken, the audience crammed around the edges of the room too, standing in close, chattering groups. It's an extraordinary turnout and Edward's heart lifts at the sight. The low hum of conversation greets him as he enters the room. A large screen stands in front of the rows of chairs, lit by a projector whirring from the back of the room. The words: *Mental Deficiency and the Criminal Mind, The Delinquent Child and the need for Eugenic Reform* are displayed in flickering black letters.

'It's a great turnout,' Leonard Darwin says, coming to greet Edward. 'We've got all manner of important people here today.' He waves a hand. 'Churchill, Russell, Keynes, Stopes, Wells, Shaw, to mention but a few. And there are two Labour members of parliament – Will Crooks and Archibald Church. They have both told me, in confidence, that they are willing to put up a private member's bill to parliament in support of compulsory sterilisation, if we are able to garner enough support. Good work eh?'

'Indeed,' agrees Edward.

'If you get this through, and your education proposals,

well, my friend, that knighthood has your name written all over it!' Darwin gives him a wink and chuckles to himself, wandering off to greet some late arrivals pushing through the door.

Edward gathers his papers, checks the projector and calls out to indicate the imminent start of the lecture.

There is a collective rustle as those that have them take their seats. When the room quietens, Edward clears his throat again, and begins.

'Good afternoon, Ladies and Gentlemen, and welcome. It is truly heartening to see so many of you here today. I will speak for the next hour about this important subject,' he waves a hand in the direction of the screen, 'then there will be an opportunity for questions, discussion and,' he lets out a self-conscious laugh, 'to purchase any of my published works, or those of my friend and colleague, Major Leonard Darwin here.'

He flicks on to the next slide.

On one side of the screen is the picture of an unsavoury young fellow. Sallow-cheeked, a cigarette hangs from his lips and he stares insolently into the camera from beneath a cloth cap, clothes rough and cheap-looking. The look of him is enough to make the audience visibly shrink with distaste from the image. Edward has not forgotten Harry's words of wisdom about the power of visual images. The other side of the screen lists the topics he will cover in his lecture, namely:

1. Inheritance and Intelligence.
2. Emotion, Character and Criminality in the sub-normal mind.

3. The efficacy of correction clinics.
4. Methods of teaching the backward, the dull and the defective.
5. In support of compulsory incarceration and sterilisation.

'Time, my friends, is running out,' he begins gravely. 'If we do not adopt a radical policy to reform our entire society along eugenic principles, we face the bleakest of futures. It is crucial to the health of our nation and, indeed, to that of the British Empire. And the time to act is now. Our economy is suffering. Our way of life, threatened...'

Edward delivers his lecture with his usual passion to the enrapt audience. He could give these talks in his sleep, he has done so many of them. But he finds, as he speaks of the unwanted in society, Mabel hovers at the edges of his vision. Mabel rolling in the long grass of Butterfly Meadow. Mabel with a daisy chain circling her fair hair. Mabel laughing as he tickles her belly. Mabel crying when old Patch died. Mabel fitting on the back lawn, her eyes rolling back, her limbs stiffening. Mabel – but not Mabel.

There is a hard lump in his throat and he stares at the screen. What had he been saying? He has no idea. He turns to look at the audience with a sudden panic. The room is silent. How long since he last spoke? He clears his throat, wonders which part of the lecture he had reached.

'Any questions?' he asks hopefully.

There is some shuffling and a cough from the audience. Edward takes a drink from his glass.

No questions.

Instead of Mabel he tries to think of the madman who killed Eleanor's mother. He gathers himself together.

'But I must not digress.' He points at the screen behind him. 'As any of you who has attended my previous lectures will be aware,' he continues, 'I am able to prove the strong correlation between the criminal mind and low intellectual ability. As you will see from my next slide,' and a series of graphs appear on the screen, 'of all the psychological causes of crime, the commonest and gravest is the defective mind. You will see here,' he points a baton at a graph lit up bright, 'that whilst there is a range of general intelligence, the mean mental age of the juvenile offender, once he has reached adulthood, will be that of a child of about thirteen.'

Edward returns to his lecturing flow with relief. 'Given the current statistics on crime and future projections, I would say it is imperative to ensure children of the lower orders are subjected to psychometric testing to ascertain their intelligence levels. This is the clearest indicator we have as to the inherent likelihood of their possessing a criminal leaning. Furthermore, it is for reasons of protecting *our* children's futures, and those of following generations, that, in particular those falling into these groups,' he points to those labelled, *Feeble-Minded, Imbeciles and Idiots*, 'are detained automatically under the Mental Deficiency Act into suitable labour colonies and asylums. This will ensure safety and security for the general population. But to be absolutely certain these defective genes won't be passed on to the next generation, a programme of compulsory sterilisation is, ultimately, the only answer. It is for this reason we must introduce urgent legislation to this end.'

Someone raises a hand in the audience. 'And what

would be the cost to the public purse of locking up all these individuals?' asks a male voice. Edward cannot see its owner against the light of the projector. 'It would surely be prohibitive and the country can hardly afford to be building new, expensive institutions to house the enormous numbers of the unfit.'

'It would, of course, be an initially greater expense, but one which would naturally decline over time, for obvious reasons.'

'Put a number on it, please,' presses the voice.

'I'm sorry,' Edward says, 'I don't have a figure to hand. But my understanding is that a Royal Commission has been appointed to look at all aspects, including cost of the implementation of such a policy change. But I think, with respect, the question you ask is the wrong one. What you should be asking is: what would be the cost of *not* carrying out this policy.'

'I'm quite against sterilisation,' calls out another voice. 'If we are to look at the example from our American friends, once the sterilisations are carried out, these people are released back onto the streets. Then they continue to prove a pest to society with their immoral and criminal ways. What reassurance can you give us that these imbeciles won't be allowed to roam the streets once sterilised?'

Edward fields the questions with facts and figures, or deft side-swipes of the questions he doesn't like or doesn't know the answers to. He is becoming quite the politician. When it is over, there is rapturous applause and claps on his back, offers of drinks at the club – St James's, naturally – followed by dinner.

Stepping through the revolving doors of Queen's Hall,

deep in conversation with Leonard, he fails to notice the young woman until she is right beside him, tugging at his arm.

'Captain Hamilton, sir! I need to speak with you, urgently!' He is momentarily confused as he recognises the woman's face, but she is not well dressed and her hair is askew; he wonders for a moment if she is a beggar, or a prostitute and if so, how could she possibly know his name?

Then with a sudden stab of recognition he says, '*Violet?*' loudly in surprise.

For a moment the three of them stand in silence, blocking the entrance, Edward looking at Violet in horror, Leonard peering at her with interest. Violet looks embarrassed then mouths, '*Could we talk?*'

Edward recovers himself. 'Leonard – do go on ahead. I'll meet you at the club; this young woman has been a patient at one of my psychology clinics, I'll just deal with her and be along in a moment.' He takes Violet by the arm and propels her down the street as quickly as possible to avoid anyone else he knows seeing them together.

'I'm sorry, sir, for shocking you like that,' she says rather breathlessly as they walk, 'but I needed to speak to you urgent-like and, well, we weren't due to meet up for another couple of weeks and I was worried it'd be too late but then I saw your name advertised that you were giving lectures here so I thought, well, I wouldn't normally do this but...' She stops to take a breath.

'Yes,' Edward says tersely, 'it was something of a surprise to see you.'

He spots a public house on the corner of the street and guides her across the road. It looks like a rather downmarket establishment, but that is probably for the best, as he is unlikely to encounter anyone he knows here.

He places his gloved hand against the small of her back, ushering her inside the warm, smoky fug of the pub. Fortunately it isn't busy and he pulls out a chair for her at a table close to the fireside in the saloon bar. Even this side of the pub is decidedly seedy. Avoiding placing his hands on the sticky surface of the bar, he calls his order out to the bored-looking landlord.

By the time he returns with a pint of real ale for himself and Violet's usual, gin and lime, she has removed her hat and coat, revealing a relatively smart blouse and jacket, which he takes to be her Sunday best. She has patted and tidied her hair into a bun at the back of her head. She is rubbing her hands in front of the fire, and it's only then that he sees, with alarm, a faint blue tinge to her lips. How long must she have been waiting out in the cold for him? Edward takes a draft of his beer, and his heart softens a little.

'Well,' he says, 'what has happened? Why the urgency?'

He looks into his beer glass, peering into its rusty depths, an easier task than looking Violet in the eye.

'It's him,' she says finally, but not unexpectedly. Of course it had to be about *him*. 'He's been terribly ill. He has influenza. They said, with his lungs...' She swallows and takes a ragged breath. 'They said with his lungs, he might not... Probably won't recover.'

'Oh God, I'm so sorry.' He has the urge to reach out, take her hand in his, but he doesn't. There is the inevitable pang of guilt, but something else, to his shame. A rising sense of relief. Without Porter in the world, there will be no risk of Edward's secret ever being revealed. The horror of that happening has hung over him for ten years; how ruinous to his life if it were ever to get out. It would, at least, be one problem solved.

'Actually,' Violet is saying, 'I have a letter for you, from *him*.' She rummages in her handbag, and pulls out a thin envelope. Edward's heart bangs at the sight of *Captain Hamilton* scrawled across it in a childlike hand. He notices a couple of dark blotches of ink where the writer held the pen for too long on the paper, or pressed the nib too hard. Edward experiences a rush of nausea as she holds it out for him to take.

He slips the envelope into his pocket with a shaking hand.

'As you know,' Violet says, 'I've not been able to get down to see him of late, the baby being so young an' that, so we've taken to exchanging letters. Neither of us are the best writers, you understand, but it's good to keep in touch. Any road, he knows I see you regular-like and he asked me to give it to you.' She hesitates. 'He was worried he'd go without ever having been able to say, well, what he wanted to say. You don't have time to visit, I understand, but if you could find a few minutes to write back, it'd mean the world to him to receive a letter from you. And to me, too.' She stares down at her hands in her lap.

Edward's throat has closed, strangulating any possible words from coming out. He turns to stare into the fire to break the intensity of the moment. As he watches, the glowing coals slip lower, sending a shower of burning embers onto the pile of ash below the grate.

'Do you know, Violet,' he says, turning back to her, the tension falling away, 'I *will* make time to go and see him. I should have done it long ago. But now... well, now I really must.' He rubs his hands along his trousers and watches Violet's eyes widen. 'Yes,' he nods. 'I will write and let him know I'm coming.'

'You are a good man,' Violet says, tears pooling in her eyes. 'The very best.' She wipes her tears away and looks him squarely in the eyes, a smile rising up her face like a wave, until her eyes crinkle and disappear, and Edward is reminded, once again, of the pretty girl she had once been.

Later, after dinner at the club with Leonard and the others from the Eugenics Society, during which they discussed which members of parliament could be relied upon in a free vote for the proposed legislation, and those who might need further persuasion to vote it through, Edward returns to his flat in Bloomsbury. He feels guilty about the time he spends here, away from Brook End, away from Eleanor and the children. He tells himself it is for convenience, and it is true that it is. It is also true that his workload places enormous demands on his time. But the truth of it is that home, Brook End, is too full of pain to be the sanctuary it once was. And Edward is better at running than facing his problems.

Finally alone, he slips the letter from his pocket and opens it.

Dear Sir,

I hopes you and the family are well.

I'm sorry to tell you that I'm not doing so good these days. I've got a terrible bout of winter influenza, you see. It runs riot round the place each year, but I've got it bad this time and my lungs being what they are, well you know.

But they treat me well here. Matron can be fierce, but the nurse is kind. I try me best. Thinking of you and all you have done to help me makes me try harder. I'd like to think you are proud of me. So's I'm not going to give up, just like you didn't, when push comes to shove.

I dream of coming out of here for a holiday. In the summer when it's hot and I could sit by the sea with sand between my toes and watch the waves. I don't suppose it shall come to be, but it's nice to dream.

I just wanted you to know I'm very grateful for all the risks you took for me. You saved my life and I never got the chance to thank you proper and that.

Yours,
Reginald Porter

A lump, huge and uncomfortable, forms in Edward's throat as he crumples the letter in his hand.

15

Eleanor

My Dear Eleanor,

Of course you are entirely forgiven for your sharp words when I came to visit, you silly old thing. Rose tells me you are still upset. She says you think I am angry with you. What utter poppycock! Darling, you know that I shall always love you like a faithful old dog, even if you shut me out in the rain and scold me.

Now please don't be angry with her, but Rose filled me in about poor darling little Mabel. I know it was against your wishes, but she is so worried about you, she felt I should know. It also explains why you were on edge when I saw you. Eleanor – I am here for you. To bear this alone is too much.

Now, I suppose I should have told you about Marcel coming to see Rose, or at least I shouldn't have let it pop out when you had just given birth and were emotionally vulnerable. So, if you like, this letter is an apology from me too.

So there it is. We are all square and everything is well

*between us. The point is, darling, when on earth are you
going to come and visit me in London? Surely you can
leave that baby with his nanny for a couple of days – a
day even! I'm quite certain I got shot of mine within a
month. Don't get me wrong, I love my children, I really
do, but we can't let them take over our lives, now can we?*

*Name your date darling. We can shop. Eat. Drink.
Smoke. Party till we drop. Whatever takes your fancy.
I think with dear Mabel being so poorly (Please don't
worry, I shan't tell a soul) and Edward working away so
much you need cheering up.*

All my love,
Sophie.

Eleanor smiles and puts down the letter. She is surprised
to find that she isn't angry with Rose, not one bit, for telling
Sophie about Mabel. In fact, she feels relief that her dearest
friend knows – she will keep their secret. Eleanor's heart
lifts knowing Sophie has accepted her apology and they can
carry on as usual again. How she could do with Sophie's
cheerful and blasé approach to the world right now. The
memory of Mabel's horrific seizure that day she took her
daughter out in the trap is still vivid. A wave of nausea
overcomes her. She hasn't dared to take Mabel out again.
And trying to talk to Edward about it is so hard. Even when
they are together, he is monosyllabic if she tries to speak
about Mabel with him. The only person she can truly speak
to is Rose, and with her in London too now, revelling in
her time at the *New Statesman*, she is quite alone with her
agonising fears. Rose is staying with Sophie, and Eleanor
aches with the thought that they are there together and she

is here, alone. She had been quite content with the peace and solitude of Brook End until Mabel became sick. Now it feels like a punishment.

She is sitting in Edward's study this Friday morning, Rose due back home this afternoon to spend her weekend at Brook End as usual. To pass the time, Eleanor is determined to catch up on some long-overdue correspondence. During his extended absences, she has made Edward's desk her own. He is a tidy man, everything in its place. There is never a stray letter or document left lying about. Edward's life is ordered, she supposes, as a leftover relic of his army days. Efficiency and precision are prerequisites both for the military man and the scientist. Edward must be no doubt just as meticulous in his research and the collection and analysis of data.

Eleanor glances around the shelves of files, labelled and colour-coded for their relevance to whichever research project they relate to. There are floor-to-ceiling bookcases lining two of the walls of the room filled with academic books written by Edward, neat stacks of copies of the *Journal of Psychology*, and shelves and shelves of academic tomes. She reads the spines of some, *The Kallikak Family: A Study of the Heredity of Feeble-Mindedness*; *Conclusive Evidential Intelligence Data of US Recruits*. She reaches and pulls it off the shelf, delaying the moment when she must get on with looking through the household accounts. She flicks to the introduction and reads, *In this greatest, most wide-ranging study of intelligence amongst American army conscripts, one million, seven-hundred-and-fifty thousand American men have been subject to the most rigorous intelligence testing ever carried out. The results are*

*profound and will guide policy for years to come. They show,
concerningly, that the average intelligence of the ordinary
white male recruit is only just over thirteen years of age.
More concerningly, thirty-seven per cent of white recruits
fall into the category of moron, being less than twelve years
of age. The average intellectual age of immigrants, mainly
from Southern European, Slavic or Eastern European
backgrounds is only eleven, whilst the average of the Negro
is less than eleven, almost ninety per cent of whom fall into
this moron category.*

Can this really be true? Eleanor wonders as she replaces
the book. Could there really be such innate differences
between human beings? She sighs and returns her attention
to Sophie's letter, picking up her pen to draft a reply.

After several letters are written and sealed, Eleanor rings
the bell for Alice to take them to the post office in the village
in time to catch the midday collection.

While she waits for Rose to arrive, Eleanor stares out
of the window. Spring has begun to arrive in the garden
of Brook End. Carpets of crocuses have appeared beneath
the big beech tree, and there are signs of daffodils making
an appearance in the borders. Ordinarily by now, Eleanor
would have donned gardening gloves and been out there,
planting bulbs and nurturing her seedlings in the greenhouse.
But she has neither the inclination nor the energy this year.

She is looking forward to seeing Rose, but it's odd and
empty not to have Edward home this weekend. She feels
sick at the memory of his visit to the nursery last weekend.
It won't be an exercise they will be repeating.

She and Edward had gone up together to take Mabel
and Jimmy downstairs for tea in the drawing room. They

had collected a smiling Jimmy first and Eleanor was happy to let Edward carry him. Mabel had been sitting, her back resting against the wall, as she so often did now, staring listlessly into the middle distance, Prudence clutched in one hand. She looked sickly, pale and puffy from the drugs, her skin covered in ugly, raw lesions. There is nothing pretty or delicate about her any more, and yet, at that moment, she had looked more vulnerable and tragic than ever before.

Miss Cartwright-Jones was in the process of mixing up Mabel's next dose of medicine.

'How is she doing?' Edward had asked, and Eleanor had caught the shaky emotion in his voice. 'Any signs of improvement?' Eleanor, meanwhile, had rushed to Mabel and pulled her onto her lap, hugging her tightly, wishing she could somehow absorb the monstrous illness herself and take away all of Mabel's pain.

Miss Cartwright-Jones had said curtly, 'No improvement at all, I'm sorry to say. She's had countless minor seizures already this morning, and one major one, only an hour or so ago. She's just woken, groggy as you can see.'

'Oh.' Edward had jiggled Jimmy on his shoulder and blanched at her words.

'And getting this medicine down her,' she'd added, 'is very hard. Makes her sick and she cries. Takes me best part of an hour to administer, then barely a break before the next lot.'

'I see,' was all he managed.

'Edward,' Eleanor had called. 'Do bring Jimmy over here. Mabel wants to see him.'

She could tell he'd been reluctant, but he had brought Jimmy over.

'Baby,' Mabel had said, pulling her thumb from her mouth and pointing. There was the first hint of a smile Eleanor had seen for a long time on her lips.

'Give him to her to hold, Edward,' Eleanor had instructed. 'She wants to cuddle him.'

'I'm not sure that's safe,' he'd replied, clutching Jimmy a little tighter.

'Of course it is. I'm right here, so I can hold him at the same time,' she'd said, fury building inside her. What had he thought would happen? That Mabel would pass her unfortunate affliction onto Jimmy? How utterly ridiculous. How bloody awful. Poor Mabel had no joy in life any more and Edward was prepared to deny her *one thing* which made her happy. He'd be taking Prudence away next, for fear the doll might catch it too.

They'd locked eyes and for a long moment neither of them moved, but then Mabel reached out with eager arms for Jimmy, letting Prudence fall to the floor. The agony of the whole desperate scene must have had some effect on Edward because he had finally relinquished Jimmy's small, warm wriggling body onto Mabel's lap. Eleanor had held them both while Jimmy lay awkwardly across his sister, looking like a huge, fat chrysalis, resting against her delicate frame. The baby had been quiet, staring avidly into Mabel's face.

Mabel had let out a delighted laugh and cried, 'Baby!'

'Jimmy,' Eleanor reminded her. 'Baby Jimmy.'

'Jim, Jim, Jim, Jim,' Mabel had repeated, then she leant down and kissed Jimmy's forehead with such tenderness that Eleanor felt tears form in her eyes. How fast she had lost all her language skills. How ferocious this disease that her mind be reduced to that of a baby. She had wondered how long it would be before Jimmy overtook Mabel.

'Right,' Miss Cartwright-Jones had interrupted, 'I'm afraid it's time for Mabel to have her next dose of bromide.'

'Already?' Eleanor had said.

'The doctor said I have to stick carefully with the timings of the doses, so the concentration in her blood is as stable as possible. She's on the maximum dose now, and it's such a bind to get it down her so I really must do it now.'

'Well,' Eleanor had said, her voice choked, 'it doesn't seem to be doing any good, does it? So why are we even bothering with this?' She'd looked to Edward, but he'd turned away, refusing to meet her eyes.

'Of course she must have her medicine now,' he'd said, while Miss Cartwright-Jones stood awkwardly by, the cup and spoon balanced in her hands, her face reddening.

In the end, the nurse had been firm. 'I'm under doctor's orders. It would be dangerous to stop the medicine without the doctor first sanctioning how. These things are most delicately in the balance, you understand?'

'Exactly,' Edward had said, a harshness to his voice. 'We can't just stop, Eleanor.'

'No!' Mabel had shouted as Edward prised Jimmy away. 'No, no, no!' She'd begun to cry as Jimmy was pulled from her arms.

With Mabel propped up in a highchair, the nurse had tried to give her the bromide mix but she had shaken her head violently back and forth, lips pursed shut.

'Come along, darling,' Eleanor had tried to coax. 'You can have a lovely spoonful of honey afterwards to wash it all down.'

'No!' says Mabel. 'Hurts. No medicine.'

But then, with lightning speed, Miss Cartwright-Jones had tilted Mabel's chin back and prised her mouth open, shoving in a spoonful of liquid. Mabel had gagged and Miss Cartwright-Jones tried to pin her lips closed with white-knuckled fingers. Mabel had coughed and choked, her face red, features scrunched up, liquid seeping from the corners of her mouth.

'No, no, Mabel!' Miss Cartwright-Jones had told her sharply. 'You're to swallow it all down.' She'd roughly scooped up the medicine from where it had dripped down the front of Mabel's dress and shoved it back in. Then again and again, forcing the medicine in, Mabel howling, shaking, coughing and spluttering, the disgusting bromide liquid spraying out between Miss Cartwright-Jones's taut fingers.

'Let's go,' Edward had growled, pulling Eleanor away. 'We must let her do her job.'

Eleanor had allowed herself to be pulled away. Away from Mabel's choking and retching, away when Mabel had tried to turn and reach up to Eleanor. 'Mama, Mama, Mama,' she'd cried as they backed out of the room.

Mabel's cries of distress had followed them all the way along the corridor, down the stairs and into the hallway, rattling and wounding every cell in Eleanor's body.

Edward had turned to her then, fury flashing like she'd never seen before in his eyes. 'That,' he'd thrown at her, 'is not in *my* genes.'

She gasped. 'And you are saying it's in *mine*?'

He'd not replied, his mouth a hard line. He was visibly shaking with anger? Hurt? She had no idea. He had bent down with Jimmy still in his arms to greet Byron who'd arrived to join them.

'This is hardly helpful, Edward, is it?' Eleanor had said, watching him as he caressed the dog. 'Trying to apportion blame. But a second opinion might. I want a second medical opinion for Mabel. This can't go on, Edward,' she'd said, her voice cracking, before she'd run out into the garden, unable to hold back the gush of tears a moment longer.

A creak startles her out of her reverie as the door is pushed open and Byron appears, wandering towards her with a waving tail and lolling tongue. He presses his wet nose into the palm of her hand, demanding a stroke.

'I'm not taking you for a walk if that's what you think,' she tells the dog, now almost fully grown, long-legged, rangy, with a smooth, wavy golden coat and deep, black, mournful eyes. He was meant to be Mabel's dog, but he favours Edward, although heaven knows why, he is so rarely home. The dog is always so ecstatic with joy when he returns. 'I'm sorry you have to make do with me,' she murmurs into his furry ear. They are slowly becoming better friends. She strokes Byron's head and is rewarded with a lick. He lets out a big sigh as he flops down at her feet, resting his head on his paws, but not taking his eyes off hers.

Eleanor rings the bell and, in Alice's absence, Mrs Faulks appears with tea. Rose should soon be here. Sipping it, she thinks about Sophie's letter and how nice it would be to escape to London for a day or two. With the growing acrimony between her and Edward, she needs her friendship more than ever. Perhaps Sophie is right and he *is* having an affair. It's a form of escapism, after all. And conjugal relations have barely returned since Jimmy was born, which isn't surprising given Edward's lengthy absences. It doesn't feel healthy, and part of her craves his touch, but there is such a distance between them, it seems impossible to bridge.

She puts down her cup and surveys the study. His presence in here is strong – it's why she comes when he isn't here. There is the faint scent of him, his woody cologne, the hint of sweet cigar smoke. It makes her feel close to him. But perhaps there is something hidden here, something about his life she is ignorant of. To him, his study is his inner sanctum, a safe place to hide secrets.

With a lump in her throat and her heart beating faster, she opens the drawers of the desk. There could be letters, or notes or poems or something. She rifles through the contents of Edward's desk at first tentatively, knowing it is wrong, half expecting he will poke his head around the door and catch her at it. But as she goes through each one, her confidence increases. He is miles away, doing heaven knows what with heaven knows whom. She opens envelopes and notebooks, checks through files and the stacks of correspondence, but finds nothing.

She sits back in the chair unsatisfied. She had almost hoped to find something. It would be devastating, but at least it would explain the distance that seems to have grown between them.

She gets up and walks over to the bookcases where there are some files containing articles he has written, and ledgers. She takes a closer look. Of course, here are all their bank statements. She knows she is clutching at straws, but it might shed light on something untoward that Edward is up to.

For the next half an hour, Eleanor checks through Edward's bank records. She is familiar with the household accounts – these are the ones *she* manages – but the statements she is rifling through relate to Edward's private accounts. She fingers the pages as little as possible. Her palms are sticky with nerves as she flicks each one over with just the tip of her forefinger and thumb. It feels illicit, like rummaging through someone's underwear. At every sound in the house she jumps, wondering if Alice, back from the post office, might come in to dust, or could Miss Harding be returning with Jimmy from their walk? How will she explain herself? She doesn't have to explain herself, of course she doesn't, she is the mistress of the house!

It doesn't take her long to find it. The amounts are so extraordinarily large they jump out at her. And there they are, regular as clockwork. Every month Edward makes a large withdrawal of cash. Twenty-six pounds, to be precise. That's three hundred and twelve pounds each year. Enough for a working man to live off! Certainly enough to keep a mistress. She sits and stares at the numbers, her mind numb. Then she checks the previous year, and the year before that. She checks each year, going back to before they were married. The same withdrawal of cash is there, twelve times a year, every single year, although rising each year by a small amount.

Eleanor replaces the bank records on the shelf with shaking hands. There can be no mistake. Such a large sum, in cash. Edward has been hiding something from her for a very long time, not just the last few months. Whatever it is had begun before they were married.

Something explodes in her chest and a helpless, crushing loneliness knocks the breath from her lungs. She sinks onto Edward's chair and puts her face in her hands and weeps, as silently as she is able so as not to be heard. Her husband, the rock she has relied on more than she realised until this very moment; the man who picked her up and rescued her and Rose after their mother was so cruelly taken, who she had thought had loved and worshipped her, is a mere fantasy. He cannot ever have loved her. How could he, if he has carried on with a mistress all this time? How could he have lied to her from the beginning and lived this double life? It seems impossible, like some twisted, fantastical, non-existent world. But she saw the figures with her own eyes. What other explanation could there be?

First Mabel, and now Edward. Everything Eleanor holds dear is slipping through her fingers like fine, dry sand.

16

Edward

Edward pushes aside the draft thesis by one of the PhD students he is supervising and rubs the tiredness from his eyes. A full, dreamless and refreshing night's sleep has been a rare luxury for years. Last night was particularly bad and now he is paying the price for it.

He digs his fingers hard into the place behind his ears, where his skull meets the top of his neck, pressing slow circles, which is both excruciatingly painful and deliciously relieving at the same time. He contemplates the piles on his desk. His workload seems to do nothing but grow. It's no longer possible to find the time to get home to Brook End during the week, and now here he is, working a weekend too. So much to do, so little time. The student's thesis can wait. It's not due in for months.

It suddenly strikes Edward as rather ironic that his students regard him with reverence and hang off his every word. Nobody ever mentions Edward's own lack of a doctorate qualification, which he still finds mildly surprising. He cannot think of a fellow lecturer without one. But, he supposes, the intervention of the war and his academic reputation seem to have alleviated him of the need to prove his worthiness of the title in any examination or theoretical sense. There has never been any question over his intellectual capacity to achieve a PhD; he would have been abundantly able, that's clear. He has practised his own intelligence tests upon himself and he has scored in the top 1 per cent of the population.

And anyway, isn't real-life experience and work on the ground so much more important than theory? What he has learnt over the years is that if one speaks with conviction, backed up by facts – statistics and analysis – one can bring around the most reluctant of politicians.

He releases the draft thesis with a sigh and stares at the different projects littering his desk in the cramped university office he shares with Professor Littleton, whose desk is similarly disordered. Professor Littleton, however, will not be in today. Because today is Saturday and Professor Littleton will be at home with his family. Which is where Edward should be. But he has put this visit off long enough. He had promised Violet faithfully that he would visit Porter, and somehow the weeks had passed by. Porter didn't, after all, succumb to the flu. He survived. But when he met with Violet last week, for their usual monthly transaction, she seemed quite uncommonly distressed, seemed to think his visit more urgent than ever.

And there are other reasons he must go besides. And those reasons became all the more apparent last weekend. His heart contracts when he thinks of the incident with Mabel. Perhaps it isn't only work keeping him away from Brook End. What is there, now, is almost too painful to confront. As Eleanor so succinctly put it, they can no longer go on as they are. He cannot think how she can bear it. It is hard enough to see each time he goes home.

He has two hours until his train leaves Victoria station, bound for East Sussex; two hours of uninterrupted peace to get something done without risk of intrusion from Prof Littleton or any of the students.

He runs through the competing projects in his head. There is a half-finished article on psychometrics; there is his work for the London County Council to produce a battery of tests for assessing children in order to place them in the appropriate educational establishment, and following the publication of his book, *The Delinquent Child*, he is in demand to design a programme of correction for delinquent youths.

But perhaps most importantly, is the research he must report on for the Royal Commission, his part in the push for it to recommend a new law for compulsory sterilisation of the feeble-minded, all of whom must be incarcerated at suitable institutions. It is a large project and it is not going well. He thinks of the words of Bushy-Brows at that committee meeting about education policy, when the old man said the proposals would be an enormous gamble without *irrefutable* evidence. He stares gloomily at the piles of paper. He needs more. Something more.

He knows that once it is done it will prove his theories correct and, applying his own principles, he and Eleanor should not have any more children. His stomach drops at the thought. But it cannot be *his* genes. The memories of Eleanor's three miscarried babies flicker across his mind and he goes cold. Could this have been nature's way of getting rid of the unwanted? They should have heeded the message. And where does that leave Jimmy? He feels weak at the thought of Jimmy getting sick too. But Eleanor has vehemently denied having epilepsy in her family and the faintest footsteps of doubt creep up his back. Could it be that this has nothing to do with *either* of their genes?

Damn it! Damn it all.

Stop thinking! He should know by now that a wandering mind is a dangerous thing.

The Royal Commission project. He forces himself to think of the project. How will he get it all finished in time? He needs an assistant. A student perhaps. But he is not comfortable with the idea of allowing them the freedom to draw their own conclusions from the collected data. No, access to such a valuable resource like this must remain restricted. People can be biased, and with statistics it is always possible to weld the numbers into supporting an altogether different conclusion. He cannot risk this. It is his life's work to progress that begun by Darwin and continued by Galton.

And then, a marvellous idea comes to him. Of course! Why on earth did he not think of it before?. It will be a solution to so many things, not least of all his marriage. If he engages *Eleanor* to help with his work, they will, by necessity, have to spend more time together. Involving her will mean he can reduce his workload and give her an interest. They will be able to rebuild their relationship. When he had first met her, Eleanor had been an excellent secretary and research assistant. She is, unquestionably, in possession of a good intellect. It is one of the things Edward admires about her. And *her* loyalty is without question.

She wouldn't even need to travel to London. She could work in his study at Brook End and it might be just the distraction she needs from Mabel's illness. He can picture it in his mind: Eleanor sorting the raw experiment results and making neat graphs, as per his instruction and under his supervision, of course; the two of them, sitting side by side at his big desk, sharing a pot of tea, or possibly a bottle of good wine. He smiles at the image, resolving to suggest it to her when the moment is right. He picks up his pen and dips it into the inkwell, pauses for a moment, then begins to write.

The journey down to the Heath Colony of Epileptics is slow and tedious. As the train puffs its way through the outskirts of London out into the Sussex countryside, *A Passage To India* lies unread on his lap. His earlier enthusiasm over the idea of asking Eleanor to help him has waned as he recalls the row over Mabel the last time they were together. His guts churn at the memory and he inwardly laughs at his own stupidity to think this might repair things.

It had just been the two of them at dinner that evening, Eleanor clearly still rattled from watching the hateful medicine being forced down Mabel's throat. She'd barely touched her food and his attempts at talking about other things had failed.

'Eleanor, I think we should think seriously about a plan for Mabel's future,' he'd said at last. Finally he'd had her attention.

'I want her off that awful medicine, Edward. You have to agree, it's doing no good!'

'It doesn't seem to be.'

'And... And it's *cruel* –I can't bear to see her suffer so...' She'd choked back a sob and his throat had tightened at the sight of her distress. He remembers reaching for her hand. What could he say that could possibly make it better?

'We need to get a second opinion. Fast,' she had said.

'Yes,' he'd agreed. 'We must do that. In fact, I have found someone. A Sir Charles Lawson. He is, I am told, *the* expert on childhood epilepsy. There is nobody in the country who knows more than him and I am hoping to get an appointment next week.'

Eleanor's head had jerked up and she'd looked so hopeful. He hadn't told her that he had already had a fairly lengthy discussion with Sir Charles over the telephone only last week or how, once Edward had described their daughter's condition, the doctor's prognosis was utterly grim. It was far better that this first meeting be with him alone. Eleanor should be shielded from the full horror of it all.

'There must be a better medicine,' Eleanor had said, 'there simply must!'

'Darling,' he had said, as gently as possible, 'apart from the medicine, I do think we need to talk about Mabel's future in general.'

'What do you mean?' She had looked genuinely puzzled.

'What I mean is...' He remembers bracing himself for what came next. 'It is unlikely that *any* doctor will be able to cure Mabel. In which case, we need to make some decisions. She won't be able to go to any ordinary school,' he had said. 'She won't be able to go out in public. Play with friends. We will have to keep her out of the public eye, partly for her own safety, of course, but also because of me – us. My reputation and my work. We cannot let it get out that we have a daughter with epilepsy, an inherited condition. Imagine the fallout? I can't—'

'*What!*' She'd blown up like a lit grenade. 'How dare you make this about you? It's *Mabel* who matters here, not your precious work or your reputation!'

'Of course it is,' he had said, trying to calm her. 'But we must think of the future. Of Jimmy too – how will he feel growing up with a – with... Well. We should think seriously about where Mabel would be best taken care of...'

And that had been that. Eleanor had shouted and cried and screamed. '*Over my dead body does Mabel leave this house!*'

He hasn't dared to tell her what he is up to today. She would be hysterical at the thought. But if, as Sir Charles Lawson has advised him, this really would be the best way to go forward, then he will allow Sir Charles to feed her the idea. It will be so much better coming from him.

At Croydon, Edward changes trains for the country line out to the village of Crawley. From there he takes a pony and trap to the colony. As they approach the high wall and stone pillars of the entrance, Edward begins to feel a little sick.

Once through the tall pillars and iron-gated entrance, the journey up to the main cluster of brick-built buildings is long. The colony is huge, far more extensive than Edward had imagined. The pony plods up the long, straight, pot-holed driveway and Edward surveys the extensive fields to the left and right. Beyond bare ploughed earth, cows and sheep graze on undulating hillsides. The low, rounded tops of pigsties come into view followed by a jumble of mismatched hen houses.

'Where to, mister?' the boy driving the pony turns to ask him.

'Is there a main building? I'm visiting someone in the Red Cross Centre.'

The boy studies him. 'Would that be a patient, sir?' He turns in his seat and points along the lane in front of them. 'The Red Cross Centre is all the way along the lane, then up that hill, to the right, in the far distance. Shall I take you up there?'

Edward hesitates. 'But I also have an appointment with the senior doctor, Sir Charles Lawson. Have you any idea where I might find him?'

The boy sucks air through his teeth. 'I'd 'ave no idea about that, sir. Tell you what, I'll take you there,' the boy points to their left, towards a long, low building with a tall clock tower at one end. 'It's the place I normally drop visitors. Someone in there'll help you.' He twitches the reins and clicks his tongue at the pony who changes direction, plodding up the path towards the clock tower.

Edward jumps down when the pony halts in front of the building. 'Will you come back for me? I don't expect I'll be more than an hour. I'll pay you well for your trouble.'

'Sure,' the boy says with a gap-toothed smile, adjusting his cap a little on his forehead.

The large hall is gloomy after the daylight outside. Edward announces himself to a man putting chairs into rows facing the front of the hall. The man leaves the room and returns a few minutes later with a large-framed woman dressed in a nurse's uniform.

She regards Edward with a furrowed brow.

'Good afternoon, Mr…?'

'Hamilton.' He reaches out to shake her hand. 'Professor Hamilton.'

She nods without smiling. 'I'm Sister Hogget. How can I help you?'

'I'm here to see Sir Charles Lawson, as well as to pay a brief visit to one of your patients in the Red Cross Centre. In a, er, professional capacity. I do have appointments for both,' he adds.

'Of course, come this way.'

Sister Hogget leads Edward over to the large, leather-bound visitor's book laid on the table near the front door. He adds his name to the book then follows the woman down a maze of corridors until they reach a door. She knocks briskly and disappears inside, leaving Edward outside. The building is Victorian, the corridor badly lit, functional and cold. Tunnel-like. He shivers. The door snaps open and Sister Hogget is back.

'Sir Charles will see you now,' she says, opening the door wide enough for him to see two grey-haired men in the room who stand to greet him as he enters. Sister Hogget announces tea will be brought and closes the door behind her.

'Professor Hamilton...' The shorter, stouter of the two men approaches him, extending his hand and smiling warmly. 'Very pleased to meet you. Allow me to introduce Superintendent Glover.'

The taller man steps forward and shakes Edward's hand in his own. This man is thin, with gold-rimmed glasses perched halfway down his aquiline nose. He is bowed at the shoulders, as though a lifetime of stooping to greet a population always inches shorter than him has left him permanently trying to shrink.

'Ah,' says Superintendent Glover, 'the elusive Professor Hamilton! We are delighted you have at last been able to come.' He waves at a chair and Edward sits, wondering how he will find the courage to mention what he has really come about...

He clears his throat. 'Gentlemen. I'm sorry, indeed, that it has taken me such a long time to respond to your request for me to visit. As you will be aware, my work is of such volume, it could occupy that of ten men.' The other men laugh politely. 'But that is not to say the work you do here is not of utmost importance. I want to assure you that I am fully behind your campaign for legislation, not only for the compulsory detention of all epileptics, but also for sterilisation of them too. This would, indeed, bring us in line with other nations who have, or are in the process of, passing legislation to this effect.' He pauses and the men nod encouragement.

'I want to reassure you too—' But Edward is interrupted by the door opening. A teenage girl enters, carrying a tray of tea and cake. The girl, by the look of her, is imbecilic or feeble-minded. She smiles at him in a stupid fashion and puts the tray clumsily on the table.

'Thank you, Vera,' says Sir Charles Lawson. 'How are you today?'

'Better, Doctor,' she speaks slowly. 'It was a bad day for me yesterday.' She shakes her head. 'I had pains here...' She presses her hands into her stomach and looks around the assembled company as if for sympathy. 'I had to go to bed.' She has a childish way of speaking.

'I'm sorry to hear that,' says Sir Charles, addressing her as he might a child of six. 'But I'm glad to know you are better today. I shall pay you a visit later, when I am finished with my guests here.'

The girl looks at Edward and Superintendent Glover with an intent, unsettling stare.

'Would you like me to pour out the tea, Doctor?' she asks, turning back to Sir Charles.

'No, no, that's fine, thank you,' he says. 'I can manage from here. You should go back to the kitchens now, Vera, or the cook will be missing you.'

'All right then,' she says. 'Bye-bye, Doctor. Bye-bye.'

The pathetic figure leaves the room and Sir Charles says, 'Vera has been with us for some years now. She is mostly amenable and quite harmless, although simple and childlike. She is an epileptic imbecile, as you will have gathered, but she is willing to work, and therefore quite suited to colony life. She works in the kitchens – simple tasks, cleaning dishes, scrubbing potatoes and so forth. We don't trust her with the chopping since she sliced her thumb and needed stitches. She works in the laundry some days too. Not all of them are as good-natured as her,' he adds. 'Tea?'

'Please,' Edward and Superintendent Glover answer in unison. They watch Sir Charles organise tea and slices of marble cake.

'Er, as I was saying,' Edward continues, trying to push a hateful image of a teenage Mabel in place of Vera from his mind, 'I want to reassure you that my interests in this area are completely aligned with your own. As you may or may not be aware, I have been conducting widespread and comprehensive studies on the links between heredity and disease, delinquency and intelligence, and the epileptic mind and criminality – and the evidence is overwhelming.

I will soon be reporting my findings to the Royal Commission who, in turn, will recommend the legislation for institutionalisation and sterilisation of these unfortunate individuals. A private member's bill is likely to be introduced to this effect, hopefully in the next parliament. I believe we have enough evidence to silence the detractors from this policy.' He pauses to drink his tea, hoping the other men don't notice how the liquid almost spills in his shaking hand.

'Excellent,' Sir Charles says. 'Excellent news indeed.'

'Now, I must confess, my reasons for visiting today are not solely in relation to the matters we've discussed.' He puts his cup and saucer down for fear of dropping something from his unsteady hands. 'I have also come about other... delicate matters. I must be assured that I have your complete confidence before I'm able to divulge the details.'

The two men lean forward ever so slightly in their chairs.

'Of course, my dear fellow,' Sir Charles says. 'We are not unused to matters which require privacy. You can trust that whatever you say here will go no further than these four walls.'

Edward exhales and begins, with unusual inarticulacy, to tell Sir Charles some of the facts which are keeping him awake at night.

Once the meeting is concluded, Sister Hogget is called to take Edward to the Red Cross Centre. They head out of the building, past a large duck pond and up the hill towards the farm buildings scattered in the distance. The woman prattles as they walk, Edward, silent, barely hearing anything she says.

'I wonder,' he asks suddenly, cutting her off mid-flow, 'how are the children treated here?'

She glances at him in surprise. 'I've not much to do with them, I'm afraid, sir, I work almost exclusively with the war veterans, bless their souls.' They walk another few steps. 'That there,' she points to a wooden building on their right, 'is the schoolhouse. Over there is the boys' living quarters, and the girls are there, next to the women's house,' she indicates a cluster of buildings close to the one she says is the laundry. 'And that,' she points to what looks like a rather run-down cottage, 'that is the Babies Castle, where all our youngest children live. The ones not yet old enough for school.'

Edward tries to imagine Mabel here. The vision is impossible to conjure. 'Do their parents visit?' he asks.

'Not usually,' says Sister Hogget. 'Most would rather not – and besides, it only upsets the mites. Better that they forget they ever had a home. This place is their family now.'

The Red Cross Centre is a sprawling building, surrounded by a covered veranda. Sister Hogget leads Edward through to a small entrance hall and suggests he waits there. He stands in the dark hall, every cell in his body urging him to turn and run. The air is stale with a faint odour of wood polish mingling with something medicinal. The silence in the building is unnerving. In all the six years Porter has been here, Edward has not once made the effort to come. Nausea rises with the shame and guilt of self-loathing.

A sudden slamming of doors and Sister Hogget is back, this time with a younger nurse, who sports ruddy cheeks and a startled expression.

'Captain Hamilton?' she breathes, looking at him as though he is an apparition.

'Yes,' he says, 'although I go by *Professor* Hamilton these days.'

'Oh, good heavens!' The nurse is blushing violently and seems all of a flutter. 'I am so happy to meet you.' She half curtseys as she takes his proffered hand to shake it with trembling fingers. 'Reggie – Mr Porter – has spoken of you so often and so much, you are quite the legend around here!' she laughs. 'The stories he's told... We began to think you couldn't possibly be a real person. And look! Here you are, larger than life! Everyone will be so desperate to meet you!'

'Please,' Edward says with growing desperation. 'I don't want any fuss. I just would quietly like to see Porter – Reggie – alone. It's only a quick visit. I have to be back in London for the early evening.'

'Of course, sir,' the nurse says, visibly deflating in front of Edward's eyes. 'I shan't make any fuss. It's good of you to visit. Poor Reggie's still recovering from a bad dose of flu. Oh, he was so very ill,' she says with knitted brows, 'miracle he recovered. Delusional, he was, at the height of it. Not the usual trouble with his nerves, you know, but different. Muddled. And it's not gone away. We think the illness has played havoc with his memory. Perhaps it'll help, seeing you.'

Edward follows the younger nurse through a day room where a dozen or so men are enjoying the afternoon warmth, sitting in small groups, smoking and playing cards or lying propped up in daybeds. The nurse leads him to the far end where Porter sits alone, looking out over the garden to the fields beyond.

'Reggie,' she says, tapping him on the shoulder, 'I've

someone here to see you. You'll never guess who!' She hesitates a moment then slopes away.

Porter, from behind, looks like any young man. Neatly cropped brown hair, broad shoulders, a little on the thin side, perhaps. He shuffles around in his chair to turn and look.

'Hello, Porter old chap,' Edward manages, despite the growing lump in his throat. He'd tried to prepare himself during the journey for this encounter, but seeing Porter in the flesh, after all these years, is like receiving fifty volts of electricity through his body.

Porter raises a shaking hand and lets out a noise, somewhere between a gasp and a groan. 'Captain Hamilton? Sir?'

'Yes, although it's Professor Hamilton now.'

'Can it really be you? Sir? You came!'

'Yes, Porter, it really is me. I'm here and I'm just so... Sorry.' Edward looks around for a chair and pulls one over to sit next to Porter.

Porter lets out a laugh and the muscles in one side of his face move in an attempt to smile. 'You're sorry?' His hand flops back into his lap.

Edward gathers the courage to look at Private Porter properly. The man stopped wearing his mask years ago. It was heavy and painful, he'd explained to Edward the very last time he saw him, before he married Eleanor and before Porter came to live here, at the Red Cross Centre for injured, shell-shocked war heroes, within the walls of Heath Colony. The state of Porter's face then, and now, even after all this time, is shocking to see. One side of it has been blown away, leaving a cave where his eye and cheek should be. Edward would readily have paid for surgery, were it an option, but even the most talented of surgeons who'd examined him had declared it impossible to reconstruct. The other side of Porter's face is horribly burnt, the skin taut and shiny, criss-crossed and puckered with the jagged white lines of scars. The sight in his remaining eye was miraculously saved, although it is poor. Edward knows that, beneath Porter's clothes, his burnt flesh is similarly scarred and shrivelled. Porter is in constant pain and his life is one on-going hell. While the rest of the world seeks to forget the war and put it behind itself in an ever increasing pursuit of pleasure and wealth, Porter, and those like him, have been left behind. They will *never* escape the tragedy which befell them.

'I hope they treat you well here,' Edward comments as the nurse comes back to deliver a pot of tea and fruit loaf. Edward pours the tea and slices the loaf, hands both to Porter.

'Like a king.' Edward senses Porter's attempt at a smile. His words are slurred and slow. It's clearly an effort to form them. 'Thank you for coming. I know from Violet, that you pay for this place. She's all I've got, y'know?' The man's voice breaks. 'An' you being my saviour an' all...'

'Please, Porter, stop.' Edward says, placing a hand gently on the man's arm. 'Really, there is no need.'

'Thing is, Captain, sir,' he fixes Edward with his one good eye, making him squirm, 'I'm hoping you can clear something up for me. I ain't a well man. My lungs... damaged, you know. And this flu's near finished me off. Think it'd only take a dose of pneumonia and that'll be it for me. Put me out of me misery, I s'pose.' He gives a hollow laugh. 'Anyway, I've always had nightmares, you know, about that day, that battle – but no waking memory of any of it. But just suddenly, since I've been ill, stuff is coming back to me. Stuff which don't make sense in my head. Can you help me, sir?' he implores. 'Can you help me remember?'

Edward stares at him, his blood curdling in his veins. Whether he chooses to tell the truth or perpetuate the lie, either way, Edward thinks to himself, he faces damnation.

V

It was always going to come to this. Once you admitted to yourself it is me *you are fighting through the battlefield of your child. And* me *who is winning the war.*

The girl, of course, must be hidden away.

Away from the unkind stares, the whispers and the judgement. Away from the disgust and the distrust. Oh, how easy it is for you to justify yourselves!

And so, here we are at the Heath Colony of Epileptics. Just one of the many places you build to hide away your unwanted.

Behind its high walls, which keep the residents in and the decent public out, there is a stench to the place, a stink which hangs permanently in the stale air, permeating the thick walls, the cold dark rooms, the very fabric of the buildings. Stale cabbage and old socks. Privies and dirty laundry. Sickness, misery and loneliness.

A prison in all but name.

Behind these walls live the unfit, the unwanted — the dregs of society you lock away to keep the better people safe. And this is what you plan for my girl too. The poor, sweet thing.

I see how it will be: her, tiny and confused, lost amidst all the other abandoned souls. Souls whose world will never extend beyond the two hundred acres from the farm to the laundry, the kitchens to the workshop. The men's house, the women's, the staff quarters. The Red Cross Centre, where the shell-shocked soldiers live inside their shattered minds. High up on a hill it sits; how fitting an elevation for those who gave up their useful lives in the trenches! And then, of course, the children's schoolhouse and the Babies Castle for those too young to understand what they are doing here.

They are all the same to me. For most, I am the only visitor they will ever receive. You see? I possess more humanity than you!

And so I travel from soul to soul, bringing misery to some, enlightenment to others. Occasionally oblivion, an end to all the suffering.

And when it comes to be, I shan't forget the girl, the little mite who will sit all alone on her bed, crying for her mama, a scrappy doll clutched to her chest.

I am not the one without compassion, do you see?

17

Eleanor

Rose strokes the back of Eleanor's hand with the tips of her fingers as though she were a cat. Thank God, at least, she has Rose. Her sister, when it comes down to it, is the only person she can truly trust.

'I'm *certain* Edward would never be unfaithful,' Rose says. 'There *must* be another explanation. He utterly adores you, Ellie, everyone can see that. It doesn't make sense. It truly doesn't – all those years? Not Edward, I *know* he wouldn't.'

'But do we ever really know someone, Rose?' Eleanor asks through her wash of tears. 'Even those closest to us, we only know the part they choose to reveal. I'm not sure we can *ever* truly know a person.'

Rose shifts on the sofa and frowns. Is she thinking of how she hadn't confessed to Eleanor the secret visits from Marcel? It is late afternoon and they sit side by side as the light fades outside and the sitting room grows slowly darker, neither of them daring to move to turn on the lights. Rose has promised to stay until Monday morning rather than returning to London on Sunday afternoon as she often does. Eleanor can't bear the thought of her leaving at all. She watches her take a sip of sweet sherry from her glass.

'Rose, dear,' Eleanor says on a sudden whim, 'please pour me a glass of that sherry too. I think I could do with a drink.'

Rose smiles and jumps to her feet. 'Of course, that's the spirit.' She snaps on the lamp and walks over to the drinks cabinet. 'Now that you and Sophie have made it up,' she begins, taking out another glass and uncorking the bottle, 'she told me *specifically* to get you to agree to come and visit us in town.'

Rose hands her the glass of sherry and gives Eleanor an encouraging smile.

'I think it would be just the thing to cheer you up.' She bites her lip. 'In fact, Marcel is going to be in London this week and Sophie has promised to hold one of her famous evening soirées... Perhaps you could come too?' she asks tentatively.

Eleanor takes a large gulp of sherry. The liquid is sweet, burning her throat and warming her insides as it slides down. She had felt guilty for not telling Edward about Rose and Marcel, but seeing as he has been keeping much bigger secrets from her, she suddenly doesn't feel so bad. Why shouldn't she go to a party? Why shouldn't she meet her sister's *amour*? She shan't tell Edward any of it.

'I think that is a tremendously good idea,' she says, taking another swig of sherry.

Rose laughs out loud. 'That's the spirit!' She jumps up, rubbing her hands with pleasure. 'I'll put on some cheery music!'

'How is Sophie?' Eleanor asks.

'Stoic. Henry's still up to his old tricks. He's dumped the last girl and moved on to a new squeeze. Been photographed around town with an actress of all people. Poor Sophie.'

'Yes. Poor Sophie.'

Which rather neatly brings them back to Edward. Rose is fiddling with the gramophone. It's easier to say while Rose's back is turned. 'The thing is, Rose, about Edward. Since Jimmy's birth, and, well, a long time before that, we weren't having... *relations*, of a husband and wife nature. So you see, it's perfectly feasible he's gone off and f-found someone else.'

'Sex, Ellie. You mean you weren't having *sex*.'

Eleanor winces at the word, and Rose laughs, turning to look at her as the dulcet tones of Jane Green singing 'We're Back Together Again' flood the room. She swings and sways her way back to the sofa to the rhythm of the music. Christ, Eleanor thinks, is she really such a prude? No wonder Edward keeps a mistress! Perhaps she is a great disappointment in the bedroom. Rose seems so comfortable in her own skin, so comfortable with the word *sex*.

'W-we weren't,' stutters Eleanor, 'because the doctor said we shouldn't. Just in case. I mean, I'd lost three babies after Mabel, so...' She takes another sip from her glass, the sherry soothing from the inside out, the music from outside in. 'Anyway, since Jimmy was born, Edward's been staying away more and more. It's as if he doesn't want to be with me any more. I could almost accept that. The bit I *can't*,' she says with some ferocity, 'is the fact this seems to have been going on since before we were married. And at the beginning, well, we were at it like rabbits, really.'

Rose giggles, takes Eleanor's empty glass from her hand

and refills it. 'Cigarette?' she asks, pulling a packet from her pocket.

When on earth did Rose start smoking? Eleanor shakes her head and bites her lip. Is that Marcel's influence? She won't say anything about the smoking. She won't.

'Ellie,' Rose says, after lighting up and tossing the match in an ashtray. She takes a deep inhale of the cigarette, then throws her head back and blows out a plume of smoke. 'It *doesn't* mean that at all. You are jumping to conclusions. Besides, it makes no sense, if the money has been going out of his account since before he even *met* you, I mean, if he'd been having an affair, why would that person put up with him marrying *you*?'

'Perhaps she didn't have a choice. Perhaps she was a woman of ill-repute, a woman of the *lower orders*!' She spits out the words. 'Who knows?'

'But I thought Edward detested women like that.'

'He does.'

'Well,' exclaims Rose, 'there you are then! There *must* be another explanation.'

'But perhaps he only tells me that to cover his tracks, trying to put me off the scent of his dirty, sordid life!'

'Oh, really!' Rose jumps up again in frustration. 'This is all total conjecture.' She puts down her glass. 'You know what I do when I'm feeling down or sad?' Eleanor shakes her head and takes a larger gulp from her glass, her head beginning to swim pleasantly. Rose jumps to her feet, swings her hips and rolls her head, twisting her shoulders, her bobbed hair falling over her face. 'I put on some music and I *dance*, I *smoke*, and I *drink*! Ellie, you need to live a little. I think you've forgotten how. Come on, dance with me.' She holds out her hand and Eleanor drains her glass and stands, the room swaying slightly.

'All right,' she says, allowing herself to be pulled away from the furniture. She kicks off her shoes and allows her body to move with the music. Perhaps Rose is right. But even if she is, Edward is still keeping something secret from her and she is going to find out what, or who, the secret is.

'Rose,' she says, her words slurring a little, as she looks her sister in the eye, 'have you had sex with Marcel?'

Rose collapses with laughter. 'Of course I bloody have!' she says.

There is a nasty hammering inside Eleanor's head when she wakes the following morning. She groans and rolls over onto her back, her tongue sticking to the roof of her mouth. But the pounding in her temples worsens. *Need water*. She pushes herself up to sit; the morning light seeping around her curtains is too bright. *Dear God*! How could she have allowed herself to get so drunk last night?

With shaking hands she pours herself some water from the jug on her bedside table and gulps it down, immediately feeling a wave of nausea. Stupid, stupid, stupid. She rests her head back, her heart pounding too fast in her chest. She tries taking a few deep breaths and remembers the two bottles of wine she and Rose shared last night. Did they have a cocktail afterwards? She can't quite remember. Snippets of conversation return. Theories about Edward and that damned money. Rose and… yes, Marcel and she are lovers! She has visions of him creeping down Sophie's corridors in the dead of night to make love in her room. The details of what her sister divulged last night make Eleanor's toes curl. She places the palm of her hand on her forehead, feeling beads of sweat at her hairline. She thinks she remembers agreeing to meet this man who has stolen her sister's heart. She thinks she even invited him down to Brook End – and who cares a damn what Edward thinks of it all? Did she really say that?

More of the conversation returns. They had talked about their mother and of all the things which for so long had gone unspoken. The grief, the anger which Eleanor had buried deep still burns strong and is so easily stoked by the mere mention of her name. That's why she hates to talk of it. That's why she tries not to even remember her mother. She had cried last night. Cried over her mother and over Mabel. Rose had told her she hadn't dealt with their mother's murder. Hadn't grieved. Hadn't let go. They had talked so long into the night, she recalls, that they had even watched the sky lighten towards the east. Eleanor, Rose had told her, needs to let go of her hatred. Rose has accepted and forgiven the man. Somehow, some way, and it has freed her up to live her life, to enjoy her life. Then there had been laughter, and music, and loosing herself. Despite the throbbing head, she feels a sense of unburdened peace. She drinks more water and, closing her eyes again, allows her mind to drift.

Eleanor is thirteen, running barefoot on the beach at West Wittering after her brothers, one two years older, one a year younger, but both always stronger and faster than she. Four-year-old Rose is trailing behind and Mama's voice, faint against the breeze – 'careful of the sea, Rosie! Take care of your sister, Eleanor, boys!' – the fierce wind carrying with it cries of gulls and the taste of salt, sharp on her tongue. It lashes her hair and pounds her body as she pushes against it, desperate to reach the great grey sea, chopped with white, silver spray whipping so high it's hard to tell where the sea finishes and the air begins. The joyful cries of her brothers as they reach the sea's edge, pushing and shoving one another into the boiling waves. She and Rose hold their skirts high, hesitating at the water's edge then venturing into the shallows, legs quickly numbing in the freezing foam, clothes soaking anyway. The boys are much braver – leaping into the waves, heads bobbing up and down, appearing and disappearing between the undulating walls of water. Eleanor remembers clinging to Rose's hand, eyes roving the water, heart thumping, checking she could spot two heads, always two heads, fearing that if she didn't watch, one might disappear forever.

The vividness of the memory brings more. A kaleidoscope of images from her youth. Their comfortable home on Richmond Hill; endless summer afternoons playing hide-and-seek in the garden, climbing trees and teaching Rose how to make chains of daisies to dress her pretty hair. Mama laughing at something Papa says over the breakfast table, beyond her understanding, which makes it not funny at all. Mama looking beautiful, dressed in fine clothes for an evening out, her hair swept up on her head, the daintiest of curls around her ears and at the nape of her neck, jewels glittering at her throat and in her ears. Mama reading in her soft, warm voice from an armchair by the fire, while the four of them sit around her, listening with rapt attention to *Anne of Green Gables,* the fire crackling in the grate, Papa not yet home from his work in the City.

But then in her mind, as in life, the idyll cracks. The pain of cascading memories digs like a knife into her flesh and she screws her eyes tighter, gripping her blankets in her fists as if to prevent them coming. But they are a flood now, and she cannot stop them.

It's 1914 and Papa is standing before them in his new uniform, ready to go off to fight, ruffling her hair and promising to be home for Christmas. A cheery wave and he is gone. That happy, kindly man never to return. The one who did come back to them was reduced, shrunken and hollowed out, whose haunted eyes had witnessed inexpressible horrors. This wasn't the same Papa who had teased and tickled them, who'd been larger than life and full of vigour. And now she sees her brothers, eager to do *their* bit for King and Country, hugging a weeping Mama in turn. That was the last time Eleanor remembers being truly happy. First one telegram, then the other, announcing lost in action in harsh, bleak letters being placed in Mama's hands. And then Papa, whose lungs had been scorched by mustard gas, had coughed and gasped and clung to life as he lay on the sofa for months while the maids were sent away and Mama, Eleanor and even little Rose had taken over Papa's care and the household duties to save money and their father's dignity, as death slowly claimed him, day by day, cell by cell until he, too, was gone.

They'd had to move, of course. The war pension was far too small for Mama to keep the house in Richmond and the servants needed to run it. She'd sold up and moved Eleanor and Rose to a modest flat at the wrong end of Bell Street. In Marylebone, Mama had described it, but it was Paddington really. Mama had got herself a job, working in an upmarket fashion store in Regent's Street, working long days to see the girls through school and to keep them all in nice clothes and with pretty things to brighten their existence. As soon as she could, Eleanor had got herself a job too, taking shorthand and typing classes at night school. She'd been bright and quick to learn and somehow caught the eye of the teacher who knew someone who knew someone and so, within days of finishing the course, she found herself working at the War Office.

And suddenly, this window in her mind has opened and she is back in that terrible day when the police had knocked on her door and announced the murder of her mother. Hot anger flares in Eleanor's chest, making her gasp with its ferocity. Rose's words come back to her from last night. 'You must learn to forgive, Eleanor. If you do not, it will continue to eat you from the inside. The man who killed our mother had had a terrible life – I have looked into his case. He was of simple mind, given to bouts of violence he didn't understand the consequences of, and he had been so cruelly treated in the workhouse, didn't know what he was doing. Ellie, he was as sick as Mabel is. You simply must forgive if you are to move on...'

A knock at the door brings Eleanor back to the present. She takes a last swill of water and pats her hair in an attempt to look decent.

'Come in,' she calls, her voice croaky, wishing her brain would stop its incessant pounding against her skull.

Alice's head appears. 'Morning, Mrs Hamilton. I thought I should check to see if you were all right. It's almost eleven and I wondered if you might want some breakfast. Miss

Carmichael went out for a walk and even though she told me not to disturb—'

'Rose! Oh, thank you Alice, eleven!' Another thought slices. 'The baby! I should have fed Jimmy by now!' Her awareness strays to the discomfort of her full, hard breasts. 'How could I have slept so long?'

'It's OK, Miss Harding gave the little 'un a bottle of condensed milk this morning. Thought it best to let you sleep off – I mean...' Alice's cheeks flush in embarrassment and she bustles to the window to draw the curtains.

'Oh, it's all right, Alice,' Eleanor says, closing her eyes against the light and rubbing her temples with her forefingers. 'I've made an utter fool of myself, haven't I? Well, this headache serves me right and I shan't be making *that* mistake again. Still, perhaps it's time young Jimmy was weaned onto the bottle in any case. He'll be coming up for three months, soon.'

'Yes, Mrs Hamilton,' Alice says, opening the window a little before leaving the room. 'I'm sure you'll feel better with a few slices of bacon and some fried egg inside you.'

Downstairs, Mrs Bellamy, with her clicking tongue and pursed lips, makes her feelings very clear at the audacity of being asked to prepare a second round of breakfast, and so close to lunch.

'Exceptional circumstances, Mrs Bellamy, you understand,' Eleanor mumbles, backing out of the kitchen, and wondering why she is so apologetic to the woman who is in her employ, after all. She speeds away from the kitchen, wincing as she hears poor Alice receiving a tongue-lashing for some minor misdemeanour.

Mrs Faulks is polishing the best silver cutlery in the dining room.

'Good morning, Mrs Hamilton.'

'Good morning, Mrs Faulks. I'm awfully delayed this morning. Rose and I talked late into the night, I'm afraid.'

'Ah, well. I'm sure you had much to talk about, with her working up in town now. You'll be hungry I expect. Shall I speak with Mrs Bellamy—'

'Heavens, no. I just asked her. Best not to bother her again.'

'Righto.' She puts the polished cutlery back in the dresser drawer. 'Thought I'd best get these polished up, in case you and Mr Hamilton are planning on having any dinner parties soon. It's been a while...'

'Oh. Yes, thank you, Mrs Faulks. What a good idea. We've rather got out of the habit of having guests since Jimmy's arrival, but I suppose...' She lets her voice drift and there is an awkward silence.

Eleanor sinks into a chair, her head swimming, stomach churning and wonders if she can manage any breakfast at all.

'I'll fetch some coffee,' says Mrs Faulks, and bustles out of the room.

'And please could you ask Miss Harding to bring Jimmy to me?' Eleanor calls.

'Of course,' Mrs Faulks says, poking her head around the dining-room door. 'I expect you're missing the bonnie lad.' She smiles and disappears again.

It's time I picked myself up, Eleanor thinks to herself, as she waits. Time I sorted quite a lot of things out.

A few days later, Eleanor steps down from the cab outside Sophie and Henry's elegant town house in Berkeley Square. It's dusk and warm light spills from every window into the darkening and chilly square. Eleanor pays the driver and makes her way up the steps to the front door, glancing at the upper-floor windows. A muted patter of conversation reaches her above the faint resonance of music and tinkle of laughter, gay and inviting.

A maid, smartly dressed in black with a white pinafore and cap opens the door. Sophie keeps a full household of staff and Eleanor does not recognise this one. The butler must be upstairs, taking care of the partygoers. She follows the maid through the lamplit, amber-hued entrance hall, catching the familiar scent of wood polish and old tobacco smoke, and up the sweeping staircase to the first floor.

Sophie's *soirée* is in full swing when Eleanor enters the main reception room. It's so long since she has been to a party, even longer without Edward at her side, that anxiety strikes with a vice-like grip, pulling her up short on the threshold. She stands for a moment, surveying the room and resisting the urge to turn right around and leave. There must be forty people there at least. *Small intimate gathering*, Rose had assured her. The perfect opportunity for her to meet the Frenchman. Nerves flutter in her belly like birds in a cage.

The guests mingle in messy, noisy groups, some around

the gramophone, others draped languorously over Sophie's sumptuous furniture. The room itself is intimidating, after the simple, rustic charm of Brook End, all ostentatious elegance with its deep green walls and splashes of vibrant colour from the large oriental vases, drapes and rugs, decorated with exotic birds and flowers. From the look of some of the guests, this *soirée* has been going on since lunchtime.

She shouldn't have come. She'd said as much last night on the phone to Rose, having tried on most of her wardrobe for something suitable to wear. There was only one half-decent dress she could squeeze into that looked almost presentable. After much persuasion, she had agreed she would come only for one night, leaving Brook End mid-afternoon and returning by lunchtime the following day. Mabel and Jimmy would barely notice her absence that way. She'd hugged and kissed them both before she left, but instead of the elation she had imagined she would feel, as the train chugged her further and further away from her children, she felt a tug of separation, like a strap pulling tighter and tighter around her chest.

But she is here now, so she had better make the most of it. She takes a deep breath and steps into the room, sweeping a cocktail the colour of a summer sunset off the tray held out to her by the butler. Something cognac-based, she thinks, taking a large gulp for courage. Most of the men are gathered at the far end of the room, plumes of cigar smoke rising above their heads. The women, and a smattering of younger men, are in the centre, on the sofas and swaying to the music near the gramophone. The room is filled, as it always is at a party of Sophie's, with the young and beautiful; the ugly and important. Eleanor feels dour and puffy. After ten weeks, her body has yet to fully return to her svelte pre-pregnancy shape.

'Darling! There you are.' Sophie appears, sparkling from neck to knee, in a gorgeous sequined black dress. She pushes her way through the throng, grinning her perfect, white-toothed smile. 'Goodness!' she exclaims, holding Eleanor at arm's length. 'You look quite divine.'

'Oh, I really don't,' Eleanor laughs nervously.

'I beg to differ,' a voice says behind her left shoulder. A slightly balding man, with a round face and sagging jowls, shuffles round to face her. 'Thomas Stapleton,' he says, 'at your service.' He gives a slight bow. 'Now, Sophie, do tell who your delicious friend is.' Without shifting his eyes from her face, he twitches his nose, reminding Eleanor of a dog sniffing out a tasty morsel. Out of the corner of her eye, she catches Sophie rolling her eyes and stifles a giggle.

'I'm afraid my delicious friend and I have some catching up we need to do,' Sophie says firmly, taking Eleanor by the arm and leading her away from the hungry Thomas Stapleton.

'It is just so wonderful to have you here,' Sophie says. 'There are some people I *cannot* wait for you to meet – they will absolutely love you. Oh God no, not like that lech, Stapleton, they are *nice* I tell you. We have so much to catch up on. You, with poor little Mabel...' Sophie drops her voice to a whisper. 'I want to know how you are coping. As for me, I'm having terrible trouble with Henry. He's dumped that awful girl, you know, the very young one, thankfully, but now has another squeeze. He was decent to me in the space between, but he is *utterly* vile now. An actress, would you believe, and he is literally *flaunting* her around the place. The press are having a field day – have you seen in the papers? Damned fool. I'm furious with him, can't bear to be in the same room. Thankfully he has buggered off to the house in Derbyshire with her. Heaven knows what the staff think, but he couldn't care a jot!' She finally pauses for breath. '*Anyway*, I don't want to bore you with my troubles!'

'Oh Soph, I'm truly sorry about Henry. These men...' Her voice trails off. *These men, indeed.* Can Edward be just the same? Are they all the same? For all her friend's blustering and making the best of things, she knows how deeply hurtful this whole mess with Henry is. Doubly bad being played out publicly in the newspapers.

'Listen, darling,' Sophie says, placing a hand on Eleanor's arm, 'we will have plenty of time later to talk. Right now we must be *happy*. I have specially arranged for some gorgeous friends of mine to come and play live music so we shall have dancing! Look!'

Beside the grand piano, two men are taking instruments out of cases, and a third is taking his place on the piano stool. 'A special treat in your honour,' she giggles. 'But first... Ah, so *this* is where you are hiding!'

And there she is. Rose, looking more beautiful than ever in understated, pale-blue organza, shimmering slightly in the lamplight, her short, sleek hair tucked behind her ears.

In her imagination, Marcel had been a tall, dark, swarthy man with smouldering good looks, Valentino-esque. The man standing next to her sister couldn't be more different. No taller than Rose, Marcel is slight and clean-shaven, sports large, round-framed glasses. He has a prominent nose and close-set, intelligent brown eyes. Eleanor is momentarily lost for words.

They stare at each other before Marcel extends a hesitant hand for her to take. His skin is deathly pale, as though he barely sees the light of day, but his grip is surprisingly warm and firm.

'Madame Hamilton,' he says, his accent thick and slow. 'It is the greatest pleasure. I have waited such a long time to meet you. *Enchanté.*' His eyes meet hers and she is struck by the depth in them. A serious, deep thinker comes to mind, rather than the philandering cad she had imagined. He brushes the skin on her hand with his lips.

'Monsieur Deveaux...' she hesitates. *It's a pleasure,* hovers on her lips, but it feels inappropriate after all the fuss with Rose. 'How long are you staying in London?' she asks instead.

'I arrived only this afternoon. I visit several galleries tomorrow and the day after who are interested in my work, and then I return to Paris. So, a fast visit, you might say.' He gives a little laugh. 'But still a little time to see your wonderful sister.' He smiles at Rose.

He is so far from the image Eleanor has held of this mysterious Marcel that she is struggling to think of what to say. This funny little man, not in the least bit handsome – what does Rose see in him? Fleetingly, she thinks perhaps this is a good match after all. Surely this Marcel will dote on her sister and would be most unlikely to stray?

'And apart from art, what are your interests, Monsieur Deveaux?' she asks.

'Marcel, please,' he says with a little bow.

'Marcel,' she repeats.

'Learning,' he says, 'is the first and most important, don't you think? We have so much to learn of the world, of nature and all that is in it. An enquiring mind is everything.' His eyes sparkle. He looks at Rose. His devotion to her is clear. 'Rose and I have much in common in that regard. And much more besides – we both lost our mothers at the same age. Mine to cancer and... Well, there are other commonalities about our families. But that discussion is for another time. We are both drawn to art, to literature, and to how to make the world a different, better place. When we were in Paris together, we spent many hours in the museums and galleries.' *Is that so?* Eleanor thinks, but he seems so sincere, that her mind is having to do a swift recalibration of Monsieur Deveaux. 'And much time also debating politics!' he continues. 'We French enjoy politics. You English, how do you say... You are less open about these things, I think?' He cocks his head on one side.

Sophie laughs. 'Indeed. Politics is regarded as rather distasteful in this country.'

'But perhaps you, Madame Hamilton, might like to join Rose and I for dinner tomorrow night?'

'Oh! Eleanor, please?' Rose claps her hands together as if in prayer.

Rose and Marcel stare at her, waiting for her reply.

'I would like that very much,' she says, exhaling, realising with surprise that she means it. 'But I have to return home tomorrow morning, for my children. My son is only a few months old...'

'Of course, I understand. Next time perhaps—' He says something else but his words are drowned by the sounds of a saxophone and a cello tuning loudly just behind them.

'I can see we must continue our discussions later,' Marcel laughs, as the musicians pause before beginning their first number of the evening.

'Time for dancing!' Rose cries with excitement. 'Come along, Ellie, dance with me!'

She holds out both hands and Eleanor takes them, finding herself reflecting her sister's laughter. Rose leans in close, 'I knew you would like him, Ellie. I just *knew*.'

18

Edward

'Morning, darling.' Edward lowers his newspaper a fraction to greet Eleanor over the top of its pages. He is pleasantly surprised to see she has Jimmy in her arms.

'And good morning to the little fellow,' he says, pulling the newspaper lower. 'Joining us for breakfast then, young chap?' he adds, addressing the baby. Jimmy, who at almost four months is still rather small, on account of his early arrival, is nevertheless bright and alert this morning, his big eyes trained on the spread of food on the breakfast table, his little hands waving in the air as though he can't wait to grab some toast and get stuck in.

'Miss Harding has a rather nasty headache. I told her to go back to bed for an hour or two, so Jimmy and I shall have breakfast together today.' She sits down, Jimmy on her lap. He immediately slaps both hands on the table and tries to grab her knife. She hands him her teaspoon which he pops straight in his mouth. Eleanor looks rather pale and tired herself. Perhaps once she has had something to eat, he will share his clever plan to get her involved in his research. 'Sleep all right?' He asks, going back to his newspaper. He scans the foreign news headlines: *First Presidential*

Proclamation by U.S. President H. Hoover; Tightening of penalties for violating Prohibition; Fascist Party predicted landslide victory in upcoming Italian general election; Trotsky Interview in Turkey; New Land Speed Record set at 231 mph! Two hundred and thirty-one miles per hour! Good lord, one would need excellent goggles and a strong nerve. He gives the paper a shake, turns the page.

'No, I didn't sleep well,' Eleanor mumbles.

'Orange juice? Coffee?' Alice asks, coming into the room, followed by Mrs Faulks.

'Both, thank you, Alice,' Eleanor replies, 'and just a little toast and some honey, please.' She shifts Jimmy on her lap, pulling his hands away from her coffee cup.

'Here,' Mrs Faulks offers, holding out her hands, 'let me take the little mite while you eat your breakfast in peace. Mrs Bellamy and I can manage him in the kitchen for a while.'

'Oh, would you? That's very kind. Just for twenty minutes or so. Thank you.'

As soon as the door is closed, she turns to Edward. 'There is something I must speak to you about.'

There is something sharp about her tone which makes him look at her. She is rigid in her chair. He thought she was a bit off when he came back late from London last night. Two weeks' absence has clearly not made her heart grow fonder, or however it is the silly saying goes. He desperately wanted to go to her last night but thought it best not. Perhaps, in retrospect, that was the wrong decision. It hadn't occurred to him she might want him too. But if she did, why didn't she just say? Why does he always have to guess? And the messages are always so mixed, he spends his whole life being confused. Women. Such a conundrum. Still, once he gets her involved in his work, they will have more to discuss. More time together. Things are bound to get better between them.

'Of course, my dear.' He folds the paper and puts it to one side. Helping himself to a second slice of toast, he says, 'I didn't sleep too well myself,' through a mouthful of toast. 'But nothing new there.' He sighs. He always makes a point to tell her how much better he sleeps when he is with her. Just so she knows. He never gets the same messages in return. But then, he probably isn't the same attractive night-time proposition, what with his cries, sweating and thrashing limbs. But she's always seemed happy to put up with the disturbances, to shush him, hold him and stroke his hair; to remind him he is safe, here in bed with her, and not still on some wretched battlefield under enemy fire. But not, it seems, any more. Her face is flushed and she eats in silence, her jawbone visible through her pale cheek as she chews.

Edward watches his wife, aware of his heart thrumming in his chest. She's always had that effect on him: to heighten him, replenish him, excite him. In short, she makes him *better*.

Eleanor exhales.

'I know what you're up to,' she says at last, angry-eyed and thin-lipped.

'Sorry?' Oh God, she must have found out about his visit to Heath Colony. He was trying to save her from worry. Yet again he has got it wrong. 'Eleanor, I—'

'It's been going on for years, hasn't it? From way before we were married. Before we'd even *met*.'

He stares at her. Not about the colony, then. 'I honestly don't know what you are talking about.' All the stress of Mabel, it's clearly getting to her. Perhaps they should take a holiday somewhere? Is Jimmy too young to leave with the nanny? The South of France would be nice. He imagines them strolling along by the startling blue of the Mediterranean, eating lunch in hidden-away bistros, drinking wine at lunchtime and then having slow, luxurious sex with the windows thrown open, allowing a warm breeze to cool their naked bodies. They could reconnect...

'You never thought I'd find out, did you?' she's saying. 'Well, I did. I searched through your things. I *knew* there was something going on. And I found them. The bank accounts. I *know* about the enormous sums of money you have been withdrawing, Edward, every month, year after year.'

His heart plunges.

'You weren't supposed to find those.'

'Bloody hell, Edward, that's poor even for you!'

He swallows hard, trying to gather his shattered thoughts. 'I mean... At least, what I meant to say was, I *should* have told you. I know I should have, but I'm a coward. Eleanor, please. Believe me, I never meant to hurt you. The longer time went on, the harder it seemed to talk about it. The less relevant it was.'

'What?' Her cheeks are flushed. 'How could it be less relevant? Relevant to *who*? It's bloody well relevant to *me*! I'm your *wife*, for God's sake. And you've not finished it, have you, you stupid bastard?'

'No. No I haven't finished it. I have no idea how I could. Not now, it would be cruel to do that.'

'*Cruel!*' Eleanor jumps to her feet. Tears begin to course

down her cheeks. 'And what about me in all of this! How can you justify treating *me* like this? Is this whole damned lie not cruel to *me*?' She strides around the room, crossing her arms over her belly, stifling sobs.

'I – Eleanor. I'm sorry, truly I am. But this began long before I even *knew* you. I *should* have told the truth but it's in the past and—'

'But it *isn't* in the past, is it? You're still paying her, aren't you? Whoever she is, keeping her in some luxury I should imagine!'

Her words sink in and suddenly he realises what she is thinking. He laughs and jumps to his feet, running to her. 'I think you might have the wrong end of the stick, old girl.'

'What are you saying?' she sobs. 'I've seen all the money you've taken out, every month, for years and years. If you hadn't taken it to keep a woman, then what else would it be for?'

Edward grabs Eleanor's arms, pulling her into an embrace. She sobs all the harder, her tears soaking his shirt until Edward fishes his handkerchief from his pocket and hands it to her. She wipes her eyes and blows her nose. 'Oh, my poor darling! I am truly sorry. That isn't it at all! You've got it all wrong!'

She looks up at him, wet-eyed, heart thumping. 'N-not a woman?'

'*No!*' He looks down at her, tenderness in his eyes. 'Never anyone but you. And before you ask, no, there are no illegitimate children either.'

'Oh!' She slumps against him, collapsing. Shrinking like a deflating balloon. 'So… You *haven't* been unfaithful? Not even lately?' He catches the note of hope in her voice.

'Eleanor, you are everything to me. I don't want anybody else. How could I, when the most beautiful, most wonderful woman is here in my arms?'

'But Sophie said...'

'*Sophie?* What does she know?'

'She suggested... And I thought, because we weren't, well, you know... You would go looking elsewhere, and—'

'So you went looking for evidence?'

'Yes, I'm sorry.'

Edward sighs. 'I suppose it is human nature to do such a thing. We have a theory, and we search for evidence to prove it.'

'I looked at the bank accounts. I shouldn't have snooped.'

'No,' he strokes her hair, her cheek, smiles into her eyes, 'you should have asked me,' he says gently, 'before leaping to conclusions.'

Eleanor draws away and looks steadily back at him, her tears drying. 'But if the money isn't going to a mistress, or a mistress's child, then where has it been going? It's a good deal of money, Edward. There *is* something you are still not telling me.'

'All right,' Edward admits, 'that part is true, and I owe you an explanation for sure. It's – it's just a part of my life I had hoped was behind me. I've struggled to cope, Eleanor, with what happened back then, and I've tried so hard to forget, that's why I've never spoken of it. But I see that it is time, and perhaps it will put some ghosts to rest.'

He takes her by the hand. 'Come on, let's walk. Mrs Faulks won't worry about minding the baby a little longer – I'd rather do this outside.' He whistles for Byron and the three take the path across the lawn towards the woods.

'Do you remember,' he begins, 'not long after we first met, how I'd been invited, more than once, to collect the medals I had earned during the war?'

'Yes,' she says with a frown. 'Of course I remember. I could never understand why you didn't want them, especially when you had been so brave. They sent them in the post in the end as I recall.'

'I wasn't brave,' Edward forces the words through gritted teeth. 'At least,' he says, 'I simply did what anyone would do in my situation. I protected my men. My boys. Everyone would have done the same.' He takes a deep breath. 'I didn't want *medals*. My boys didn't make it so how could I possibly want medals? It would simply remind me how I'd failed them.'

'Oh, Edward! You didn't fail them! You did what you could, and that's all *anyone* could do! You were hardly in a position to single-handedly fight off the entire German army, were you? Remember, I lost two brothers and a father. I'd never blame a *British* commanding officer for their deaths, so why would anyone blame you?' She strokes his arm and he stops himself from tossing her hand aside. She will never understand and her sympathy sickens him. It's why he can't bear to talk about it.

'You mustn't be modest, Edward,' she is saying. 'Please tell me, what *exactly* did you do?'

He presses her free hand with his, keeping his temper in check. This is a conversation they must have. Once it's done, it will be over and he'll never have to repeat it. 'You have a right to know. I'm sorry. It was towards the end of the fight for Passchendaele, in early November 1917. I was a captain, in command of a company, charged with advancing on German positions. We'd been under hours of heavy fire and the men were exhausted and utterly demoralised. The whole company had been suffering heavy casualties all morning. We were almost completely surrounded by enemy positions and on the brink of collapse.' He stops as they reach the garden gate. Holds it open for her.

They walk close together as the path is narrow, just room for two, side by side, Byron rushing off, pale tail waving in delight as he goes in search of rabbits. Edward takes himself back to the heat of the battle. 'I realised that a machine gun on our flank was causing the bulk of the casualties. I also knew we couldn't hold out much longer. So, I did what any good soldier should do, I quickly assessed the situation and noticed an opening on the flank. It was a now-or-never chance...' Edward stops talking.

'What happened next?' Eleanor prompts.

'I didn't hesitate,' he says, eyes on the path in front of him. 'I had to try to save my men. There was the tiniest chance of success, but it *was* a chance, and I had to take it. So I shot out of the safety of the trench and rushed the machine gun. There was a crew of four. One was taking a piss, two having a smoke and the fourth was practically asleep on the job. Fortunately for me, they were too slow to see my ambush. I screamed and fired on them mercilessly. Got the pissing guy straight away and the others, just young boys too, I suppose, were somehow paralysed by fear from the ferocity of my attack. Single-handedly, I managed to kill the whole crew of four.'

'No!' Eleanor gasps. 'But Edward, that was unbelievably brave. Was that what they awarded you the medals for?'

Edward nods. 'That was part of it, yes. But there is more.'

'Go on,' breathes Eleanor.

'I had control of the machine gun and I was angry, Eleanor – you understand?' He turns to her, searching her face. Are her eyes moist?

'Edward,' she says, 'I don't judge you harshly for killing those men. It was war, and you did what you had to. You were protecting yourself and your men.' She squeezes his hand in encouragement. 'What did you do next?'

'I turned the gun on the Germans' own lines. I fired and fired which enabled, not only a platoon, but the whole company, or what was left of them, to gather themselves and advance, raining fire on the enemy. The pathetic Huns then turned and fled back to their own lines. I was exhausted by this time, but I went on, trying to protect my own men with the captured machine gun, taking out snipers and deterring any thoughts the enemy might have had about any further advance.'

'Goodness! But Edward, you were incredibly brave! I simply don't understand why you don't accept that.'

Edward shakes his head. 'But none of it did any good, Eleanor. After that offensive, the Hun came back at us, revengeful, full of hatred. I lost all my boys in the end, Eleanor. Each and every one. I failed them. Hours and hours of hauling injured men, under fire, out of the mud where they lay wounded and dying, dragging them back to safety in the hopes they could be rescued by the Red Cross. Most of them died in the most awful way. But I can't speak of it, Eleanor. I simply cannot.' He realises he is shaking. Eleanor has tears rolling down her cheeks. 'What I saw – it was indescribably awful. And nothing I did made any difference. So why would I want accolades for my part in any of it?'

They walk in silence, just holding hands.

Then she pulls him to a halt and turns him to face her. She takes Edward's face in her hands. 'You don't need medals. You did your best in horrific circumstances. You *know* in your heart that you did all you could. That's all that matters. But Edward, you still haven't told me about the money!'

He smiles weakly at her. 'Ah, yes, that. One of the men – boys – I pulled out of the mud was only seventeen at the time, a boy called Porter. Private Porter. He'd been hit by an exploding shell. It's a miracle he survived at all, he lost so much blood, and was burnt so badly... But he *did* live, although his body was damaged horribly – and his mind was worse.

'To cut a long story short,' he continues, 'Porter was not in a fit state to take care of himself. He had several operations and stayed a long time at Queen's Hospital in Sidcup and other institutions where the doctors tried to put his mind and body back together. It didn't work. He went, in the end, to live with his sister, Violet. But she was married and had little ones to take care of and the family is not wealthy. She couldn't cope. She wrote to me in desperation to see if there was something I could do. So I did what I thought was the right thing. I paid for Porter to be taken care of at the Red Cross Centre at Heath Colony. It's actually a colony of epileptics, but it has this centre which looks after the war damaged. I've paid for Porter's care there ever since.'

Eleanor stares at Edward, her mouth wide open as though in astonishment. He suspects this is far from any of the scenarios she had imagined. 'But,' she says after a pause,

'I simply do not understand the necessity for such secrecy. Why?'

'I didn't want a fuss. I didn't want medals. One life. That's all I saved. All the others – gone. How could I be celebrated for that? I didn't want to speak of it, or think of it, or have any praise for it. It was better that nobody knew. Violet was happy to keep it all secret too. It made things awkward. They're a proud family and don't want to be seen accepting charity.'

'My God! Oh, Edward, how could I *ever* have doubted you.' She cups his face in her hands and pulls him in close.

'I should have told you,' he says softly, stroking her cheek. 'I'm sorry. I'm not the best at...' He hesitates, picks his words carefully. 'Opening up. And I have been away from home too much lately. So it's no wonder...'

She smiles and takes his hand. They begin to walk again.

'Listen,' he says, 'about my workload keeping me away from home; I have an idea, which might help just a little.' She looks up at him. 'I'll be presenting the findings of my large research project in support of the proposed legislation to the Royal Commission in just a few weeks. It's an awful lot of work and I need help – but I'd rather not take on a student for the job because it's important that the analysis is done correctly, the right conclusion reached. Students are prone to going off on tangents of their own, thinking they'll impress by reaching some controversial conclusion which doesn't tally with mine. This is too important, Eleanor,' he presses. 'I need someone I can trust *absolutely* to get it right because the risk of assuming the wrong inference from this vital research is too great. So I was thinking, perhaps you could help? You are so clever and efficient at this sort of thing and it would really make a difference. It would also mean we could work on it together – here, at Brook End. It would be a wonderful excuse to spend more time at home, with you.'

Her eyes shine with excitement. 'Really? Do you mean it?'

'Yes,' he laughs, 'I mean it! You used to work with me before we married, so I do know what you are capable of!'

'Oh Edward! But that would be wonderful! I loved my job with you. Of course, I love being married to you, but I do miss working and we were a team, weren't we, you and I?'

'Yes,' he smiles, 'we were, and we still are.'

And then, with a leap, she is in his arms, kissing him, full and tender on the lips.

Kisses him like she has never kissed him before.

Edward lies on his back, Eleanor tucked, still fast asleep, into his side. Her head is on his chest, her hair falling over his shoulder, tickling his skin. The soft light of early morning seeps in around the curtains and he stares at the ceiling, allowing the pleasures of their lovemaking last night to replay in his mind. A wave of desire surges through him and he wonders if she'd object if he woke her, so they can do it all over again.

He peers at the clock hanging on the wall. He can just make out the hands. It isn't yet six and he doubts if she would be too happy if he wakes her so early on a Sunday morning. He is content to wait. It is enough just to be here, back in her bed, her body touching his, listening to her soft, even breath as she sleeps.

The hour may be early, but Edward is refreshed. Gone is the muzzy head he so often wakes with. A new energy surges through his veins. He slept better last night than he has in months. Things *will* be good again. Today he must tackle the subject of Mabel – and how much better to do this now, when they are on good terms again. Eleanor shifts, her head sliding off his chest and onto her pillow. He props himself on his elbow and watches her sleep.

A cold wave of shame washes over him. He had intended to tell her the whole truth, he really had. But when it came to it, he couldn't do it. The words wouldn't come. The version of the truth which *did* come is the one he has trotted out before, many times. It's the story that earned him the medals which he couldn't bring himself to collect, and now lie hidden for the shame of it in his drawer anyway. Has he made a terrible error? Will she discover this latest lie?

It is impossible, he decides, and allows his head to fall back onto the pillow. There are only two people in the world who know the truth, and only one of those possesses the capability of telling it. What harm could there possibly be in allowing her to know this version of what happened? And for the most part, what he told her *was* true. Just... not all of it.

Eleanor stirs and her eyes flicker. Edward watches consciousness return to her features as she wakens. Her almost-violet eyes fix on his and she smiles sleepily at him.

'Hello, you,' she says.

'Good morning.' He kisses her gently on the forehead. 'It's lovely to have you here. I've missed you.'

'And I, you.'

'Oh, Edward. I feel such a fool about everything,' she says, more awake now. 'You do forgive me, don't you?'

Edward scratches his head. 'Hmm, I'm not sure. I think you will have to be *very* nice to me before I can properly consider it.'

She laughs and digs him in the ribs. 'Oh really. And just *how* nice do I have to be?'

'Incredibly nice.' He nuzzles his face into her neck. 'And I can think of a few ways to begin with...'

She rolls on top of him, her hair falling either side of his face as she lowers her lips to his, her soft breasts meeting his chest.

'Like this?' she murmurs, kissing him full on the mouth, so he cannot answer.

He melts into the kiss and pushes the wave of guilt away as his fingers trace their way up her thigh. The best thing is, he has his wife back. Nothing can be more important than that – and he will not risk anything which could undermine it.

19

Eleanor

Sir Charles Lawson is an impressive-looking man with a smattering of fine grey hair encircling an exceptionally large, shiny bald head. Natural or polished, Eleanor wonders suddenly, as he extends a hand towards her.

'Professor and Mrs Hamilton...' He limply clasps Eleanor's gloved fingers with his own rangy digits. 'Please,' he says, indicating the two armchairs in front of his desk, 'do sit down.'

Once seated, the doctor regards Eleanor with sad, hooded grey eyes. His expression is serious and Eleanor's heart swoops. *Please* let him have an answer. Please let this most eminent of neurologists, as Edward has described him, the man they have engaged to provide them with a second opinion on her treatment, fix her poor, broken Mabel. Mabel, who with each passing day slips further and further away, becoming a shadow of her former self.

Lawson sighs and shifts his gaze towards Edward. 'I trust you had a good journey here this morning,' he begins lightly. He pulls at his collar. 'Unseasonably hot for June, isn't it? And the traffic in London grows worse by the day.

Such shocking hold-ups at the junctions.' He shakes his head. 'They really must do something about it.'

'Indeed,' Edward answers. 'But my wife and I have been staying in our flat in Bloomsbury while Mabel has been in hospital.' He glances at Eleanor. 'She didn't want to be too far away, and she's enjoyed spending time with her sister and friends. Haven't you, darling?'

Sir Charles grunts. He looks down at the papers on his desk. Purses his lips. Clears his throat. 'I know you are keen to find out the results of my observations and investigations into your daughter's condition.'

'Yes.' Edward rubs the palms of his hands along the tops of his trousers, a nervous gesture she has seen in him before.

'We hope you can help her, Sir Charles. You are, to be honest, our last hope,' Eleanor says.

'Well,' Sir Charles begins, 'I've observed Mabel closely since she has been staying at St Mary's hospital this past week, both during the day and at night while she has slept.' He stares at his notebook with its tight, neat lines of handwritten notes. He taps his pen on it. 'Mabel, as you already informed me, is experiencing a worrying, and increasing, number of fits, or convulsions, as we in the medical profession prefer to call them. The child's situation, I'm sorry to tell you, is grave. Epilepsy is a complex condition and no two cases are the same. But we know there are some general patterns which apply in almost all cases. The progress of the disease tends to follow the same stages of progression, so to speak. Where the condition begins in early childhood, as in Mabel's case, there is an initial, early stage, when the convulsions first begin. If medical and other interventions are taken sufficiently early, it is possible that such convulsions may be cured and remission from the disease can happen. If, however, the epilepsy becomes established, then unfortunately, in the majority of cases, it becomes a progressive, degenerative malady. In these instances, mental deterioration is, I'm afraid, the usual outcome.' He pauses, letting his words settle. 'In Mabel's case, in just a few short months, her deterioration has been fast and severe.'

'But – can she not grow out of it?' Eleanor asks.

Sir Charles shakes his head. 'For some mild epilepsies, it is possible that the child will grow out of the condition. But in cases of convulsions with the severity Mabel has been experiencing, that is a highly unlikely outcome, Mrs Hamilton. Indeed, Mabel is suffering from many varied types of fits. Unhappily, she is experiencing some of the more unusual types, including hallucinatory convulsions and absences, as well as those where she falls unconscious. This is not a good sign. These types of convulsions often progress in their severity and do not respond well to medical interventions. And in a young child, they do, I regret to say, almost certainly affect the child's development. It's for this reason that Mabel is losing certain skills. It would appear that the constant fitting is causing damage to the areas of the brain controlling her speech, hence the reason Mabel is struggling more and more to find words, and it is possible she will lose the ability to speak altogether. Then there is the stumbling and tripping, the increasing inability to control her bladder. I'm afraid to tell you that these are all symptoms of a generalised epilepsy affecting her whole brain, and the damage the convulsions are having on Mabel's developing brain is extremely serious.'

The doctor's words crash and rattle in Eleanor's head. His lips are wet and glisten in the light of his desk lamp. She can taste something bitter as she watches the doctor's tongue, raw-steak pink, push against his teeth, spilling useless words about the catastrophe befalling their daughter.

'What we need to understand,' Edward says, face taut and drained of colour, 'is how she developed this condition in the first place. My understanding has always been, and you are aware of my work in this area, that there is a strong link to inheritance. But epilepsy is not known in either of our families.' He glances at Eleanor and she wonders again if he quite believes her protestations of innocence in this matter.

'Indeed, I am aware of your work, Professor Hamilton. And yes, there is, of course, a strong hereditary link, but sadly we don't always know the cause of the malady. We believe there are many complex causes – shock, or a fright of some sort. Possibly, even, a fright experienced by the mother before the child is born. Or a difficult birth, or family situation. Sometimes the cause is simply unknown.'

'So,' Edward's voice falters, 'it may not be faulty genes after all? And there may be no reason why our son, or even subsequent children, should get it?'

'None at all. But forgive me, I thought this was your area of expertise?'

Edward shifts uncomfortably in his seat and mutters something incomprehensible.

'But surely,' Eleanor says, 'whatever the cause, there is *something* more you can do for her. In this day and age there must be a better medicine than those dreadful bromide salts – they do nothing but make her sick and upset.'

The doctor looks down at her, taps his pen on his notebook as he speaks. 'Mrs Hamilton, these are the early stages of Mabel's disease. My advice is that we take all possible steps to arrest the development of the condition to prevent further deterioration. But I must warn you, the outlook is bleak. And it is no longer appropriate, I'm sure you will understand, for Mabel to live at home.' Eleanor sees him exchange a look with Edward and she wonders if they have discussed this previously. The stuffy room suddenly feels hotter. Sir Charles continues, 'She should be admitted as soon as possible to an institution, away from the prying eyes of the public, where she will be given the best, most advanced treatment to help her.' His voice is slow, patient. He speaks as though she is a small, and not very clever, child.

She turns to Edward but he is staring straight ahead, impassive.

'What institution?' she hears herself ask, a prickle of sweat spreading across her skin. She thinks of Edward's work, of all the lectures she has attended, delivered by the Eugenics Society, the sudden, inevitable, nature of it all. She looks again to Edward, but he stubbornly doesn't look her way.

Sir Charles is also looking at Edward, as though to gain his permission to speak openly. Edward nods his consent.

'There is a colony of epileptics, not too far from where you live, in the county of Sussex. It is within easy reach of London and I visit regularly. Mabel would continue to be treated under my care. Really, it is the only solution. Treating the epileptic child is about more than the simple application of medicine. Living in a quiet, tranquil environment, free from corporal punishment is key—'

'Our home is tranquil! And Mabel has *never* been subject to corporal punishment!' Eleanor exclaims.

Sir Charles holds his hands up. 'I wasn't suggesting for a moment that she was,' he says. 'But for many of our patients, who are perhaps not from such… refined and enlightened homes, this is not always the case. I am merely trying to outline that the entire environment of the colony is set up to be optimal for the epileptic, whether adult, youth or child.'

Eleanor opens her mouth to protest, but Edward reaches out and gives her hand a squeeze. 'Please,' he says to the doctor, 'do go on.'

Sir Charles folds his hands together. 'Medicine, as I say, is only part of the picture. There are many other important factors. Ensuring a healthy digestive tract is essential. Constipation is the enemy, so regular laxatives and the application of enemas and douches is essential. A simple, healthy diet is also vital. Not too much food – epileptics have a tendency to overeat, to the detriment of their health.'

'But Mabel *does* have a healthy diet,' Eleanor begins.

'Please, darling, let the good doctor explain.'

She shuts her mouth, the flush of humiliation burns hot on her cheeks.

'Mrs Hamilton, I'm not for one moment suggesting that your care of Mabel has been anything but exemplary; however, there are some very particular aspects to the epileptic and their diet. Let me explain. Nervous energy has its source chiefly in the albuminous and nitrogenised principles of foodstuffs.' He gives Eleanor a stern look and she pretends to have complete understanding of the doctor's words. 'Put simply,' he says, 'substances – proteins, enzymes, etcetera – produced by the liver which interact with the elements and substances contained in the food ingested, become even more critical when we introduce medication. Thus, for example, when we combine a controlled diet with bromide salts, the results are far better than if we do not reduce the intake of common chloride salts. Likewise, when bromides are used in combination with a purine-free diet, the benefits are very substantial indeed.'

'Purine-free?' queries Edward.

'Foodstuffs where the purine or alloxur bodies are absent or negligible. I'm talking about substances which produce excess uric acid, such as alcohol, although of course that doesn't apply to Mabel, but other foods such as sweetbreads, liver or beefsteak. In other words, Mr and Mrs Hamilton, at Heath Colony, unlike in your home, we are able to adjust the diet to ensure the highest chance of the medication's success.' He pauses and regards both of them with solemn eyes.

Eleanor says nothing, stunned into silence by the paralysing prospect of Mabel being sent away. Her mind freezes at the thought of her tiny daughter being placed in a colony of delinquents of the very nature described during Edward's lectures on the subject. Every single cell in her body is screaming, *no, no, no!* How could she bear such a thing? How could Mabel? It is unthinkable.

'Would you consider changing Mabel's medication?' Edward is asking. 'And what are the chances that she... That she might recover?'

'We will start by continuing with the bromide salts. These, combined with the right diet and environment, have been widely used to a decent level of success for many years. The tricky thing is to get the balance right in the blood.

Not enough bromides, and there is no therapeutic effect. Too much saturation and,' his eyes flicker over Eleanor. He hesitates for a blink, then says, 'well, that can result in unfortunate outcomes.'

'You mean fatal?' The word slips out as an accusation.

Sir Charles nods and doesn't meet her eyes. 'In extreme cases, yes. But that is rare and, as I say, she would be very closely monitored and the dose adjusted long before—'

'Death!' Eleanor snaps. 'What else might occur? What other side effects can there be? The stuff makes her vomit, surely that's her body's way of expelling a poisonous substance?'

Sir Charles leans forward. 'The medicine really can be most effective in children when properly administered, not by an amateur *nanny*. Especially when combined with the other lifestyle changes I will recommend. To answer your earlier question, Professor, if we can catch the epilepsy early enough in its development, we can achieve full remission in around 50 per cent of cases, initially, although long-term remission is more like 25 per cent. However, around 28 per cent will, long-term, experience a significant reduction in convulsions. That said, I must warn you that in just under 50 per cent of cases, there is no reduction at all.'

'Dear God, those are not great statistics!' Eleanor breathes. 'And in such cases?'

'If there is no benefit gained from the bromide treatment, there is a relatively new drug we can try, which has been in active use at the colony for three years now. It is a drug called phenobarbital. We have seen some good results with this medicine, although, as with any other treatment, it does not work for all.'

There is a pause. An idea begins to formulate in her mind. 'What are the other lifestyle changes you would impose?' Perhaps this is something they could manage at home. They could hire a properly trained nurse. Mabel would be safe and away from prying eyes at Brook End. 'As much detail, if you could, please, Sir Charles.'

He clears his throat. 'Well,' he says, raising his eyes to look out of the window at the square of bright sky and leafy green tops of the plane trees, just visible from his third-floor consulting room, 'apart from the concentration on a healthy, working bowel,' he turns his attention back to his visitors and begins counting points off his fingers, 'daily exercise, fresh air, spinal douches, massage, regimented sleep routine. For children, education within the normal system is completely out of the question. In the colony, we teach children in accordance with their capabilities. We combine the physical with the mental. It's a regularisation of the senses, focussed on coordination and mental exercises. Over-excitement and stress are to be avoided in all circumstances, thus ordinary school and education is unsuitable.'

Edward nods his approval.

'In later life,' the doctor shifts uncomfortably, 'it is most likely, and indeed advisable, that Mabel does not lead a life outside the colony. Even if we are fortunate enough to arrest the development of her condition, which, as I said, is far from certain, it is important that she avoid marriage. There is, as you know only too well, a strong likelihood that the condition would be passed down to future generations via the burden of her defective genes. This is why the colony will be the best place for her, as marriage is strictly forbidden. Suitable activities can be found for her within the confines of the colony. For example, quiet, indoor pursuits, such as drawing, sewing or even a little office work, if she were capable.'

'And if she were not?' Edward asks.

'Well, then there is the laundry, or the kitchens. The colonists must keep the houses and the school room clean and tidy. The men do the bulk of the farm work, but there are the chickens and pigs to feed.'

Bile rises in Eleanor's throat and she lurches in her seat, ready to run for the door if she really is going to be sick. She manages to force it back down.

'Surely,' she gasps, 'it needn't come to that?'

'You must know,' Sir Charles continues, looking at Eleanor, 'given your husband's work, what a diagnosis of this nature means in practice.' Why does she feel as though this is a rehearsed speech? As though his job here today is to convince Eleanor, and Eleanor alone, of the advantages of his proposal. 'The adult epileptic mind, is, I'm sorry to tell you, prone not only to criminal tendencies, but also to, well... I shall try to put it as delicately as possible... to a rather lewd and obsessive interest in sexual activity.'

'For God's sake,' she bursts out. 'Mabel is only *five*!'

'Ah, yes, but she will grow into a woman and it is as well to know these things in advance. Sexual activity in the epileptic must be avoided. It overstimulates and risks making the condition worse. Sterilisation really would be the best cure.' He pauses. 'Whilst it is not compulsory at the present time, *voluntary* sterilisation is, of course, an option. As her parents, and while she is underage, this is something you should seriously consider.'

The air contracts and Eleanor is finding it hard to breathe.

How can any of this be happening to them? All the work that Edward does... It feels like a punishment. *Sterilisation.*

'We do know only too well,' Edward's voice is distant, as though in the next room. 'And given the nature of my work, it is of utmost importance that we adhere to all that we believe in.' He glances at Eleanor but she is numb. 'I don't think we should be too hasty with the proposal of sterilisation. We have time to consider this matter, given Mabel's age, but I do wish to mention another, delicate, issue. I'm sure you will understand that there must be absolute discretion. It would be an impossible situation for me if it were to come to light that a child of mine has developed epilepsy, even though the cause is blatantly not hereditary in our case.'

The room swirls back into sharp focus. 'No!' Her voice thunders in her own ears. 'Mabel is only five years old! She is from a *good* family! I cannot – I *will* not let her go to such a place. She cannot be with degenerates and criminals and fully-grown, sexually deprived men. The place sounds terrible!' Her voice cracks. She stands up on impulse, steps towards Sir Charles's desk and leans on it, staring at him, panic rising inside. 'There must be some way we can keep Mabel at home. We needn't tell a soul about it! We can hire a nurse to administer whatever diet and medicine you decide is best. We can bring her here, every week, to see you. Please, I *can't* send her away. I won't!'

'Mrs Hamilton, don't upset yourself. Hysterics will not help.'

'Eleanor, please, sit down.' Edward has his hand on her arm. She allows herself to be directed back to her chair. It feels as though she is in the midst of a nightmare. If only she were back at Brook End, with her books and Mabel – happy, normal, *healthy* Mabel – playing on the floor at her feet. And Jimmy too, of course.

'It's out of the question,' Edward says, giving Eleanor a warning look to stay quiet. 'She cannot be cared for at home, can she, Sir Charles?'

Sir Charles regards them with his gloomy eyes and shakes his head. 'I'm afraid not,' he says. 'Mabel's condition is too advanced and remission is highly unlikely. It is probable that her condition will continue to progress and that she will deteriorate further. Should she survive into adulthood, Mabel will need to be cared for – for the rest of her life. Given this fact, and Edward's occupation, I really don't see that you have any choice in the matter.'

Eleanor stifles a cry and reaches into her pocket for her handkerchief, balling her fists to stop herself from allowing the tears to fall.

'I don't like to give false hope,' Sir Charles Lawson says after a pause. He clears his throat. 'Besides, we must look forwards, rather than back. I would say the feelings you will have when you let Mabel go are rather akin to grief. Mabel is not the child she once was. That child is lost and you must grieve for her. But you also have a healthy new baby, and no doubt will go on to have more. You must focus on him and future children. Mabel will be safe and secure in the colony. She will receive the best, most advanced care and treatment. She will be free from the inevitable stigma and judgement of wider society. Nobody need know whose child she really is and your own lives need not be adversely affected as they would be by keeping her at home. It really is the best solution for all.'

Edward stands and Sir Charles follows suit. 'Well,' Eleanor hears him say, 'that's settled then.' They shake hands, discuss niceties, make plans to visit Heath Colony. Whispered plans. But Eleanor's ears buzz and her body is weak. She is to lose Mabel. Sweet, darling Mabel is to become one of the *unwanteds*. She will experience none of life's taken-for-granted pleasures: a husband, a family, a home. There will be barely any school. No freedom, no learning, *no love*.

It is a life sentence. One that neither Mabel nor Eleanor will ever be released from.

Perhaps it would be better if she *were* dead.

Out on the street, Eleanor lets loose her fury on Edward.

'You knew about this, didn't you?' she throws at him, heat and anger coursing through her blood. 'You'd already discussed it with Sir Charles but couldn't bear to break the news yourself, so you got him to do it.'

'No,' Edward says, his tone measured and reasonable as if to counter her hysteria, 'I did not know what he was going to say. How could I? He's only just been able to assess Mabel.'

'I don't believe it.'

Edward shrugs. 'Believe it or not, his advice remains the same. You heard him. We have no choice. Mabel must go to the Colony.'

'Damn it, Edward!' She turns to him, hot, angry tears coming now, pouring down her cheeks. 'I won't let her go, I won't!' He stands there in front of her, his face devoid of emotion. How can he be so cold? How can he not care!

A yowl of pain escapes from deep inside her and she is battering his chest with her fists.

'Eleanor!' He seizes her wrists, drawing her towards him. Dimly she is aware of passers-by staring at them, treading a wide circle around them.

Edward wraps his arms about her tight so she cannot hit him. She struggles against his hold for a moment, then, as fast as it came, her anger melts away and is replaced by a plunging devastation. She sinks into his chest, heaving and sobbing. If he wasn't holding her upright, she would not have the strength to stand but would crumple like a ragdoll onto the dirty wet pavement beneath her feet.

'I swear to you,' Edward says softly into her ear, 'I will do everything I can to make sure Mabel is as well looked after as possible. We will *pay* for her comfort. But, Eleanor, you must know Sir Charles is right. Mabel has to go. It is for the best.'

'But surely,' Eleanor speaks into his shoulder, her voice shaky with emotion, 'there is another way. We have money. Why can't we keep Mabel with us? We can hire a nurse, keep her hidden away. The Royal family did it with Prince John – they hid him away but kept him at home. If they did it, why the hell can't we? I can't bear to send Mabel away, I simply can't!'

She looks up into Edward's face, distorted through the wash of her tears.

'And look how it turned out for Prince John,' Edward says, a note of urgency entering his voice. 'Shame on the family and, fortunately perhaps for him, escape by an early death. And it's worse for me, Eleanor. Surely you see that? With my reputation, with my work, we cannot risk

Mabel's condition getting out into the public domain. We will keep her real identity hidden and our daughter will receive the best treatment in the colony. She'll have fresh air and freedom within its walls, she'll have other children to play with. What will she have if we hide her away at home? No freedom, no friends. What if people were to find out? It would be ruinous. Besides, how could we watch her deteriorate?' Edward's eyes bulge and his cheeks are flushed pink. His breath is quick and heavy.

They stare at each other and, in that moment, she wonders if she knows Edward. *Really* knows him. Her husband, the Edward she thought he was, surely wouldn't be saying this.

'I'm doing this for you, Eleanor,' he whispers, as though in answer to her thoughts. 'I only want the best for you. For us. I love you. Eleanor, I *love* you.'

But his words light a match and something explodes inside.

'No!' she yells at him. '*No. No. No!*' Her fists are hammering his chest once more. She doesn't care that people have stopped and are staring open-mouthed. Edward is trying to catch her arms but she wriggles free and stumbles away from him.

'Eleanor!' he's pleading, 'calm down! This is crazy!'

'You can't do this!' she shouts as she turns and runs away from him. 'You cannot send my child away. I won't let you!'

20

Edward

Mabel is curled beneath the sheets, her mop of blonde hair the only visible part of her, spread fine as silk thread, across her pillow. Eleanor sits heavily on the side of the bed and strokes her hair. Mabel's face, pink and puffy, appears from beneath the sheets where she'd been hiding from this cold ward of iron beds, crisp, white-uniformed nurses and furrow-browed doctors. This is the first time they have been permitted in to see her since she was admitted to St Mary's hospital last week. Her face, at first pinched with fear and confusion, relaxes into a smile when she sees her mother's face.

'Hello, my darling.' Eleanor's voice is soft and low.

'Mama.' She sits up and wraps her fat little arms about Eleanor's middle, resting her cheek on Eleanor's stomach. She clings tight, as though she knows instinctively what is to become of her.

Edward looks away. The sight of the two of them, clinging onto each other is almost more than he can bear. After the showdown in the street, and after Eleanor had calmed and they had spoken of the matter once again, he had managed to convince her that his desire for Mabel to go to the colony wasn't so much to do with his work as that the colony was the right place for Mabel to go. It was in Mabel's best interests for her to live there. They could administer the drugs so much better, they were experts – and she would be with other children like her. Surely, if it gave her the best chance of recovery, that is where she should be, just for now. She would have playmates and Edward would ensure her care was the best there could be. Hopefully this would only be a temporary arrangement and then Mabel could come home again. He had managed to make his wife understand that if they went on as they were, their daughter was only going to deteriorate – and what mother wouldn't try anything to make their child better, however painful that separation might be?

'I have some good news for you, some great news,' Eleanor says, her voice breaking. She swallows hard, stroking Mabel's hot cheek. 'The doctor says you can leave the hospital. What do you think of that?'

Last night, as they ate dinner in the flat, they discussed over and over how to handle this moment. It was just the two of them, except for Mrs Timms, the daily, in the kitchen. She'd excused herself to get off home once the peaches and cream had been served for dessert. In the end, after much hand-wringing and tears, Eleanor had agreed, exhaustedly, to Edward's suggested approach. It would be for the best and less upsetting for Mabel. Children were adaptable and she'd soon settle into her new life.

Now, cuddling into her mother, Mabel neither moves nor speaks. Edward imagines how it has been for her this last week, prodded and poked by strangers, watched over by the unsmiling matron. It must have felt like a lifetime to a five-year-old who had no idea what was happening or why. She looks dazed, her eyes cloudy; her skin has a deathly pallor about it, and those unsightly lesions – God, he can barely look at her! Fresh country air will do her the world of good.

Edward pictures Mabel at Heath Colony, playing in a field of fresh green grass studded with wildflowers. She has buttercups tucked behind her ears, highlighting the golden tones of her hair. She is laughing with other children, watched over by a smiling nurse.

But he knows that vision of Mabel is ridiculous. That was the Mabel who now exists in his imagination alone. That is the one he wants to hold on to, the one he wants Eleanor to hold on to. That is why they cannot watch her deteriorate further. It would be too painful for them both. And that is the reason, although of course there are more, why they must never visit Mabel once she is in the colony...

Mabel raises her chin and looks into Eleanor's eyes. 'Mama, home?' She tugs on Eleanor's jacket. 'Home?'

'Shhh,' Eleanor says, stroking her hair.

Mabel suddenly winces and then cries out, bending forward, clutching her tummy. 'Hurting,' she says, pain etched into her face. 'Hurting, hurting.'

Eleanor opens her mouth to speak, then snaps it shut. She shakes her head. Beneath the harsh lights of the ward, her wet cheeks glisten. She gently rubs Mabel's tummy and the pain seems to lessen, the creases in her face easing away.

'Right!' Eleanor says in a falsely bright voice. 'Let's pack up all of your things.' She prises Mabel away and stands, busying herself, folding the child's few clothes and putting them in her case.

Edward takes her place on the bed and holds Mabel's small hands in his own.

'You'll be home before you know it, my little princess,' he says. 'But first, you are going to stay in a lovely place in the country where you can run around outside and get lots of fresh country air, not like in here.' She rewards him with a weak smile, her eyes cloudy with confusion. 'They'll give you some medicine to help you, and tasty fresh food, and when you are all better, then you can come home. But first you must be a good girl and get lots of sleep and be helpful to all the nurses. You will get better much quicker, especially if you are good.' She stares up at him, eyes wide, then she pops her thumb into her mouth and begins to suck, the fingers of her other hand stroking the flesh between his thumb and forefinger.

'You understand, Mabel?' he says.

No response. They sit in silence, then Mabel's thumb comes out with a pop. 'Baby,' she says. 'Jim, Jim, Jim.'

Eleanor stifles a sob and Edward speaks loudly to cover it up. 'Yes, baby Jimmy. Well done, my girl. You'll be home in no time and you can play with Jimmy when you're back.'

She nods once, then puts the thumb back in.

'Good!' Edward says. 'It's good that you understand and that you are such a big, sensible girl who is going to be very good for the nurses, yes?'

Mabel nods again.

'Professor and Mrs Hamilton?'

Edward looks up to see the stiffly starched ward sister standing next to the bed. He meets her cool, grey eyes and strongly suspects the woman has never smiled in all her long and tedious life.

'Yes?'

'It's time to say goodbye to Mabel now. Sir Charles has organised for a car to take our patient direct to Heath. Nurse Jameson here will accompany her.' She beckons over a wispy young girl Edward had not even noticed standing there to come closer. 'The car is waiting by the back door. It's easier this way. Minimum fuss for all concerned.'

She stands stiffly, poised, as though ready to pounce if Eleanor or Edward should dare to disagree.

Eleanor, head bowed to hide her tears, closes Mabel's little suitcase. 'I'll send the rest of her things on from home,' she comments to nobody in particular. Her lips lightly brush the top of the little girl's head and, it appears to Edward, using every ounce of effort, she says, 'Well, darling, Papa and I will see you very soon. You be a good, brave girl now, won't you?' She kisses her again and turns, quickly wiping away the tears with the back of her hand.

Mabel lets out a wail. Thumb forgotten, she begins to scrabble around on the bed, as though looking for something. 'Mama!' she says. 'Mama!' More tears and she throws her pillow to the ground, her face reddening as she becomes cross and frustrated. Eleanor turns to Edward, her face etched with agony.

'Mabel!' Edward scolds, 'that is not a way for good princesses to behave.'

'Oh!' exclaims Eleanor, 'wait. Look, she's lost Prudence.'

Sure enough, the ragdoll is found beneath the bed and Mabel smiles at the sight of her, immediately quieting and calming, snatching the doll to her chest and putting her thumb back in her mouth.

'There.' Eleanor pats Mabel's arm as she clings to Prudence. 'All better now.'

She picks up the pillow from the floor and places it back on the bed, then turns and sweeps away, walking fast between the lines of beds, as though, if she doesn't leave this instant, she will change her mind.

'Thank you,' Edward says in a rush to the ward sister. 'I think it's better if we leave quickly,' he adds in a low voice.

He turns one final time to Mabel. 'Don't forget now, my princess,' he says, 'to be good for the nurses, take your medicine and don't fuss. That way, you will be home in no time.'

Without a backward glance, he heads after Eleanor, hoping she isn't hearing the plaintive calls of her daughter echoing behind him as he hurries away from the ward: 'Mama, Mama, Mama!' And the soft sobbing that follows when she realises her mother isn't coming back.

Afterwards, Edward and Eleanor take tea in a Lyon's Corner House. Eleanor sits, pinch-cheeked and white-knuckled, gripping the handle of her teacup so hard he wonders if it will shatter in her hand. The stony silence between them is unnerving.

'It really is for the best, darling, you do agree, don't you?' he tries in a careful, gentle voice.

'No,' she replies tightly. 'You may be right, Edward. But I don't feel it. Not for one single second. It's as though my heart and guts have been twisted and wrenched out of my body. I can hardly bear the pain of it. I don't think I can bear the pain of it.'

'I feel it too,' he says. It's as though she assumes he suffers nothing. 'Let's hope it gets easier. We must keep reminding ourselves, it's giving Mabel the very best chance,' he reiterates, because they have been over this many, many times. 'And if we stay away and don't visit, at least for the foreseeable future, it will be much less upsetting for her. And like Sir Charles said, we must avoid as much upset for her as possible. He knows these things. He's seen hundreds of children moved into that colony.'

She shoots him a look, one where her eyes flash hot with fury. 'How long, exactly, is the foreseeable future?' Eleanor asks, her voice tight.

He hesitates, knowing he is walking a tightrope. Say the wrong thing and she could fly into an angry rage. 'I think it's hard to put a time frame on it. It rather depends on each child, Sir Charles says. We must be patient and wait until they tell us she is settled.' No response. Edward lights a cigarette and smokes it while they sit, Eleanor staring wordlessly out of the window, her tea undrunk.

She turns to him then, her mouth a tight, ugly line, her voice bitter. 'So, if we are no longer allowed to see Mabel, and we must keep her very existence quiet for fear of her whereabouts being discovered, why don't we simply imagine she is dead? She may as well be.'

Her words shatter inside him like a pane of glass. Dead. Mabel, dead, in all respects but fact. She is not in their lives any more, nor is she ever likely to be again, however much he dresses that up now. Eleanor has put into words what they both know, but he has been too cowardly to say, or even think. The sooner they both accept this, he supposes, the better. It's clear to anyone who looks at her, medically trained or not, there really isn't any hope. So now it boils down to how each of them comes to terms with the new reality. Each must deal with the grief in his or her own way, he knows that. It's how they deal with others they must still work out. The staff. The village. Their friends. It will have to be brushed as quietly as possible under the carpet. It will become an unmentionable and, over time, with luck, no one will remember, or only vaguely so, that they once had a daughter called Mabel.

It's how it must be, and, as angry as she is for now, Eleanor will come to accept it. She will have to. He shudders at the thought of the press getting their hands on the story. Headlines flash through his mind: *Daughter of Prominent Eugenicist Admitted to Colony of Epileptics!* Or, *Will Epileptic Daughter of Ardent Sterilisation Supporter, Edward Hamilton, Be Subject to That Fate?* Or *Does An Eminent Professor of Genetics and Inheritance Himself Carry Defective Genes?*

He tries a new tack. 'I think it will be important for you to keep busy over the next few weeks, Eleanor. To take your mind off—'

'*Nothing* can take my mind off Mabel,' she retorts.

'No. No of course not. But you have Jimmy to think of.' She doesn't react.

Night is Edward's enemy, an enemy he is powerless to control, and this night is no exception. His dreams are filled with nightmarish visions of Porter's disfigured features, somehow morphed into Mabel's face on his damaged body. There are disjointed pictures, like some warped tableau, of Mabel silently screaming, being pulled out of her mother's arms, Porter writhing in agony; the two of them descending into some Dante-esque hell of never-ending torment.

He snaps on his bedside lamp. Two thirty in the morning. The silence presses in as he sits, knees hugged into his chest, his cold, damp pyjamas sticking to his back. He gets up, strips them off and finds a fresh pair. The dry cotton feels smooth and comforting against his skin. He treads along the corridor to the bathroom and drinks a glass of water, staring back at his reflection in the mirror. A middle-aged man stares back at him. Hair greying at the temples, crow's feet around his eyes. How did he get to be old? It's a nothing face. Just a face, two small eyes, thin lips, a receding hairline. Why does he think he is more deserving of accolades than the next man? The water is not enough.

He fetches a tumbler of whisky then pads back to his bedroom. All alone in this soulless flat in a quiet corner of Bloomsbury, now that Eleanor has returned to Brook End, he knows there must be a reckoning. It feels like time is rushing relentlessly towards him. It's coming for him and he is powerless to stop it. He climbs back into his bed, props up on his pillows, and stares into his glass.

For a moment he is the little boy, aged seven, who first went off to boarding school. Small and terrified, he'd been cast adrift into a harsh and merciless sea of strangers. He'd been bullied ruthlessly by the bigger boys for his bookish, non-sporting ways, for his lack of aristocratic breeding and his unrefined accent. Edward's father had thought that sending him to a prep school, then to a famous public school, would open doors for him, hoped it would enable him to get on in the world and be accepted into genteel society. School society, however, turned out to be anything but genteel. It was brutal and unforgiving. As Edward grew and it became clear he would never be accepted as *one of the boys*, he kept his head down and worked hard. Fortunately, he was clever. It was the thing, in the end, which saved him. He used his intellect to survive – and in agreeing to write other boys' essays, and by impressing his masters, he found a way through. But he hated every moment – and so desperate was he to leave that he completed his final two years in just one, fleeing to the hallowed towers of Oxford to begin life as an undergraduate.

But Edward's vision of himself became moulded over time into that which the other fellows saw: wholly inadequate, too delicate and lacking in bravery to excel on the sports field, too serious and shy to be popular, deficient in good looks and wit and pretty much all the virtues by which his fellow students judged and ranked each other.

Things improved once he had left and began to be judged by his work and his intellect rather than for anything else. He gained a reputation for his valuable research and for his work with delinquent children and their re-education. He had found a place, a reason for being – and his battered ego dared to show in delicate green shoots.

But then, just as everything was beginning to go well, came the war. Edward's work in education had initially been considered of national importance. But as 1915 rolled by, it became clear that as an unmarried, healthy, relatively young man, it would only be a matter of time before he would be forced to go. With the growing numbers of casualties and new recruits, the demand for officers to lead these young men was high. Edward was neither a natural soldier nor a natural leader, but he was of the right class and he had to step up. He had to become a Man.

And from that day on, Edward acted a part. He pretended to be the man he wasn't, the man these rough young teenagers should look up to and respect. He acted like the person they imagined he was, and he got by. He almost began to believe he *was* that person, the man who didn't fear and who didn't run away in the face of danger. Until that fateful battle...

He takes a gulp of the fiery whisky and it burns the back of his throat pleasantly. It reminds him he is alive, here and now. But his mind drifts back to the war.

Edward had quickly been promoted from lieutenant to captain. Not through any talented leadership but through desperation on the part of the army. He had gone from having fifty to two hundred men under his control. Men, but not men. Most of them were boys, the eldest in their early twenties, and from all walks of life, from the sons of doctors and teachers, to those of shopkeepers, road sweepers and factory workers. Edward sometimes felt he had to be father and teacher as well as leader.

Private Porter was just an ordinary young boy of seventeen. As ordinary as you can get. After leaving school at twelve, armed with only the most basic reading, writing and arithmetic skills, he'd worked as a labourer at a builder's yard. Like many of the others, he'd joined Edward's company as soon as he'd finished his basic training. The poor young buggers hadn't a clue. They came out to the front, half of them not even possessing the proper kit, expecting it to be all gung ho and giving the Hun a good bashing. Instead, they found themselves descending into the stinking pits of hell.

But Porter was something special. Nothing was ever too much trouble. He'd go about whistling and singing, cheering everyone he encountered.

'Aye, aye, sir,' he'd say, his face appearing in the entrance of Edward's dugout. 'What can I get ya this morning? Fresh brew, natch, but how's about bacon, eggs and sausage?' He'd chuckle as instead he'd served the inedible bread made from turnip flour and a tin of bully beef. But somehow, those little jokes and his bright, cheery disposition made things, for a few moments at least, a little more bearable.

But the fight for Passchendaele was the day when Edward's world changed forever and the lie was born. Because there *was* no brave Captain Hamilton who saved the day. Captain Hamilton was, in reality, a quivering, pathetic creature who lost his nerve when it mattered most. The truth of it was that Edward lay useless and shaking in the trench, unable to move and to fight, unable to lead his men, and so it was Private Porter who had risked his skin. It was brave Porter who assessed the situation and noticed the opening in the enemy's flank. It was Porter who ran at the machine gun and killed the four crew with his own gun at close range. And it was Porter who took control of that gun, turned it on the Germans and demonstrated extraordinary bravery for the sake of his fellow men until backup and the Red Cross arrived to take the injured to the hospitals.

There. The truth, at last.

Finally, he has admitted it to himself.

Now all he has to do is admit it to the rest of the world. To his wife, who was attracted to him under false pretences.

To the authorities in London, who considered him to be a worthy hero and promoted him to a level which made everyone sit up and listen. Brave Captain Hamilton was a man worth listening to. A man worth marrying. A man worthy of adulation.

Meanwhile, Porter lay injured, almost beyond recognition, twitching and quivering and staring into the abyss in a hospital bed. Nobody expected him to survive. To this day Edward has no idea who hauled Porter to safety from where he lay in the mud of no man's land. The commanding officers and the Red Cross assumed it was Edward, who by then was wandering around like a dazed idiot, muttering and crying. They congratulated him wholeheartedly on his bravery and he never dissuaded them of their misinterpretation of the situation. He let the world think he, Edward, deserved all the praise.

But Porter *did* survive, albeit with no memory of the event whatsoever. He was fed the same false story as everyone else and believes he has Edward to thank for his life – or what's left of it.

People treated Edward differently when they considered him to be brave and worthy and he wallowed in their respect. For the first time in his life, he mattered. Women noticed him, *flirted* with him. It was a whole new world and he revelled in it.

And then came Eleanor. The moment he had set eyes on her, he'd been in love. Before his foray into hero-hood, she would never have given a second glance to the man he really was – is. She would have glanced at him and moved on quickly. Indeed, it was the false Edward who had made that brazen approach in the first place, depositing the note on her desk. No girl would have gone to meet a coward in the café. What girl wouldn't have wanted to come to work for the dashing captain whose name and picture had been all over the papers? He'd made sure Eleanor had sight of those... All these years built on a lie.

It had been fortunate, for him at least, that he had encountered her just when she needed someone most. She'd been grieving for her murdered mother. Murdered, almost fortuitously, if he can bear to think of it like that, by a man of the lower orders – an imbecile. Just the type he was hoping would soon be expunged from society altogether. And now, from his studies of the great followers of the Darwinian theories of inheritance, he is making this his life's work. Her experience and his interest in the subject had drawn them together, given them a common cause, and he, like the man he so longed to be, had been able to swoop in and rescue her and Rose.

Outside, the light strengthens and Edward drains his whisky glass, his head now pleasantly muzzy. He flattens his pillow and lies down. The room dips and sways. His eyes drift shut and behind the lids is Eleanor's smile, Jimmy's toothless grin, Mabel, pale and wan, Prudence clasped to her chest. There's the enraptured faces of his audiences as he spreads his expertise, his friends and colleagues at the very highest levels of government and society, the whispers of the title to come – *Sir* Edward Hamilton.

He is on the very edge of losing his grip on it all.

VI

Just as I foresaw, they've put her in the Babies Castle.
She's my girl now. Why not? Her parents have sent her away, so I shall keep watch over her instead. She's here all on her own, albeit under the watchful eye of Miss Manners, the matron and her rotating staff.

She staggers, woozy-headed, weak-limbed with muscle pain and nausea from the doses of bromide you give her. Why do you do it? The sickly drug doesn't stop me, and it makes her ill.

Babies Castle. This is not a fluffy heaven with toys galore, pet rabbits and entertainers. It sits on raised ground, across the courtyard from the main building of this colony of epileptics with its tall clock tower and the low brick-built hall, bedecked with flowers and cheery bunting. The hall is the only place you, the pompous public, are invited into. A showcase of good works of which the founders, with their warm Christian hearts, were proud. The founding fathers' vision: a training colony for the unemployable, and a home and school for epileptics. It was to be a place of secluded sanctuary and specialist care for those who your society would rather pretend did not exist. A lofty ideal, no doubt, but as always with you humans, your foolproof ideas and your grand plans fall short and become twisted into something else altogether.

The Babies Castle, even in the height of summer, has a chill to it. In winter, the rooms are positively frigid. How easy it is, as the dense night falls and the frost rises, to pass soundlessly from tiny head to tiny head lined up, as they are, in their side-by-side beds. What havoc I cause, pulling dozy-eyed nurses from the warmth of their beds to tend to their distressed charges.

The nurses and the doctors are kept busy here, with frequent visits from the likes of me and my friends – influenza and pneumonia, diphtheria and sepsis, mumps and tuberculous – and the odds of survival are not so high.

But there is another recent arrival who catches my interest. No, not an inmate – a doctor. A young and arrogant one, if I'm not much mistaken.

A Dr Eversley, who thinks he has solutions at the tips of his perfectly manicured fingers. Who believes in his own pale-faced, pockmarked greatness.

Who thinks he can get the better of me.

Ambition roars in this young doctor's blood. I see the danger that lurks behind his dome-shaped skull and in the fastidious attention he pays to the inmates of the Babies Castle.

I've seen his sort before. I've seen the cruelty they inflict with their experiments in pursuit of the greater good.

And as he asks the young nurse for child patients, the severest cases only, for those who have no visitors and would not be missed, there is a twinge of concern for my girl.

PART III

July 1929

21

Eleanor

Eleanor buries her face into Jimmy's hair, soft as kitten fur, smelling faintly of Pears soap and warm milk. At six months, he is bigger now, chubbier, his personality emerging every day. He is a jolly chap, full of smiles and enthusiasm for life. But he isn't Mabel, and the loss of her remains unbearable. Hugging him close, she screws up her eyes and tries to sing him a goodnight lullaby, as she always did with Mabel.

Lullaby, and goodnight, with roses bedight
With lilies o'er spread is baby's wee bed

Her voice wobbles and cracks as the vision and feel of Mabel in her arms comes crashing into her mind. She swallows hard and tries to concentrate on Jimmy, whose soft cheek now rests against hers, his breathing shallow and even in her ear.

Lay thee down now and rest, may thy slumber be
*   blessed*
Lay thee down now and rest, may thy slumber be
*   blessed...*

She kisses him gently, laying him in his cot. 'Goodnight, little Jimmy,' she says, as she tiptoes out of the nursery, 'sleep tight,' and she wipes the tears from her cheeks before anyone can see.

After dinner, Eleanor goes to Edward's study where a large rectangular table has been moved next to the window for Eleanor to work at. The raw data relating to Edward's research are spread in neat piles and she has a typewriter set up at one end in order to type up the findings which will be added to Edward's final report, backing up his recommendations, which in turn will be presented soon to the Royal Commission, in support of the proposed legislation for the mentally defective.

She frowns. It is hard to study this subject matter knowing how their own daughter's intellect has been affected by her illness. Edward seems able to separate his intellect from his emotions and lose himself in the numbers. She is finding this increasingly difficult; the more she learns about each of these children, the more she is reminded of Mabel's deterioration – which she is briefed on monthly in Sir Charles's reports to Edward. She can see the pain on his face when he hands them over to her. A boot in the belly would be less painful. The latest one arrived only yesterday.

Mental Assessment Notes – Mabel Hamilton, aged 5

Noticeably backward for age. Feeble-minded, mental reaction slow. Has difficulty in answering yes or no correctly to simple questions. Does not remember instructions. Uses only simple words. She couldn't be induced to do anything purposeful or take part in proper conversation, running around the room in an uncontrolled way chattering disjointed words. Couldn't name coins or count on her fingers. No change from previous mental assessment.

She had not been able to read on and feels sick at the memory of it. She forces herself to look back at the paperwork. She promised Edward her help. So she must. She takes a deep breath, gathers her strength and picks up the summary sheets. She must try not to see each of the children and the adults who form part of the study as individuals. Instead, they must become a case number. A case number isn't a real person any more. Identified by age, class, educational attainment, they are transformed into data. Something which can be analysed, chopped and categorised, a tiny number, devoid of any feeling or personality, an infinitesimally small element of a much bigger story.

From that story, nationwide policy will be formed.

Edward has given her clear guidance on what he has set out to prove with this research. 'What we need to show, in essence,' he told her, 'is that a *minimum* of 80 per cent of intelligence is inherited. A high percentage of accuracy is necessary to reassure both Parliament and the public that, what some will see as a drastic measure, is highly necessary if we are to save our population from its steady but assured descent. The least intelligent in society have the highest fertility. The most intelligent, the least. It does not take a genius,' he'd chuckled at his own joke, 'to work out how things will go if we allow this situation to go on unchecked. Now, this has been a complex study and environmental factors play a role, but a minimal one in comparison to the hereditability factor. I am also keen to convey the strong hereditability of disease and the link between all of these and the criminal mind.'

Eleanor knows full well what he had meant in that last statement. The link between the criminal mind and the epileptic. One aim of his research is to prove the generally accepted view that epileptics are predisposed to criminal tendencies is correct Neither of them speak the word *epileptic* out loud any more.

Eleanor has spent the last few weeks systematically working through Edward's meticulously recorded case studies to pull out the data and write it into neat columns for his analysis. The case studies are divided into boys and girls, men and women, age categories and class within the population. Each subject had been put through a battery of tests and was observed for certain variables, namely: speed, accuracy, persistence and discriminating powers. Those charts of data are passed to Edward who performs complicated mathematical factor analysis to determine correlations, variables and common factors.

Thus far, Edward's results have been incredibly consistent. Of most interest are the results of children who have been taken away from birth parents and adopted. These invariably have come from the lower orders and been placed with middle-class or upper-class families and given every educational advantage. But their outcomes, overall, remain consistent with their birth class. They do not perform as well as the birth children of those parents in the higher orders, which proves Edward's theory is correct.

Just before nine, Mrs Faulks knocks on the door and asks Eleanor if she wants anything. Eleanor accepts her offer of a hot cup of cocoa.

Eleanor goes back to her case studies. There is something odd... Perhaps she is just tired, but Edward has highlighted in his report that a battery of intelligence tests were carried out on one hundred and twenty cases of adopted children and young adults, but fifty-three of them are missing. Eleanor can find the raw data for only sixty-seven of them. The results from the sixty-seven are consistent with Edward's findings, so what has happened to the rest? She re-examines all her piles of paper. They definitely aren't there. But how could they have got separated? When Eleanor had worked for Edward before they were married, he had always been so careful, so organised. She scratches her head. Has she somehow mislaid them?

Mrs Faulks delivers the cocoa and it's rich and thick.

Eleanor tells herself Edward must simply have refiled the missing data. She wanders over to look through the files neatly stacked on the bookshelves. There is nothing there. A fear begins to stir in the pit of her belly that she got rid of them by mistake two days ago when she was clearing out a load of scrap paper. Edward had been scrawling equations in his messy, spidery writing over endless sheets to ensure he had the correct model and methodology for his study.

'For any useful factor analysis,' he had explained to her, 'one must include variables. For example, if we administer a problem to different subjects, they may all solve it, but take differing speeds to do so, or they may only partially solve it, or abandon the attempt rather than try and fail. One must factor the most important of these variables into the results.'

He had spent days working on which factors and variables to include in his model, and she had asked if she could get rid of the abandoned workings. Could it be possible that she got rid of all raw data in error?

Her pulse quickens and her skin grows cold as she examines every inch of the study. Finally, in desperation, she begins to search Edward's desk and the boxes he has yet to unpack, just in case they were mistakenly filed in there.

Biting her lip, she wonders how on earth she is going to break this to Edward. Without this missing data, is the entire study in jeopardy? God, what is she to do? Barely able to breathe, she checks through all the drawers in his desk, although she knows there will be nothing there.

But hang on, there they are! Why on earth has Edward put them in the bottom drawer, beneath a pile of scrap paper? It must have been a mistake, she reasons, as she pulls them out.

She exhales with relief. It's odd, because she had always thought Edward to be so regimented and meticulous about everything he did, from his wardrobe to his work. But now she has begun working with him again, she can see there are little inconsistencies – mistakes, even – or a general lack of attention to detail. He has seemed to have developed a tendency towards slapdashery in his work. Undoubtedly the result of the combination of a genius mind combined with overwork. Another reason why he most definitely needs her help with all of this. She will get him organised and will make sure this, well, *negligence*, in his work practices is carefully managed, without him even noticing it is being done. That is where a good woman can excel – by supporting a man in his work, she is enabling him to become better! She nods to herself.

She takes the bundle to her own desk. There is too much to go through now. Indeed, from the looks of it, it will take her several days to plough through it all. No, she will leave it for now and come back to it in the morning when she is fresh. She will find a way to apologise to Edward at some point that this data wasn't tied up with his report sooner, and blame herself for mislaying them, although it was unquestionably Edward who must have shoved them in there by mistake.

It isn't until Friday that Eleanor manages to get back to the fifty-three missing records. As she examines them, she sees that something doesn't appear to be quite right. These test results relate to the adopted children, although not all. There are additional, unaccounted for results here, as well as the missing fifty-three. But all of the missing records concern children from the most deprived backgrounds – the worst of the social classes, whether adopted or not. But despite the children's backgrounds, the results in every one of them are wholly inconsistent with all of the other findings.

Unless she has made some sort of mistake, which is quite likely given her lack of mathematical ability, these records show scores much higher than they should, if the 80 per cent correlation between intelligence and inheritance is correct. Edward's report, which specifically refers to these fifty-three, makes this correlation clear. Or perhaps she has mixed up the parentages of some of these children? Or whoever collected the data has not categorised the samples correctly. She will need to discuss it with Edward, but first she wants to see if she can identify the error.

With a pot of freshly made tea, she settles herself at the desk and goes through each case study again, checking the details against her list to ensure she has correctly transferred the data. That all appears to be in order. She then checks the names of each child or young person against their background data to make sure they have been properly categorised. She has a separate file of the blood parents and their adoptive parents where relevant, their educational attainment and their social class and occupations. Even for the adopted children, their parents' lineage has been investigated to the fullest possible extent. There are only a handful of cases where these details are unknown or there is scant information available.

She separates these out from the rest, but even without these included in the numbers, the results still do not correlate with Edward's supposed findings. Fingers of doubt crawl up Eleanor's back. Could it be that the researchers have been slapdash and incorrectly categorised these children? None of the results are as one would expect, and some have performed far higher than they, by rights, should. Of course, this is to be expected, but only in a minority of cases, that is, less than 20 per cent. These results indicate that in the vast *majority* of these missing cases, children of the lower orders, despite the stated IQs of their parents, have performed in a similar way to those born of middle-class parents with a much higher average IQ. How can this make sense?

Eleanor does not want to accept the possibility that

Edward has removed these test results on purpose, so that overall, the accuracy of the results in all categories remain at 80 per cent or above. If these fifty-three are included, plus the additional ones Eleanor has found, that percentage of accuracy will be reduced greatly below 80 per cent.

Eleanor sighs. Edward's report is pretty much finished and he is finalising his recommendations. All he has to do now is write the introduction to his paper and it is ready to go. But now what are they to do with all of this? Her blood slows in her veins. Surely Edward can't put his report forward with these recommendations given her discovery?

Her stomach twists. She stands and paces the room, wondering when Edward will be back. He is probably on the train at this very moment, chugging his way back to Surrey. How on earth is she going to tell him?

She leaves the study and goes to Jimmy's nursery to spend a few minutes with him before he goes to bed. The door to Mabel's room remains firmly closed. Eleanor cannot bear to go in there and she passes it quickly, fists and jaw involuntarily clenched.

Jimmy is sitting on the rug chewing on a wooden teething ring. His hair is neatly brushed and he is pink and glowing from the bath Miss Harding has just given him.

'Evening, Mrs Hamilton,' she says cheerfully as she pulls the curtains and lowers the lamps so Jimmy knows it's bedtime. Is Miss Harding ever *not* cheerful, she wonders? 'Will you be reading his story tonight?'

'Yes, of course,' she replies, and picks her son up off the carpet. She draws her fingers over his soft cheeks and he coos appreciatively, still chewing on the teething ring, wet from his drool.

'What shall we read tonight?' she says, carrying him over to the bookcase.

'I'll leave you to settle him down then,' Miss Harding smiles, and gently closes the door behind her.

'Right,' Eleanor says, as she and Jimmy peer at the books together. 'How about some nursery rhymes?' He reaches out and grabs a handful of her hair. She pulls the book from the case and they settle down together in the armchair, Jimmy still with a fistful of Eleanor's hair in one hand, his teething ring in the other. She reads, Jimmy coos, squawks and chatters, flaps his arms and slaps the book a few times in appreciation.

'Well,' she says after they finish '*London's Burning*', '*Three Blind Mice*', '*Humpty Dumpty*' and '*Twinkle, Twinkle Little Star*', 'it's time to go to sleep now.' She kisses him and lays him in his cot, switches off the lamps and tiptoes out of the room, silently saying her goodnights, as she does every night, to Mabel too.

When Edward finally does arrive home, Eleanor hands him a glass of crisp Chablis and suggests the two of them have a drink on the terrace as the weather is so fine.

He sinks down onto a chair beneath the wisteria-clad pergola, and looks exhausted. He takes a slug from his glass and sighs. 'It's good to be home,' he says.

'Edward,' Eleanor takes a drink from her glass too, and, despite promising to herself she would wait until after dinner before she mentioned the data, she says, 'I wonder if I might have a word? It's about the project. I'm afraid there may be a problem. It could be that I've made some sort of a mistake. I mean, I've checked my work carefully, but it's still all wrong. The thing is, I noticed some of the case studies were missing, many of the most important ones. You know, the ones involving the adopted children. But it wasn't just them, it was some of the others too. I looked everywhere. With such a large amount of backing data missing, well, it puts the whole authenticity of the project at risk. I mean, such a study cannot be validated if you can't present the evidence, can it?'

He shakes his head. 'No, of course not, but—'

'And without it,' she ploughs on, 'how can you prove the very essence of what you set out to do? I mean, the 80 per cent correlation simply isn't there.'

'Yes, yes, Eleanor, I do understand the purpose of my own research project!' he snaps. 'Look,' he says more kindly, 'you should have asked me about this before. I know exactly which cases you are speaking about. I filed those separately *precisely* because of their importance. If you'd known that, you needn't have had all this worry. I've already included that data in my report and have the records to hand in the event anyone should wish to examine them.'

'What?'

'Yes,' Edward chuckles. 'You see, all this worry for nothing.'

'But... isn't the end result that they don't conform to your predictions? I mean, I thought they showed, on the contrary, that the correlation was significantly *less* than 80 per cent?'

'I've no idea what you are talking about, Eleanor,' Edward says, his voice tight. 'The results prove beyond doubt that the correlation is in fact *above* 80 per cent. Really, darling, do we have to discuss this now? I'm going to have a bath and change for dinner.'

Edward disappears inside the house leaving Eleanor staring after him in astonishment. She checked all that data with total care and the numbers are too perfectly conclusive. There's no deviation amongst them at all. Something so neat... It simply *couldn't* be right. It's as though Edward is trying to back up his theory only with the evidence that agrees with it.

Which means he must be trying to hide the truth behind the numbers.

22

Edward

Edward dresses after his bath with clenched jaw and jerky movements. How *dare* Eleanor question his methodology? He sits on the edge of the bed and ties his necktie so tightly it restricts his breathing. He jabs a finger behind it and tries to tug it looser. Damn, damn, damn! He shrugs on his jacket and hurries out of his room, seeing her door is firmly shut as he passes on his way downstairs.

In the study he goes straight to his desk and pulls out the bottom drawer. The records are gone. Double bloody damn. His pulse surges as he moves to Eleanor's table and yes! There they are. The audacity of her to search through his desk without asking! He flicks through the pages of her notebook. Pages and pages of neatly written notes, the data all carefully organised into columns and graphs in accordance with his instructions. He sinks into her chair and stares at them. At the question marks and queries she has written in the margins. He thumps the desk then goes to the small drinks cabinet and flings open the door, grabs a tumbler and searches for the whisky bottle.

Of course she wouldn't understand any of this. Why didn't she just ask him, rather than waste all this time going off on this hunt of her own? This is precisely the behaviour he was hoping to avoid by employing his wife for this job, rather than any of his students. And now he is forced into making some awkward explanation, as if he's been caught on the back foot. But it isn't like that. The knot of frustration hardens in his belly. She'll never understand...

But he need offer no explanation. Eleanor's discovery changes nothing. There is ample evidence everywhere to back up this policy. If they don't implement it, there will be no hope. America has surged ahead – look at how well their economy is doing. And all the other countries with this in the planning. Look at the research going on in Germany, fully supported by the up-and-coming National Socialist German Worker's Party under their leader, Adolf Hitler.

Edward finds the whisky and pours an inch into the tumbler, recapping the bottle.

This is *his* life's work, not Eleanor's, and sometimes things must be done for the sake of the greater good. A little bit of tweaking of the data to prove what they all know is correct isn't so wrong, is it? There are always anomalies and it's his job to interpret the data and account for such irrelevant bits. That's what Harry Laughlin and his colleagues did, so why shouldn't he do it too? Edward thinks about all the funding and support Davenport and Laughlin get from their wealthy benefactors – Rockefeller, Carnegie, Kellogg. He doesn't have any powerful backers behind what he does. He's got where he has, achieved the results he has, through sheer hard work and dedication to the cause. He won't let Eleanor and her inability to understand the bigger picture undermine all of this. He simply won't.

The door swings wide and Eleanor stands, dressed in a

dark-green evening dress, on the threshold. 'Ah, there you are!' he says. 'Would you like a drink?'

Her face is pinched and she doesn't reply. She shuts the door behind her and comes over. 'Edward, I'm sorry, but we have to speak about this.'

'Gin and tonic?' He turns back to the drinks cabinet.

'Please.'

Eleanor is hovering over the table as he returns with the drinks.

'I just don't get it,' she says in a rush. 'I mean, at first I thought you had forgotten to give me these records, or that I'd made some awful mistake and thrown them out. I was beside myself with worry. But then I checked your report and I could see you'd included data for the missing fifty-three. When eventually I found the records, they simply didn't tally. None of it makes sense.' She turns to face him, her eyes searching his. 'Edward, I've thought and thought about it. I've barely thought of anything else.' She swallows, her throat contracting and expanding. 'These results, the real ones – they tell a different story, don't they? One which doesn't reflect the hypothesis you were so certain of.'

He looks away, his skin burning beneath the intensity of her stare, clears his throat. 'You know, Eleanor, it would have been so much better if you had simply asked me, rather than dug around of your own volition. This is, after all, *my* research project, and consequently, I have all the answers.'

'Well, I'm sorry, of course. Perhaps I should have done that but—'

I have had to exclude them from my report.'

'What do you mean?'

'There was no consistency. Tests must be fair and equally applied, with the same variables so they can be properly measured. In the cases of the excluded test results, the variables were not consistent, so they had to be discarded.'

Eleanor is silent. He continues, 'To save time and unnecessary expense, I replaced the data from the discarded tests with data I gathered from different, but similar, studies, where I feel the variables were more consistent. By lucky chance, some of those studies also involved a high number of adopted children, too.'

'Edward...' She seems for a few moments at a loss for words. 'Surely you can't... I mean, that doesn't sound right. The tests on the children would have had to be exactly the same to be comparable? *Similar* can't be enough. I mean, just *how* similar were they? And where are these tests? Why haven't I seen them?'

'I've no idea where they are. They must have got lost.'

'*What*?' They stare at each other. 'Wait a moment.' She puts down her drink and picks up his draft report.

Edward takes a large swig of his whisky. With fumbling fingers, he lights a cigarette, breathes in deeply, waiting for its effect to calm his jangling nerves. Eleanor is being too smart for her own good. He watches as she flicks to the back of the report and reads, '*When one takes into account the results from the combined cases of adoption and children from the lowest orders, one can clearly see the correlation between hereditability both of intelligence, and the aforementioned conditions and behaviours, including delinquency.*' She looks up at him, open-mouthed, searching his eyes with her troubled ones.

'Yes, and?' He can't hold her gaze.

'*And*,' she says, slapping the report on the table in front of him, 'the bulk of those cases, Edward – the examples you have relied on to reach that conclusion – are precisely the ones you have excluded and replaced.' She moves towards him, her voice sharpening. 'Isn't that rather convenient? How could it be possible that cases you *previously* studied, and never mentioned, are so remarkably similar to these? How could you have got hold of two such large samples of children, of the same age, class and background, and placed in such similar households, but with such different results?' Her voice cuts like a razor and Edward begins to sweat. 'How very neat that they correctly fit into your hypothesis. How odd that my careful Edward has lost all of the raw data! The thing is, having seen all the other tests, it seems to me that the variations in these missing ones, even if they were carried out correctly, are too small. The differentials are too neat. It doesn't make sense unless…' Her voice is rising, along with her gesturing hands.

'Unless *what*?' He braces himself for the accusation.

Pink cheeked, body braced with hostility, Eleanor takes a deep breath. '*Unless you have falsified the results.*'

And there it is.

He stares out of the window where the setting sun is bleeding scarlet across the sky. 'That is some accusation,' he breathes, wishing they could put an end to this skin-crawling conversation. 'The fact is, the fifty-three cases you saw were incorrectly carried out and—'

'In what way were they incorrect? In what way did they show inaccurate answers?'

'Well,' he pulls again at his too-tight collar, 'in many

ways. I don't intend to go into all the technical details with you now.'

Eleanor shakes her head and lets out a snort. 'I can't believe it! You are not seriously going to send this? People will rely on this "evidence" to make laws. Laws on how to treat people. *People*, Edward, like your own *daughter*. It's too important! Can't you see that?'

Edward turns back to the window, to the darkening garden, trees sculpted against the fiery sky. He is mute, the lump in his throat threatening to suffocate him. He forces the last of his whisky down, relishing the burn.

'There would be no shame in asking for more time,' Eleanor is saying, softer now. 'If you want to rely on the earlier studies, well, maybe I can help? I will need to catalogue and check each one just as I have for these—'

'That won't be possible,' he says quietly, keeping his back to his wife. 'There *are* no records. There were no earlier tests.'

The tick of the grandfather clock from the hallway fills the yawning silence as his words hover between them.

'Dear God,' Eleanor groans, at last. 'How could you? I thought you were a morally upstanding man!'

He whirls to face her. 'Of course I am! But don't you see, Eleanor,' he pleads, 'the result justifies the means!'

'No!' Eleanor's eyes are bulging, her chin thrust out. Her hair is becoming unkempt and she begins to pace the room. 'No, I don't see. Edward, you must face up to this. What you are doing is wrong. It's *completely* unethical!' she screams at him. 'This is false data!'

'Now calm yourself, Eleanor! You're being ridiculous. It's not *false*, it's merely... adapted.'

'Adapted? Edward, I can't believe I'm hearing this!' She is fast becoming hysterical.

'Eleanor, Eleanor,' he adopts his most placatory tone. 'You are taking this out of all proportion. I am hardly making things up. There is evidence from all over the world which backs the same conclusion as mine. The results in the excluded tests were wrong, they must be. What we are looking for in science is trends. We take a small sample and sometimes it doesn't fit the overall picture.'

'Then widen the study! Increase the testing. What if your theory is wrong? What if the entire eugenics movement is wrong? The consequences for all the people affected – people like Mabel – is terrible! You have to be *absolutely* sure, don't you? Take more time.'

'We don't *have* more time. I'm presenting my report to the Royal Commission on Monday! This is the result of *years* of work. You are only seeing a snapshot of it. Do you honestly think I would be proposing any of this if I wasn't certain of its efficacy and value? There would be no point, would there? Think about it. Adopting such a policy would be an expensive act of foolhardiness. No, I am absolutely sure the facts stated in my report are correct. These small numbers of samples form only a tiny percentage of a much bigger whole. We need to act *now*, Eleanor. We must make policy which reflects the bulk of the bell curve of normality. We can't allow the odd piece of outlier data to steer us away from the necessary course. I am certain what I am doing is right.'

'Right! What the hell is *right*? I honestly don't know any more!' Eleanor clasps her head in her hands. She is trembling and shaking, whether with rage, or anxiety or nerves,

Edward cannot tell. But she is incapable now of listening to reason and is rapidly losing control of herself. He wishes to the depth of his being that he had never allowed her to help him with this damned project.

He reaches out to take her into his arms but she slaps him away.

'*Don't!* You cannot seriously think I will allow you to present that report to Parliament, when it is full of inaccuracies and discrepancies and falsified data?'

Edward sighs and puts his hands in his pockets, returning to the window to look out at the sunset. 'Eleanor,' he says with a supreme effort of patience and control, 'this will go off as planned on Monday to those who are looking into the viability and potential benefits of legislation for sterilisation of certain sections of the community. They will be looking at a range of issues and this will form only one of those parts. The information in this will also be used by the Board of Education to change education policy going forward and to introduce the testing of children at the age of eleven to ensure they attend a school commensurate with their ability. This will happen, with or without this report. You need to put this into perspective; it is but a tiny part of something so much bigger. It's a means to a necessary end.'

'I thought I knew you, Edward Hamilton,' Eleanor says, her voice low and tremulous. 'I thought you were an upstanding man, someone whose integrity was beyond reproach. I don't know what to think about all this. I honestly don't.'

'But Eleanor—'

'Lies have a habit of catching up with people, you know.' She stares at him, unblinking, then, through lips stretched thin, she says, '*The truth, Edward, is a platform that will never let you down.*' With that she turns and slams her way out of the room, leaving Edward staring after her, his drink resting in one hand. He exhales slowly. Women! Eleanor will calm down and see that this really isn't worth her getting so het up about. He will make sure, however, not to discuss the topic with her again. A man needs harmony in his home; rows like this are for other married couples. Not his.

He picks up the post from his desk and makes his way to the dining room to eat his evening meal alone.

After he has finished, he slices open the letters with the cheese knife, Eleanor not being there to chastise him for its improper use. Bills mostly, an invitation to dinner with the Leytons and a letter asking for donations for the tombola at the annual village summer fête. He opens the last letter. It is from Sir Charles and contains the latest summary of Mabel's condition and progress with the medication. It always makes for painful reading, and today's letter is no exception.

31st July, 1929

Dear Edward,

Further to my correspondence of 28th June, I summarise below the situation to date in respect of your daughter, Mabel.

As mentioned in my previous letter, having increased the bromide salts to the maximum dose possible, and despite making the necessary changes to Mabel's diet and lifestyle, her condition has continued to deteriorate at exceptional speed.

I mentioned we were considering starting Mabel on the new medication, phenobarbital. We are withdrawing the bromides gradually and have begun to introduce the phenobarbital. It is too early to gain any meaningful insight into its effects as the introductory doses are currently below the therapeutic level. The dose must be increased gradually over time. We carry out regular assessments on Mabel, and she is officially now classed as weak-minded.

In respect of her future at Heath Colony, as I'm sure you are aware, to function well, we have to have a minimum intelligence quotient level of colonists. Anyone below the required level must be sent to an asylum instead. IQ is assessed regularly, and I do not need to appraise you of the tests as undoubtedly these will have been designed by your good self! For now, do not concern yourself with the matter which will be taken to the board. I will ensure Mabel's situation at the Colony is secured, at least until such time as we can be more certain of her future prospects.

Yours,

Charles Lawson, KB

Can the evening get any worse? How is Edward going to pass this bleak piece of news onto his wife after their awful row? He thinks of Mabel and her deterioration. If this legislation *is* passed, then there really will be no prospect of her ever leaving an institution. She will be caught within its reach. All it would need, when she reaches her teenage years, would be a signature from Edward and then she would be destined for the operating table too, to cut away any prospect of her having a family. And he wonders then about all the other countless families like his, who have an unpalatable secret in their midst.

He thinks of Eleanor's fury with him. And his stomach churns uncomfortably as he considers the faint possibility that she might be right. *Could* those test results be showing a more complicated picture than he had imagined? No, he tells himself firmly. He cannot let their own personal tragedy with Mabel cloud his cold reason. He must not allow his own emotions or Eleanor's to take hold.

VII

*O*h this crazy game. This spin of the dice.

Sometimes the mouse gets away. The cat loses interest, just for a second, and its prey sees its chance.

For the cat, there is always another mouse.

But in our game, I'm not losing interest. Not yet. Not with this girl.

And so I watch as the doctor, the old one with the grey beard and sad eyes, Sir Charles Lawson, shakes his head as he looks at her. She's a shadow of her former self, no longer lively and gay, as she once was when she laughed and sang with her mother and the doll named Prudence.

Prudence now lies on the floor beneath the girl's iron bed, skinny cloth arms and legs flung out, yellow wool hair covering the face. The girl herself hovers on the edge of sleep and wakefulness, her head whirling and muzzy from the medicine. She has the sensation that the bed dips and spins as though on the high seas. Nausea rises and she gags a little, swallows it down.

I know what you're thinking. That it's me who's reduced her.

But you're wrong. It's you and your medicines that numb her, slow her, slur her words and turn her into this floppy, pathetic creature who curls on her bed and faces the wall.

She wakens a little, lifts her head. 'Mama,' she cries out softly. It's one of the few words she has left in her shrinking vocabulary, and she feels around with desperate hands.

The old doctor spies the shape of the doll on the floor, sweeps it up and hands it to the girl. She snatches it and clutches it to her chest. With a groan, she turns over and falls back to sleep.

23

Eleanor

Eleanor plunges the trowel deep into the soil, scraping aside stones and dry earth, a folded picnic rug tucked beneath her knees to keep her day dress clean. Yesterday she worked all day removing the scraggly old roses in the border next to the patio at the back of the house and, in the holes she is digging, she will soon be planting the new ones. The August sun is high in the sky and Eleanor wipes sweat from her brow with the back of her wrist, leaving a trail of soil across her forehead.

She has taken to gardening again with renewed passion. It gives her something to do and the physicality of it is tension-relieving. She tries so hard to exhaust herself during the day, hoping that it will help sleep come at night, but so far it hasn't. Her feelings towards Edward are so confused and mixed up. She loves him, that can't be denied, and each time she thinks of him there is a physical pressure in her chest. But equally, she can only be so disgusted with his behaviour it feels akin to hate. She is furious with him for falsifying data which could spell what is, essentially, a lifetime prison sentence on those who, through no fault of their own, have some sort of *affliction*, for want of a better word, which society judges to be undesirable. Two days ago, despite her pleading with him, he presented his report to the Royal Commission. There is nothing now she can do. Unspoken between them is the fact Eleanor will no longer be helping Edward with his work.

The soil is dry and digging is hard work. She's sticky with sweat and her back is sore, but she pushes on. A vision of Mabel hovers. She is so angry with Edward for sending her away, angry for still forbidding her to visit. Does Edward ever think of Mabel the way she does? When he plots and plans against the unwanted in society, is there not a small part of him, as there is in her, a part whose voice is growing, little by little, day by day, asking: is what the eugenics movement stands for *right*? How can it be? She had always been so doggedly certain because it all made such perfect sense: better humans, less crime and disease. But through Mabel she can see it's not so simple as all that. And now, with this data which possibly proves at least some of the theories may be plain *wrong*, she doesn't know what to think any more.

And what about liberty and freedom and humanity? Should this not be a right of every man, woman and child, regardless of their state of health? How hard it is to reconcile and make sense of the desperation she feels for Mabel, with the hatred she has for the man who murdered her mother. They are both weak-minded. But Mabel isn't criminal, a murderer. How can it be that they should be treated in the same way?

She has not seen Mabel for weeks and, instead of getting easier, the loss of her is growing day by day like bindweed, clogging and choking, threatening to strangle her. So she has tried to fill her days to the brim with correspondence and pointless tasks around the house. When there are gaps in between, she gardens. And now, unable to bear the idea of spending next weekend alone with Edward, she has decided to invite Sophie and Henry, Rose and the Leytons for a weekend party. It's been almost two weeks since she last saw Rose.

She drops her trowel and goes in search of a cool drink. Really, she should be getting dressed and making sure the house is ready for today's visitors, due to arrive shortly.

Rose, who has been granted a day's holiday from the paper, is bringing Marcel. She telephoned last night, breathless with excitement to say that Marcel had travelled to London especially to see her and Eleanor on a matter of great importance. Since Eleanor had told Rose she approved of Marcel, at least after their initial meeting at Sophie's party, she wonders if they have become engaged. It would seem a little hasty, especially as Edward hasn't met him yet and Rose did declare she had no intention of marrying. With everything else that has happened, Eleanor has not found the right time to talk to Edward about Rose and Marcel's rekindled relationship.

Eleanor sighs. Rose seems determined to stay with this man and she is finally beginning to accept that this decision should be Rose's alone. By the time Edward returns to Brook End next weekend, Marcel will be back in Paris, so really, there is no need to mention anything to Edward until she has had this chance to meet him again and made up her own mind about him completely.

She drinks cool lemonade in the shade of the kitchen doorway, Mrs Bellamy clattering, more, Eleanor is pretty sure, than is strictly necessary, in the kitchen behind her, when the distant clip of Dilly's hooves on the road echo across the garden. The little bay pony appears at the top of the drive, two figures sitting on either side of Bertie in the trap.

'Oh lord, look at the state of me!' Eleanor exclaims and rushes to the bathroom to wash her face and hands.

They are already in the hall when she emerges.

'Welcome!' she says with a smile to Marcel after hugging her sister. 'Come in and make yourself at home, Marcel. Lunch won't be long. Would you like something to drink? I'm sure you're thirsty after the journey. I always find trains so dusty, and the smoke dries one's throat so, don't you think? I'll have Alice bring some refreshments.'

'Your hospitality is most gracious,' Marcel tells her as he follows her on his short legs into the sitting room.

'Please,' Eleanor says, 'do sit down.'

He sits beside Rose on the sofa and Eleanor settles herself into Edward's armchair after ringing the bell for Alice.

'It is wonderful to see Rose's dearest sister again!' Marcel exclaims, leaning towards her.

'Her *only* sister,' Eleanor retorts without thinking, then smiles, hoping to take the sting out of her words.

Marcel's eyes flicker. His hesitation is momentary and he laughs. 'But of course,' he says. 'I understand. She is very precious to you, and you wish to know that I am worthy of her, *n'est-ce pas*? Madame Hamilton, I assure you, I will take the best care of Rose. She is very precious to me also. I only hope I am worthy of *her*.' He smiles at Rose, and she blushes. Eleanor holds her breath. They *are* going to announce their engagement.

'That is sweet, Marcel,' Rose says before he can say any more, 'but don't be bashful. Of course you are worthy of me. And I know that Eleanor will soon love you as much as I do.'

Eleanor turns to look at Rose with raised brows. 'Did I miss something here?' she says, unable to bear the suspense any longer.

Rose blushes and glances at Marcel. She frowns. 'I'm sorry, Ellie. I really have no idea what you are talking about. You've not missed a thing. Marcel has come to London,' she explains, 'partly to see you – we will come to that later, but also to meet a big fan of his – a gallery which wants to hold an exhibition of his work. It's a big deal for him, isn't it, Marcel?'

Marcel gives a quick nod and a blush blooms on his pale cheeks too. Eleanor is certain she has never seen a man blush before. She exhales with relief. No engagement *yet* then.

'Anyway,' continues Rose, 'it means Marcel might have some real money coming in soon,' she announces triumphantly.

'I see.' Eleanor shifts uncomfortably in her seat. Discussing money like this is awkward and distasteful. 'Well,' she says, wondering fleetingly what Edward will make of it all, then dismissing it from her mind. Really, it doesn't matter what he thinks. 'That is good news. I'm pleased for you, Marcel.' She stops. She mustn't forget all the reservations she and Edward discussed when Rose first dropped her bombshell. 'Although...' How best to put this?

'What?' asks Rose. 'Although *what?*'

'Well, it's a dicey business, isn't it, the arts? One minute you are flavour of the month, the next, poof! It's on to the next new thing. Rather like authors and actors.'

'He'll do brilliantly. Won't you, Marcel?'

Before he can answer, Alice enters the room.

'Ah, Alice,' Eleanor says, delighted to have the chance to change the subject. 'What would you both like to drink?'

While Marcel confers with Rose before answering, Eleanor gives him a closer inspection. Dressed in a shirt, tie, slacks and blazer which look too thick for a summer's day, his appearance is more librarian than artist.

'Where is Jimmy?' Rose asks after giving Alice an order for a lemonade and a glass of red wine. 'I'm desperate to see him. He's such a dear – Marcel wants to meet him, don't you, darling?' He nods obediently but fails to look overly excited by the prospect of babies.

'Miss Harding will bring him down at teatime,' Eleanor says. 'Now, tell me Marcel, what exactly is it that you paint?'

'Has Rose not mentioned? I undertake experimental pieces. The genre I work in is an anti-art movement. We call ourselves the Dadaists. Do you know of the Dada movement?'

How can you be an artist, who is anti-art? Eleanor wonders. What a ridiculous notion. 'That seems rather… confused.'

Marcel smiles indulgently. 'It is an exploration of the wonders of the unconscious mind, an area being explored not only in art, but literature and poetry and free-thinking. But it raises the question too: "*What is art?*" It is a challenge to the viewer, to the art critics and to society. The idea is to engage discussion. To provoke a shock reaction. Above all, it is about thought and consideration of the world around us.

We are in the midst of a time of profound change, Madame Hamilton. We live in a world where the establishment is being challenged like never before. What is frightening to some, is exciting to others. The man on the street is gaining a voice, perhaps for the first time in modern history. I could talk of the subject at much length, Madame Hamilton. How much time do you have?'

Eleanor laughs. 'How very intriguing you are, Marcel.'

'Ellie, you *must* come and see Marcel's work. He is so very busy with commissions, but if this London exhibition goes ahead in the autumn, it will be an enormous success. He also has a large winter one planned in Paris. You and Edward should *both* come to that.'

'Well, I'm not certain it really is Edward's thing, him being a man of science, you understand. But of course *I* shall come,' Eleanor agrees. Edward would probably rather die than go to such a thing, but she has to admit, the whole concept sounds intriguing.

'Marcel is going to be known throughout the world one day, Eleanor. You'll see,' Rose adds, looking proudly at her man as though he were a prize catch.

Eleanor smiles at her sister, but doesn't reply. The age gap between them has always been there, but at this moment it feels like a generation, not merely nine years.

'Listen, Ellie,' Rose says, taking a glass of wine and waiting for Alice to leave the room. Her expression is serious. 'There is a good reason why Marcel wanted to come here today. An important and urgent one...' *Oh heavens, she's pregnant!* The room sways and Eleanor grabs the arm of her chair to steady herself. 'Marcel,' Rose continues, 'thinks he knows of a way to help Mabel.'

'Mabel!' That was absolutely not what she was expecting. She turns to Rose in confusion. 'Whatever do you mean?'

Rose snatches Marcel's hand in hers and gives it an urgent shake. 'Tell Ellie, Marcel. About Marie.'

Marcel clears his throat. 'It's a winding story, I'm afraid, Madame Hamilton,' he says, 'so please humour me. But I will try to be short. To put you a little in the picture, although I now live in Paris, my family actually come from a small town in the South of France. It is not a place you will have heard of, but my family have lived there for many years. Like most towns of a certain size, there are a few wealthy parts and many poor parts.'

'You're supposed to be telling her about Marie!' Rose nudges him with her elbow.

'Yes, yes. Apologies. I know I talk a little too much, but I come to the point. You see, my father is a well-regarded doctor in this town. For years he was, how do you call it here, a family doctor, I suppose, with his own practice. He had wealthy clients who paid his bills and kept him and his family – that is me, my younger sister, Marie, and our mother – in a comfortable lifestyle, but his real love was working in the poorer communities. He was deeply sympathetic with these people who could not afford his fees, so he did what he could for them and charged his wealthy clients a little more which helped to fund this work.'

'A real Robin Hood character, then,' Eleanor murmurs.

Marcel gives a little shrug of his shoulders, clearly having no idea about Robin Hood. 'As a youth, I used to accompany my father after school on his visits into the poorest areas. I saw the hardships and the problems. I also saw the way they were treated – with mistrust and disdain – by the wealthy people, who thought themselves to be altogether superior. Life was a daily battle, for food, for a job, against disease which always hovered in the background. There was no leisure, no let-up. Just the day-to-day matter of survival.'

'It is what influenced Marcel to become a socialist, Ellie,' Rose interjects, and Eleanor freezes in horror at the word.

'Go on,' she says, her jaw clenching involuntarily. She really wonders what Edward, the purest of capitalists, would make of this man – although, for a red revolutionary, he seems remarkably mild-mannered.

'Well,' Marcel continues, 'after some years, my father was asked to work in a large mental institution on the outskirts of the town. There are many different types of patients in this hospital. Some are suffering from depression illnesses, some from hysteria, or retardation, or they are epileptics. The problems are very varied. My father began to have a special interest in the patients who suffer seizures, in particular, the children. He did not believe, as the other doctors did, that their seizures are brought on by weakness of mind or hysteria or bad genes. The reason was because, and he kept the matter very much a secret, his own daughter, my sister, Marie, had begun to suffer from seizures at the age of eight.

'My father knew from his work that the therapies they were using often did not work. Some were, how do you say, *crazy*, old remedies. The bromides had horrible side effects, so he began to read widely on the subject, both as to methods tried further back in history and also the most modern trials in America.' He takes a sip of his wine. 'Well, to keep the story short, my father found, after some years of study and his own testing of these theories, that seizures, particularly in children, can be effectively treated through *starvation*. The method has worked for hundreds, if not thousands, of years on calming fits, although nobody really understood why.'

Eleanor stares at him, a sudden flare of anger in her chest. 'You are suggesting I starve my daughter?'

'No, no, of course not. The period of starvation is temporary. After that, if the diet is moderated sufficiently, the benefit is not lost. He tried these methods with Marie and for the next three years, she suffered no further seizures. They did return, unfortunately, when my sister reached puberty, but, with the help of the starvation diet, not with the viciousness of before. She is an adult now, still following the controlled diet, and she has very few attacks.'

'Oh!' Eleanor sits back in her chair, suddenly weak as Marcel's story unfolds.

'I didn't take so much interest in my father's work,' Marcel continues, folding one leg neatly across the other, 'and once I reached adulthood I decided, to my father's disgust and disappointment, that art, not medicine, was where my heart lay.' Marcel rests his fist on his chest. 'I'm an artist, deep in *here*, you see, and not so interested in matters of science. Indeed, my father considers me to be a failure in the highest order since I turned my back on the profession. But I believe the human spirit grows and develops through the arts, not the sciences. I am happy to leave the health of the body to other men. I am interested in the health of minds and *hearts*.' He thumps his chest and his voice grows louder. Rose nudges him, and he stops. '*Je suis désolé*. I get too...'

'Carried away,' Rose finishes.

'Passionate,' he corrects. 'Anyway, I left our town and

went to live in Paris, but this is another story, for another time. When Rose told me, only recently because she was afraid to be indiscreet, about her little niece and the devastating illness, I told her immediately about Marie and my father's work.'

'I am sorry for telling him, Ellie,' Rose says with downcast eyes. 'I know we are not supposed to speak of it, but when I learnt of Marie, I thought I must.' Eleanor stares at the pair as they grip hands. 'Anyway,' Rose continues, 'I really think you should try this starvation diet, Ellie. Perhaps others at the colony could benefit too. Maybe they even already know about it?'

'Oh, Rose, I don't know. It sounds so extreme. Poor Mabel has been through so much already. She is on two lots of awful medicine and still she deteriorates. The idea of starving her as well seems inhumane.'

'No, no, Madame Hamilton, as I have said,' Marcel says, waving his hands and becoming passionate again, 'the starvation is temporary. And the other medicines would be dropped. I took the liberty of writing, first to my father, then, on his advice, to the clinic where they are carrying out trials in the United States. It is a famous clinic, the Mayo Clinic – perhaps you have heard of it? This is why it has taken some time for me to relay this to you. I am a careful man and I wanted to be certain of all the facts. Since my father's early trials with Marie, further work and studies have been carried out at this Mayo Clinic. There is much to be hopeful about. There is a growing body of significant work on this starvation therapy, and what they have discovered, as my father had also realised, is that if, after the initial period of starvation, the child is given a very restrictive diet, then the fits do not return. I have brought with me the correspondence and papers sent to me by my father and the clinic. These include the latest research papers. I thought you might like to see them. Of course, they are rather technical, but I am sure, as an intelligent woman, they will make sense to you. Please, if you allow me, I will fetch them from my case.'

Eleanor watches in stunned silence as he leaves the room in search of his bag. Rose had mentioned none of this. One thing is certain, Marcel Deveaux is becoming a far more interesting prospect than Eleanor could ever have imagined.

After what turned out to be a rather jolly lunch, Rose takes Marcel on a walk to explore the grounds and Eleanor reclines on her bed, the afternoon sun streaming in through her open windows. She pours over the articles Marcel has given her. There are four, two in French, two in English. Eleanor's French is passable, but much of what is in the articles is technical language and she struggles to understand all of it. What she does glean is that a study in 1911 in France showed some improvement in two patients who followed a low-calorie vegetarian diet, combined with fasting. She always suspected vegetarianism to be a good thing and she vows once again to adopt it. The second French article explains the role of fasting in the treatment of disease for thousands of years, as detailed by both ancient Greek and Indian doctors. The author of the *Hippocratic Corpus*, a collection of about sixty Ancient Greek medical works, even mentions how abstinence from food and drink cured a man's epilepsy.

Eleanor sits up and puts the French articles aside. She picks up the first of the American ones. Birdsong drifts in on the soft breeze and her heart lifts for the first time in months. Perhaps, within these pages, lies hope. The first study, conducted in 1916 and reported to the *New York Medical Journal*, was carried out by a Dr McMurray who claimed to have successfully treated epileptic patients with fasting and then following a diet free from starch and sugars for the next four years. This, in turn, was based on the research of a Hugh Conklin, who believed that epileptic seizures are caused by a toxin produced in the gut. *So, not bad genes at all, then,* speaks that small voice in the back of Eleanor's mind. That same voice which prods and pokes at her from time to time about the morality and efficacy of Edward's grand research project. She goes back to the article. Conklin tested a method of starvation, except for water, for eighteen to twenty-five days. An impossibly long period without food, surely? She goes back to reading the article, in which he claimed 90 per cent of children were eventually cured of the condition, and 50 per cent of adults.

The second paper focuses on the work of a Russell Wilder from the Mayo Clinic in 1923, who, by putting his patients on a diet, dubbed the Ketogenic diet, rich in fat and low in protein and carbohydrate after a period of fasting, was able to reduce or eliminate seizures. This article, written by a Dr Peterman, seems to claim a lower success rate than the previous article, but perhaps this one is more believable.

She reads on. The starvation period was shorter and the benefits were maintained because, by not reintroducing carbohydrates, the body remained flooded with ketone bodies produced by the liver. Following the low-carbohydrate diet after this initial period, the body was tricked into thinking it was still starving, ensuring the ketones were still produced. It was these ketone bodies which had the effect of calming the seizures – and with none of the nasty side effects caused by the potassium bromide or phenobarbital.

Eleanor's head is beginning to throb. It is difficult to understand all the scientific data behind the studies. But she does understand the outcomes and the theories. It represents a chance. A chance it might work, when all else has failed.

She puts the papers down and rests her head back against the pillows. She thinks of Edward's studies and his determination to prove, despite the fact that neither of them know of any epilepsy in their own families, the heritability of intelligence, behaviour, and epilepsy. Why is he so doggedly determined to prove this? The legislation which will inevitably follow, will mean thousands will be kept in institutions all their lives, including Mabel, prevented from marrying and enjoying the very basics of a happy family life. It will mean forced sterilisations. And it will mean children's attendance at vastly different educational establishments, impacting their possible futures, will depend solely on a single test of their intelligence taken on one day at age eleven. Intelligence test results which, they all know, will fall roughly along class lines.

There is something chillingly inhuman about it. As though people of lower intelligence are somehow less worthy – *beneath* human – and therefore less deserving of a good life. Is Mabel less deserving of a good life?

The sun has gone in and the room grown a little colder without her noticing. She pulls her cardigan around her shoulders. Her focus, for now, must be on Mabel. These papers have given her a cause for hope and her mind races. Has Sir Charles read about this diet? Could they try it on Mabel at the colony? And what about other children similarly afflicted? Or, and she can barely let herself think of it, could they bring her home and try the diet here? Like Marcel's father did with Marie. True, he was a doctor, but Edward has money. They can spend some of it paying for a trained doctor or nurse to care for Mabel at home and to check on her ketone levels. He has, after all, been paying for that man he saved on the battlefield all these years. Or if he refuses, well, she will do it without him. She is capable of weighing and measuring out the food. But how could she check her daughter's ketone levels? And how would she manage the food? She can just imagine Mrs Bellamy's reaction if she had to cater for Mabel in this way, on top of her usual duties. There would be much huffing and puffing and possibly a resignation. But no matter. She will find a way. And this time, Edward will have to go along with her wishes.

Eleanor gets up. It is time for tea. Rose and Marcel must be back from their walk and waiting for her downstairs. She hurries to the nursery. Miss Harding hands her a very smiley Jimmy.

'All fresh and clean from his bath,' she announces. 'Sorry, his hair is a little damp still.' Jimmy's eyes are drawn to Eleanor's diamond necklace hanging at her throat. He makes excited cooing noises.

'Oh that's quite all right,' Eleanor says, absentmindedly stroking his damp hair and holding his hand to stop him grabbing at the necklace. 'That one's not for you, young man,' she murmurs, breathing in his warm, soapy scent.

'There is someone downstairs very keen to see you,' she adds, as his bright blue eyes meet hers and she smiles down at him. 'Come on then, you.'

As she treads carefully downstairs with Jimmy in her arms, Eleanor pictures them, Mabel and Jimmy, her children, healthy and happy, playing on the lawn in the sunshine. She has not allowed herself to imagine such a scene before and her heart aches. Tears well in her eyes but she wipes them quickly away. It is far too soon and she is getting ahead of herself. None of this may be possible, and even if it is, the chances are it won't work. Besides, she knows from bitter experience, it doesn't do to become too sentimental. Not now, not yet.

But in her bruised and battered heart, hope blossoms, and she resolves to make an appointment with Sir Charles at the first possible opportunity.

24

Edward

In a cramped committee room in some forgotten corner of the Palace of Westminster, Edward's head reels, partially with tiredness, and partially from inhaling the thick fug of cigar smoke. Around the table with him are Major Church, the Labour MP keen to introduce the private member's bill in support of sterilisation to Parliament; Havelock Ellis, the prominent eugenicist and council member of the Eugenics Society; Julian Huxley, evolutionary biologist; and, of course, Leonard Darwin, outgoing President of the Eugenics Society. Churchill declined the invitation, on account of workload, but they know they can count on his support. Edward's American friend, Harry Laughlin, sits beside him.

Last night Edward had had a terrible showdown with Eleanor. Clearly still angry about what she calls his falsified data, but what Edward calls, 'necessary filling in of the gaps', she had travelled all the way up to his flat in town. First, she admitted that Rose was back in a relationship with the Damned French Socialist, as he has come to think of him, and then she had ranted on about some nonsense starvation diet for Mabel he had told her about. She waved a bunch of papers at him, claiming they were proper scientific evidence – as if *she* would know – and told him to read them if he didn't believe her. Of course he would do no such thing. Anyone can make up evidence to back up a theory. He gives a snort of laughter at the irony of that and quickly turns it into a cough when he realises people are staring at him.

He had told her it was out of the question that they would take Mabel out of the colony on the strength of what a good-for-nothing French artist had to say on the subject. The whole idea is quite ridiculous – and cruel. He isn't going to waste his time reading such nonsense. In the end, just to quieten her down, Edward promised to consult with Sir Charles about the matter. If, and only if, he agreed it was something worth trying, which he very seriously doubted, then perhaps a trial could begin within the colony. There would be no point in taking her out, would there, if it was totally ineffective?

Harry is waving a copy of Charles Davenport's latest book, *Race Crossing in Jamaica*, at the assembled men. It shows, beyond doubt, he tells them, with rock-solid statistical proof, the biological and cultural degradation which results from the cross-breeding of blacks and whites. Edward, despite his exhaustion from being up half the night, tries to concentrate.

Huxley is listening intently. He turns to Church, 'I'm not certain we are going far enough,' he says. 'In my view the reduction in numbers of the degenerate is only half the story. If we are not to experience a catastrophic drop in the population caused by the birth control efforts due to the likes of Mrs Stopes and Mrs Sanger, we must do much more to encourage middle-class women to produce more children to better the race and to ensure the population is maintained at healthy numbers to avoid disaster.'

'I think that would be rather a step too far,' Edward says. 'The whole idea is somewhat unpalatable. Women as brood mares?' He shudders and can only imagine what Eleanor would have to say about that.

'But it is the logical next step,' insists Harry, 'if you think about it.' He has dark circles beneath his eyes and pinched cheeks. His shoulders slump. 'I fear we may all be too late, anyway,' he continues. 'There are dire warnings coming from several quarters that we are heading for a financial disaster – a total collapse of the capitalist system.'

'There are always doomsayers.' Huxley waves his arms dismissively, as though seeing off an irritating fly. 'Far better to look for facts than to listen to idle gossip and rumours.'

'But that's just it...' Harry leans forward to emphasise his point. 'The warnings are coming from reliable, sensible people. They say there is huge overvaluation in the markets and that a crash of some sort is inevitable.'

'Ah well,' interrupts Ellis, 'that may be, but can we stick to the matters in hand? Corrections in the market are the concern of the Treasury. I'm sure they are well aware of these warnings and must be doing whatever it is those fellows do to shore things up if it's true. Now back to this Bill. Do we have all we need in support of it? How is public opinion on the matter, Darwin, what do you think?'

'I think support is there. But that almost doesn't matter. Look what happened in 1913! There was almost universal support for the Mental Deficiency Act in its original format. If we'd been able to get that through, we would not be needing this one as every mental defective would have already been locked away and our problems now would be manifestly less.

'So what happened?' asks Harry.

'Wedgwood's what bloody happened,' Leonard offers gruffly, narrowing his eyes and waving his cigar in the air. 'Damned decent piece of work that was too,' he adds, staring miserably at his cigar.

'Leonard Darwin here wrote most of its major provisions,' Edward explains as Harry's brow knits in confusion.

'Ah,' he says.

'That dratted anti-Galton, anti-Darwin Liberal; namely Colonel Josiah Wedgwood, led a public, vocal campaign against our proposals, partly on the grounds of the enormous cost of running a Eugenic state, and partly around how many people would fall under the definitions of unfit and feeble-minded. With the help of a few powerful voices outside Parliament, he managed to split opinion, and the bill got so watered down, it's simply too weak to make a difference.' Leonard grinds the remainder of his cigar into the ashtray. 'And then, of course, came the war, and for the few years after that, with the country recovering from the shock of it, the time wasn't right for trying again.'

'But now,' interrupts Church, 'we believe the tide is turning once again in our favour.'

'And what makes you think there will be a different reception this time?' asks Laughlin.

'It's not going to be easy,' says Ellis, 'but Church and I have discussed this at length. We believe that to make the proposition sound more palatable, the sterilisation proposals should be voluntary rather than compulsory. Of course, it will be the women who will be subject to the sterilisation programme; once again, a more palatable proposition.'

'And the objections over categorisation?'

'Ah,' says Church, 'well, that is where my friend Professor Hamilton here comes in. Edward, could you elaborate?'

Edward clears his throat. The room suddenly feels too hot and he is conscious of sweat pooling in his armpits. 'Of course. I have this week provided my findings to the Royal Commission on the link between the hereditability of intelligence and delinquency.' He gathers himself to go on. 'I'm confident they will, once they have considered all the evidence, make a recommendation to Parliament in favour of the proposed legislation.'

Edward is only vaguely aware of the words uttering from his mouth. It is as if a section of him is speaking, while the other parts watch on, waiting for him to stumble and fall. Waiting for him to come unstuck and for the men around the table to see him for what he really is: a fraud.

Somewhere deep in his mind, Eleanor exists, shocked and chiding, 'The truth is a platform that will never let you down.' He hears her voice, clear as if she were standing right behind his left shoulder. Beneath her judging gaze, he knows he should confess all.

But how could he do that? It is far too late for honesty.

He has chosen this path and now he must continue plodding down it, as he has always done before – and hope the destination it leads him to is not ruination and disaster.

It's mid-afternoon as Edward strolls along the bank of the Thames. The sun warms his back and the steady rumble of traffic along the Embankment, the clanking of machinery, shouts and cries of workers calling to each other fill the air. The sound of London at work.

A woman emerges from the tunnel of the tube station, a little girl with blonde hair skipping at her side. His heart lurches. *Mabel.*

Only of course it isn't. Like Mabel, but not her.

He has begun to glimpse her in unexpected places. Sometimes, when he is working, he might glance up and there she is standing before him, picture-perfect in a flowery dress. She beams at him before melting clean away. Or he might catch a ghost of her, running between the flower beds at Brook End, her curls tumbling about her shoulders, laughter on the breeze. And now, it seems, he sees her face in every child he encounters on the streets of London.

Violet is waiting for him on their usual bench. Now that Eleanor knows of their encounters, and now he has her blessing for what he has done and continues to do, these meetings should be easier. But his belly still knots when he sees her look up as he crosses the patch of grass towards their bench. She stands, bobbing a little curtsey, dipping her chin in deference. He wishes she wouldn't do that.

'Good day to you, Violet.'

'It is a lovely one, sir,' she says, taking her seat again. He sits next to her, allowing a person's space between them, as he always does.

He recalls from their previous meeting how worried she'd been about her baby, three months older than Jimmy, who had seemed to be developing whooping cough. 'Tell me,' he asks, 'how is the little one?'

'Oh,' she laughs, looking much more relaxed than she had done last time. 'He's fine! It was croup, after all that. Cured with a few boiling kettles. He's bouncin' and bonny enough now, thanks for asking.'

'That's wonderful news.'

'And your little ones, sir? How are they? I were in such a tearing rush last time, I didn't even ask, which was mighty rude, I'm sorry.'

'No, no. You had a good deal on your mind.' He swallows hard. 'Jimmy's doing very well, thank you.' He stares out over the busy traffic on the river, slow-moving barges carrying coal; large passenger vessels puffing out steam; rowing boats, all jostling for space.

'And Mabel?' Violet goes on. She's trying, he knows, to be polite and interested in Edward's life, so that this interaction between them becomes more than merely a financial transaction. 'She must be five now?'

Edward's mouth is dry. He can feel Violet waiting for his reply.

'I've not really mentioned it before,' he says carefully, testing out the words to see how they feel. He can't talk about his daughter to anyone. Least of all Eleanor, with whom whenever there is any mention of Mabel, it only seems to end up in a row. 'But Mabel has been – has been taken ill.' He draws a deep breath. 'Gravely ill,' he adds.

'Oh!' Violet turns in her seat to look at him. He continues to stare out across the river, screwing his eyes against the glare of the sun on the water. 'I'm so sorry to hear that.'

'It turns out,' he says, his words beginning to flow, 'that she's an epileptic.' The word catches in his throat, sours his tongue. He feels, rather than sees, Violet tense at the word. 'It's very bad. We had to make the difficult decision that it would be best to send her away, so that she can receive the most advanced treatment. And so she can be taken care of, away from the public gaze.' How can he be saying all of this? How, when he has made it absolutely clear that not a word should be said to anyone. People are gossips, and there is nothing better to gossip about than news which could bring a great man down.

But now he has started, the words won't stop. They gush inexorably out of him, unstoppable, like the river before them. Suddenly he is telling Violet everything: Mabel's visions of the fire lady, the nanny leaving them, spouting about curses and evil spirits, the desperate visits to doctors who all shook their heads and adopted the same pained expressions. He tells her of Mabel's deterioration; of the fits growing in severity; how her eyes would roll back and saliva would run from her slack lips. How the violent force of the seizures would propel her across the room, and of the cuts and bruises she sustained as she fell. He tells her how Mabel's speech and steps faltered. How her personality disappeared before their eyes. The whole sordid story streams out of him like dirty sewage into the river.

Violet sits bolt upright and listens, mouth half-open, in silence. His story spent, Edward slumps back against the hard wood of the bench. The speech has exhausted him, but it's also a relief to voice the churning emotions which have gathered inside him like poison, unsaid, for weeks.

'Dear God, bless her soul. I am so, so sorry, sir. That's a truly awful thing to happen.'

'And before you ask,' Edward says, knowing how inevitably this conversation will go, 'Mabel has been sent to Heath Colony, in Sussex.'

Violet takes a sharp intake of breath. 'But that's where Reggie is!'

'Quite.'

'Your daughter, she's with my brother?' She gives an ironic laugh and shakes her head. 'Well, ain't that something?'

Ain't that something indeed. Edward's heart thumps in his chest as he allows his mind to properly explore, as if for the first time, the information he has just imparted. He's never believed in fate. But it seems he was wrong. His two worlds are colliding as though they were meant to all along, and he has been powerless to stop them.

He has done a terrible wrong and this, in the end, is how he is to be punished.

Elgar's *Serenade for Strings* plays softly on the gramophone. The lamplight is warm and muted, candles flicker down the centre of the dining table. It has been a long time since they entertained dinner guests. Edward watches Eleanor in the candlelight. Never has she looked more beautiful, nor more out of his reach, than tonight.

It is Saturday evening and the house is full of guests. Eleanor had arranged this before their argument last weekend and he wonders if he will ever get the opportunity to speak to her alone. He must apologise, ask her forgiveness. He can't bear her disapproval. Her disdain. Not only about the *adaption* of the research evidence, which neither of them have mentioned, but about Mabel. She remains furious with him, but she says nothing, which is almost worse. Her fury is transmitted through her eyes, the stiffness of her limbs. It oozes from her skin and pricks at him like static electricity. It's as if she blames *him* for Mabel's illness. For everything that's happened to her. But really, what choice did they have? They have done the thing any right-minded, well-to-do family would have done. They have sought the most advanced treatment for her and put her in the best place she can be. But no amount of explaining that makes any difference.

Barton and Lizzie are here, together with Sophie and Henry, who has abandoned his latest squeeze to spend the weekend with his wife. Of course, Rose is here as well. She and Eleanor appear closer than ever. Edward's guts twist at the loss of Eleanor's trust. She has stopped confiding in him. Instead, she and Rose sit close and comfortable, side by side. The ease between them speaks of secrets shared. Could she have told her sister about the false data? He drinks his wine and looks away.

Tomorrow there is tennis planned, followed by a picnic in the meadow, perhaps a dip in the river if the weather holds. Just like happier times, only a facsimile. This isn't real. They are all just actors in a falsely jolly play.

Over the consommé, Barton taps his glass, then raises it. 'A toast,' he proclaims, 'to good friends and better times to come.' He gives Edward a sad smile and, in the unsaid words, he feels a warmth. The old bugger is more sensitive, more thoughtful, than he lets on. He is one of the few who understand the searing pain the loss of Mabel has cut through this family.

'Here, here,' Henry agrees, raising his glass, clearly

having no idea to what Barton is referring. 'To a bloody good night,' he says, downing the lot. Sophie rolls her eyes.

'I sold a parcel of land yesterday, Edward, old chap,' Barton announces. 'Made a decent amount on it, as it happens. Lizzie has plans to use some of it to spruce up the old place, but I thought I should put the rest of it in stocks and shares, or what not. Looking for a bit of advice. Would you recommend your banker chaps?'

'Coleroy and Mack? Yes, been with them for years. Solid and trustworthy. I can make an introduction if you like.'

'No, no,' Henry interrupts. 'You want something a bit more dynamic than that fusty old set-up. If you want to make a *real* return, you want to have your money in America. That's where the big bucks are.'

'Oh yes?' Barton says, raising an eyebrow. 'What do you think, Edward?'

'Really,' Edward says, 'I'm not in favour of taking risks. But then I'm not really the man to ask. As you know, I'm a man—'

'Of science,' interrupts Barton. 'Yes, yes, I know. But you do seem to know an awful lot of Americans. Rich ones too, like that Rockefeller chap. They must know a thing or two.'

Edward laughs. Barton's funds would be small change to Rockefeller or Carnegie. 'I should listen to Henry, he knows far more about all this than I do. My bankers assure me my funds are in steady, safe investments. I shan't make a fortune, but that suits me just fine.'

'Ha!' exclaims Henry. 'No risk, no reward! Now that Rockefeller – he *does* know a thing or two. Rockefeller senior, anyway. Very smart chap, buying up all the logistics networks. Created a monopoly. Genius. Anyway, Barton,

I'll introduce you to my American bankers, no problem at all. They'll make you a very wealthy man,' he chortles.

'Really?' Lizzie says, plunging her spoon into her soup. 'How?'

'On the backs of underpaid workers,' Rose pipes up, her cheeks reddening. Oh God, please not this socialist claptrap. Straight from the mouths of Sidney and Beatrice Webb, influenced by that awful Frenchman too, no doubt. This job at the *New Statesman* was a truly awful idea. 'The rich make their money because countless workers who make money *for* them take home a wage they can barely live off,' Rose is saying. 'And that's those who have a job! Surely everyone deserves enough money for a comfortable living?'

'Ha, ha!' Henry rolls in his seat with amusement. 'Here speaketh the little socialist worker. If only it were that simple!'

There is an awkward silence around the table as Rose and Henry glare at each other.

'Which part, exactly, in that is *not* simple?' Rose says.

'All of it,' Henry drawls. 'I wouldn't expect a woman to understand, mind you. *Life* is not that simple. Unemployment, my dear, is due to advancements in mechanisation, lack of demand, exports being overpriced, multiple reasons. Many businesses can't afford to pay their workers more. The market will right itself, eventually, although it might be painful along the way.'

'Not painful for you,' mutters Rose.

'*Rose,*' warns Eleanor.

'Well, I, for one, think she has a valid opinion,' Sophie cuts in loudly. 'Why is it such a bad suggestion? Surely paying a decent wage for people to live on is better than paying out welfare?'

'Never discuss politics with a woman, that's what I say.' Henry laughs loudly at his own joke.

'Well, there are a handful of us in Parliament, in case you hadn't noticed,' Sophie snaps back.

'Indeed, what a hoot. Shame they aren't a little younger or more attractive. That would certainly brighten up the place a bit.'

'Oh, shut up, Henry.' Sophie rolls her eyes and turns to Eleanor. 'God, don't you sometimes miss the war years, Eleanor? When we were both young, and free, and we actually *mattered*?' Edward can see his own discomfort at the turn of the conversation reflected in the eyes of his other guests as they all fall silent. Eleanor mumbles something inaudible in response to Sophie.

'Here we go...' Henry drawls. He opens his mouth to speak again, but Rose swiftly interrupts.

'Actually, Henry,' she says, her spoon clattering onto the plate. She leans forward, her back rigid, 'It wouldn't hurt, would it, to listen to opinions which may be different to your own? Perhaps looking at the evidence from *all* angles, with no fixed opinion, *before* making a decision about something, could be a good way to go about business. And that includes having a preconception about the value of a woman's opinion on affairs of the state in Parliament or indeed, outside of it!'

Sophie sniggers.

'*Rose!*' hisses Eleanor, finally meeting Edward's eye. 'Please, not at the dinner table.'

'Oh, no bother!' Henry looks around the gathered

company, amusement rather than offence in his expression. 'I'm quite used to hot-headed women. I've enough experience of them in my life.' Sophie snorts and everyone lapses into silence, with only the clink of cutlery and background music to break it.

'Excellent soup!' Barton says after a few minutes. 'Do pass that on to Mrs Bellamy. Excelled herself this evening, wouldn't you say, Lizzie?'

'Oh yes!' Lizzie springs into action. 'Edward, I've been meaning to ask, how have you been getting on with training the dog? Barton is utterly useless with our hound. What a beast it's turning into! Never comes when it's called, steals food off the table and eats every other shoe in the house!'

Out of the corner of his eye, Edward sees Eleanor pat Rose on the hand and wink at Sophie. What a conspiracy of females around his table. The three witches of Macbeth spring into his mind. No, that's unfair. He rings the bell for the next course.

He'd always felt rather smug about his marriage compared to Henry's. But now, feeling the antipathy emanating from his wife in his direction, he wonders gloomily if they really are any better.

VIII

*A*nd what of my girl?
        She's still here. Hanging on, despite your despicable treatments. Here, beneath her ruined skin and swollen flesh, present behind her dull, glassy eyes and deep within her mind, sedated and deadened by your sickening administrations.

My precious girl, with her visions of fire-haired women and dogs with flaming red fur. To make up for your hateful medicines, I'm determined to counter them. I redouble my efforts to bequeath her my greatest gifts. I shower her with more and more. Unlike you who rein her in, diminish and deflate her humanity, I am not ashamed. Where you turn her world into a colourless barren land, I do the opposite. I plunge deep into her mind and fill it with relentless visions.

I'm with her when the visions are too much. I'm with her when her stomach gripes and twists with pain, and her throat burns from the bromide salts you force into her, when the phenobarbital dulls her. I'm with her when she cries for her mother, or reaches out to grasp at a vision through empty space. It's me who's here as she twitches and jerks, when her limbs fly out and her head snaps. I'm with her when she crashes into walls and collapses to the floor.

And it's me who is here when, finally exhausted, she curls up into a ball and falls asleep.

But there is someone else here too.

The young doctor, the ambitious one. Dr Eversley, you call him. Dr Eversley whose close attention to the girl sets my nerves on edge.

Dr Eversley who hovers over her, examining her face, her lesions closely, like a lion breathing hungrily over his prey.

She'd be perfect for my trials, *he mutters to himself.* Just perfect. If only Sir Charles will let me have her.

25

Eleanor

The letter arrives, in a handwritten envelope, by the morning post. It is in a hand Eleanor doesn't recognise, with a Sussex postmark. A stab of fear. Heath Colony is in Sussex. But they never write to her. Sir Charles writes once a month to Edward with reports on Mabel. She hates those depressing reports, detailing as they do in detached, unemotional tones Mabel's state of health, numbers of seizures and deteriorating mental state.

She sets the letter to one side and quickly looks through the rest. Nothing of any interest. She lets them drop onto the hall table and fastens her hat and coat, pulls on her gloves and slips the strange envelope into her bag. She rushes out to the car which Wilson has brought to the front of the house to meet her. She can't risk missing her train to London.

Settled in her seat in the First Class carriage Eleanor pulls the envelope from her bag. An elderly lady and gentleman share the carriage with her, hands folded neatly into laps. The two sit silently staring out of the window at the countryside speeding past.

Strictly Private and Confidential

27th August 1929

Dear Mrs Hamilton,

I do hope you won't mind this direct contact, but I have some concerns about Mabel's welfare. I think it may be a good idea if you were to visit the colony at your soonest convenience. I believe your daughter may be at risk.

I write this letter with genuine concern. Please do not mention my name as having alerted you to this matter. I would, in all probability, lose my position if it were to become known I had written to you.

I am, yours sincerely,

Miss A. Manners,
Matron, Babies Castle,
Heath Colony

Eleanor strides into Sir Charles Lawson's consulting rooms. He stands to greet her, his back slightly stooped, lined face solemn and unreadable.

She sits, he sits, and they regard one another across the expanse of the table between them.

He clears his throat. 'What can I do for you, Mrs Hamilton?'

'I've come to discuss Mabel, of course.'

'I see. And no Professor Hamilton to accompany you

today?' he enquires with a sniff. Irritation rises up her spine like quills on a hedgehog's back.

'No. Edward is busy.'

'Of course. I'm sure he is always very busy.'

'Indeed he is.'

He folds his hands together on the desk and regards her with what she can only deduce is disdain.

She takes a deep breath. 'I would like to hear how Mabel is getting on with your programme of treatment. I understand from Edward she is now on phenobarbital and I should like to know if there is any improvement. As her mother,' she adds in a slow deliberate voice, 'I take it I am permitted to make such enquiries.' She finishes with a smile.

Sir Charles returns a weak version of his own. 'I so appreciate, Mrs Hamilton, that it must have been a great wrench to have been parted from your child. But it will get easier.'

'I didn't come to discuss my feelings,' Eleanor snaps. 'I came to find out about my daughter's health!' She is a different woman sitting here before the great man. Last time she had sat in this chair, she'd been numb with shock; helplessly reliant on Edward and his sensible thinking, or so she thought. She bites her lip. Banishes the negative thoughts which will do nothing to aid Mabel now. In her bag are the folded notes she has made, and the salient sections of the articles she has read, in the event she needs to refer to them. But she doubts she will; having read them over and over, she could practically quote them, word perfect.

'Also,' she says hesitatingly, 'I've received a letter which concerns me greatly.'

'Oh?'

'It's a note, really. Rather short and anonymously written. It says the person, whoever they are, has concerns about Mabel's welfare.'

'*What!*' Sir Charles appears to be genuinely shocked. 'Let me see it.'

'I-I don't have it on me.' Eleanor says, wishing she could show him Miss Manners' letter, but it's impossible. Miss Manners asked her not to and she can't risk exposing the one person who seems to care about Mabel's welfare getting the sack.

'Well.' Sir Charles sits back in his chair and gives her what she takes to be a suspicious look, as though he doesn't quite believe her. 'Mrs Hamilton... Frankly this is complete nonsense. Mabel is perfectly safe and well cared for, I assure you. Such a note will have come from a troublemaker, no doubt about it. Your husband has a high profile and, unfortunately, people like your husband attract unwanted attention.'

'But I thought nobody knew that Mabel is our daughter?'

'As far as I am aware, nobody does. But who knows where such information comes from?'

Eleanor shifts uncomfortably in her seat. 'And how *is* Mabel?'

'Your daughter has settled nicely into colony life,' Sir Charles is saying. His demeanour has relaxed. She senses less hostility, but there is still a guard, a lack of openness about him. 'I have been sending regular reports of her progress to your husband,' he adds.

'Yes, I am aware of that, but I wanted to come myself, you see. To hear everything from the horse's mouth, so to speak.' She smiles at him again. 'Sir Charles, to be frank, I do think enough time has passed for me to be able to visit Mabel on a regular basis. It can be discreet. Edward needn't come, so the secrecy of her identity will be maintained. In light of the letter, I simply must satisfy myself as to how Mabel truly is.'

'I see,' Sir Charles says, cocking one silver eyebrow. He spreads his hands, palms up. 'What would you like to know, in particular?'

'How is she in *all* ways? Does she have friends? Is she happy? Is she learning anything at school?'

There is a pause.

'She has formed a good attachment to the nurses who tend to her,' Sir Charles answers in a flat voice. His eyes no longer meet hers. 'I believe she enjoys drawing and painting, visiting the farm animals and, I imagine, playing with the other children,' he says, obviously having no idea about such things. He clears his throat. 'Mrs Hamilton, as you'll be aware from my reports, Mabel is not doing well. School is out of the question for her. Our programme ensures the child suffers no undue stress. It is important that epileptics are kept in calm, well-ordered environments. Too much excitement is liable to increase the propensity to suffer fits. For this reason we discourage visiting. Seeing her mother, while there remains any expectation she might be taken home, could cause unnecessary stress. Furthermore, the majority of our children do not receive visitors. If they see one of their number being visited by their mother, well, it will cause anxiety to the rest of them, and that is not to mention *your* distress at seeing the sad state of your own child. Truly, it is better for all parties if you save yourself the trauma.'

Eleanor opens her mouth to say what she *really* wants to say, but shuts it again just in time. Better to keep that thought to herself. 'And what about her seizures – the medication. You mentioned this new wonder drug. Is it having any effect?' She sits forward, heart thrumming. Perhaps, miraculously, Mabel will be improving anyway.

Sir Charles shakes his head, assuming a saddened expression. 'Mabel's condition is of the most serious kind. I feared it was too late for her to respond to either bromides or phenobarbital and, I'm sorry to say, my predictions are being borne out.' He pulls out a register of names and numbers. Sir Charles traces a line beneath Mabel's name. 'It's not been a good quarter,' he says. 'Four hundred and seventy-five major seizures this quarter, three hundred and forty-eight minor. That's a huge number, and up on the last quarter. That said, she is not yet on the maximum dose of phenobarbital and we can adjust the combination with the bromide salts if—'

'Sir Charles, this is why I have come to see you.' Eleanor shifts in her seat, her heart banging in her chest. 'The treatment you have recommended is clearly not working. I want to discuss something with you. I have heard of an alternative treatment I want you to try with Mabel.'

Sir Charles leans back in his chair and fixes her with a stern expression.

'Mrs Hamilton, I'm afraid to say that there are some crackpot remedies out there, none of which will work.' Just as last time Eleanor was seated in Sir Charles's consulting rooms, he adopts the tone he would for a troublesome child who can't quite grasp an easy lesson. 'I assure you, the treatment plan I am recommending for Mabel is the latest, most effective on the market.'

'Sir Charles,' Eleanor says, her voice firm, 'the treatment I'm proposing is certainly not crackpot. It has been extensively tested and used on children in America. I am sure that, if you are as up to date on the latest research and evidence as you say, then you will no doubt be aware of the Ketogenic diet.'

Sir Charles blinks and twitches, almost imperceptibly. Is that irritation? Surprise? But his smoothness is back as quickly as it left him. 'The diet we administer our epileptic patients is very carefully controlled, as I informed you last time you were here,' he says.

'But have you heard of the Ketogenic diet, Sir Charles? This is something very different from that which you spoke of last time.'

'No,' he admits after a pause, 'I have not heard of that one, but,' and he laughs a little, 'I do not pay much attention to the myriad of crazy ideas which pop up every now and then.' He raises his eyebrows. 'Some defy belief!'

'This is not crazy, I assure you.' Eleanor unclips the clasps on her handbag and pulls out the papers. 'As you will see, the results of their tests are extremely encouraging.' Eleanor slaps the carefully written notes and the highlighted sections from the articles in front of the old doctor.

Sir Charles stares, as if in shock, at the papers before him. Everything about him speaks of resistance, from his knitted brows to his arms crossed over his chest. He gives the papers a cursory glance, then shakes his head and clears his throat.

'Such a diet would be very extreme and bad for the body of an adult,' he begins, his voice soft and slow, laced with patience, 'but a small and delicate child?' He lets out a laugh. 'It could be the death of her! A few months in and she would be gravely sick from lack of vitamins and nutrients. She would have severe constipation and her system would fast become poisoned with the detritus the body would be unable to expel. I can only advise you, Mrs Hamilton, that this diet could be catastrophic for Mabel, and I would avoid it at all costs. What is considered right and appropriate in America may not, indeed, is certain to not, be considered appropriate in London.' He pushes the papers back towards her and looks at his watch. He grimaces. Eleanor is about to be dismissed, her time up. She's failed in her mission.

'Please,' she pleads, her voice quieter now. 'Please look at these research papers. I appreciate, in any normal circumstances such an extreme diet would be considered detrimental to health, but for the epileptic it might be a saviour. Everything – the details of the trial, the evidence of its success – it's all here.' She taps the papers. 'It might benefit other children too,' she says as he picks up the pile as though it were itself infectious. 'Not just Mabel,' she presses. Sir Charles does not respond.

She pulls on her gloves and gathers her bag to leave.

'Do you really want your child to be an experiment? A laboratory rat?' Sir Charles is suddenly furious. 'Some of the experiments carried out on epileptics in America – there are no bounds to the cruelty over there, Mrs Hamilton, I assure you. There is no knowing what the side effects could be, particularly long-term, on the growing child. I would not want to subject *my* child to such treatment,' he adds finally and gets to his feet, as though his opinion must be the end of the matter. 'I do have another patient waiting, Mrs Hamilton.'

'Yes of course.' She stands and offers him a gloved hand. She looks him straight in the eye. 'I shan't drop this, Sir Charles, you know. I will give you a call in a day or so to see what you think once you have actually read these papers.'

He takes her hand. 'And Professor Hamilton? What does he think of all of this,' he asks, studying her face closely.

She hesitates. 'Well,' she says, 'for now I would rather keep matters between the two of us, Sir Charles. Once we are agreed, I shall of course discuss it with Edward. But he is so very busy with his work right now, I do not wish to bother him with this.'

'Ah.' The doctor releases Eleanor's hand. 'I see…'

'I'll telephone the day after tomorrow.' She flashes him the briefest of smiles. 'Good day to you.'

And with that, Eleanor turns on her heel and sweeps towards the door, her head held high.

Sitting alone in a café, sipping sugared tea in an attempt to calm her nerves, Eleanor ponders her next move. Her hand trembles as she lifts the cup to her lips. Sir Charles is the expert; she has merely read a few obscure reports. But then, all his years of experience and his self-assured manner have got him nowhere with helping Mabel. And Marcel, after all, has personal experience with his own sister.

Everything she has ever known feels as if it has been swept from beneath her feet and she is floundering. The row with Edward is rumbling on, unspoken, but always present in the room between them, like a bad smell.

She imagines he cannot see the problem with what he has done, so utterly certain is he of his own theories, that his way of looking at the world is right. It seems he will stop at nothing to succeed. She knows he has a knighthood in his sights and it has twisted him, made him lose his sense of reason and morality. What is it they say of men and power? Something about power corrupts and absolute power corrupts absolutely? Does Edward have power? She's never thought of it like that before, but she supposes he does. Power over those whose lives he will affect by virtue of his influence. Power over her, certainly. He's always been her rock since she lost her mother. She's come to rely on him, totally and utterly, to trust in his judgement to the extent she has almost forgotten she has her own.

Are things so difficult between them now because she is trying to assert herself? If so, she can only imagine how much worse it will get if he finds out she has been to see Sir Charles without him. He will be furious to hear she has suggested a treatment not advocated by this doctor he seems to admire so much. Edward has too much faith in these people.

Or is it that she has simply lost faith in him? He lied to her all those years about Porter. Why? It doesn't make sense. He must have known she would have supported him paying for Porter's care. And now this falsifying of evidence. The refusal to listen to her about the treatment for Mabel, to let her take her from the colony or even visit her. What other truths may he be concealing? The whole edifice that is Edward is crumbling before her eyes.

Eleanor's mind flits unwillingly to the memory of the man who murdered her mother. The day she first saw him, sitting in the dock, rocking back and forth, his big frame so at odds with his childlike mind. He seemed to have no idea what he was even doing in the courtroom, let alone an understanding of the terrible crime he had committed. Back then she had been shocked by his lack of remorse, certain he should never be permitted to roam the streets again. Not long after that she'd gone along with Edward to a talk by the Eugenics Society and had thought what perfect sense it all made.

Now she sees it's not so simple. She thinks back to her conversation with Rose and how she had looked into that man's life. How he had always been of simple mind and couldn't speak. How he had been filled with a rage nobody could understand or control. How he'd been locked up and beaten in an attempt to knock it out of him, for most of his young life. Eleanor isn't sure she can ever forgive him, but she can see how it wasn't so straightforward as she imagined, how the way he had been treated could have contributed to how he behaved.

She thinks of Mabel and her disease. How there could be a cause other than her or Edward's bad genes. What if this science of eugenics is wrong? What if the diseased, the criminals and the feeble-minded might still be born to those with supposedly superior genes? Indeed, is there even such a thing as superior genes at all? Does that disprove the whole theory? And isn't the result of that possibility that the personal cost to individuals like Mabel is too great in pursuit of something which might or might not work? What if, indeed, there are others like Edward, who have delved into the realms of falsehood to find evidence to back up their beliefs? Beliefs which may be based on false ideas in the first place. None of it bears thinking about.

Clearly, there are people who have disease and mental illness; there are criminals and alcoholics and those with reprehensible behaviours. But what if these things are not always caused by inheritance? And what if there are possible treatments which may help or even cure these conditions? Surely this is what the clever scientists should be focusing on. Surely *this* is a better way forward.

With a sick lurch she knows in her gut that Edward will never listen to her about any of this. He will believe Sir Charles over her instinct any day. She will never be able to persuade him to take a different course, because Edward has a closed mind to anything he does not want to know. And in that moment, Eleanor knows what she needs to do. From her bag she pulls out some paper and jots down the text of a telegram she plans to send to Dr Peterman, the doctor who wrote the article Marcel had brought her, at the Mayo Clinic in Rochester, Minnesota. She fumbles in her purse for money for the tea which she drops onto the table for the waitress, then heads towards the post office. On her way she stops at a phone box.

She drops the coins into the slot and gives the operator the instructions. After a few agonising moments, she is through.

'Sophie,' she says breathlessly into the receiver. 'How do you fancy a little drive?'

26

Edward

Edward is tucking into a plate of cold ham, potato salad and pickled beetroot, when a knock at the door almost makes him jump out of his skin. He's alone in the flat in Bloomsbury, Mrs Timms having left before he got in from his last clinic of the day.

It's gone seven in the evening, so who on earth could this be? The caretaker did not call up and announce a visitor and he isn't expecting anyone.

The knock comes again, followed by a woman's voice, muted by the door and the distance between it and him several feet away in his dining room. 'Edward! It's me, I haven't brought my key. Are you there?'

Eleanor!

He jumps out of his chair, sending his fork, together with the stabbed beetroot, skittering across the table to the floor, spilling its blood-like juice onto the cream carpet. *Damn it.*

Eleanor is standing outside the door, flushed and looking bedraggled. On his walk home it had been threatening to rain, and from the sodden state of her hat and the shoulders of her jacket, it would appear the weather followed through.

'Darling! What on earth are you doing here? I had no idea you were coming to London!'

'Can I come in?'

Edward hastily moves to the side to let her through the door. 'I'd have asked Mrs Timms to leave you some supper too, if I'd known you were coming,' he says, following her through the small hallway as she discards her shoes, wet jacket and hat, and into the dining room. She walks straight to the drinks cabinet and helps herself to a glass of the Burgundy he decanted earlier. 'Is everything OK?' he asks carefully. Her behaviour is most un-Eleanor-like.

She gives a hollow laugh. 'Well,' she says, turning to him, 'what do you think, Edward?'

Not OK, then. His momentary joy at finding his wife on his doorstep evaporates.

'Would you like to share my dinner?' he asks.

She slumps into a chair and shakes her head. 'Edward. We need to talk.'

'Of course.' He picks his fork off the floor and dabs at the stain on the carpet with his handkerchief, spreading the deep purple mark even more. Sitting down again he wonders if he should continue eating or if that will annoy her. He puts down his cutlery. She wouldn't have come all the way to London to discuss something trivial and he feels a sharp stab of pain at the thought of what she might be about to say.

'Jimmy?' he asks, suddenly afraid he has things wrong. 'It's not Jimmy is it?'

'No,' she says, frowning, 'Jimmy is fine. Miss Harding is a wonderful nanny. He's better off with her than me.'

'Don't be ridiculous.'

'No, I mean it. She is so good with him. She's always jolly

and makes him laugh. I'm so miserable I'm not sure it's good for him to spend too much time with me.'

'Oh, Eleanor, that's simply not true! He likes you, *loves* you. You're his mother—'

'I didn't come here to discuss Jimmy,' Eleanor says between gritted teeth. 'I need to discuss Mabel. But first, first Edward, I need to know, to *understand* why you lied to me for all those years.'

'What?' Edward's heart begins to beat a little faster, his palms begin to sweat. He feigns ignorance but he knows what's coming.

'Why did you never tell me about Porter and the fact you were paying for his care in the colony? The secrecy doesn't make sense. Don't spin me any more lies, Edward. I want the truth.'

Her face is taut, her eyes pleading as she examines his. She's so young, hopeful – as though she is daring to believe that there is an explanation she will be able to forgive. Dear God, he cannot bear her disapproval, but here she is, asking him for the truth. He cannot spin any more. She will have what she is asking for.

They go into the sitting room, where Edward turns up the lamps and places another log on the fire. It's only early September, but there is already a chill to the evening air.

They sit opposite each other and Edward, fortified by another glass of wine, tells her everything. The best he can hope for is her forgiveness. He can't look into her shocked eyes as he falters through his self-justification for not putting the officers and the Red Cross team right when they made their false assumptions on the battlefield. How can she understand the confusion, the horror of the scene? She is silent as he explains how, as time went on, with Porter not expected to live, the truth hardly seemed to matter, and then later, when he did survive but remembered nothing, it was too late. People thought Edward was the sort of person he wasn't, but he wanted to be. How could he possibly put them straight so long afterwards? And then, of course, everyone moved on, wanted to forget and focus on the future, him included. Did he really do so wrong? Wouldn't others have done the same in his position? Could she find it in her heart to forgive him?

Finally, he forces himself to look into her eyes. Disappointment. His stomach plunges. So much worse than anger.

'I remember so clearly,' she says, staring at his shoes, 'the day you walked into the War Office. So tall, handsome and brave. I couldn't believe that you even noticed my existence. You looked distinguished and important. And of course you were. How I admired you, Edward! How incredibly lucky I felt that I was the one you picked, when you could have had *any* girl.'

'But I only ever wanted you, Eleanor! Don't you understand? I love you so very much, and... and I've never lied about that!'

She shakes her head, tears glistening in her eyes. 'Oh, I believe you, Edward. I know how much you love and want me. But it's just like everything else that you want, you falsify the truth to get it. Me, your career, your reputation. All of it. I thought I knew you, but I didn't! I don't...'

'Now that's going a bit far, Eleanor. You make me sound like a total fraudster! My work is meticulous, I promise you that.'

'But you call yourself "Professor", and you aren't one, not really.'

'I didn't finish my PhD, that's true, but the war intervened. What could I do about that? And I'm an expert, as good as any professor with or without a PhD.'

'You falsified evidence.'

Edward sighs and raises his eyes to the ceiling. 'Not this *again*. It was a small thing. Insignificant amongst the vast amount of other evidence.'

'Not to me.' Eleanor's eyes are glinting in the firelight. She leans towards him. 'If you were brave, Edward – and sometimes admitting you were wrong, or standing against the tide of opinion takes a great deal of courage – you would retract that evidence. And you would take your daughter out of the colony and allow me to trial her on the diet I have told you about.'

Anger swells suddenly in his chest. She is asking too much. He is prepared to be more careful in the future, but you can't undo the past. And as for Mabel, she really is in the best place, under Sir Charles's care. Sir Charles is the country's leading expert in paediatric epilepsy. Eleanor is clinging to ridiculous false hopes. Promises being made by charlatans preying on the vulnerable.

'I am not taking my daughter out of a place where she is safe and secure,' he says firmly, 'to allow her to be starved and subject to some quack treatments due to the say-so of your sister's boyfriend! The idea is cruel and preposterous, Eleanor. I know you want her to be better – so do I, more than anything. But you are desperate and clutching at an impossible dream. I'm sorry, but at some point you will have to accept the truth. Mabel is not going to get better.'

'This is not some quack treatment, Edward,' she spits back at him. 'This treatment has been developed over years, *centuries* even, and finessed by the famous Mayo Clinic in America, by *real* doctors, *real* scientists, just like you!'

'Eleanor, Eleanor, come on. America has its fair share of charlatans and fake treatments, just like anywhere else. It's all about the mon—'

'Is that so!' Eleanor jumps to her feet. 'Well, Edward Hamilton. You are a fine one to talk, aren't you? I could throw the same accusation back at you, couldn't I, falsifying the results of experiments?'

'How dare you!' Edward has had enough. Now he is on his feet too. It's true, he did swap some of the test results, but only to ensure *irrefutable* evidence behind facts he is certain are correct. 'I did what I did for excellent reasons and I am confident in the overall results. I will not stand here and let you accuse me of being a fraud!'

'Has it ever occurred to you, Edward,' Eleanor is controlled now in the face of his anger. Calm, her voice steady and even, 'that you *might* be wrong? That there are other ways to improve lives than through the narrow ideas of Edward Hamilton?'

'Don't be ridiculous, Eleanor. These ideas do not originate from *me*. They are accepted medical science and supported by multiple other experts.'

'But even the experts don't always agree.'

'That's true, but—'

'So can't we give another way a chance?' She is pleading now, almost in tears. His own anger dissipates. '*Please.*'

'We said we would see what Sir Charles thought of the diet.'

'He doesn't want to try,' says Eleanor, now pacing the room like an agitated cat. 'I went to see him.'

'You went to see him? Without me?'

'Yes, Edward. I can do things without you, you know. And I wanted to present the *evidence* to Sir Charles in a neutral, unbiased way.'

Edward watches her with new eyes. *She went to see Sir Charles behind his back!* The way she is speaking to him – she seems so different. Someone has stolen his sweet wife and replaced her with this confrontational, assertive one.

'All right, Eleanor. I understand you want to do your best for Mabel, but you must see sense,' he says, trying to take the heat out of the argument. 'You must listen to Sir Charles's advice. If he thinks this treatment is unlikely to make any difference, why would you think he is wrong? What benefit is it to him not to use it if it is as efficacious as you say? He, believe it or not, has no wish to keep children in a permanent state of sickness!' Surely she must be able to see the sense in that?

Eleanor looks exhausted suddenly and he steps forward, tentatively reaching out a hand for her to take, to try to repair things between them.

She looks at him for a moment, ignoring his proffered hand. She opens her mouth as if to say something, but then closes it again. He gets the feeling there is something she isn't telling him. Then in a weary voice she says, 'You aren't going to change your mind about the diet, are you?'

'No.' Edward speaks as gently as he can, not wishing to rile her again. But he doesn't want to give her false hope either. 'I have spoken to Sir Charles about it myself, as it happens, after you mentioned it to me, and he is thoroughly against such an inhuman treatment. Eleanor, darling, Mabel is in the best place she can be – in the colony under Sir Charles's care. Please see sense here.'

'Best for whom, Edward?'

'Best for all of us. Mabel, us, Jimmy...'

And she allows him to take her into his arms for a moment, looking up into his face. Her eyes are full of pain and hurt, before she pulls out of his arms and turns her back on him.

In that movement, Edward realises, with sudden sick clarity, that his wife is distancing herself from him.

IX

Like an owl swooping silently down to snatch its prey, I come for the girl. She is no longer in her usual place in the Babies Castle.

Something is wrong. I sense it from afar, but I cannot be sure. I close in, watch her sleep. And then I know it for sure.

Dr Eversley has taken her for his cruel experiments. Now, instead of leaving her to slumber her nights in peace, he, with his trickery and treachery, has stolen her away.

In the game of cat and mouse there is no knowing quite which way it will go.

This time, this girl is slip, slipping away, out of my grasp, out of my reach.

This dear, sweet girl.

Soon, for her, there will be an eternity of oblivion, a universe of emptiness. There will be no more scent of burning. No exotic taste. No heightened hearing, feeling, seeing. No more electricity misfiring in her brain; surging across the synapses, bursts of it flying down the highways of her nervous system.

Now I see she becomes confused and befuddled. There is a terrifying strangeness in the new, cold, dark room. There is no comforting pale light of the moon through the high windows of the dormitory in the Babies Castle. Instead she floats in velvet black, disorientated and alone.

There is nothing I can do for her now.

I leave her to her fate.

The battle for this girl may be lost, but my war with you goes on.

PART IV

September 1929

27

Eleanor

Sophie takes a corner too fast, and the great weight of the Mercedes-Benz lurches so violently, Eleanor is certain they are going over. But somehow, amongst a good deal of swearing about the state of the bloody roads, hard braking and grinding of the gears, they defy gravity and the car rights itself.

'Are you sure you know what you're doing?' Eleanor calls above the wind. She had thought Edward a bad driver, but Sophie is in another league altogether. 'Couldn't we slow down just a little?'

'Of course I know what I'm doing, darling! We are on a tight schedule,' Sophie shouts back, gripping the steering wheel hard as she fights to control the car. 'You are quite safe, I assure you!'

Eleanor sinks a little lower and grips the sides of her seat, wondering if it would be better to close her eyes. The road is not a good one and it's getting worse. Narrow, with too many potholes and sharp bends. It doesn't do to think about what might happen if a car comes in the other direction. Sophie is going at such a pace there is sure to be a terrible collision. She takes a few deep breaths in an effort to calm herself.

The car ferry is booked, hotels arranged and the final destination prepped and ready for them. The staff at home had been the last to know. It was better that way. Eleanor couldn't risk Edward finding out and she didn't want to put any of them in a difficult position. She'd been buoyed and heartened by their support.

'It's the *right* thing to do,' Mrs Bellamy had said, surprisingly wet-eyed and even going so far as to touch her arm in sympathy. 'I miss the little scrap,' she'd sniffed. 'Them poor mites in them institutions, you 'ave to feel sorry for 'em. And don't worry, I'll make sure nobody 'ere breathes a word. They'll 'ave me to answer to. And they won't risk *that*,' she'd said firmly, and Eleanor didn't doubt it. Mrs Bellamy had even packed them a basket groaning with food, as though they were travelling to the uninhabited wilderness, not France. A sudden fondness for Mrs Bellamy swells in her chest. She will miss her. She will miss them all.

Lizzie had been harder to convince of the merits of Eleanor's plan. It was alien to her nature to go against the wishes of her husband, the heavy expectation of convention and society's norms gave her all sorts of internal dilemmas. 'But what about Edward? What about Jimmy?' she had questioned, her eyes wide, forehead crimping with concern. 'You can't leave him, surely?' She had looked horrified. 'He's only a baby, he can't do without his mother for goodness knows how long, and you'll be so far away!'

In the end Eleanor showed her the letter from Miss Manners. She had watched as all the colour drained from Lizzie's face. 'My God,' she had said at last, looking up at

Eleanor. 'Of course you must go! Tell me what I can do to help... But, Eleanor, what if you're too late?'

The possibility had crossed Eleanor's mind too. But she couldn't think of it now. She'd moved as fast as she could and dearest Sophie had dropped everything to help her.

'It's an adventure, darling,' she had insisted. 'I wouldn't miss it for the world!'

Eleanor had a sneaking suspicion she was happy to have an excuse to get away from Henry and all their troubles for a while.

Eleanor's anger towards Edward has percolated and simmered, growing in strength the more she dwells on every action, every lie. It has begun a trial of her husband in her mind. Things he has done and said over the years which are now debated over by the prosecution and defence in her brain. Judgement is yet to be reached.

There's a stab of regret and pain at the parting with Jimmy, a knot of anxiety not knowing exactly when she will see him again. Miss Harding is a competent nanny, but what if he comes to some sort of harm while she is away? She would never forgive herself.

She almost had second thoughts when she went to say her goodbyes just before they left. As she cuddled the little boy she thought she may never love as much as Mabel, she realised that, even as that thought flickered in her brain, it wasn't true. She *did* love him. Enormously. As much, if different, to Mabel. And she was allowed to love him. Guilt about Mabel being sent away, she understood in that moment, had prevented her from fully acknowledging her feelings for Jimmy. Now she was going to bring Mabel back, she had given herself permission to let go.

She had cried then and Jimmy, searching her face with his big eyes, reached out a chubby hand to touch her wet cheek. 'Darling boy,' she had whispered to him, 'I wish I could take you with me. But it's impossible. Mabel needs me now, *all* of me, just for a short time. As soon as we can all be together again, we will be. Somehow, some way I will make it happen. I promise you that.'

He had giggled as she kissed him on the cheeks, on his non-existent neck and his round little tummy, just as he liked it. He chuckled, a deep-throated belly laugh, and that, at least, had made her smile through her tears.

Lizzie promised to look in on Jimmy and Edward every day, but especially this evening when Edward gets home from work and finds out what Eleanor has done. She pictures the scene when he reads her letter and she curls up small inside. A jolt as the car hits a pothole Sophie hadn't spotted in the gathering gloom brings Eleanor back to the present.

'We must be nearly there now, surely.' Eleanor peers ahead, but the road seems to be disintegrating into a dusty farm track. The car pitches as the wheels rise and fall over uneven ruts. They had been told to use the back entrance, coming into the colony via the farm, rather than the front which is too conspicuous, and now their mission risks being forfeited at the eleventh hour.

'Please do slow down, Sophie,' Eleanor cries, 'or you're going to lose a wheel or send us flying right out of our seats!'

'Fine, fine,' Sophie mutters, mercifully easing off the accelerator and steering around a large crater in the road.

Eleanor is steeling herself for the worst. Mabel may not

even remember her. According to Sir Charles's latest report, she has lost almost all of her speech. She communicates now by crying, shouting in frustration, pointing, shaking her head, or taking the nurse by the hand and leading her to whatever it is she wants. She sleeps a good deal, is dull and drowsy most of the time due to the medication and no longer shows any interest in playing. She cries and whimpers for no apparent reason. She keeps her ragdoll with her all the time, and if she ever loses it, she is distraught.

She eats, sleeps, exists. That is all.

A wave of nausea overcomes her when she thinks about that letter and what may happen to Mabel if they don't get her out of the place fast. Mabel needs her mother's love and protection now more than ever, and if Edward can't bear to have her home on account of his work and reputation, then so be it. She will live with Mabel somewhere quiet, away from him and his work. She has come to detest his work. Not only because, after what he did with those records, she has now come to question the very concepts he told her were rock-solid scientific facts, but also because of what it means for people like Mabel. Innocent people who may not all be the kind who murder innocent mothers.

So now, in what feels like a scene in a moving picture, she will pull Mabel from behind the dark walls of this institution and restore her to the light. They will seek help from a doctor who *is* willing to try, Marcel's father, and Eleanor is braced to be nurse and cook. And if it doesn't work, and if, like poor, dead Prince John, Mabel does not make it to adulthood, well, Eleanor will have done her best and she will find some peace in the knowledge that she did everything she could for her daughter.

And let polite society be damned for judging her for that.

'Look!' Sophie suddenly exclaims with excitement. 'Those buildings over there – could that be it?'

'Yes, it must be,' says Eleanor, leaning forward in her seat. 'There is the farm and that must be the clock tower in the distance, just as Miss Manners described.'

'Hurrah!' cries Sophie triumphantly.

'We've not got Mabel out yet,' Eleanor mutters. 'Best not celebrate too soon.'

The colony is vast. They pass farm buildings, cottages, larger houses, what looks like sprawling Victorian boarding houses and a school building. Sophie stops the car before they get too close to the main long, low building with the clock tower. Eleanor pulls the plan of the buildings Miss Manners has drawn and sent to Eleanor out of her handbag. She tries to work out which of the buildings is Babies Castle. Her eyes fix on a run-down-looking cottage, very un-castle like.

'Looks haunted to me,' Sophie says with a shudder, slowing the car to a crawl.

Eleanor checks her watch. They are right on time. It's 7.30 p.m. Miss Manners explained that this is when the patients are back in their rooms and the majority of the staff will be having supper. The plan is to go straight to Babies Castle where Miss Manners will be waiting. By then, the youngest children will be in bed. Sophie will turn the car around and wait by the front door, engine running, ready to scoot as soon as Eleanor has collected Mabel and her things. Then, safely on board, Sophie will drive them straight to Dover where they will try to sleep for a few hours in a hotel next to the docks. At ten o'clock tomorrow morning the car will be winched on board and they will be en route to Calais.

Sophie cuts the engine and the two friends sit in silence for a few moments. Eleanor's nerves fizz. Her heart pumps strong and quick and her ears are primed to pick up on any sound, near or far. The growing darkness feels like a friend. It is the right time to say what needs to be said.

'Sophie,' Eleanor begins, eyes fixed on the buildings in front of them, 'whatever happens after this, I need you to know how grateful I am. I know how much you must be sacrificing to leave Henry and the children.'

'Not Henry,' Sophie's voice is low and even. 'I've made up my mind, you see. Henry and I are miserable together. Watching you take control of your situation made me realise I should do the same. I'm leaving him, Eleanor. As soon as I'm back in London, I'm breaking the news.'

'Oh no!' Eleanor turns to look at Sophie, who continues to stare resolutely straight ahead. 'There will be a terrible scandal – it will cost you so much…'

'My mind is made up. I need to do this for my sanity. Just like you,' Sophie says. 'I needed a kick and your example is it.'

Eleanor places her hand on her friend's arm. 'Well,' she says, 'I'm here for you whatever you need, whenever you need it.'

Sophie turns to her and laughs. 'As if you don't have enough on your plate! Now go and get that child of yours. GO!'

Taking a deep breath, Eleanor leaves the car, creeping silently towards the old cottage. Her heart is beating so fast, her legs as weak as water, and she wonders if she might faint. *Mabel needs me,* she reminds herself and pushes on. She passes what must be the dining hall, as a low hum of conversation can be heard through the partially open windows. Holding her breath, she ducks low, keeping beneath the ledge.

A sudden bang of a door at the end of the hall stops her in her tracks. Frozen, she watches a figure, a man, short and bedraggled-looking, emerge from the dining hall a few feet in front of her, walking in the direction of an adjacent building. She wills him not to look around, for he will surely see her if he does. But he seems deep in thought, his hands shoved in his pockets, and his head, thankfully, doesn't swing around. He reaches a door, flings it open, light flooding out, and the man is silhouetted in the entrance way. For a terrifying moment, he stands still, and Eleanor wonders if he somehow senses her presence and will turn around and shout, 'Who's there?' She holds her breath, her heart crashing in her chest, and then he moves, steps through the door and with a bang he vanishes and the square of light is extinguished. Exhaling with relief, she moves off again towards the Babies Castle.

As arranged, she knocks on the door, three sharp raps. Time ticks and Eleanor wonders if she has got the right building after all. She looks around in desperation but the door swings open and a young nurse stands on the doorstep, looking at her in surprise.

'Hello,' she says, 'can I help?'

Eleanor's heart sinks. This cannot be Miss Manners.

'I, umm, I'm looking for Miss Manners...'

The young woman shakes her head. 'I'm sorry, but Miss

Manners was suddenly taken very ill last week. And you are?'

'Oh no! She didn't tell me... Will she be OK?' Eleanor exclaims, deftly avoiding the question.

'I'm sorry you weren't told. She has a very bad case of influenza.' The woman shakes her head. 'Disease travels through the colony like wildfire.' A sudden stab of fear for Mabel. The young woman frowns, leaning against the door frame. 'It's very late for visitors. Are you lost? Who did you say you were?'

'I didn't.' Eleanor's mind races. She looks closely at the nurse. She has a pleasant, open face. She can't be more than nineteen or twenty. Rose's age. Can she be trusted? With Miss Manners taken ill, she doesn't have much choice. 'Might I come in for a couple of minutes? I had an appointment with Miss Manners this evening.' She hesitates. 'My daughter is a patient here.'

'You'd better come in, although it is very much against the rules,' the nurse says, looking over Eleanor's shoulder, as if to check nobody is watching. 'You're lucky almost everyone is at dinner,' she adds, stepping to one side to let Eleanor pass into a long, dark narrow hallway.

She leads Eleanor along to a dreary little sitting room, lit only with a couple of gas lamps. In the shadowy corners Eleanor can see wallpaper peeling where the walls join the ceiling. Damp, she thinks. There is a wet chill to the room.

'Please, take a seat,' the nurse says, pointing at the uninviting-looking furniture, but Eleanor declines.

'My name is Nurse Baker,' the girl says. 'Which of the children is yours? I should probably telephone Superintendent Glover, although he has gone home for the evening. Or I can direct you to the main hall and the duty matron. I can't leave the children.' She looks worried.

'No!' Eleanor exclaims. Nurse Baker shrinks from her harsh tone and Eleanor holds her hands out. 'I'm sorry,' she says. She has no choice but to plead with this girl for help. 'I'm Eleanor Hamilton,' Eleanor says. 'Mabel's mother.'

The girl's face visibly blanches at the mention of Mabel's name and Eleanor's heart plunges.

'What is it? Is Mabel ill too?' Dear Lord, that wasn't something she had considered. What if *she* has the dreaded influenza, or scarlet fever or mumps? Or worse, diphtheria or pneumonia? *Diseases run through the colony like wildfire*, the nurse had said. Oh God, she is too late! What if Mabel is too poorly to travel or what if she has already passed away?

'No,' Nurse Baker says quickly, 'no. She's not ill.' She blinks rapidly a few times. Eleanor notices her hands are shaking. She clutches them together as though willing them to be still.

'Then I should like to see her. Now, please.'

'It's far too late for visiting!' The nurse stares at Eleanor, eyes stretched wide. 'And I was told Mabel would never have visitors. They said she was one of those who...'

Her voice trails away.

'Who, *what*?' Eleanor feels sick.

'I'd better telephone Superintendent Glover.' Nurse Baker glances towards the door. Eleanor has the urge to grab hold of the girl and shake out of her whatever it is she is clearly holding back.

'That won't be necessary.' Eleanor fights the panic and tries to keep her tone even. 'I'm here to collect Mabel. I am her mother and I have every right to come here at whatever time I choose and take her home. So, are you going to show me where Mabel is sleeping, or do I have to search the rooms myself?'

'No!' Nurse Baker springs towards the door as though to block Eleanor's way. 'Mabel isn't in the Babies Castle any more. I'm afraid she is in the medical wing.'

Oh sweet heaven.

Miss Manners was right. A wave of nausea hits Eleanor and she leans against the back of an armchair for fear her legs might buckle.

'But why? You said she wasn't sick?'

Nurse Baker is shaking her head, looking stricken. 'She's... Dr Eversley is...'

'*What!*'

'She's been taken for Dr Eversley's experiment!' the girl blurts out. Her words hit Eleanor like gunshot.

'Where is she?' Eleanor gasps. A wave of nausea rises. 'Tell me where the hell she is, *now*!'

28

Edward

Wilson is waiting, as usual, outside Mayfield station when he arrives on the 6.40 train.

'Evening, Professor.' Wilson greets him with a smile. 'I do hope you've had a good day.'

'Not particularly,' Edward answers with a sigh. He's become rather used to offloading his week's happenings to Wilson on the drive home.

'I'm sorry to hear that, sir.' Wilson opens the passenger door for Edward to climb in. 'Anything I can help with?'

Edward wonders at Wilson's cheerful optimism, envious of his buoyancy. Early this afternoon, he had received a panicked telephone call from Coleroy & Mack and the unsavoury news has sat in his belly like a sickness ever since.

'It seems,' Edward tells Wilson as the Sunbeam pulls out into the road, 'that there were large falls on the London stock market today, set off by some chap – Hatry, was it?'

Wilson shrugs. 'Can't help you there, sir, I'm afraid.'

'No, I don't suppose you can. Well, it doesn't matter, anyway, this chap, or his company, had invested in some American steel venture but it turned out to be fraudulent.'

'The steel venture, sir?'

'No, the investment. Or the collateral for the investment. Oh, I don't remember the detail. Anyway, the long and short of it, Wilson, is that it caused an almighty crash in the stock market and the result of *that*, is apparently everyone wants to take their money out – not only of the stock market, but also the banks, which means everyone is panicking, most especially the banks.'

'I see,' Wilson says, a little frown forming beneath his cap, clearly wondering where Edward is going with this.

'Anyway,' Edward continues, 'until Mr Coleroy, my banker chappie, called me, I was blissfully ignorant of all of this. But he telephoned in quite a state of high excitement and told me that I needn't worry and that I must hold firm and keep my money where it is. He said the markets would recover in a few days, once they got over the shock of whatever it was this Hatry fellow had done, and things would be back up to what they were. He said that because of my risk averse choices, my investments are quite safe.'

'I see,' repeats Wilson, even though he clearly doesn't. 'So... everything is all right then, sir?'

'Well, the problem is,' Edward says, as the reassuringly solid pillars of Brook End come into view, 'until Coleroy told me I shouldn't worry, I *hadn't* worried. I'd been perfectly content that my money was in safe hands. But once a person receives a phone call telling him not to worry, that is exactly what the person will then do. So, I am left to wonder, if Mr Coleroy telephones all his customers to tell them not to worry, and they do, are they all going to rush to the bank in the morning and remove their funds? And if they do *that*, will the bank collapse? Well of course I'm now thinking should *I* be taking my money out and stuffing it under the bed like everyone else?'

'Oh dear,' Wilson comments, as they crawl down the drive towards the house. 'And what did you decide to do in the end, sir?'

'Nothing,' Edward says. 'When in doubt, Wilson, doing nothing is always an option. But an uncomfortable one, all the same. My nerves are in shreds, I can tell you.'

'I'm sorry to hear that, sir,' Wilson says, but adds nothing more, clearly unable to think of a way to save Edward's nerves from shredding further. Edward wonders if he has concerns for his own job if Edward has to cut his expenses. He considers expressing some sort of platitude as the car rolls to a halt outside the front door. 'Are you expecting Mrs Hamilton back this evening, then?' Wilson asks, before Edward can say anything further, seemingly keen to find a different topic of conversation as he walks around the car to open Edward's door.

'Pardon?' He hadn't realised Eleanor had plans.

'Only I saw her leaving in Lady Grant-Parker's car earlier,' Wilson says jovially as he pulls Edward's briefcase from the back. 'Looked like they were off for the weekend, car stacked high with luggage.'

Edward takes his briefcase from Wilson and wonders if he has forgotten something, but mention of luggage sets off alarm bells in his head. Where on earth would Eleanor be going with luggage?

'Well, thank you.' Edward avoids answering Wilson's question. 'Have a good evening, Wilson,' and he turns towards the house. Faulks or Mrs Faulks will be able to solve the mystery.

He knows something is off the second he steps inside the front door. The air in the house is different. Even the dog who comes to greet him is less exuberant than usual.

'What is it, Byron?' he asks, patting the dog's golden sides. 'What's going on here, old fellow?'

'Ah, Professor Hamilton, you're back at last.' Mrs Faulks bustles into the hallway as he puts down his briefcase, hangs his hat on the stand and removes his jacket.

'Am I late?' He wonders again if he has forgotten something he was supposed to remember. Has the nonsense with the stock market knocked something crucial from his memory?

'Not exactly.' She turns on her heel and disappears back down the corridor, muttering something about a letter.

'Good evening. Can I get you a drink, sir?' Faulks appears from the dining room.

'Ah! Faulks. Most definitely. Never been in need of one more. A double whisky is in order, I think, don't you?' Faulks smiles thinly and disappears to fetch the drink.

There is an urgent knocking on the front door. In Faulks's absence Edward opens it himself to find Barton and Lizzie on the doorstep. He really is losing his memory – he had no idea they had guests this evening for dinner.

'Oh, Edward, sorry to turn up unannounced, but we thought you wouldn't want to be alone this evening. You must be beside yourself with worry, old chap.' Barton steps through the door and gives Edward a squeeze on the shoulder.

Good lord! Someone else who is fraught with worry. This stock market thing must be much worse than he realised.

He begins to feel a little sweaty as he shuts the front door behind him. Could it be that he actually *has* lost all of his money? Does everyone else know something he doesn't? Is this why Eleanor has taken off on some bizarre getaway with Sophie?

'How are you, Edward?' Lizzie asks, her face the picture of empathetic kindness.

'Well, I...'

Faulks is back and hands him his glass. Edward takes a deep slug of whisky and it burns hard and fast in his throat. Its pleasing warmth spreads.

'Shall we go into the drawing room and sit down?' he asks Barton and Lizzie once they have given their drinks orders to Faulks. 'Are you staying for dinner?'

'If you'd like us to,' Lizzie says gently. 'We'll do whatever you prefer. We weren't sure if you'd want company or not, were we, Barton?' She turns and nudges her husband, who is giving him a peculiar look. He nods his agreement.

At that moment a breathless Mrs Faulks returns. 'I'm so sorry, Professor,' she says breathlessly. 'I put it in a safe place you see, but then could I remember where that was? Anyway, I found it eventually. Here you are.' She holds out a sealed envelope with his name on it in Eleanor's handwriting.

'Oh bless me!' Lizzie's hands fly to her face. 'You haven't read the letter! So you don't know?'

Edward is becoming agitated. Everyone is talking in goddam riddles. He takes the letter from Mrs Faulks and looks around the room. Barton, Lizzie, Mrs Faulks – they are all staring at him with their mouths wide open, looking like idiots in an asylum.

'Know *what*?' he asks irritably, waving the letter in despair. And then it hits him. Eleanor has left. She's left him.

She is so angry about the data *fraud*, as she called it, over his lies about Porter, she's gone to stay with Sophie.

The room sways and he almost drops his glass. He sinks down into his armchair, staring at the envelope in his hands.

'I think you'd better open that,' Barton says.

'Yes,' Lizzie agrees. 'You really must. But we should give you some space – Barton, let's go somewhere. Leave Edward to read the letter in peace.'

'No,' Edward says. 'Please. Stay. It's – it's good of you both to come. I'd appreciate the company.'

'Excuse me,' Mrs Faulks asks, 'but will you be staying for dinner then, Mr and Mrs Leyton?'

'Yes. I think we had better stay,' Lizzie nods.

'Right you are,' she says, backing out of the room and closing the door gently.

Edward takes a deep breath and opens the envelope.

Darling Edward,

By the time you read this note, I will be a long way away. I cannot tell you where I am going, for reasons I hope you will understand. But those reasons are not only so that nobody can find us, but also to protect you and your good name.

I know we haven't seen eye to eye over things lately. But the most important of these is Mabel and her treatment. I have found it unbearable to think of Mabel being locked up in the epilepsy colony, where she must be so scared and lonely. I have tried to convince you and Sir Charles Lawson about the efficacy of the new dietary treatment I have spoken of to you. You were not interested. Sir Charles dismissed me entirely.

Worse still, I received an unexpected letter from someone at the colony who is concerned for Mabel's welfare and urged me to come.

I cannot sleep at night thinking Mabel may be harmed, and also knowing that there is a treatment, some say a very effective one in children in particular, without giving it a try. Further, I will also say that I cannot live with myself knowing that I have sent my child away with the prospect that I may never see her again. I know this is what people do and that this is what everyone expects of me, but Edward, I, Eleanor Hamilton, cannot do it. I have no desire to live unless Mabel is at my side, for however long she has on God's earth.

And so I have set up, in a secret location, a place where we may live comfortably and well, and I have engaged an experienced doctor who will help me to administer the diet. With all my heart and soul, I hope it will work. If it indeed does not, please know that I will not send Mabel back to that colony.

I know it is wrong to do this without you, Edward, but I also know that you would not have agreed to my plan. You have been a kind and generous husband, and you granted me the ability to have access to our bank accounts. I have therefore wired sufficient funds to a local bank so that we may have something to live on for the time being. I trust you will, in time, come to accept and respect my decision in this regard.

Edward, I know you will be thinking, how can I leave one child for another? I have thought long and hard about this. It would be cruel and unkind to remove Jimmy from his home and to bring him would be too *complicated and difficult. I need to devote my full attention to Mabel to care for her and nurse her. I could not give Jimmy the attention he needs, just now, but I know leaving him in Miss Harding's care he will be in the best hands, and he has you too of course. Lizzie has promised to look in on you both and make sure you are OK. I think it has been difficult for me to love Jimmy as I should have done, when my heart has been torn in two without Mabel. I do love Jimmy, of course I do, but not in the way a mother should. I hope in time, once I have done what I need to for Mabel, I will be able to be the mother Jimmy deserves.*

And so, that leaves me only to say, as for us, I cannot tell you what the future holds. I do not know if we, you and I, can make a new start sometime. I do not know if you will ever forgive me for doing this. I also don't know if I can forgive you for insisting we send Mabel away in the first place. Indeed, for all the work you do in respect of people like our daughter. I urge you, from the bottom of my heart, to reconsider your position on eugenics and the movement. I have changed my views completely, as you know. I think for us to be reconciled fully, you would need to take a different position in your professional life. Rose has helped me to see things differently. I was so full of hate for the man who killed our mother, I could no longer see clearly. Now I understand so much more. We cannot treat all people who are unfortunate to have some kind of affliction of the mind or body in the same distrustful way. Everyone, wherever they come from and whatever abilities they have or don't have, is human, and deserves to be treated so.

*Please do not try to contact me. Not yet. Perhaps when
the time is right, you and Jimmy may even be able to join
us. I will let you know when we have safely arrived and
will send a post office address soon.*
  All my love,
  Eleanor.

Edward stares at the letter in stunned silence. Of all the
things it could have said, this was not at all what he would
have imagined. His brain is struggling to compute. Eleanor
has been planning this and not said a single word to him.
Does she distrust him this much?

Of course she does! She knew he would forbid her to
take Mabel out of the colony. Indeed, he *did* forbid it. But
he did it out of concern for *her*, knowing how bad it was
before Mabel had gone into Heath, how awful the effect
was on Eleanor – and him – in seeing her deteriorate. Surely
it is better that they don't have to watch that? Besides, Sir
Charles really does believe it is best for her to be in a place
with others like her, where they are used to dealing with
epileptics. Where she can live in peace and tranquillity
and not be mocked or judged or treated badly by normal
society. This poppycock about someone writing to Eleanor
being concerned for Mabel's safety – who was that? Some
troublemaker, no doubt, who, knowing Edward's line of
work, perhaps found out that Mabel is his daughter. Damn
them, whoever they are!

But to him, the worst of it is, how can she leave her
baby son? How can she love poor, damaged Mabel more
than perfect, healthy Jimmy? It seems Eleanor has lost her
mind, or Rose and that bastard Frenchman have warped

her into thinking she can carry out this ridiculous notion of a miracle cure. Of course it won't work. What then? Will Eleanor come back, even more heartbroken?

'Edward?' Lizzie's voice brings him back into the room. He looks up, startled that his neighbours are sitting staring at him with worry in their eyes. They knew. Everyone knew except him. A sudden flare of anger at Eleanor. At all of them. How dare she make him look such a fool!

'So, is there anyone apart from me who wasn't in on the big secret?' he asks, the bitterness seeping into his voice.

'We only knew this afternoon,' Lizzie says quickly. 'Eleanor came and told me. I begged her not to go, begged her to speak with you, but her mind was quite made up. She was worried about you, though, and so we promised we would help in any way we could.'

'Yes, old chap,' says Barton. 'Anything we can do, just shout.'

'Did she give any hint about where she was going?' Edward asks Lizzie, glancing at the letter again in case he missed some clue hidden between the lines.

'No, nothing. I did ask, but she wouldn't say...'

Edward looks at his watch. It's 7.30 p.m. He springs from his chair and finds Mrs Faulks in the dining room

'What time did they leave, Mrs Faulks?' he asks.

She stares up at the ceiling. 'Well, let's see. Alice had just finished laying the fires and I was just back from the village having bought some silver polish and dusters. Mrs Bellamy hadn't begun the supper... I imagine it was about 5.30...'

Edward's pulse quickens. That was only two hours ago! Chances are, she hasn't yet left the colony with Mabel.

Surely they wouldn't allow his daughter to leave without his express permission anyway?

He runs to the telephone in the hallway. He'll call Superintendent Glover now. There is still time to stop this madcap idea of Eleanor's. Heaven knows – if she takes Mabel out of the colony without the medication, she could kill the girl. Sir Charles had warned how dangerous it was simply to stop it without phasing it out. Unwittingly, Eleanor could be putting Mabel's life at risk if she goes through with this terrible plan.

29

Eleanor

'Did Sir Charles sanction this – this *experiment*?' Eleanor demands. 'And Superintendent Glover?'

'No!' The nurse looks alarmed. 'They didn't know about it. I'm sure they would not have agreed to it if they did.'

'But this is an outrage!' Eleanor is shouting. 'How can such things happen? My child, *any* child, can't be taken for experimentation without the parents' permission! And if Sir Charles can't know? Christ! What can this doctor be doing to her?'

Nurse Baker shrugs and looks helpless. 'It happens all the time, Mrs Hamilton. Only usually the families don't care. What they don't see, they don't worry about.'

'What sort of place is this?' Eleanor grabs Nurse Baker's arms. 'Where *is* Mabel?' Eleanor asks her desperately. 'Please, just tell me where she is!'

'Dr Eversley has a suite of rooms next to the medical wing but I'm not allowed to leave the Babies Castle – the children would be unattended.' She glances up at the ceiling as though she can see the sleeping children through it. 'I will telephone Dr Eversley.' She checks her watch. 'He'll be finishing dinner just about now...'

'No,' Eleanor says. 'Don't. Just tell me where to find my daughter.'

'The medical rooms are in the basement. At the end of the corridor. In the old days, they'd have been the old kitchens when that building was a private house.'

'Is there a back entrance?' Eleanor asks. Time seems to be passing too fast. If the staff have finished their dinner, how will she get to the medical wing unseen? She peers out of the window, trying to make out the shape of Sophie's car in the shadows of the barn it is parked alongside. Should she get her friend to help?

'Well, yes,' Nurse Baker says, pointing across to the left of the main building, 'but only on the ground floor. The outside entrance to the basement has long since been blocked off. You'd have to come all the way through the house to get to the staircase down to the basement. There is only one way down there.'

Damn! Eleanor turns to leave.

Nurse Baker follows her to the door. 'Mrs Hamilton, you can't take your daughter. The experiment Dr Eversley is carrying out – it would be dangerous to—'

'I've heard enough,' Eleanor says, pulling open the front door. 'Nothing will stop me removing my daughter from this place.'

As she runs from the building, she hears Nurse Baker pick up the phone, hears her say, 'You need to find Dr Eversley – quickly!'

Eleanor doesn't wait to hear any more. There is no time to fetch Sophie. She sprints towards the building the nurse had indicated and through the door she saw the short, dishevelled man enter earlier. Inside is a large, vaulted hall, thankfully empty. Eleanor glances around. A light is on in a room on the left. Eleanor peers in. It is some sort of staff sitting room and several are in there, apparently having after-dinner coffee and a smoke. She creeps past, holding her breath, and heads down a corridor in the direction Nurse Baker indicated the medical wing lies.

A telephone rings loudly from an office as she walks by, making her jump. The light is on, papers piled high on the desk and the chair has a jacket hung over the back, its occupant thankfully absent. But clearly not for long. She doubles her speed, breathing a sigh of relief when she sees a staircase ahead, leading downwards.

She takes the flight of stairs, two at a time, almost falling in her haste, then she is in a long, dark corridor, dimly lit at each end. Which way? Eleanor shivers and turns towards the direction furthest away from the house. She feels certain that was what Nurse Baker had meant.

There is a maze of rooms in the basement, many of the doors locked. The ones Eleanor can open are empty and all have bars on the high windows, bars around the beds. One has padded walls. With rising panic, Eleanor realises Mabel must be behind a locked door and she has no way of getting her out.

At the final door she stops, chest heaving, and lets out an anguished sob which echoes along the corridor. She is defeated. How stupid; how foolish was she for thinking this crazed mission could ever work?

She stands, unsure what to do next. Perhaps she should go and find Sophie. Explain what is happening. Perhaps she will have some bright ideas.

She begins to walk back up the corridor when she

hears footsteps clattering down the stairs. She stops in her tracks.

A man appears and as he swings towards her, his ill-fitting jacket flying out behind him, she realises it's the same rumpled man she had seen enter the building earlier. He yells something, which sounds like *hey there!* at her and waves his arms. Her heart bangs wildly in her chest. Something tells her this is the despicable Dr Eversley and every muscle in her body tenses. Nothing will stop her from getting her daughter back. Nothing.

'Mrs Hamilton!' The man skids to a halt in front of her, his three-piece tweed woollen suit accentuating the broadness in his chest and belly. His dress and hair, thoroughly unkempt, indicate a man who is uninterested in his own appearance.

'Yes,' she replies, squaring up to him. 'And you are?'

'I'm Dr Eversley.' He is breathless from running. 'I've just received a call from Superintendent Glover telling me your husband telephoned him in a great state of agitation. He was worried you would show up and try to take your daughter away from here. And well...' He takes a deep breath. 'Here you are.'

'*Edward!*' Eleanor exclaims. He's read the letter. He's told the Superintendent not to let her take Mabel. At the very last moment, she is thwarted. She bites her lip to stop herself from crumbling.

'Kindly take me to my daughter,' she says, doing her best to keep her voice calm. 'I do indeed wish to take her away from here, and you shan't stop me.'

'Ah. That is unadvisable. Perhaps we could have a little chat in my office first?' he says. He pulls his handkerchief from his pocket and dabs sweat off his forehead. 'Professor Hamilton,' Dr Eversley continues, 'wanted all the staff alerted, to ensure you didn't do anything rash. I told the Superintendent I'd not seen you, and doubted you would come so late. He is fully expecting you to show up in the morning.'

Eleanor swallows the lump in her throat. 'I suppose you wish to telephone him back then,' she says.

The doctor fixes her with hooded dark eyes. 'I have no wish to bother him again this evening,' he says slowly, 'if you would rather I didn't.'

Eleanor's legs turn to liquid as she remembers Nurse Baker's words. How his *experiments* were being kept secret from Sir Charles and Superintendent Glover. She wonders, fleetingly, what Nurse Baker is getting to keep this a secret.

'I... I just want my daughter to be OK,' she says finally. 'I want her safe.'

Dr Eversley smiles then. A warm smile. 'As do I, Mrs Hamilton. As do I.'

'Sorry?'

'Let's talk in my office,' he repeats. 'We don't want to be found talking here, do we?'

Eleanor allows him to propel her along the corridor and up the stairs, back to the lighted office she had passed earlier. It crosses her mind that if nobody knows she is here, could he lock her up, or do something unspeakable to her? Thank goodness Sophie is waiting for her outside. She'd raise the alarm. Although she may already have done so. Eleanor has been gone longer than they had planned.

Dr Eversley waves her into a chair and seats himself behind his desk. He clears his throat. 'Can I offer you anything?' he asks. 'A drink?'

She shakes her head, watching him. Not the demeanour of someone wanting to do her in. But neither is there any shame or awkwardness for taking her daughter as a laboratory specimen. Eleanor almost chokes with anger.

'As I said,' he begins, 'I'm Dr Eversley, one of the doctors here, and I've been treating Mabel.'

'I really would like to see her now, Dr Eversley,' she says as politely as she can muster.

Dr Eversley frowns. 'When is the last time you saw her?'

'More than three months now, although not for want of trying. My husband wouldn't—'

'I must warn you,' Dr Eversley says, at last meeting her eyes. 'Mabel has deteriorated very much.'

'I have been made aware,' Eleanor says in desperation. 'Sir Charles has reported Mabel's condition to us; we know the situation is bleak. And that's why I'm here! I want to try—'

'I know exactly what you want to try,' Dr Eversley exclaims, 'and this is precisely what I wish to discuss with you too! First I must explain that Sir Charles told me about the treatment you wanted to try with Mabel. He told me with derision. With shock and amazement that any mother would wish to try something so ridiculous and cruel on her own daughter. He showed me the papers you left with him. Told me to dispose of them.' He pauses.

'Go on,' Eleanor says.

'Well, fact is, I had heard of this starvation treatment before. Read about it a few years ago in a medical journal. So of course, I read the papers and I was excited about what I read. This could really help them, I told Sir Charles. But, to cut a long story short, he and I had a disagreement.' He stops. Removes his glasses. Puts them on again. 'Here's the thing. Sir Charles is, without doubt, the eminent expert of our day. But, and please understand I am not in any way bad-mouthing a friend and colleague, a superior, indeed my employer! You understand, yes? But you see, Sir Charles is, how can I put it...' He drums his fingers on the desk as though trying to judge how much to divulge. '... *old school*, in his thinking and unwilling to take risks. But in my opinion, in life risks must be taken if we are to make progress. To advance medicine. Yes?' He beams at her.

Eleanor is struggling to process his words. It feels as though he is working up to telling her something unpleasant. A queasiness takes hold in her belly.

'I'm not sure I follow, Dr Eversley.' She looks desperately at her watch. Could he be stalling, waiting for Edward to arrive and then what?

Dr Eversley fixes her with his bright brown eyes and clears his throat. 'I will be plain, Mrs Hamilton. I admit, I should have made contact with you. But Sir Charles had strictly forbidden this, on the understanding Professor Hamilton would be against it too. Therefore, I took a liberty. A liberty which is for the greater good. Sometimes one must grasp that bull by the horns, bite the bullet, seize the day. Do you follow me?'

Eleanor simply stares at him, waiting for him to come clean about what he has done.

'The experiment... Well, it is early days but we mustn't be without hope. I've weaned her off all the drugs. You should know that how you find her now is solely due to the new programme. Before I began treating Mabel, her decline had been swift and decisive. She had lost control of her bladder, ceased playing, speaking and interacting normally. Her intellect was deteriorating fast into feeble-mindedness – imbecility.'

Eleanor's heart is hammering so hard, she is certain the doctor must be able to hear it thumping.

'So,' Dr Eversley hesitates, glancing at Eleanor, 'I got in touch with the same Dr Peterman at the Mayo Clinic in Minnesota, who wrote the article you had left with Sir Charles. He runs a programme there. I decided to run my own research programme here and requested their help in terms of the most suitable patients to select and how to run and test the candidates. Well, Mabel was a perfect candidate – she wasn't responding to any of the medication, is young and with several unusual seizure types. I have ten on the programme in all.'

'But – but why didn't I hear of this? I've been in touch with Dr Peterman too! I should have been included on the decisions you were making. I simply don't understand how you could take Mabel without our permission!'

'When you put Mabel in the colony,' Dr Eversley says in gentle tones, 'you gave us permission to treat her in the way we thought best. In my professional opinion, this is it.'

Trembling, Eleanor leans towards him. 'I would like to see her now. Please.'

He nods and grabs a set of keys from his drawer. Eleanor follows him across the passageway to a room just across from his office. He turns the key in the lock and flings open the door, disappearing into the room in a flap of tailcoat.

Eleanor takes a deep breath, stunned into silence by his revelation, and follows him in. She has buried the last painful memory of Mabel, but now she allows it to flood back; that pathetic sight of her in the hospital before she was brought here. Her face, puffed and swollen from the medication, her previous baby-smooth skin puckered and spoilt with an ugly rash, her very soul stolen by this monstrous disease. Given what Dr Eversley has said about her decline, she braces herself for an even more unpleasant encounter.

The room is pitch black. Mabel hates the dark, Eleanor thinks, as the doctor fumbles around, knocking something over. He swears and then, finding the lamp cord, he switches on the light.

A nurse appears behind them, bustling in and saying, 'I've only just got them off to sleep, Dr Eversley.' She sounds more than a little disgruntled.

The room is large. The beds are arranged at one end of the room. At the other stands a rocking horse, a dolls' house set on a low table, and a rug with wooden blocks, toy cars and dolls neatly arranged at one side. It looks much like the contents of any nursery room.

A couple of the children shift in their beds and poke their heads out of the covers, blinking at the sudden bright light.

'Mabel?' Dr Eversley says, striding towards the end bed. Eleanor's throat closes. *Mabel.* Her daughter is pushing herself up to sit, her face sleepy and confused, quiet and pale – but she is quite obviously Mabel. Gone are the swollen features, the sunken, sad eyes. Gone is the terrible skin rash and the floppy, dead look about her. This Mabel bears a striking resemblance to the one she was before she became ill. Delicate and slender, her complexion peachy in the soft light; big, bright eyes. Well, not quite that, perhaps, but closer than she ever imagined might be possible again.

She is hugging her ragdoll to her chest, rocking her a little, as one might a baby. Eleanor cries out and rushes to her, slowing as she reaches the side of her bed.

'Mabel?' she says, her voice choked with tears.

The little girl looks up and says, unmistakeably, 'Mama!'

Eleanor is on the bed, Mabel in her arms, and her daughter is repeating, over and over, *'Mama, my Mama, my Mama.'*

Mabel is warm and soft pressed against her, her skinny little arms wrapped tight around her middle, as they cling to one another. *I shall never let you go again*, Eleanor thinks fiercely. *Never again.*

'I'm here, darling,' she murmurs. 'I'm here and I shan't leave without you. You are coming with me, Mabel. OK?' She rocks her gently back and forth, just as she did when Mabel was a baby.

She vaguely hears Dr Eversley say above her head, 'We are only in the very earliest of stages of the diet – a week in – but I am delighted with the results so far. Indeed, of all the cases, she has responded most dramatically...' His voice fades in and out as Eleanor is only half listening. 'I would dearly love to have the funding to expand this project... To help more children like Mabel. She has not experienced a single seizure for *four* days.'

Dr Eversley's words filter slowly into Eleanor's brain. *Mabel has not experienced a seizure for four days.* So many questions crowd into her mind, but she is speechless. She looks down at Mabel, who peers up at her and smiles. Behind her wide blue eyes, she can see the girl she was before. Gone is the cloudy, inward gaze. The spark she can see makes Eleanor's stomach flip. *Mabel is back.* She strokes her hair, oh so gently, and fights the tears which threaten to cascade with relief down her cheeks.

Mabel hasn't experienced a seizure for four days.

Those are the best words she has heard in a very, very long time.

'Mrs Hamilton,' Dr Eversley's voice carries a tone of urgency, 'once I was certain I was seeing positive results, I was going to present them to Sir Charles, and then to you. But right now it's too early.' He steps a little closer, his voice a little firmer. 'Of course I cannot stop you taking your daughter away from here, but I do urge you not to. We are at a critical stage and she needs an expert to administer this treatment.'

Eleanor stares up at him. 'I can't leave her here. Not now. I promised and – and Edward…' She clings to Mabel a little tighter. 'It's too complicated to explain.'

Dr Eversley sits on the side of the bed. 'I understand, Mrs Hamilton. And in time, when we are sure the diet is working on Mabel, with luck you will be able to take her home. But in the meantime it would be foolhardy to—'

'No! You don't understand. I had plans to start Mabel on this diet myself, under the guidance of a French doctor who has past experience with it, and I have been in correspondence with the same Dr Peterman from the Mayo Clinic, as I said.' Eleanor explains to him what she has learned about the Ketogenic diet and how she has arranged things in France. 'I've been working for weeks to sort this out. The fact is, Dr Eversley, whether the diet works or not, I do not want Mabel to be away from me one minute longer.'

Dr Eversley studies her in silence. She has no idea what

is going on in his head. 'You are determined,' he says at last, 'not to leave here without her tonight?'

'That's right,' she says. 'My husband will stop me if I don't.'

Dr Eversley is silent again. 'Right,' he says finally, giving a quick nod. 'As I say, I cannot stop you. You are clearly a resourceful woman as you have all this planned and you understand the mechanics of the diet. So,' he rests his fingertips on his forehead, 'the best thing I can do is to make sure I give you all the information you need to make it a success.'

He turns to the nurse. 'Pack up Mabel's things and help her to dress,' he instructs, then says to Eleanor, 'Come with me.'

Leaving the nurse to collect Mabel's few clothes and possessions, Eleanor follows Dr Eversley back to his office. As they walk, she is struck by sudden terror. Everything has gone so well in Dr Eversley's trial. What if she messes it all up? Is she really doing the right thing?

It's too late now. She has to go through with this.

'It is crucial to follow exactly my instructions,' Dr Eversley is saying. 'You must have a good set of scales then it will be easy to follow. I will detail how to measure the body's ketone levels as well as meal plans written for the two nurses who have been assisting me. I will also write to the doctor who will be helping you – we can make this work, do not worry.'

She watches him scribble instructions, his face wrinkled with concentration, then with a broad smile he places a sheaf of papers into Eleanor's hands. Alongside the terror of responsibility, her heart swells with gratitude. 'Thank you,' she says, her eyes filling with tears. 'Those words aren't enough,' she adds. 'I'm so grateful that you took a risk on Mabel. I do hope you don't get into any trouble for all of this.'

'Ach, I'll be fine. Go,' he says, brushing off her thanks. 'Any questions, you know where to find me. I'm keen to help these children,' he adds. 'I don't want them to be locked up here forever. They should live full lives out there in the real world.'

Minutes later, Dr Eversley carries Mabel, bundled in warm clothes and wrapped in blankets, to the car, Eleanor beside him carrying her case. He lays her gently on the back seat.

'I thought you'd been locked up in there too,' Sophie exclaims, leaping out of the car. 'I was about to find a telephone to call the police!'

'Dr Eversley, this is Sophie.'

He raises an eyebrow. 'Your driver?'

'My friend,' she says firmly. 'My dear friend who has agreed to drive us to our destination in France. She'll leave us there and then return to her own family.'

'We all need friends like Sophie from time to time.' Dr Eversley smiles and slaps a hand on the bonnet. 'Go safely.'

'Thank you.' Eleanor climbs into the back seat and rests Mabel's head gently on her lap.

'Please write to me soon, so I know how Mabel is getting on,' he says, then Sophie pulls away, the engine roaring, navigating once more the bumpy track.

As the colony buildings recede behind them, Eleanor feels herself begin to relax. Mabel is on the road to recovery. With her arms wrapped around her daughter and Prudence, she leans her head against the back of the seat and allows her eyes to drift close. Whatever happens next, she knows she has done the right thing.

30

Edward

Darling Edward, he reads. He wishes she wouldn't call him that. Fact is, he isn't her darling any more. If he was, she would never have gone. Never have left him. He regrets not having listened to her, regrets shutting her down when she suggested hiring nurses and cooks and whatever else was needed to administer this treatment to Mabel. It had simply seemed so far-fetched and preposterous, too good to be true. And he had thought he was protecting *her* from the pain of watching Mabel's deterioration and, perhaps himself too. In truth, though, however hard it is to admit it, all his actions, now and in the past, have really been to protect himself.

It seems he is, with every passing event in his life, adding to his list of regrets.

Over three weeks have gone by, and so far, Eleanor has not given up and come home. Still has not let on where she is, although he knows from the postage she is in France. Or at least, he thinks she is. Unless there is an elaborate ploy to cover up her location because the dates on her letters don't tally with how long it is taking for the letters to arrive, nor the Paris postmarks on the envelopes. He imagines the letters are being sent to the Frenchman, Deveaux, in Paris, who forwards them on. He sighs, and goes back to the letter.

20th October 1929

Darling Edward,

How are you? I think of you every day and wonder how you are faring. Please do write to the PO address at the top of the letter. I am desperate for news from home. Perhaps you think I have no right to hear it, but I know that you are not unkind and that you will write when you are able. Please, above all, give me news of Jimmy. I find I miss him far more than I ever thought possible. Now that Mabel is with me again, it's as if a door in my heart has been opened and all the love for Jimmy permitted to flow out. I'm sure he is well and happy, but oh, what I would give to hold him in my arms!

As for Mabel, I am happy to tell you that so far, at least, and I know it is still early days, she does very well. The best news is that she has not had a convulsion or fit at all. Not once. We are extremely strict about the diet and stick to it to the tiniest percentage. We measure her ketones daily and these, at the moment, are steady and at the perfect level. Although it is some work, at least at the beginning, to measure and prepare 100 per cent of everything Mabel eats, it surprises me that she isn't in the least bit hungry. Most importantly, she seems happy. So, Edward, I dare to hope.

For the rest, well, she remains a very sick child. She can barely speak, just a smattering of words and hardly knows how to play. It is as if she has reverted to babyhood. But I nurse her and spend every waking hour with her and today, Edward, you are the first person I wanted to tell – she called for me to look at a book. And so she sat on my lap and I read to her and Prudence – and she smiled! It was the first time she has properly showed interest in something. That's good, isn't it?

I do reflect, though, on the other poor children left behind in the colony. I think sometimes about how their mothers might wish they could have their children at home but don't have the means, financial or otherwise, to do what I have done for Mabel. It makes me impossibly sad if I dwell on it and I suppose there is little I can do to change things at this moment. And so I thank the stars at night for our good fortune and your wealth, without which I could never have been reunited with our daughter. For that I will always be grateful.

I otherwise lead a very quiet life. It is peaceful here. But I do miss you, Edward, I do.

This is all for now.

I will write again soon.

Your wife,

Eleanor

There is no hint of smugness, or *I told you so* between the lines Eleanor has written. What a fool he has been!

Edward folds the letter and places it in the top drawer of his desk, with the two other letters he has received from her. They are all he has left of her, just ink marks on paper, the faint scent of her in her bed and when he opens her wardrobe. The fact of her absence is so strong he is breathless with it, doubled up by the pain of it – he almost doesn't know how to live if she isn't here.

She used to beg him to be home more. She could never understand the constant pressure of his work, how the travelling back and forth to Brook End during the week ate too much into his time. Nor how he couldn't bear to be there and witness Mabel's decline. Back then, *before*, he didn't see that he had any choice. The work was relentless, the need to achieve and succeed, to bury the pain of things he would rather not face, was like an unstoppable force driving him on and on. But now that it is too late and she is gone, he can see he was wrong. It *was* a choice, his choice. And the irony is, now that Eleanor isn't here, he is home almost every night because it makes him feel closer to her. And it means he gets to see Jimmy, the one shining light in all of this mess.

Of course, he could try to find her; bring her home. He knows it wouldn't be too hard – he could hire a detective. But what would be the point? If she comes back, it will need to be because she wants to, not because he insists on it. The shock of her leaving has made him reassess his life and he has had three weeks of thinking, painful thinking, since she has gone. He has had to face the thing he has spent so many years hiding from. The truth. *His* truth. And what of his work? What of his reputation which he has fought so hard to protect? That is partly why she has stayed away, he knows that, but without Eleanor in his life, he realises, nothing else matters. Not his work, not his reputation.

Thankfully, his finances are secure after the shock of the stock market crash in September. Things appear quiet – at least he hasn't had Mr Coleroy panicking on the telephone, but he reads in the papers that everyone remains jittery.

Staring out across the leaf-strewn lawn, Edward ponders his future. The woods beyond the lawn are clothed in their full autumnal glory and the sight soothes him, nature a balm to his tortured soul. October is his favourite month, a month of glorious golden light and colour, of woodsmoke and early morning mists, of damp grass scattered with acorns and conkers from the huge ancient oaks and horse chestnut trees which shed their bounty, year after year, without the concerns of man. Edward is taking a good many walks through the woods and the fields, Byron by his side. Walking, he finds, is good for thinking. And he has done a lot of that this past month.

When Edward had telephoned Superintendent Glover the evening he discovered Eleanor had gone, Glover had assured him Eleanor had not arrived at Heath Colony; if she did, Glover would immediately let Edward know and they agreed it was likely she would come the next morning. But early the following morning Sir Charles had telephoned. He was too late. Eleanor *had* arrived the night before and taken Mabel away, which that maverick, Dr Eversley, had kept quiet about. He should have seen to it the man was fired, only he hadn't had the energy. All he had felt in the days that followed was despair, together with the growing sense that it was what he had deserved all along for gaining Eleanor's affections under false pretences.

Edward goes to the drawer in the display cabinet where, right at the back, are the medals he keeps in their presentation box, the medals he had worn proudly on his uniform the day he went to be decommissioned. The day he met Eleanor. He pulls out the flat, blue box, runs his hand over its smooth surface. Can one ever really right a wrong?

He climbs the stairs to the nursery. Jimmy is sitting on the rug, stacking his wooden blocks, or at least, Miss Harding is stacking his wooden blocks and Jimmy is knocking them over, flapping his chubby little hands and deep-belly laughing as they tumble down. He looks up as Edward comes over and bounces with joy.

Edward sweeps him up and kisses him, just where the fluff of his baby hair meets his neck. Jimmy chuckles and coos, wriggling like a fat worm in Edward's arms.

'Hello, young man,' Edward says, looking deep into his son's eyes. 'I hope you are behaving for Miss Harding this morning?'

'Oh, yes,' Miss Harding says from her position on the rug. She gathers up the bricks, piling them back into a tower. 'He never gets bored of this game.'

Edward blows a raspberry into his son's belly, sending him into another round of giggles.

Miss Harding smiles. 'It's lovely that you spend so much time with him,' she says. 'There's not many fathers who play with their babies,' she adds thoughtfully. 'He clearly adores you.' Neither of them mention the glaring absence of his mother.

'Well,' he says. 'I have to go now. I'll see you later, young man.' He puts Jimmy back on the rug. In the last few days the little boy has begun to wave and say, recognisably, the word 'bye'. Incredible, the speed of his development. Was Mabel the same? He has no recollection. An hour at teatime was the most he spent with her. His heart aches for the missed moments.

Two hours later, Edward pulls up at the front of Heath Colony. Sir Charles isn't here to greet him – Edward deliberately chose a day Lawson has a clinic in London.

Dr Eversley shakes his hand with great enthusiasm. He is much shorter, plumper and sweatier than Edward had visualised him to be. Younger, too. Edward suddenly feels old and jaded in the face of the man's bubbling energy.

There is a moment of awkwardness as they stroll together towards the Babies Castle where Edward has asked to be taken.

'I, er. Look, it's not for me to get involved in the… delicate matters between a husband and wife,' Dr Eversley mutters, looking at his toes. 'I hope… What I mean is… I didn't set out to cause trouble. I only wanted to help a *child*. Sir Charles and I… Well, it's no secret that he's trying to get rid of me. Personally, I've nothing against the fellow. He sees the people who live here as a problem we'd be better off without. There's plenty of people like him – of the lock 'em up and throw away the key point of view, society better off without them and all that.' He pauses for breath. 'But me, I see colonists as patients – individuals who need treatment. Who perhaps *can* be helped and made better. But if they can't, well, we should make their life, their time here, as stimulating and enjoyable as we possibly can.'

They reach the door of the Victorian building and Dr Eversley bangs on the door. 'Anyway,' the doctor continues, 'it seems that Superintendent Glover and Sister Hogget are rather more fans of mine than I had realised. They have blocked Sir Charles from getting rid of me, and we are trialling a new entertainment programme for *all* the colonists – trips to the seaside, a sports programme, theatricals and parties. Who doesn't like a party?' His face cracks into a wide smile. 'But most importantly, the children. I have all of the children, like Mabel, the ones for whom the medication has failed, on the Ketogenic diet, with varying degrees of success. It's not for all, I grant you, but we've seen an improvement in around half. That's worth an investment, isn't it?'

The front door opens and a young nurse, Nurse Baker, as she introduces herself, invites them in. Edward follows Dr Eversley on a tour of the place where Mabel lived for the past few months with the other youngest of the colony's children. The building, with its peeling wallpaper, high-ceilinged, freezing rooms, could not be less suitable for small children. It's a soulless place, with mouldy carpets and snotty-nosed children who stare up at him with wide, solemn eyes. Edward tries to imagine Mabel amongst them and he shudders.

'And these children?' he asks Dr Eversley. 'What hope is there for these?'

Dr Eversley crouches down. 'I don't know. But it is up to us adults, isn't it, Professor Hamilton, what sort of life they will live?' He looks up at Edward. 'I'm no politician, but I challenge all the lawmakers who decide how these people should live – each and every individual here – to come and see. Come and spend time, get to know them. Only then would it be right to decide.'

He brushes his hand over the head of one tiny boy, who

can't be more than three. 'Good day to you, Charlie.' Charlie says nothing. There is a twist to the child's open mouth, a blank look in his slightly crossed eyes. Edward resists the urge to avert his own. The boy looks from Dr Eversley to Edward and back to the doctor again. 'Charlie has suffered terrible convulsions since he was a baby and his development has been severely affected. I don't suppose he'll ever go home, assuming he survives to adulthood. Mother couldn't cope – father left and he was one of seven children.'

Edward cannot help but think the thoughts he has always had about families like this. Surely it would have been better had he not been born in the first place?

'But,' Dr Eversley is saying, 'Charlie loves cars, don't you, young fellow? How would you like to come with me and play in my car for a short time?' The boy's face cracks into a wide, wide smile. 'There now, provided Nurse Baker agrees. What do you say, Nurse?'

She looks down at Charlie. 'Oh, all right, just for half an hour until snack time – as long as the others can come too; we don't want any special favours in the Babies Castle, do we?'

'No, no. That wouldn't do at all,' Dr Eversley confirms.

And so Edward, Dr Eversley, the nurse and nine small children trail across the car park and pile enthusiastically into a black Austen 7. Edward winces, imagining them crawling all over the pristine interior of his Sunbeam, but Dr Eversley doesn't appear bothered at all. They watch the children in silence for a few moments. Like any *normal* children, they are engrossed in their exploration of the car. Charlie has hold of the steering wheel and is making car noises. He looks so happy, and Edward wonders, in that moment, whose right it should be to decide what is a *valuable* human life? Is this little boy any less valuable than Jimmy? Who is Edward, who is *anyone*, to decide that?

'Well,' Edward shoves out a hand, 'thank you so much for your time, doctor. I have learnt a good deal. I would stay longer but I have an appointment I must keep at the Red Cross Centre.'

'Come back any time,' says Dr Eversley.

After a moment, 'I will,' says Edward.

Too many thoughts are spinning. He needs time to think them through, come up with a plan. But first, there is something he must do, something he should have done ten years ago.

The only part of Porter visible above the pile of blankets is his head. He sits outside on the terrace of the Red Cross Centre, tucked against the wall beneath the overhand. From where he sits, the Centre being positioned on top of a hill, he has a sweeping, uninterrupted view of the woods and fields. Edward watches him for a few moments. Porter is entirely still, his body so small and shrunken beneath the blankets that Edward can barely make out his shape. He must literally be wasting away. Edward wonders, with a horrible stab to his conscience, just how long the man has left on this earth.

The enthusiastic young Nurse Dyer is fetching tea and cake. Edward imagines she will be less enthusiastic about Captain Edward Hamilton, as she still refers to him, once she learns the full truth.

'Hello, Porter.'

The man winces as he turns his head. When he sees Edward, he nods a fraction, almost as though he has been expecting him.

'Sir.'

'I, er, I said I would come back and see you again.'

'You did, sir. And here you are.'

Edward pulls up another chair and sits facing Porter. 'How are you bearing up?' he asks, although he can see the answer clearly enough in the poor man's pained expression.

'Can't complain,' Porter mumbles; then, quieter, 'Can't complain.'

Edward nods and smiles weakly at the man's fortitude in the face of all he bears, each and every day. 'Porter – Reggie,' he begins. 'When I was here before, you mentioned you had some memories. That things were coming back to you, which you couldn't make sense of. You asked me if I could help.'

Porter nods again. 'That I did,' he says.

'Well, I think I can,' Edward says. 'In fact, I must. I have done a terrible thing, Reggie, and somehow I need to make amends.'

After a moment of silence, Nurse Dyer steps out onto the patio with a tray of tea and Victoria sponge cake, jam and cream oozing from the middle.

'Here we are,' she says cheerfully, laying it on the table. 'Shall I pour you both a cup?' She smiles.

'It's fine,' Edward says. 'I'll manage.'

She looks a little disappointed but smiles again and disappears back into the building, leaving the two of them alone.

'What do you think makes a hero, Reggie?'

Porter shifts his position and looks properly at Edward for the first time.

'I don't rightly know, sir,' Porter says. 'Does it matter?'

'Yes.' Edward forces himself to look straight into Porter's eye. 'Yes, it matters very much. Because, you see, it should be me, Reggie, sitting in that wheelchair. Me, with the broken face and the painful body. It should be you, not me, who lives out there,' he points across the open countryside, his voice cracked with emotion, 'with a wife and children, a proper home and family.'

Porter stares at Edward, frozen.

'My life, Porter, you see, has been based on a falsehood. For ten years I've lived a hallowed life. I came back a hero from the war – or so everyone thought. It brought me respect, gave me confidence, emboldened me. With these medals,' he holds out the blue box, 'I gained a wife and a following. People listened to me, held me in high esteem. I am supposed to be a member of the officer class. I'm supposed to be genetically superior. I'm the one who was supposed to show the lesser men, the boys from the lower orders, how it should be done. But while I lay, shaking and useless with fear at the bottom of the trench, you, a boy of barely seventeen, proved me to be the coward and *you* to be the possessor of the superior genes. It is you who should be passing them on, not me.'

'Sir!' Porter is suddenly alert as though he has woken from a half-sleep. 'Don't. What is the point of this? Please, stop.'

Edward feels his face crumple, his whole body fold inwards. He *can't* stop. Porter needs to hear it all, the whole sordid secret which has soiled his past and now his future. It has to come out. He has to know that he is the one who deserves so much and that Edward has taken it all.

'You were badly wounded,' Edward says, 'after you had so bravely and heroically saved, not only my life, but many others too. A grenade landed close – too close to you. It blew up in your face and your clothes were set on fire. I didn't think you would survive and when the platoon arrived to relieve us, they made the assumption it was I, the commanding officer, who had been the hero of the hour. But the truth of it is, I'm a coward, and I didn't correct them otherwise.'

Edward stops. His cheeks are wet as tears roll freely from his eyes.

Porter pulls a hand from beneath his blankets and reaches up as though to touch Edward's face. His fingers twitch and hover in mid-air. 'Stop, please,' he says. 'Pour the tea, sir, would ya?'

With shaking fingers Edward does what he's told and hands the cup and saucer to Porter.

'Sir—'

'Please. I don't want you to call me that.'

'Can't call you anything else, I'm used to it. Fact is, sir, since I had that bout of influenza, some memory of that day has come back to me. What you say, it makes a lotta sense. But sir, whatever you did or didn't do, really it don't make much difference, does it? If you'd gone out there, you could've landed up dead, and I could still have been injured and stuck in here. Fact is, we none of us came out of that place with normal bodies nor minds. You, not any more than the next man.' The speech has exhausted him.

His breath is ragged and he struggles to get more air into his lungs.

Once calmer, he goes on, 'I don't expect to last much longer, y'know. My lungs are very bad. Next dose of influenza will carry me off, I reckon. Truth is, I'm ready for it. I've had enough of this life and I'm looking forward to the next one.' He takes more deep breaths. 'You should go and live your best life, sir. Make my sacrifice worthwhile.' His face winces in pain. 'Wouldn't be much point, would there, if we're both misery guts?'

Edward stares at Porter through his wash of tears. This is the boy he remembers, the gung-ho, upbeat, see-the-best in every situation, Porter. This is what had drawn him to the boy in the first place.

'No,' he responds at last. 'No, you are quite right. What *would* be the point of that? I *will* live my best life, Porter, I promise you that. But you will get the recognition you deserve. I won't let you down this time. I promise you that too.'

31

Eleanor

It's late October but there is still enough heat in the middle of the day to eat out on the terrace. Imagine that! But then, this is the South of France. Eleanor looks out across the vines stretching as far as the eye can see, painting the hillsides golden brown.

Rose reaches for the carafe of rosé and tops up Eleanor's glass. She never used to drink wine at lunchtime, but here it's drunk like water with lunch and dinner. It isn't hard to get used to.

On the blue tablecloth, Marie has spread plates containing slices of juicy fat tomatoes sprinkled with herbs and bathed in local olive oil and vinegar; tapenade; hunks of bread; sliced cured meat and local soft cheeses. Eleanor studies her as she sits, Mabel tucked onto her lap. With her thick, dark hair, olive skin and long, slender limbs, she couldn't look less like her brother, Marcel, who sits across from them, head buried in the morning newspaper. Flitting between Paris and London, between his work and visiting Rose, Marcel has decided to stay in Provence for a little while, and Rose, who has been granted a few days' leave, has travelled down to see them all. The light at this time of year is particularly *impressionnant*, apparently, and Marcel has taken to working on an enormous canvas, propped up at the end of the terrace, which is hauled inside in the evening to avoid the damp. To Eleanor, the work – can it really be called art? – with its oddly juxtaposed shapes and boxes, bears almost no resemblance to the stunning scenery surrounding the old stone farmhouse they are staying in. Apart from the colours he thickly applies, which, she admits, are vaguely evocative of the place.

All Eleanor can currently see of Marcel are his paint-crusted hands. The occasional tutting and expletive comes from behind the rustling pages of the broadsheet and Marie shakes her head, smiling, and shrugs at Rose as though to apologise for her brother's manners.

'*Alors*,' she says, 'Mabel… *Mange, s'il te plait, chéri.*' Marie's lack of English and Mabel's lack of any language doesn't seem to prevent the two of them getting on handsomely. It is good for Mabel to have someone who shares the same carefully controlled diet as her and together, Eleanor and Marie, under Dr Deveaux's supervision, weigh and measure the daily allowances for Mabel. Marie and Mabel's lunch consists of a slice of meat, a hunk of cheese, and a smattering of fresh walnuts with a dollop of cream. Twice a day they check Mabel's urine for her ketone levels.

It is not difficult. Time-consuming, perhaps a little, although that seems less problematical in the sleepy hamlet just outside the town of Brignoles. Here, there are no other pressures on a person's time, other than the daily business of existence. Most people don't have much here, they work on the land, or in small craft businesses. Twice a week Eleanor accompanies Marie into the town to visit the market and stock up on everything they need, and it feels as though she has stepped back half a century.

But lovely though it is here, Eleanor aches for England. For Brook End. But more than anything, she misses darling little Jimmy and his gummy smile. If she stays much longer, will he even remember her?

The question is, what to do about Edward? Poor, darling, misguided Edward. He has always tried to do the right thing, she knows that, and in her heart she believes he isn't a bad person, just a weak one, from time to time, perhaps. But can she reconcile her differences with him, or will she follow in Sophie's footsteps? Sophie, who has begun the messy process of divorce from Henry, amid all the hateful media attention and wrangling over the children that will bring.

Eleanor turns and smiles as Mabel reaches up to pop a walnut into Marie's mouth. Mabel giggles as Marie returns the favour. It's incredible how her daughter has changed even in these short weeks, showing a growing interest in the world around her, she is filling the empty shell she had been reduced to by the disease and by the harsh effects of the medication. Mabel, tentatively, step by step, is becoming a person once again.

Marcel lowers the newspaper and peers at Eleanor over the top of his little round reading spectacles. Sometimes he gives the impression of being fifty, rather than thirty.

'Did you read the morning papers?' he asks.

'No,' she says. 'Should I?'

He folds the paper and hands it to her. 'I believe you should,' he says. 'The end of Capitalism is nigh,' he nods wisely. 'It is as we have been predicting – the world as we know it is over and a new era must begin.'

'Whatever has happened?' Rose asks, a hunk of bread, amply covered in green tapenade, held in mid-air. 'Surely you are being a little overdramatic, Marcel.'

'I think not.' He clasps his hands as though in prayer. 'This will filter down, of course, so that in the end it will be the working man, as always, who suffers the most.'

'The working woman, actually, Marcel,' Rose bristles. 'Why do you always ignore her in your socialist view of the world? I think you forget that, in reality, it is the woman who is at the bottom of the pile. She is the one, most likely, who sacrifices the last slice of bread off her plate to feed her hungry children, who would rather give up the coat on her back to keep her babies warm!'

'*Chéri*! Come on, you know that when I say working man, I am including woman!'

'Really? Then why not say so!'

'Rose, my darling.' Marcel pulls a little infantile face. 'Please forgive me...'

They pucker at each other in a mawkish way and Eleanor can't look. Their sentimentality towards each other is touching, but occasionally too much. She opens *Le Figaro* and reads the headlines: *Stock Market Crisis Over!* She hadn't known there *was* a crisis, buried down here, deep in the countryside. New York, London – the financial markets might as well be on another planet. Unmoved, she reads, *After days of volatility and panic selling, followed by the worst fall in living memory on Thursday, the market rallied a little and climbed on Friday. We have seen the worst, reports the New York press. Stock*

houses have survived the worst day in history and live on.
Bankers are hopeful for a quick recovery as confidence
increases. Heaven forbid we should see anything like this
again!

Eleanor skims a few more articles about how many
billions were knocked off the US stock market, how other
countries might be affected by a change in interest rates, but
she fails to be moved. Who cares if a few wealthy bankers
have lost a pot of their cash?

She yawns and puts the paper down.

'It doesn't look that bad,' she says, finishing her rosé. 'I'm
not sure how you conclude this is doomsday for us all.'

'You'll see,' Marcel says with the assuredness of a
soothsayer. 'I've been following this story since the spring.
There are some who have predicted this, but their voices
were drowned out. They had said that the values of stocks
and shares cannot continue to just grow and grow and now
they are so high they are nothing to do with the true value
of the underlying companies. Like a big fat balloon, poof!'
Marcel uses his arms to demonstrate the bursting of the
economic bubble. Eleanor wonders how an artist can be
such an expert on the financial markets. 'I don't believe in
this bounceback,' Marcel is saying.

'But how can you possibly know?' Eleanor asks.

'*Mon dieu*, I don't. But I know something of the human
condition. And that, my friend, is to ignore the mess we make
of things and to merely hope everything will somehow turn
out OK in the end. But for sure it never does.' He crosses his
arms and puffs out his cheeks.

'Mama!' Mabel is wriggling to get down from Marie's
lap.

Marie says something fast and urgent to Marcel in French, along the lines of 'please don't talk about politics. It is rather dull.'

Mabel runs around the table and shoves Prudence up at Eleanor.

'Would Prudence like to go for a walk?' Eleanor asks. In their new routine, they take a daily stroll after lunch, so that Mabel can collect interesting pebbles or leaves and point at birds or rocks or plants for Eleanor to name, and Mabel to repeat. Mabel nods. 'Mama,' she says, and smiles, reaching out her hand.

'Excuse us,' she says to the others, 'but Mabel and I have an appointment with nature.'

Marcel puts down his paper and turns to Rose. 'Now that is a very good idea,' he says. 'Rose, perhaps you could accompany me for a walk too?'

Marie announces she will clear the lunch things and then take a siesta. Eleanor watches her sister and Marcel disappear behind the squat old farmhouse, its walls the colour of desert sand.

Hand in hand, Mabel and Eleanor wander down between the gnarled trunks and branches of the vines. Mabel is not the child she once was. She is a shadow of the vibrant chatterbox Eleanor remembers from what seems like a different lifetime. This Mabel is placid and quiet and compliant – but there are sparks. The way she giggles, the occasional mischievous look in her eye, her growing interest in the world around her. It's as though she is unfurling, turning from looking only inward, to looking out. It is a delicate, slow recovery, and there are good days and bad. They can take it only a day at a time and Eleanor must be content to live with that.

While she has been in France, she has kept up a correspondence with Dr Eversley. He has been keen to know about Mabel's progress, she having been part of his original cohort of children on the diet. Dutifully, she has written to him each week with an update and the clinical details from Dr Deveaux. Really, she is becoming quite the expert. Dr Eversley seems genuinely delighted at Mabel's progress. In his latest letter he even offered to take over the supervision of Mabel's treatment as and when Eleanor decides to return to England.

As they walk, Eleanor chats and Mabel listens. She tells her about Jimmy and Papa, Dilly and Byron. With a lump in her throat, Eleanor wonders if they will ever live together again.

A year ago, Eleanor could not have imagined life without Edward. He'd been her everything. He had plucked her and Rose from terrible grief and misery after the murder of their mother and over the years she has leant on him too much, she can see that now. She had never properly dealt with the loss of Mama, and Rose has helped her realise that. But now she has proved she can live without Edward, the question is, she thinks, as she breathes the warm, still air, tinged with woodsmoke and dying summer, does she want to?

In her pocket is a letter from Edward. She collected it yesterday from the post office and she has not told anyone of its contents. Before she does, she needs to work out how she feels about it all. And this, she can't yet fathom.

October 1929

My darling Eleanor,

I must begin this letter by saying this: I do not blame you for leaving. I understand your reasons and I respect them.

I have had a good deal of time since you left for thinking. For facing things I have not before wanted to face. It has been hard, but truly, it is something I must thank you for. You have forced me to face my demons and, although I do not know what will happen to me now, I finally feel at peace with myself.

Eleanor, you now know I had no right to win your heart, having pretended I was a man I had never been that day in the brigadier general's office. You were a salve to the terrible wound I suffered, through my own cowardice, during the war. But you know the worst of me now, you have seen all my lies.

My only defence is that this has been a pattern of my character which I came to rely upon since a young age. I was never a success as a child, nor as a young man at Oxford, not in terms of gaining the respect of my peers, in any event. But somehow, by manner of a growing list of falsehoods and subterfuge, I managed to convince those around me I had something important to say, that I was a man of honour and good standing. Nothing could be further from the truth.

So when Mabel became so terribly ill, it was my natural inclination towards covering up unpleasant truths which made me want to hide her away. Please understand, I never wanted to do her harm. I truly believed that Sir Charles was best placed to treat her. But it was also the pressures of society and my honest and true belief that people like Mabel should be kept in institutions that persuaded me to act as I did.

But now that I no longer have you to lose, for the first time in my life I realise I have a choice about who to be and how to behave. I know what I have to do – and Eleanor, I have you to thank for that. I have made the decision to change direction with my work. You are quite right. How can I preach about the efficacy of running society under the principles of eugenics, when you and I are living proof that even those who possess good genes can produce a child who, it pains me to say, is one of the 'unfit'. Furthermore, the results of my studies have thrown up anomalies enough that they require more study before any conclusions can be reached. Instead, I plan to focus on my original area of interest, namely education. It is in that field I believe I can do real good and bring about change for all children, those who are in possession of great intellect, as well as those who are not.

There is much more for me to repair in the coming months, but this will all take time. Whether I am able to come through this unscathed, who knows? But at least I have a growing peace in my heart, especially knowing, at least hoping, you will approve.

I am sorry, Eleanor, for the pain and discomfort I have caused you.

With all my love,
Edward

★★★

Later, the lamps and fires lit, staving off the chill of the evening, Dr Deveaux arrives, as he usually does at this time each evening, to check up on Mabel and Marie. Like his son, he is rather small and nondescript looking, but his kind and fastidious care of Mabel, and of Eleanor herself, is extraordinary.

She watches as he weighs the little girl, jotting the result in his notebook. He sits her in a chair and they solemnly regard each other.

'How are you today, *mademoiselle?*' he asks.

She nods and grants him a smile.

'*Très bien,*' he says. 'The smile is a good sign! May I?' He waves his stethoscope and she nods again. He places it on her chest and listens carefully, moving it and listening again. 'Well...' He smiles at her. 'This sounds very good. A strong beat, like a—'

'Pony!' Mabel shouts and they all laugh.

'I was going to say a drum. But, still, a pony is better I think.'

Behind his pale exterior beats his own warm and generous heart.

'Dr Deveaux,' Eleanor smiles when his examination is finished, 'you'll stay for dinner?'

'Of course! My house is empty without Marie.' He looks affectionately at his daughter. Eleanor recalls Marcel telling her his mother had died of cancer when he was Rose's age. She wonders why the doctor never met anyone else, although she rather suspects it is to do with Marie, who still experiences the occasional fit and he is forced to protect her from the world. How sad it is, this fear of the disease. This fear of anything different about others. Is it really so bad, not to be perfect of mind and body? And what, or who, is perfect anyway? Shouldn't kindness and spirit, or joy in the simplest of pleasures be of equal importance? Stepping away from the world for a while has given Eleanor a perspective on things she never really thought of before.

'Very good, Mabel,' Dr Deveaux is saying as he finishes checking her ketone levels and proclaims them to be fine.

'Well then,' Eleanor says to her. 'It's time for bed.' She kisses her and allows Marie to take her up and tuck her in.

'You know,' Dr Deveaux says as they watch her go upstairs, 'I think Mabel is stable enough, and you are prepared enough, if you would like to take your daughter home. I wonder, Madame Hamilton, how do you feel about that?'

'I feel terrified,' she says instantly, a lump forming in her throat. What if Mabel's seizures return? She lives with that fear every day, but it would be so much worse back in England without Dr Deveaux's kindly face to reassure her every day. Without Marie to show her a possible future for Mabel which does not involve an institution.

Dr Deveaux takes her hand and gives it a sympathetic squeeze. 'I understand you are afraid. But I think you are ready. Mabel no longer needs to see a doctor on a daily basis, and you have told me that Dr Eversley has offered his support. It is enough.'

Eleanor watches him as he packs his doctor's bag. A potential future for her and Mabel, at home with Jimmy, opens in her mind. She swallows hard. Dearest Dr Deveaux

– and Dr Eversley. Really, she has absolutely no idea how she can ever thank them enough.

Marcel and Rose arrive late to the dinner table. Rose's cheeks are flushed and Marcel appears uncommonly flustered.

'I'm so sorry,' Rose says, taking her place at the table. Eleanor sees her fingers are trembling as she unfolds her napkin. A look passes between her and the still-standing Marcel. She nods and he clears his throat.

'I would like to have a private word with you, Eleanor, if I may?' He stands stiffly and Eleanor looks at her sister. Have they rowed, these two?

'Of course.' She places her napkin on the table and looks at Dr Deveaux. He is staring resolutely into his lap and she has a sneaking suspicion he knows what this is all about.

They step into the living room. Marcel places his hands behind his back and makes a little bow. Eleanor suppresses a giggle. Poor Marcel, these moments are so very awkward for him, but she stays silent, and waits for him to speak.

'I, er, this is a little unconventional,' Marcel begins with a flash of a smile. His eyes flick from the rug to just around Eleanor's nose. 'But as there is no father, nor any mother to ask... I must, to be entirely correct, ask you, Eleanor, if you will give your permission for me to marry your sister. I have asked her, she said yes, and so now, I wonder if you—'

Eleanor cannot stay silent a moment longer. She laughs and claps her hands together. 'Oh, Marcel! Of course I give my permission! I mean, strictly speaking, I suppose Edward should agree too, but well, with things as they are...' She moves forward and takes Marcel's hands. 'I am delighted for you both. You are wonderful for Rose, just what she needs. And you two – you make a wonderful couple. You will do so much good in the world, together. I just know it.'

Marcel exhales a long breath.

'Thank you,' he says. 'I was very nervous! We are so happy. And if Rose wishes to continue working, well, that is fine with me. I plan to move to London, and we shall marry in the spring. I know she won't want to be too far from you.'

'That is wonderful news. Does your father know?'

'I told him my intentions earlier, and he is delighted also.'

'Well,' Eleanor announces as they return to the dining room, 'I think this calls for champagne, don't you?'

She goes to her sister. 'I'm so happy for you, darling Rose.' She kisses Rose on the cheek.

'Thank you, Ellie. I never thought I would wish to marry, but...' She smiles at Marcel. 'Frankly, I cannot imagine life without Marcel. I don't want to imagine it. So, I am gracefully bowing to my change of heart. I simply had to say yes!'

Watching Rose's eyes sparkle in the lamplight, Eleanor reflects on how, in the past, she had always feared this moment, been so worried about letting Rose go. But now, having got to know Marcel and the Deveaux family these past weeks, the idea of her sister marrying really does fill her with joy.

32

Edward

On Tuesday morning, Edward heads once again for the committee room of the Palace of Westminster. Tired, as he barely slept last night, but resolute, he has two stops before his appointed time with the Royal Commission. First, he detours via the War Office. As promised in the long letter he wrote last week, he is returning his medals. Well, not *his* medals – they never really belonged to him in the first place. Something he should have done long ago. The letter explained why the medals he'd been awarded should rightfully be given to Private Porter and that they should be presented to him at the earliest opportunity, given the poor state of his health. What action the War Office may take against Edward, heaven knows. He will accept whatever is coming to him, but he knows without the medals in his possession, a weight will lift from his body, and he proceeds down Whitehall with a lightness to his step as he heads towards the next challenge of his day.

'But I don't understand,' the major general says, looking in bemusement from Edward to the letter and back. They have rolled out a high-rank to receive him. His letter clearly stirred something up at the War Office. 'This is quite without precedent.' He fixes Edward with a penetrating gaze. 'It is not so unusual to strip a man of his medals, but I've never heard of anyone voluntarily handing them back.' He is a large man, his shoulders heaped inside his jacket, a thick, bristly moustache twitches on his astonished face.

'Well.' Edward clears his throat. 'As they say, there is a first time for everything.'

The man leans back in his chair. 'So,' he says slowly, 'you say you were awarded these medals in error, and by rights they should have been awarded to a Private...' He searches the letter.

'Porter,' Edward says.

'Porter,' the man repeats, looking up at him again. 'But that would mean,' he says, 'that the citation in support of your award was falsified by your senior officer, and that apparently false version of events verified and supported up the chain of command. How?' he says, 'and more importantly, *why* are you only confessing this now, more than ten years after the event?'

'That,' Edward says, 'is rather a long story, but in essence, the situation was extremely confused on the field, as I'm sure you will understand. There were no live witnesses to what took place, at least none who could string two coherent words together. I myself was in an extreme state of shock and trauma following the battle. But you are right, I should have long ago confessed my error in willingly going along with false assumptions and taking the credit for bravery which truly belonged to Private Porter. I will take whatever punishment you deem appropriate, but the most urgent matter is that Private Porter has not much time left on this earth and deserves to be rewarded for his valour. I urge you to read all the paperwork as soon as possible and expedite the procedure to present him with the medals he should have rightfully received long ago, before it is too late for him.'

The major general frowns. 'I have read the paperwork and I am willing to put this in motion. We can arrange for a presentation of the awards at his place of residence. As for you, ordinarily, following a thorough investigation, there might be a Court Martial, for an acting officer, possibly imprisonment if the offence is considered particularly heinous. Your superiors who wrote the original citation would also be investigated and might be punished—'

'Oh no,' Edward interrupts. 'I do hope not. The only person to blame should be me.'

'Well,' the major general continues, 'bearing in mind the time that has passed and the context, I don't think this will all be necessary. I will begin an investigation as to how this almighty mess came to be. Depending on the result of that, I must warn you, steps may be taken for proceedings against you, in the worst-case scenario, or your discharge status may be changed from honourable to dishonourable. Do you understand?'

Edward nods. 'I do.'

'Then I bid you farewell, Professor Hamilton,' the major general says, stacking the papers together, Edward's letter on the top, and sliding them into a file labelled, 'Captain Hamilton'. 'Good day to you.'

'Good day, sir,' Edward says, and leaves with a growing sense of relief.

★ ★ ★

Edward enters the small café around the corner from Westminster overlooking Victoria Tower Gardens. He is half an hour early and the café is not busy, for which he is thankful. He finds a table in an inconspicuous corner to await his guest. He orders tea and pulls a notepad and pen from his briefcase. He has many wrongs to right, and now that he has started, these actions seem to have picked up a momentum of their own. He writes:

Dear Violet,

I could have spoken to you in person about this matter but I want to commit my words to paper, so that you will see in the permanency of ink on the page, the genuineness in my intentions and the longevity in my apology.

Violet, I have done you, and more importantly your brother, a grave injustice. I've been so intent on putting the horror of the war behind me, that I have failed to ensure the person who was deserving of the highest honours and recognition for his supreme acts of bravery, missed out on receiving the hero's status he deserved. Instead, through a series of prejudiced assumptions by those in superior ranks, those honours went to another, who neither deserved them, nor had the strength of character to stand up and admit the mistake. The result was that the real hero has lived a life of extreme pain and obscurity, while the thief who stole his life and his veneration, has enjoyed years of good fortune under false pretences.

That hero was, of course, your brother, Reggie Porter, and the thief, the coward: me. Porter saved my life and the lives of many others through his brave actions.

It has taken me many years and tragedy in my own life to fully appreciate the harm I have done. No apology or action I can take now will make up for that, but I will do all that I can to make recompense and to ensure that your brother's remaining time on this earth is as comfortable and filled with joy as it is within my powers to arrange.

I know that my paying for Reggie's care all these years does not make up for my wrong, and I am truly sorry for what I have done, not only to Reggie, but also to you, Violet. I have reported the entire sorry tale to the powers that be in the army, and they will take whatever action against me that they see fit. In the meantime, whilst I can never make up fully for my wrong, I have requested that they honour Reggie with the medals he truly deserves as soon as possible.

I hope that, in time, you will find it in your heart to forgive me.

Yours sincerely,

Edward Hamilton.

As Edward folds the letter, Harry Laughlin bursts through the door in a flurry of hat, scarf and flapping coat. Edward folds the finished letter and slides it into his briefcase.

'Laughlin,' Edward says, and rises to greet the breathless American, here to attend a meeting of European eugenicists. Harry takes his hand and shakes it.

'Hamilton,' he says, his voice gruff, manner more agitated than usual. His brow is furrowed and it looks as though he hasn't slept all weekend. 'I can't stay too long,' he says. He turns and waves to the waiter. 'Strong coffee, please!' he calls across the café and sits down. He rubs a hand across his brow. 'What a week to have been away!' he says. 'Goddam market volatility. I'm not the wealthiest of men, but I have my share of investments as I'm sure you do too, huh? What a wreck.' He shakes his head. 'Even Rockefeller's jittery as hell. Lost *millions* last week, put our funding on hold. Thank God the bankers seem to be turning it all around. Think we'll be OK, but I'm taking an early boat back. I need a steady hand at the tiller. Can't risk too many of our research projects being cancelled. Now, what was it you wanted? How have you been faring?'

Edward is startled for a moment, so deep in thought about what he is going to say. 'I, er, I think most of my stocks and shares are in English companies. My bankers are very conservative,' he adds hopefully. The bank had written to him last week to explain what action they had taken to protect his money, but he can't really even remember what was in the letter.

'That sure is good. But hold firm, Edward. That's what everyone is saying. Hold firm and don't panic sell. *That's* the road to disaster. Anyhow, what is it that you wish to discuss?'

Edward clears his throat to begin. 'You clearly have much on your mind, so I'll get straight to the point. I've had a change of heart about supporting Church's proposed private member's bill for compulsory detention and for sterilisation of the feeble-minded. I appreciate how much you have helped with this, providing me with additional data to back up my own research, and I hate to have wasted your time, but, well, there it is...' He is aware of the tensed muscles in his jaw.

'What?' Harry stares at him as though he has grown a second head.

'As you know, I've been researching this area for many years,' Edward carries on, acutely aware of how rehearsed his speech sounds. 'Recently I've come to realise that whilst I remain convinced there *is* a strong link between hereditability of intelligence, the data I have collected is not as clear-cut as I had expected it to be. As a result, I believe the eugenics programme is of questionable efficacy and humanity. In short,' he says, 'I cannot support legislation which so fundamentally infringes the liberty of individuals in favour of the state. I am, as of today, resigning my position with the Eugenics Society, and I will be devoting myself solely to my work in education. I am no longer convinced that the vision of a future run on eugenics principles is right. I think the science itself is... unproven, and possibly dangerous in its application.'

There is a moment of stillness.

'Are you serious?' Laughlin snorts. 'Dangerous to whom, exactly?'

'To us all,' Edward says. 'We do not know the full consequences of what we try to achieve with eugenics policies. Either for the future of the race, or the individuals involved. Some of the results I have seen in my own work have made me question if the underlying theories are even correct at all.'

The coffee arrives at that moment and there is quiet while the drinks are poured, sugar added and stirred in.

'I just don't get it.' Harry scratches his head and looks genuinely confused. 'Edward, you and I have been collaborating on our research for a long time. I thought we were so aligned about all of this. What on earth is going on?'

'I've had time to think,' Edward says with a deep sigh. 'Indeed, I've been *forced* to think. I'd been so certain about the eugenics view of the world that when some of the evidence I found during the course of my research didn't back up the theory, I was so convinced the evidence must be wrong, that I invented a few case studies which would provide what I needed. What sort of person does that?' He looks at Harry. He is opening himself right up here. Laying himself on a slab. All Harry has to do is stick the knife in and twist.

Instead, he laughs. 'You are not serious?'

'Yes. I know. I mean, I don't think the theory is entirely *wrong*, but we can't base nationwide policy on something... nefarious. Do you see what I mean?'

'Christ, Edward!' Harry's face is turning pink. His cheeks puff and his eyes grow big. 'What the hell has happened to you? It's like some crazy libertarian just brainwashed you, like that!' He snaps his fingers. 'We *know* this is what must be done. Do you honestly think you are the only one who has invented cases, exaggerated data or even plain made stuff up? Sometimes, Edward, the goal justifies the means, right?'

Edward drinks some coffee. Harry is a very persuasive man. Since Edward has known him, he has found himself emulating this charismatic American. He feels once more like the little boy at school, so desperate to be liked by the popular chaps he'd have done anything.

But not today. He shakes his head. 'No,' he says finally. 'I'm not sure that it does.'

'So, after all your years of research, the reputation you have built, you're just going to *drop* eugenics, like that? You're a clever man, Edward, there is no doubt about that. I've read your papers. They constitute some of the leading work in eugenics, psychology *and* education. People have relied on the evidence you've supplied about genetics and the feeble-minded. *We* have relied on it. Goddam it, Edward, such a sudden turnaround makes no sense! What the hell's going on?' He slaps his hands on the table so hard, coffee sploshes out of his cup into the saucer.

Edward swallows hard and ignores the sweat prickling at his forehead and around his collar. *Be honest, Edward.* Eleanor's voice, warm and reassuring in his mind, urges him forward. He takes a deep breath.

'It's like I said,' Edward stays calm, 'as a scientist, I'm less convinced about the benefit of the eugenic theory. In fact,' he goes on, 'I'm beginning to wonder if it wouldn't be better to spend the money looking for treatments – ways to make people better. And to educate. Education has always been my primary area of expertise and I plan to return to that. Education for both the fit and the less-fit. Perhaps we can change the outcomes for them after all. Perhaps they can have useful, productive lives. So, alongside my plans for educating the most able, I plan to introduce special education establishments to teach those who find learning most challenging. Harry, there is something else I should tell you,' he swallows the lump in his throat, 'our daughter,' he says, 'Mabel. You remember her?'

Harry nods. 'Of course.'

Edward takes a deep breath. 'She is an epileptic,' he says.

And for what feels like the first time, Edward tells the truth. He explains the progression of her illness, how he insisted she go into the Heath Colony. How, when he tried so hard to forget she existed, Eleanor never gave up hope for their daughter. Harry listens, expressionless. When he finally stops, to Edward's astonishment, Harry laughs.

'Edward,' he says, leaning forward across the table towards him. 'I'm sorry about your daughter. Truly I am, but you can't let that stop you, *us*. You *know* this policy is right and good. What happens in your personal life should have no bearing on what is for the greater good. You *know* that reorganising society in a eugenics manner is the only way to avoid catastrophe in the future.'

'But that's just it,' Edward says, 'I'm really *not* sure any more.'

'C'mon man! Look,' Harry says, 'if we are going to go baring all today, you wanna know the real truth about me? Well, I have epilepsy too. Yes, that's shocked you, hasn't it? But it's true. It's not bad; not bad enough to be put in an institution. Fortunately, my intellect is intact, and it certainly isn't going to stop me pushing forward with what I know to be *right*.'

'I-I'm sorry to hear it.' Edward looks at Harry in amazement. How has he managed to keep this secret? And how can he possibly advocate sterilisation for epileptics when he suffers from the condition himself? 'Do you suffer much?' he asks.

'As I said, I don't have it bad and nobody but my physician and Pansy – and now you – know.' He slurps the last of his coffee and lights a cigarette, taking a long drag.

'How...' Edward asks, his head whirling with this

confession, 'how can you justify locking up others with the same affliction as you, in institutions?'

'Because they are *not* the same as me. They don't possess my ability or my intellect and I am determined to progress with our programme of sterilisation and segregation. We have to do what is right and good for society, Edward. It's not about the individual.' He sits back in his chair, triumphant, blows smoke from the side of his mouth. He looks certain he has won the argument.

Edward picks up his hat and gathers his coat from behind his chair.

'I'm sorry, Harry,' he says, 'but I have another appointment. And I'm not going to change my mind. I invited you to hear my plans out of courtesy. As a long-time colleague I wanted you to know before I make any public announcement. I'll be continuing my work in education and psychology, as I said, but I shall no longer be supporting the eugenics movement – nor any of its ideologies – and nothing you can say will change my mind on this.' He stands. 'Good day to you, Laughlin,' he finishes. 'I wish you all the best. Truly.' He feels Harry's eyes on his back, until he rounds the corner and walks briskly towards the Palace of Westminster.

Now he must tell Church he will be withdrawing his support from the private member's bill. He must also inform the Royal Commission he has discovered a problem with the data behind his evidence, that it is no longer reliable and that he has changed his mind – he can't be certain of the inheritability of intelligence and feeble-mindedness. More research is required and until there is enough certainty, this bill should not be passed into law.

* * *

Later, back home at Brook End, Edward is changing for dinner when Barton turns up unannounced.

He is waiting for Edward in the drawing room, nursing a large whisky and looking morose.

'Sorry to barge in on your evening,' he says, 'but I thought I'd better check you are all right, old chap. All this dreadful news of the stock markets.' He shakes his head and clicks his tongue.

'What a bloody mess, eh?' Edward helps himself to a whisky too, wondering if Barton really has come to check his finances are still in order, or to divulge a catastrophe of his own.

'And the newspapers don't help. They seem to *revel* in bad news, making the whole thing ten times worse, I'll bet you.' Barton's jowls shake with emotion.

The man has a point. The newspaper headlines screamed it as the afternoon editions had hit the stands: *New Wall Street Debacle: Frenzied Stock Exchange Scenes! Speculators Lose Thousand Million Pounds in Day of Wild Selling! Thousands of People are Ruined In Devastating Wall Street Crash! J.D. Rockefeller Loses Four-fifths of Worth.*

It was only then that Edward remembered the message waiting for him on his desk at the university after his visit to the Palace of Westminster. *Please telephone Mr Coleroy as a matter of urgency.* He had shoved the note in his pocket, not wanting to miss the train home. He had discussed the matter of his money with Mr Coleroy only last week, over a nice lunch in a French restaurant around the corner from the bank, paid for by his banker. Mr Coleroy had reassured

Edward that both his funds and the bank were in a good position to weather this terrible bull market. Many people, he had explained, had borrowed money to invest in stocks and shares. As the markets began to fall they had panicked and sold at vastly lower values and were unable to pay off their loans. Edward, on the other hand, had no borrowings and his money was sitting in safe investments, or in cash in their accounts.

He had nothing to worry about. Or did he? He thought about the message again and something fluttered in his chest. He checks his watch. It's past seven – too late now. Mr Coleroy would surely have gone home.

'That damned fellow, Grant-Parker. Messy divorce – you know the one. Well, it was right here in your house,' Barton was saying, waving his glass at Edward, 'that he suggested I put all my money into the American stock market. Can't go wrong, best way to make a quick buck and all that. Do you remember?'

Oh no! The conversation comes crashing back. He *does* remember it. That awful weekend when Henry and Sophie were here and at each other's throats.

'How much did you lose?' he asks, feeling a little sick at the misfortune of his friend. He hopes Barton doesn't blame him. He did introduce them, after all. He touches Barton's arm in sympathy.

'Me?' Barton looks up at Edward, his broom-like moustache twisting wildly on his top lip. He guffaws loudly. 'Oh, I've not lost a penny, thank heavens. I trusted you more, old chap, and had a chat with *your* bankers. Good old English sorts. Gave me good, solid advice. Suggested I keep my investments this side of the pond.'

'That's a relief, then,' Edward says cautiously, still thinking about the urgent telephone message.

'Fact is,' Barton says, 'I'm such a dilly-dallier. Couldn't make up my mind *what* to do, so, in the end I did nothing. Money is still locked in my safe at the back of my wardrobe. That is, unless my wife has pilfered it to spend on dresses or whatnot.' He waves a hand dismissively. 'Sometimes,' Barton says, regarding Edward with solemn, hooded eyes, 'doing nothing is the safest course of action. At least, I think that's what your banker chappie was trying to advise me, if I remember right.' He grunts, takes a slug of whisky.

'Funny you should mention that, Barton, but Mr Coleroy did try to reach me this afternoon. I doubt if he is still in the office, but would you excuse me while I telephone him?'

'Actually,' Barton says with a sigh, 'I should be getting back for dinner or Lizzie will be having my guts for garters. Just wanted to make sure *you* were quite all right. You know, being on your own and with all this financial nonsense going on.' He slugs back the last of his whisky.

'That's good of you,' says Edward, shifting his weight from foot to foot, anxious to make the phone call, but not wishing to be rude. Barton and Lizzie have been good, steady friends and neighbours. The best, in fact.

After seeing Barton out, Edward picks up the mouthpiece and receiver and asks the operator to be put through to Mr Coleroy at Coleroy & Mack. To his amazement, the man is there.

'Good evening, Mr Coleroy – I, er, I didn't think I would be lucky enough to catch you still in the office, but I'm glad I did. I received your telephone message earlier. I do hope all is well?' Edward begins.

'Professor Hamilton! I'm glad you called, but – but I'm sorry, I have some news. Quite bad news, in fact.' Edward hears him draw in a ragged breath. There is a pause on the line. 'It's over,' Mr Coleroy says. 'The bank has collapsed.' The despair in Coleroy's voice is clear as a bell.

'*What*?' A rush of heat sweeps over Edward and his legs weaken. 'What do you mean, *collapsed*?'

'Everything is lost...The markets have plummeted. Our net worth wiped out. Depositors have removed their funds en masse...'

'But I haven't!' Edward's voice rises. Pinpricks of panic scatter across his skin. 'We had that lunch. You said my investments were safe. My cash was safe!'

'I was wrong.' Coleroy's voice is low and flat. 'Nobody predicted the scale of the losses. We had no idea this was coming and your investments are, I'm afraid, worthless.'

'But what about my cash? My cash must be OK?' Edward's voice echoes back to him down the line, *OK, OK, OK*? He is sweating and feeling sick, thoughts flashing through his mind as the panic begins to take over. If he has no funds left, how will he pay for the expense of running Brook End and the flat? What about Eleanor? What about the staff – dear God, they all depend on *him*. All of them. His salary from the university and the local authority education work is never going to be enough to cover all his expenses. How will he pay for Porter?

'I'm sorry,' Coleroy is saying. 'The bank has filed for bankruptcy. It's too late. There *is* no cash. You will have to join the queue for any scraps which can be recovered like everybody else.' Coleroy continues to speak but Edward can't take it in. His mind is struggling to absorb what it means. His only heart-stopping thought is, *I have lost my father's fortune. The fortune he worked all his life to build. In one godforsaken day, it has all gone.*

Everything is lost. First his daughter, then his wife, and now his money too. Edward walks numbly back to the sitting room and pours himself another large whisky with shaking hands.

What else is there to do but drown his sorrows?

Minutes later, Mrs Faulks bursts into the room, unannounced, all of a fluster.

'Professor! She's here!'

'Who?' Edward turns to look at her, confused.

'Mrs Hamilton!' she cries, and the floor lurches beneath Edward's feet.

They sit on either side of a roaring fire in the sitting room. There is a sense of unreality about this evening. First Coleroy and the bank, now Eleanor is here, after an absence of nearly six weeks, sitting a few feet away. He stares at her, not knowing where to start. *How* to start. Should he tell her about the money? Not yet. He watches her movements warily, as though she is an apparition who may just disappear if he says the wrong thing. She takes a sip of red wine and stares into the flames. After the shock of his conversation with Mr Coleroy, emotions bubble inside him like water on the boil.

She's home. This matters more than the money.

But is she here to stay?

Does she hate and resent him, or can she find it in her heart to forgive? Will she still love him if he no longer is a man in possession of money and status?

And Mabel. *Mabel is here.* Asleep beneath his roof. Back in her room where she should be. The little girl had been fast asleep, wrapped in blankets, stretched out on the backseat of the car, when Eleanor arrived unannounced an hour ago, herself sitting beside the driver, that Frenchman, Marcel, who he has avoided meeting until this evening.

Mrs Bellamy had appeared, open-mouthed, at the kitchen door, clearly wondering just how many uninvited guests might appear for dinner. As soon as she saw who had arrived, her face had broken into the widest grin. Until that moment Edward was certain he had never seen the woman smile.

Alice had hurriedly made up Mabel's bed and, while Eleanor peeked in at Jimmy, Edward had carried the little girl up to her room. He managed not to wake her as he laid her gently in her bed. Staring down at her, he had been unable to stem the flow of tears from coursing unbidden down his cheeks. Mabel had had no seizures now for six weeks, and that was all thanks to Eleanor's courage and tenacity. He didn't deserve either of them.

After Marcel had eaten a sandwich which Mrs Bellamy quickly prepared for him with no grumbles whatsoever, he departed for the last leg of his journey to London. It transpired he had driven Eleanor, Mabel and their luggage all the way back from Provence, and now he was going on to see Rose. Eleanor told him the two were engaged. He was too numb from everything that had happened to say anything other than *congratulations*. But the man seemed genuine and had looked after his wife and daughter with care. Another person Edward must recalibrate his opinion of, he realised.

'Why didn't you tell me you were coming back to England?' Edward says now, finally plucking up the courage to speak.

Eleanor removes her gaze from the fire and studies him. She looks exhausted, but there is a peace in her eyes Edward has not seen for a very long time.

'I was planning on coming back soon, anyway,' she says slowly, 'now that Mabel is so much better. But then Marcel arrived for a few days and offered to drive us back. He really is the kindest and most generous man, and I hope in time you will come to see that. I thought about sending a telegram, but then,' she sighs, 'I wondered if you might have some objection to Marcel driving us, so…Well, here we are.' She shrugs and gives him a hesitant smile.

He's silent, trying to gather his thoughts into something he can form into words.

'How is Jimmy?' Eleanor asks, breaking the tension in the room. 'He looks so big.'

'He's… delightful. Bonny. Perfect, but…'

'But?'

'He needs his mother.'

'I know.' She shifts a little in her seat. Puts her wine on the coffee table. 'Edward I—'

'Eleanor, I'm so very sorry!' Edward jumps in before she can say whatever it is which will slice his heart in two. 'I am sorry I lied to you. Sorry I prevented you from taking Mabel out of the colony. Sorry I didn't listen. I'm so sorry for being a damned fool and I understand if you never want to see me again. But I never meant to—'

'I know. Please. Edward, let's not do this now. I *know* you are sorry. I've missed home dreadfully – and I've missed you too.'

Edward stares at her, his vision blurred by tears.

'Does this mean I'm forgiven? That you will stay with me?'

She hesitates. 'Yes. I think so.'

He exhales. 'Even though my name might still be dragged through the mud after the medals fiasco?'

'Even then.'

'Even though a knighthood really is out of the question?'

'Especially because a knighthood is out of the question!'

And suddenly she is on her feet and in his arms, her own tears soaking into his shirt.

He pulls her face up to look at him.

'Eleanor,' he says slowly. He takes a deep breath, the nausea stirring once more in his belly. 'There is something more. Something worse.'

She takes a step back, searching his face. 'What is it?'

'Coleroy & Mack have collapsed into bankruptcy. Apparently everyone else was wise enough to remove their cash, except me. I've lost it all. Or most of it, anyway. I'm not too sure of the situation. I've only had the briefest of conversations, just now, before you arrived. I am going to the bank first thing in the morning.' He swallows hard. Eleanor claps her hand over her mouth, her eyes growing wide. He feels his shoulders, his whole body sag as he speaks.

'Oh, Edward,' Eleanor says, 'this is terrible.'

He nods. 'It may mean we will have to sell Brook End.' His voice cracks and he looks around the room. How dear this house is to him. It is Eleanor and him, Mabel and

Jimmy; the essence of them all combined into the fabric of the place.

Eleanor is quiet for a moment. The sound of the grandfather clock ticking from the hallway resounds in his head. Whatever their ups and downs, whatever the earthly traumas, time still ticks on regardless. Nature cares not for man's agonies.

'Edward,' Eleanor says finally, stepping forward and stroking his cheek, 'it doesn't matter. We will find a way to manage. I love this house, but wherever we live, you, me, Mabel, Jimmy... *that* is home. I don't care if it's a caravan or a wooden hut, as long as we are all healthy, that's what matters. Besides, I can get a job. You have work and an income – we won't starve.'

'But the staff!' Edward takes her hands, pleased to have heard her including him in her future vision of huts and caravans. 'How can I—'

'Shh.' Eleanor puts a finger to his lips. 'Not now,' she says. 'We will deal with each and every problem as it comes. I've done this before, remember?' She smiles weakly. 'For tonight, let's just... Be.'

He nods. 'Yes,' he says. 'And... Eleanor. I'll try to never let you down again.' He means it more than anything he has ever meant before. 'You and the children are everything to me.'

33

Eleanor

Summer 1931

Eleanor watches Mabel lead Jimmy by the hand, weaving between the rose bushes, careful not to catch her pretty dress on the thorns. Behind the largest, the one with the perfect pink blooms, she crouches down on her haunches. Jimmy copies her, his face alive with delight, not yet understanding he needs to be concealed *behind* the bush in a game of hide-and-seek. He is just happy to be playing a game, any game with his big sister. He lets out a chuckle of laughter and Mabel sticks her head out from around the bush to see if anyone has heard. She puts a finger to her lips.

'Eight... Nine... Ten! Ready or not, here I come!' Eleanor shouts, loud enough for the pair to hear. A little squeal from Jimmy. She comes out from behind the big oak tree, Brook End standing in front of her, solid and comforting in an uncertain world. Eleanor turns and pretends to look for the children in the herbaceous border. 'Hmm, now where can they be?' she calls.

At that moment, Byron's large golden body tears down the steps from the patio and runs straight to where the children are hiding behind the rose bush, barking, wagging his tail and covering the boy and girl with his vigorous wet tongue until they squeal and giggle.

'Naughty Byron!' laughs Mabel when Eleanor arrives, feigning surprise at the sight of them. 'He gave us away!'

'Naughty Byron,' echoes Jimmy, bouncing on his short legs, tapping the dog's hairy side with the palm of his hand. 'Naughty, naughty, Byron!'

'Well,' Eleanor says, smiling and hugging them all, even Byron who licks her cheek, conveying his happiness at being included. 'I don't know about you, but I'm exhausted after all that hide-and-seek. Let's go inside and have a nice, cool glass of water and see if Miss Harding and Mrs Bellamy have your tea ready.'

The children follow Eleanor into the kitchen, wash hands and sit at the big, battered oak table, legs swinging back and forth. The back door is propped open, dappled sunlight playing on the flagstone floor. Mrs Bellamy places the children's plates in front of them, then the cook leans against the warmth of the range, taking a break while she sips her tea, rubbing a hand on her back as though to ease away an ache.

'I want that,' Jimmy says, pointing at Mabel's plate, his lower lip pouting. He stares glumly down at his own plate of sandwiches and tomatoes from the garden. Mabel's meal with its carefully weighed out egg and bacon, a dollop of cream on the side, is, as always, a more enticing proposition than his own food.

'You know that Mabel has to have special food to keep her healthy,' Miss Harding explains, pouring milk into Jimmy's glass, water into Mabel's. 'I shouldn't have to explain this every meal, Jimmy. Now, you eat up those sandwiches if you wish to become a strapping young man. If you're a good boy, your father said he might even take you fishing this weekend.'

Eleanor leaves the children to their tea under Miss Harding's watchful eyes and goes to Edward's study. Really, it is *their* study now. She has a permanent desk in it at one end, his desk at the other. They both have a view of the garden and of each other.

Sitting on Edward's desk is a photograph of him and Private Porter at the small ceremony they, and Violet and her family, all attended, just three weeks before he passed away. Eleanor picks it up and runs her fingers over the poor man's face. Just how he had survived all that time with those injuries showed an extraordinary spirit, one which was finally recognised for having been so brave that day at Passchendaele.

She remembers, too, the day the letter from the War Office had finally arrived to tell Edward of his fate. The letter had been brief and to the point.

Dear Professor Hamilton,

Following our investigations and consideration of the circumstances of the citation which was submitted in support of your version of the events which took place at Passchendaele in November 1917, which resulted in your being awarded various medals for bravery, we have reached a decision.

Whilst the circumstances of your case are regrettable and do not reflect well on you as an officer of the British Army, we recognise that you volunteered to serve your country when it needed you, that you otherwise served honourably and that you suffered significant mental trauma in so doing. For this reason, and given your voluntary admission, we have taken the decision not to strip you of your honourable discharge. However, in view of the length of time it took for you to step forward with your admission, we have made the decision to strip you of your retirement rank, so forthwith, you will no longer be permitted to refer to yourself with the title 'Captain'.

In the event you wish to appeal against this decision, please contact Major General Briggs-Norton at the above address. This matter shall otherwise now be considered closed.

Yours sincerely,

Major General Briggs-Norton

The content of the letter had been an enormous relief. Edward could finally put the whole sordid matter behind him and move on. The photograph on his desk meant he did not want to forget Private Porter, or what he did, but he sleeps easier at night, his nightmares hopefully becoming a thing of the past.

Edward is home every night now that he no longer has the London flat. After the financial catastrophe with Coleroy & Mack, Edward was left with little choice but to sell up. Fortunately, he had a few remaining government bonds which he cashed in to tide them over. They also sold off the apple orchard and Butterfly Meadow to a property entrepreneur, which enabled them to keep Brook End, managing with the smaller household staff of Mrs Bellamy, Alice and Miss Harding. Wilson retrained as a mechanic, and now fixes cars in Guildford, while Faulks and Mrs Faulks pronounced themselves ready to retire in any event. The income from Edward's work at the university and the local authority, together with a moderate income from his book sales, means they can afford to stay at Brook End, for now at least.

When the stock market crashed, things were bad, but nobody had any idea just how terrible things would get. There doesn't seem to be any end in sight, yet it's been nearly two years. She glances at the copy of *The Times* on her desk. *Labour Government Resigns! Government of National Unity, Headed by Macdonald in Place: Is consensus politics the only way to fix the economic slump?* GERMAN BANKING SYSTEM IN CRISIS. UNEMPLOYMENT IN AMERICA DOUBLES. *Car Manufacturing Collapse – Cars An Unaffordable Luxury.*

She pushes the paper aside. Truly, it is depressing reading. It really does feel as though the world is coming to an end. One does have to wonder how, or if, the country, indeed the *world*, will ever be able to pull through this crisis. In response to people's despair, lectures and debates are being organised all over the country to discuss ways in which the diseased economy can be nursed back to health. Eleanor has attended a few – some in London with Rose and Marcel – advocating a socialist vision. At these, the rich are lambasted for saving too much and not spending their wealth, resulting in mass unemployment and recession. Social justice is advocated as the only cure. But Eleanor also attended a talk given by Sir Oswald Mosley, recently resigned from the now-defunct Labour government, who talked about his Mosley Memorandum. The only way the economy can be saved, he had argued, would be by protecting Britain from growing globalisation, closing its borders and obliterating class conflict. A planned economy seems the only way forward. This idea is marching its way across Europe, from Stalin's Soviet Union, to Mussolini's Italy, to the rise of the National Socialist party's vision for Germany.

Change is coming, for good or for bad, whether anyone wants it or not.

Eleanor sighs. She has survived hard times before: the loss of her brothers and her father, the brutal murder of her mother, Mabel's illness, and difficult times with Edward. But she and Rose forged a life for themselves and her marriage with Edward has come through. The most important thing is that Mabel is well. She is not the girl she once would have been, with her lispy speech and limited words. She will struggle with her lessons and with life, but she laughs and she loves and the bright, inquisitive spark is back behind her eyes.

And that, at the end of the day, is everything she could

wish for. Whatever else lies ahead, as long as they stick together, they will get through it.

As for Edward, slowly, carefully, he is pulling the tattered strings of his life back together. He is working quietly behind the scenes, devising education policy for the nation. He is researching ways in which those considered unteachable can be taught. No longer does he focus only on the able, but he is working on setting up special schools where those less able can learn skills with which they may gain an occupation, however lowly that may be.

Eleanor checks her watch. Half an hour before Edward, Rose and Marcel are due back on the train from London.

She begins her letter.

Dear Dr Eversley,

It was a delight to receive your letter and to hear how the work is progressing on the new building to replace the Babies Castle. I am thrilled the funds we have raised from my charity campaign, 'A better life for the children at Heath Colony,' are being put to such good use. I am indebted to my dear friend Sophie, and her new husband, the generous Lord Matthews, who has provided so much in the way of publicity and backing to the project. Your description of the comforts of the new building sounds quite remarkable.

I am further delighted to hear of the expansion of the Ketogenic diet programme, as well as the plan for hiring of a full-time specialist nurse to assist with its administration. As you know, we continue with the strict adherence of the diet for our own dear Mabel, and she continues to do very well. She remains seizure-free and is speaking much more. She also enjoys playing games with her little brother. I fear he may soon overtake her as he is a bright little thing, but no matter. Daily she makes progress and that is what counts.

Finally, I must congratulate you, my dear Dr Eversley, on your new position as head consultant of Childhood Epilepsy at the Royal London Hospital. You are indeed deserving of such a prestigious post.

As for the matter we discussed when we last saw each other, I have given it much thought and I am hoping my dear sister, with her contacts in the newspaper world, can help me publish a series of essays that make the case for those of feeble-mind and for those with epilepsy to be thought of more kindly. I will also happily work with you, alongside my charitable work, to ensure the ability of the Ketogenic diet to change lives, be more widely known and accessible.

So, until we see each other next month,
Yours sincerely,
Eleanor Hamilton

There is a frantic barking and scratching from the hallway. Byron must have heard the car returning from the station.

Sure enough, there it is, Edward at the wheel of the Sunbeam, and she can just make out the heads of Rose and Marcel in the back.

'Mama, Mama!' She hears Mabel come running. 'Papa home!'

Then Jimmy, 'Papa home!'

Smiling, she takes a hand each and they run out to meet the car as it pulls up at the front of the house.

After the quiet of the afternoon, there is a cacophony of slamming doors, cries of, *Hello there!* and *It's good to be home!* and *Take care, Rose!* and Byron's panting, whining and the children laughing. Marcel helps Rose out of the car, her seven months' pregnancy visible beneath her dress. She looks radiant and happy.

Edward smiles and comes to Eleanor, enfolding her and the children into his arms. As she takes in his familiar woody scent, feels the weight of his arms around her back, she knows that, whatever happens out there in this uncertain world, in her little corner of it, with her family around her, this is all she needs to be happy and safe.

Author's Note

The origins of this book began eleven years ago with a poem. It was one I wrote at the lowest point of my daughter's illness. She had just turned two years old and, out of nowhere, she developed debilitating seizures. It turned out to be of a type which did not respond to any of the usual medications. I shan't repeat the whole poem here, but the salient verse was:

You are so young, but you put me to shame,
Your forgiving affection lifts my pain;
For I can see you will never give in,
And succumb to the monster you carry within.

That was how it seemed; a monster had taken possession of our child. Reading reports of others and how they described their illness, it was often in similar terms. They talked of 'the visitor' or 'him'. In a similar way to cancer sometimes being described as an enemy which must be fought, epilepsy had a persona, which was, I suppose, where the voice in the book sprang from.

To this day, we have no idea what caused our daughter's epilepsy. For well over a year she suffered around thirty seizures on a good day, over a hundred on a bad, despite

471

various medications which did nothing but give her terrible side effects. Our daughter had intractable epilepsy, she was in non-convulsive status epilepticus, meaning she was in a constant epileptic state, and the effect of it on her developing brain was catastrophic. We watched her regress, day by day, from the chatty, playful, inquisitive little girl she had been, with a wicked sense of humour, into a tragic shadow. She began to lose all her skills – speech, play, toilet training. She stumbled and tripped when she walked. Watching her deteriorate was torture. When her neurologist had run through all the medications to try her on (one of which was as awful to administer as the one Mabel was forced to take in the book, albeit not the same one), she mentioned the Ketogenic diet as a last resort.

It was the first I had heard of the diet, and after some research I found that it had indeed been in widespread use during the 1920s, before other anti-convulsant medications were introduced. It then went out of favour until the late 1990s when it began to have traction, again in children whose epilepsy did not respond to conventional medicines. It was a beacon of hope as the results looked promising. That beacon was quickly extinguished, however, when we learned that the waiting list to get on the diet was eighteen months. As it was so extreme, it had to begin in hospital and be supervised by specially trained nurses, who, at that time, were few and far between. We were, of course, devastated.

Our daughter was now three, and while we waited for the diet, she was put on a different, and at that time, more unusual, medication, Levetiracetam. Miraculously, it worked. Our daughter suffered her last seizure on Easter Sunday that year, and never had one again. Because of this, she never needed the diet in the end. I do, however, know of other children for whom no medication was effective, but the diet has worked. One of those children, now a teenager, is still on the diet and remains fit, healthy and seizure-free.

For us, the seizures may have stopped, but the hard part was in many ways still to come. At age three and a half our daughter had the developmental age of ten months. We were told she had profound learning difficulties and was unlikely to be able to live an independent life. In answer to my question of what we could do to help her, the consultant said, 'The more you put in, the more therapy you can give, the more you will get out.'

And so we exposed her to as many learning possibilities as we could, mental and physical. All medication was withdrawn at the age of nine and today, at thirteen, she remains seizure-free. We are lucky. Over the years, our daughter has made a remarkable recovery. It hasn't been easy and she still has a rocky path ahead, but she is incredible, and we not only have our wonderful girl with her wicked sense of humour back, but we have a tenacious, bright young lady, who excels at sport, attends an ordinary school and has many friends. Although ours is a happy story, the legacy of that illness lives on, not only in her, but in all of us. Our family carries the scars from the deep wounds that that monstrous epilepsy left on us all.

The sad fact is, had our daughter been born a hundred years ago, there is no doubt that she would have been institutionalised from a young age and, in all likelihood, would have spent the rest of her life incarcerated. Indeed, epileptics continued to be institutionalised well into the second half of the twentieth century, despite the fact that

LOUISE FEIN

the vast majority did not experience cognitive impairment. Marginalisation and stigma around the disease continued and still exist today. We certainly experienced some in relation to our daughter.

The Eugenics Movement

The general themes, notions, philosophy of thought and historical context of this book are factually accurate. Some of the specifics have been altered or adapted for the sake of the story and the timeline. Before I began researching for this novel, I had thought of eugenics solely in the context of Nazi Germany. Whilst researching my previous novel (*People Like Us/Daughter of the Reich*), which is set in Germany during Hitler's rise to power, I carried out some research into the pseudo-science of eugenics, but nowhere did I read about its origins outside of Nazi Germany. I was therefore rather shocked when I began to look into the ideas behind the inhumane treatment of people with disabilities, including epilepsy, in the 1920s, and I found that in fact Nazi Germany took its lead in this area from the widespread and accepted eugenics ideas circulating in both the United Kingdom and the United States. The eugenics movement had been born in England in the late nineteenth century and was extremely widespread in the first thirty years or so of the twentieth century. It spread decisively to the United States where many states went further than we did in the United Kingdom in enacting eugenic legislation. It was also prevalent in several European countries and, as we all know, was enthusiastically adopted by the Nazi party

474

in Germany. Unlike Nazi Germany and the United States, however, where the main driving force behind the eugenics movement was race, in England it was class.

The phrase and concept was first adopted by Sir Francis Galton, cousin of Charles Darwin, in the late nineteenth century, who took the idea from his famous cousin about breeding improvements into domestic animals and thought these should also be applied to humans, to improve their ability. The concept of getting rid of 'undesirables' and increasing the proportions of 'desirables' in the general population, gained much popularity across the entire political spectrum, with champions of the movement coming not only from the right, but also from prominent socialists, such as Sydney and Beatrice Webb, John Maynard Keynes, Virginia Woolf, George Bernard Shaw, William Beveridge, HG Wells and Marie Stopes, to name but a few.

Indeed, there were few voices of dissent. In 1907, to prevent the deterioration of Britain's population, the Eugenics Education Society was established in England to campaign for sterilisation and marriage restrictions for those considered 'unfit' to prevent the deterioration of Britain's population. In 1912 the first International Eugenics Conference was held in London and presided over by Charles Darwin's youngest son, Leonard Darwin, who headed the (later renamed) Eugenics Society until 1929. In attendance were prominent supporters including Winston Churchill and Lord Balfour. Legislation was proposed for compulsory sterilisation and incarceration of those considered 'weak-minded', a catch-all phrase for those with learning difficulties as well as epileptics, criminals, those with behavioural difficulties, alcoholics and anyone else considered 'undesirable' and ruinous to the health of the population in general.

The Bill was almost universally supported but in the end the Act which was finally put into law, the 1913 Mental Deficiency Act, was greatly watered down by the heroic efforts of the Liberal MP, Josiah Wedgwood, who managed to gain support through two main arguments: firstly, the enormous and unknown cost of segregating and sterilising huge swathes of the population, and secondly, the concept of the liberty of the individual being subjugated by the state. The other arguments – the spurious science upon which the whole concept was based, and the difficulty in defining exactly who and how people were captured under the definitions of the legislation, fell more on deaf ears.

The 1914–1918 war rather diverted attention from the eugenics movement, but by the mid-1920s, the economic bounceback after the war was well and truly over. There was mass unemployment and a growing concern about the speed at which the relative classes were reproducing. The 'poor' were producing seven or eight children per couple, the middle and upper classes only two or three. The Russian revolution was not yet a decade old and the fear of a Communist revolution in England was real. The economic and social upheaval of this decade was enormous and debates raged about the tenuous future of life as they knew it, Capitalism and Western democracy was doomed, and people were genuinely afraid. The echoes down the years with today are striking.

The eugenics movement picked up momentum again, and in the United States it was taken further, with hundreds of thousands subject to incarceration in institutions for sometimes dubious reasons and tens of thousands forcibly sterilised. Charles Davenport and Harry Laughlin (featured in the book) ran the Eugenics Record Office on Long Island, New York. Laughlin wrote the Model Eugenical Sterilisation law which went on to be enacted in various states. The case referred to in the book, that of Carrie Buck and the involvement of Harry Laughlin, was a real one. He wrote as to her suitability for sterilisation, even though he had never met her. Laughlin did include epileptics in his list for incarceration and sterilisation, even though he himself suffered from epilepsy.

In 1933, the German Reichstag passed the law for the Prevention of Hereditarily Diseased Offspring closely based on Laughlin's model. Laughlin himself was awarded an honorary degree by the University of Heidelberg for his work in the science of racial cleansing.

The concept of the superior Aryan in Germany could be traced to the idea decades earlier, cultivated in California, about the superiority of the blond-haired, blue-eyed master Nordic race. Philanthropic organisations such as Carnegie, Rockefeller and Harriman provided extensive funding. The Rockefeller Foundation also helped fund the German Eugenics programme, including Josef Mengele's twin studies before he went to Auschwitz.

Indeed, these policies made it awkward leading up to the Nuremberg trials when the crimes of Genocide and Crimes Against Humanity were being devised and prosecutions proposed for the treatment of people in the period before the war began in 1939. This was because of America's own forceable sterilisation programme of 'the unfit'. During the trials, Germany raised the Californian eugenics statutes, albeit unsuccessfully, in its defence. In the United Kingdom, another bill for sterilisation for certain mental patients was proposed in Parliament in 1931 by the Labour MP, Archibald Church. This was never enacted, but 'voluntary' sterilisations were undoubtedly carried out under coercion. In any event, the incarceration of so many under the 1913 legislation (which wasn't repealed until the Mental Health Act of 1959) effectively prevented marriages and kept 'undesirables' of all shapes and forms out of the public eye.

Characters/Location

This novel contains a mix of real and fictional characters. Eleanor and Mabel are entirely fictional. Some of the minor characters who were supporters of the eugenics movement were real, such as Harry Laughlin, Charles Davenport, Junior Rockefeller, Leonard Darwin, Marie Stopes and Margaret Sanger. Edward is very loosely based on the real figure of Sir Cyril Burt, a prominent educational psychologist and eugenicist at the time. However, I have changed so much about him that it was only right I give him a different name. Edward's background, role during the war, and personality are all figments of my imagination. Edward had a change of heart about the eugenics movement (and in reality, some prominent figures *did* change their minds), but the real Sir Cyril Burt remained a eugenics supporter all of his life. My character falsifies records relating to adopted children. The real Sir Cyril Burt, it was discovered after his death, *allegedly* falsified his twin study data to back up his theories of inheritance of intelligence. His earlier work, which was not questioned and which formed the basis for the concept of grammar schools in England and the testing of children's intelligence at the age of eleven, has been acclaimed and recognised, and for which he was awarded a knighthood. However, it is also alleged that the methodologies for his research were questionable. He has been reported as being slapdash at best, negligent or even purposefully misleading in some of the data, at worst, although such accusations remain unproven.

The colony featured in my book is a fictional one, but it is based on a real colony. I have renamed it and changed its location because the real one still exists, albeit not as a colony any more, but as a school for children with severe epilepsy. I am indebted to them for welcoming me in and opening their archives for me. The real epilepsy colony did have a Babies Castle (although it was closed in 1923, being deemed unsuitable accommodation for small children) and it also had a Red Cross Centre which housed soldiers from WWI suffering from shell shock. My fictional colony was, in fact, more of a mixture of a colony and an asylum, for I believe the real colony was a happier place than my book hints at, although remaining in the colony was dependent on a minimum IQ level of only mild cognitive impairment, below which they were not deemed suitable colonists. Parents were at liberty to remove their children if they chose, but the sad fact was, most would not have done what Eleanor did.

I did extensive research into the case files of another local colony (closed in the 1990s) and an asylum. It was gruelling and heart-wrenching reading. I read of one little girl who was told by her mother she was being taken to a children's home for the night and she would pick her up in the morning. Over seventy years later she was still there and never saw her mother again. The case notes contained pictures of the patients, each one a sad and forgotten life, apparently devoid of love and a family to care for them. They also painted a picture of a matter-of-fact attitude towards the inmates at best; at worst the staff were critical, unsympathetic, short-tempered and cruel. I felt a desire to give each of these people's lives an airing, a sense of being remembered. So this book, in part, is for them.

Continuing Relevance

Eugenics philosophies continue to find support today, whether that be in relation to arguments against people making the decision to knowingly give birth to children who have a genetic disorder or perceived disability. But disability itself is debatable – a condition one person might regard as a disability could, by another, be regarded as simply a difference. We are able to screen embryos pre-implantation, and we have the ability to predict which may be more intelligent; we have the ability to choose which to reject.

Some societies and governments also have a very different attitude to that of Britain and America, whereby the sentiment is that an individual's interests should be subordinate to those of the nation. Such nations may therefore strive to improve population via eugenic principles, a programme which is at odds with our current ideology.

My personal view is that, whilst I understand there are benefits of reducing or eliminating certain inherited diseases, we should be wary of our interference with nature, as we cannot know where it may lead. We only have to look to history to see the dangers of it, when taken to extreme.

Acknowledgements

Thank you to the incredible team at Head of Zeus for everything – most especially to my wonderful editor, Hannah Smith, whose championship, insight and vision is so much appreciated. It really has been a team effort! Thank you to brilliant copy editor, Kati Nicholl, for her careful work, checking all the research and thoughtful commentary. Thanks also to my fabulous new editor, Hannah Todd, as well as Victoria Joss, Kate Appleton and the myriad of others involved in getting this book from a germ of an idea into the hands of readers, from the talented cover designers to the printers, distributors and book sellers. I am immensely grateful to each and every one of you.

My gratitude to Caroline Hardman, agent extraordinaire, who has, especially over this last and most difficult of years, been such a calm and dedicated supporter. I'm sure I haven't been the only one to have a few wobbles during the pandemic, but Caroline has been a steady voice of reason, encouragement, and at times, therapist, throughout! My thanks to Thérèse Coen for ensuring my work is read in so many different countries, and indeed to the whole Hardman & Swainson team who have adapted admirably to these difficult circumstances.

I was fortunate to have been able to conduct the research

for this book during a time before, when we were blissfully unaware of COVID and lockdowns. I am immensely grateful to all those at The Surrey History Centre who assisted me enormously by granting access to their records of long-closed asylums and epilepsy colonies. My thanks also to Sue Turner and Alice Reynolds who so generously permitted me to look through their archives. Thanks also to someone whom I'm not permitted to name, but who advised me on the army processes for awarding medals, stripping them and the likely punishment someone like Edward might expect. You know who you are!

In terms of my research, for anyone who may be interested, other than physically looking through records, I was able to find a good deal of information about the Ketogenic diet through Wiley online library for information on the Ketogenic diet, and about eugenics through the eugenics archive in The Wellcome Library. I read the bulk of the 1925 text of Sir Cyril Burt's, *The Young Delinquent*. I also read various publications about life, politics, social change and thought during the 1920s and early 30s, as well as on the 1929 stock market crash.

One group who deserve a special mention are The D20 Authors (find us on Twitter – @TheD20Authors). We are a group who all published our debut novels during the course of 2020 when bookshops were closed and all our desperately-looked-forward-to events were cancelled. We not only bonded on weekly Zoom chats, but by supporting each other and our books across all our social media channels. This group literally saved me this year – indeed we saved each other. Together we have not only gathered together for online events and panels, festivals and promotions, but we have had each other's backs and celebrate each other's success. D20 authors – you all rock!!

Finally, my biggest thanks must go to my family. Having been locked down together for the best part of a year, and having had to write this book during a time which was difficult, in different ways, for each of you, you have been the very best. Thank you for listening to my difficulties with plot and character and helping to work those through. Thank you for being my first readers, my champions and my supporters. Thank you for the meals, the washing and the tidying. I couldn't have done any of this without you.

Reading Group Guide

1. The Hamiltons' views on the 'unfit' and the 'underclasses' were widely held of their time and class in society. It was largely their personal experiences with Mabel that forced them to change their beliefs. How much do you think our own views on what is acceptable in society are driven by the beliefs of those around us? Have you ever changed your thinking on an issue after being confronted by something on a personal level you hadn't considered before?

2. Supporters of the eugenics movement feared the human race would become less intelligent if those who they considered to have lower intelligence were permitted to have more children than those they considered of higher intelligence. Do you think intelligence today continues to be one of the highest valued qualities a person can have in most societies? Do you think this right, or should other qualities be equally valued? Can you give examples of such qualities?

3. Why do you think Eleanor and Rose handled their mother's death so differently?

4. Edward sees himself as weak and a failure, lying to cover up those 'faults', as he sees them. Do you think Edward is weak? Do you consider his actions regarding Porter to be dishonorable and unforgivable? How do you think the war affected his decisions?

5. Eleanor blames Edward for Mabel ending up in the epilepsy colony, despite the normalcy of such institutions at the time. Do you think there were alternative solutions for Mabel, given Edward's position in society and his profession? Do you think it was fair of Eleanor to blame him?

6. Many characters were forced to reckon with their preconceptions of others. Can you think of some examples? As you read through the book, how did your opinions about the characters change? Which character did you find experienced the greatest transformation?

7. Eleanor forgives Edward his wrongdoings by the end of the book. Did you think she should have done this? How would her life have changed if she hadn't forgiven him?

8. Many of the eugenic ideas that were so enthusiastically adopted by the Nazi party originated in the UK and the US. Also, both these countries embraced the widespread practice of lifelong incarceration and sterilisation of thousands of disabled people in the first half of the twentieth century. These facts are rarely discussed.

Do they surprise you? Do you think more of this history should be studied and considered? What is the benefit?

9. How do you feel about the personification of the disease of epilepsy? Why do you think the author chose to use this narrative tool? In what way did this voice add perspective and insight into how the disease affects Mabel?

10. Mabel is at the heart of this book, and yet hers is the voice not heard. Why do you think the author made that decision? How do you think the story might have shifted had Mabel's perspective been given?